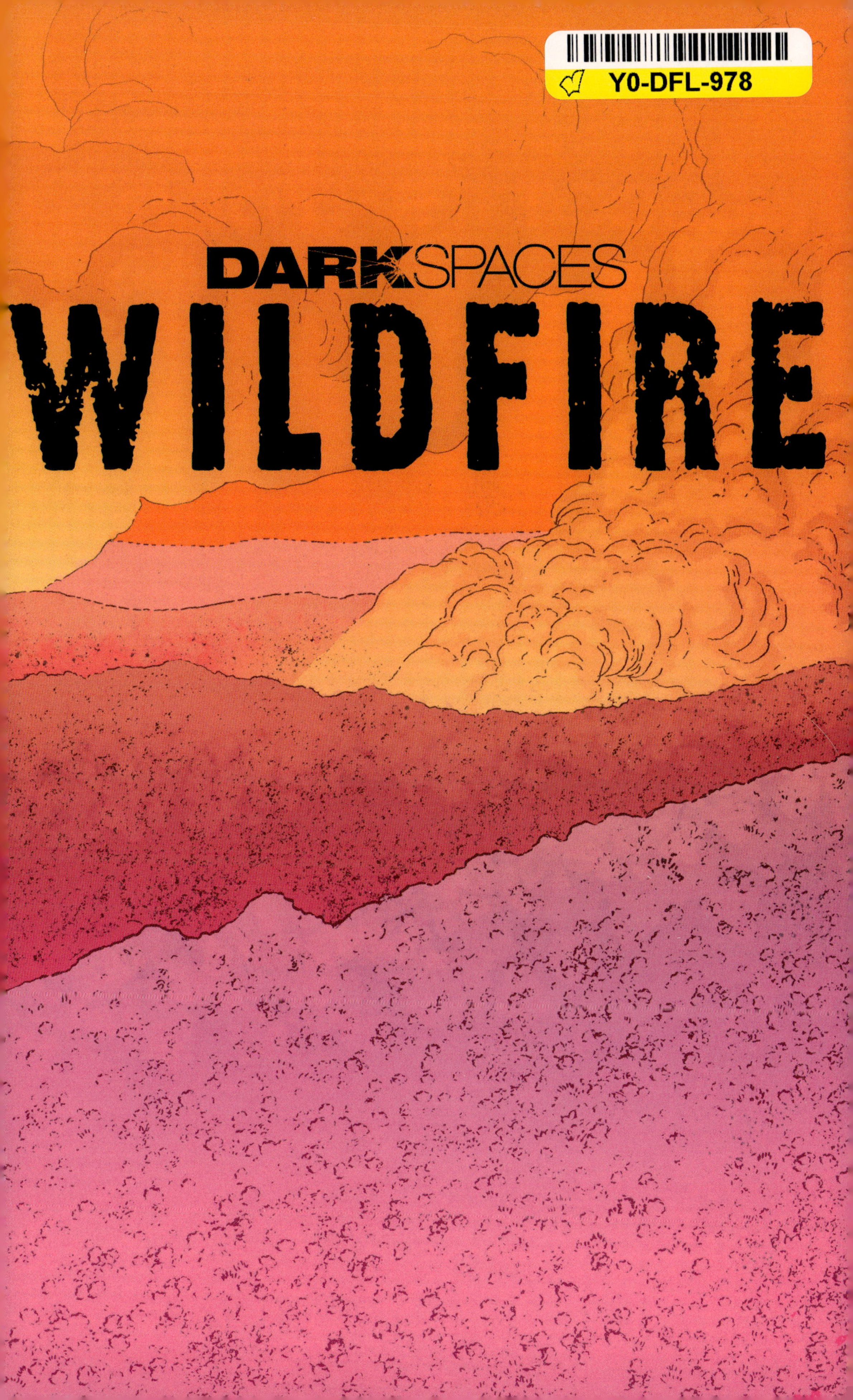
DARKSPACES
WILDFIRE

SCOTT SNYDER

WRITER

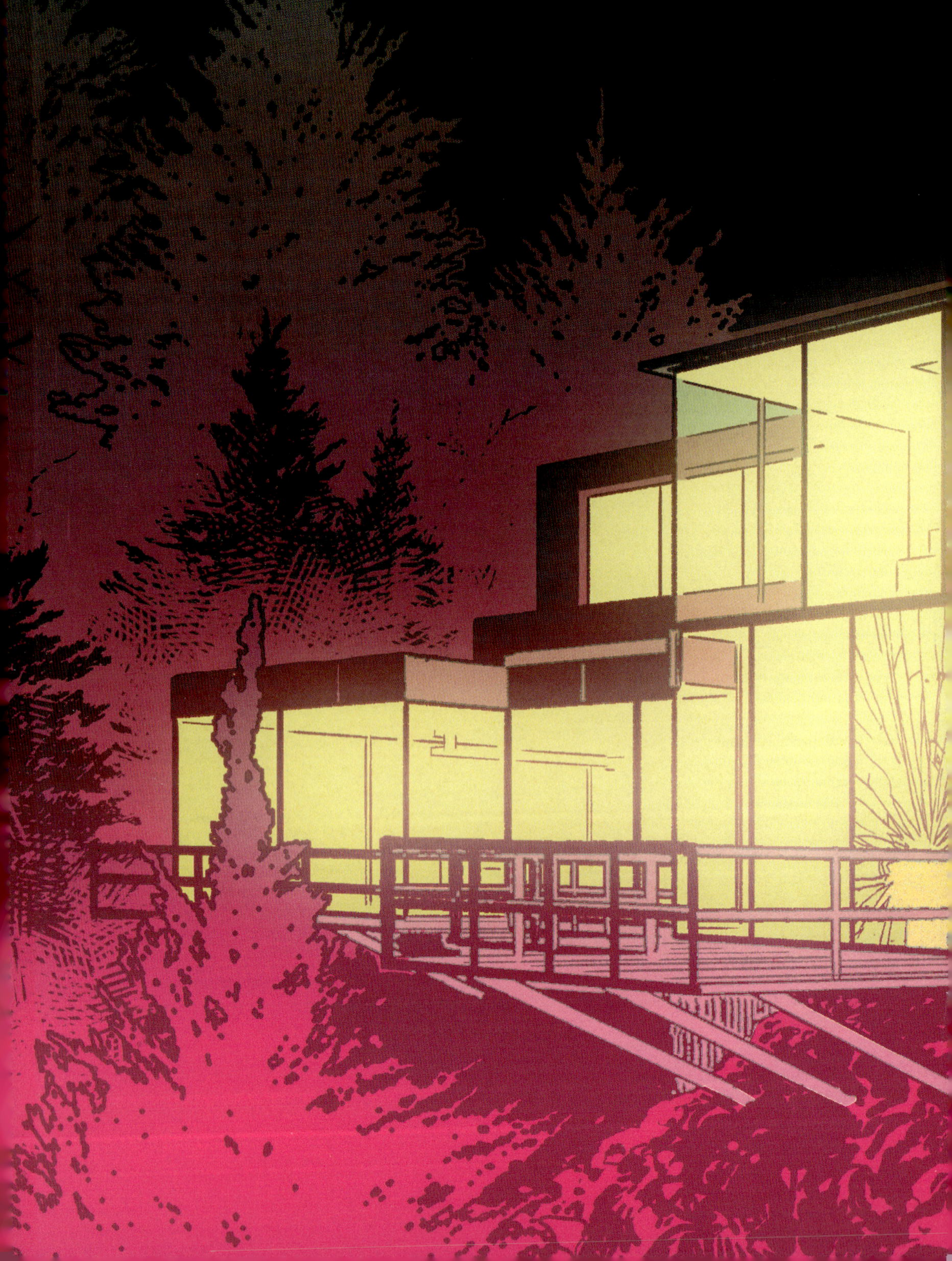

HAYDEN SHERMAN

INTERIOR AND COVER ARTIST

RONDA PATTISON

COLORIST

ANDWORLD DESIGN

LETTERER

DARK SPACES: WILDFIRE CREATED BY SNYDER & SHERMAN

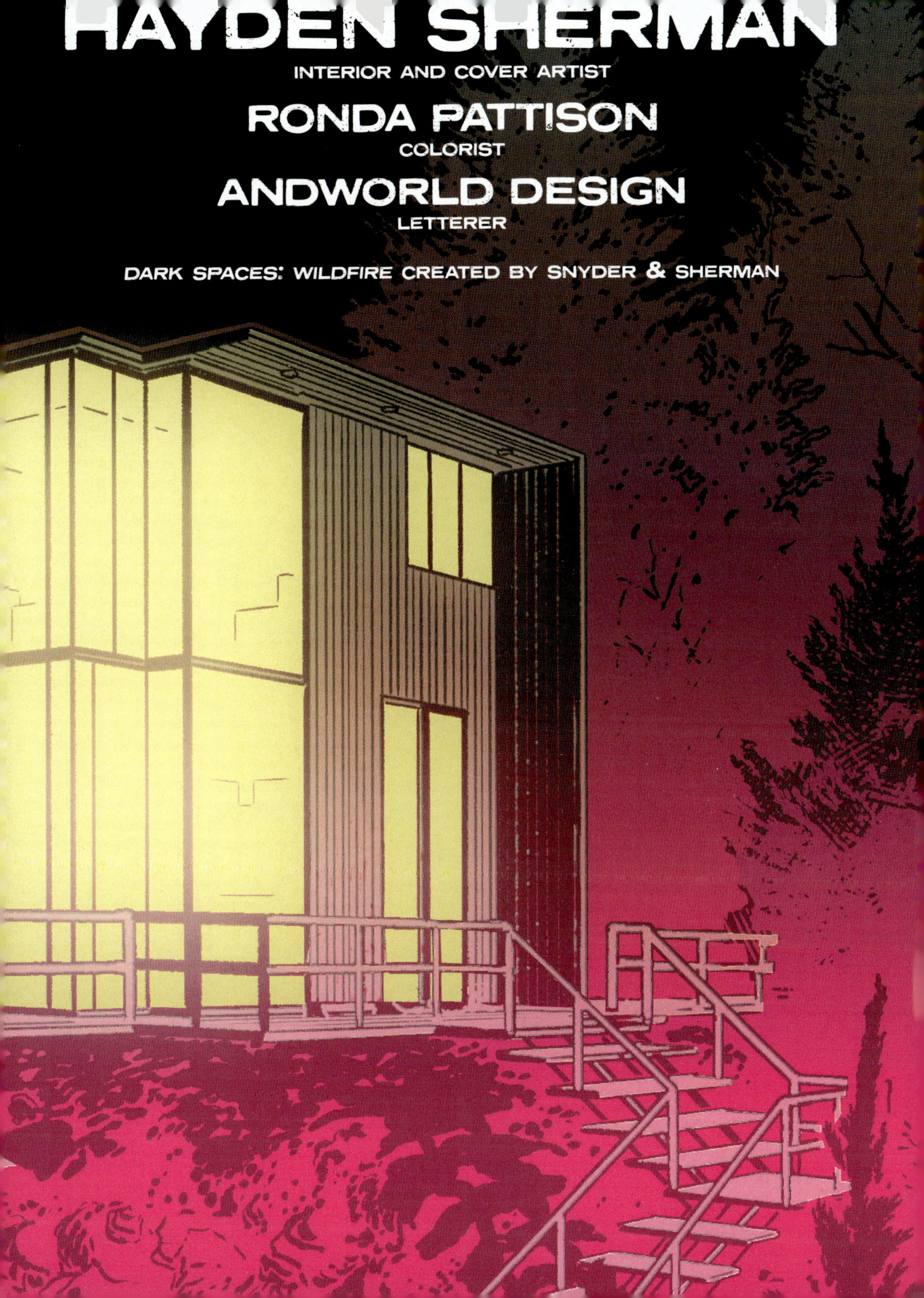

TYLER JENNES
STORY ASSISTANT

**MARK DOYLE
& MAGGIE HOWELL**
EDITORS
ORIGINAL SERIES, COLLECTED EDITION

JAKE WILLIAMS
ASSISTANT EDITOR
ORIGINAL SERIES, COLLECTED EDITION

SHAWN LEE
PRODUCTION ASSISTANCE

KRIS SIMON
COLLECTION GROUP EDITOR

**COLLECTION COVER ART BY
HAYDEN SHERMAN,
COLORS BY RONDA PATTISON**

**EXCLUSIVE COVER ART BY
HAYDEN SHERMAN**

ISBN: 978-1-68405-961-4   25 24 23 22 1 2 3 4

IDW ORIGINAL
@IDWpublishing
IDWpublishing.com

DARK SPACES: WILDFIRE. MAY 2023. FIRST PRINTING. © 2023 Scott Snyder & Hayden Sherman. All Rights Reserved. The IDW logo is registered in the U.S. Patent and Trademark Office. IDW Publishing, a division of Idea and Design Works, LLC. Editorial offices: 2355 Northside Drive, Suite 140, San Diego, CA 92108. Any similarities to persons living or dead are purely coincidental. With the exception of artwork used for review purposes, none of the contents of this publication may be reprinted without permission of Idea and Design Works, LLC. IDW Publishing does not read or accept unsolicited submissions of ideas, stories, or artwork. Printed in Canada.

Originally published as DARK SPACES: WILDFIRE issues #1–5.

Nachie Marsham, Publisher | Blake Kobashigawa, SVP Sales, Marketing & Strategy | Mark Doyle, VP Editorial & Creative Strategy | Tara McCrillis, VP Publishing Operations | Anna Morrow, VP Marketing & Publicity | Alex Hargett, VP Sales | Jamie S. Rich, Executive Editorial Director | Scott Dunbier, Director, Special Projects | Greg Gustin, Sr. Director, Content Strategy | Kevin Schwoer, Sr. Director of Talent Relations | Lauren LePera, Sr. Managing Editor | Keith Davidsen, Director, Marketing & PR | Topher Alford, Sr. Digital Marketing Manager | Patrick O'Connell, Sr. Manager, Direct Market Sales | Shauna Monteforte, Sr. Director of Manufacturing Operations | Greg Foreman, Director DTC Sales & Operations | Nathan Widick, Director of Design | Neil Uyetake, Sr. Art Director, Design & Production | Shawn Lee, Art Director, Design & Production | Jack Rivera, Art Director, Marketing

Ted Adams and Robbie Robbins, IDW Founders

For international rights, contact licensing@idwpublishing.com.

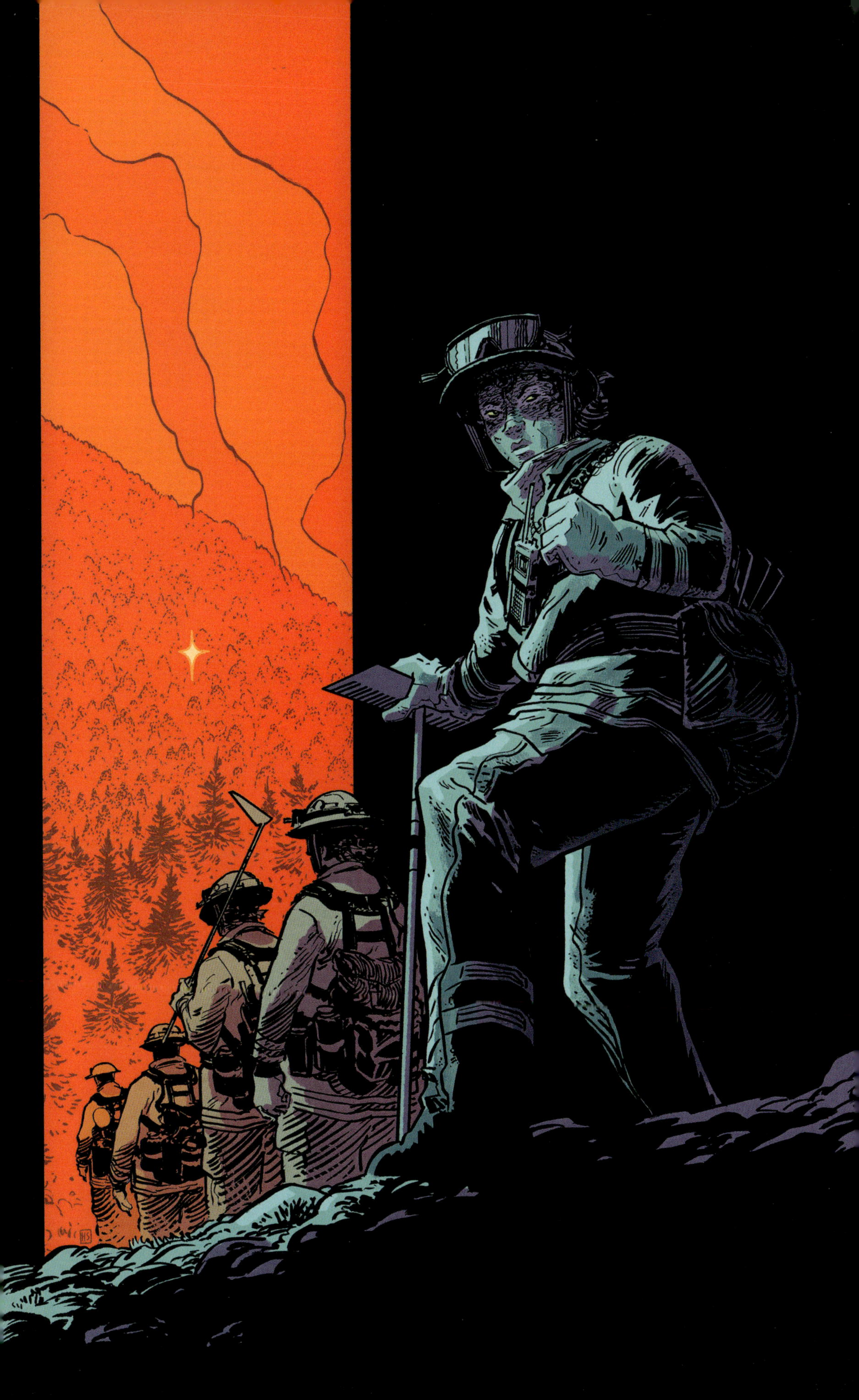

"IT'S MY JOB TO
KEEP THEM SAFE..."

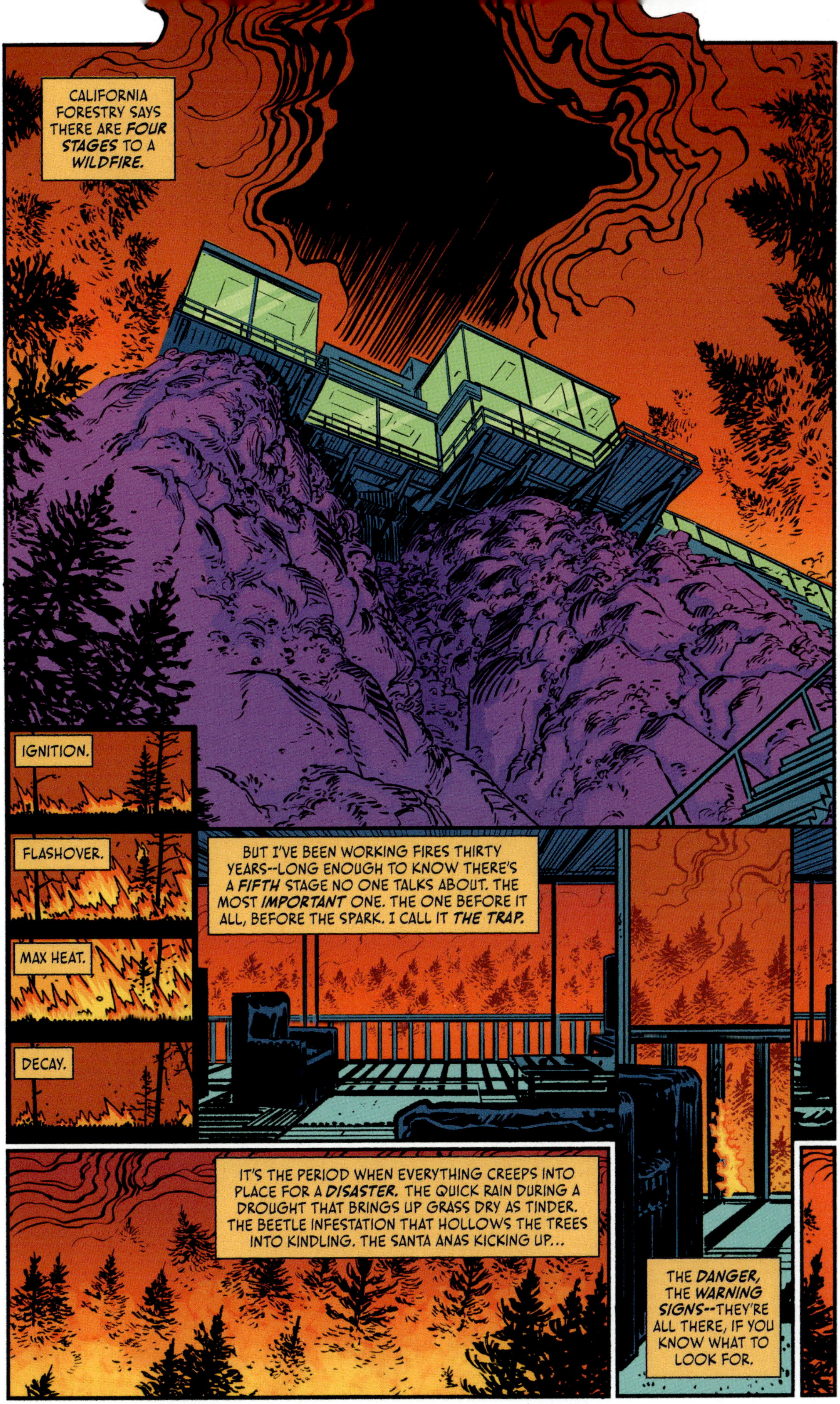
CALIFORNIA FORESTRY SAYS THERE ARE *FOUR STAGES* TO A *WILDFIRE.*
IGNITION.
FLASHOVER.
MAX HEAT.
DECAY.
BUT I'VE BEEN WORKING FIRES THIRTY YEARS--LONG ENOUGH TO KNOW THERE'S A *FIFTH* STAGE NO ONE TALKS ABOUT. THE MOST *IMPORTANT* ONE. THE ONE BEFORE IT ALL, BEFORE THE SPARK. I CALL IT *THE TRAP.*
IT'S THE PERIOD WHEN EVERYTHING CREEPS INTO PLACE FOR A *DISASTER.* THE QUICK RAIN DURING A DROUGHT THAT BRINGS UP GRASS DRY AS TINDER. THE BEETLE INFESTATION THAT HOLLOWS THE TREES INTO KINDLING. THE SANTA ANAS KICKING UP...
THE *DANGER,* THE *WARNING SIGNS*--THEY'RE ALL THERE, IF YOU KNOW WHAT TO LOOK FOR.

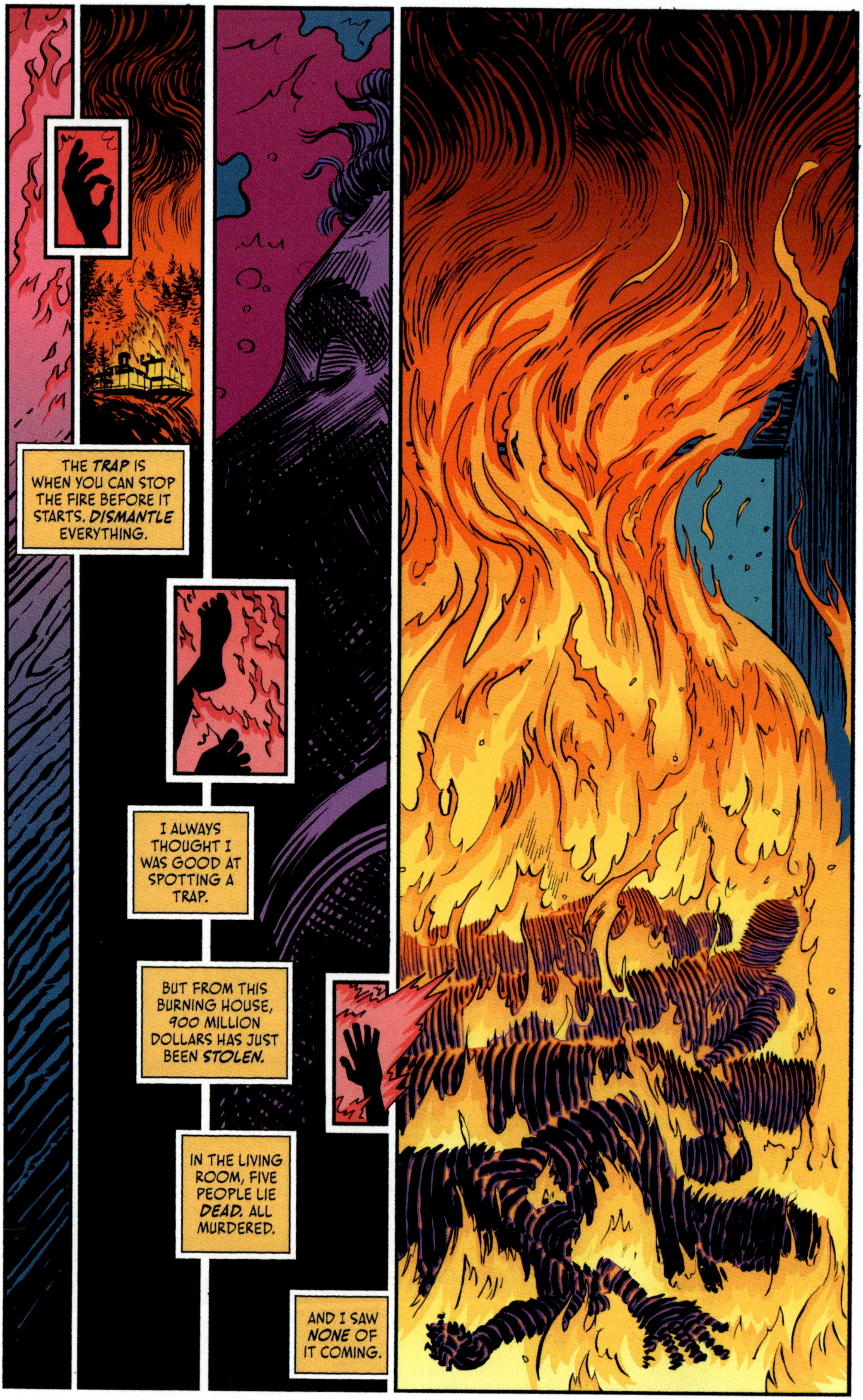
THE TRAP IS WHEN YOU CAN STOP THE FIRE BEFORE IT STARTS. DISMANTLE EVERYTHING.
I ALWAYS THOUGHT I WAS GOOD AT SPOTTING A TRAP.
BUT FROM THIS BURNING HOUSE, 900 MILLION DOLLARS HAS JUST BEEN STOLEN.
IN THE LIVING ROOM, FIVE PEOPLE LIE DEAD. ALL MURDERED.
AND I SAW NONE OF IT COMING.

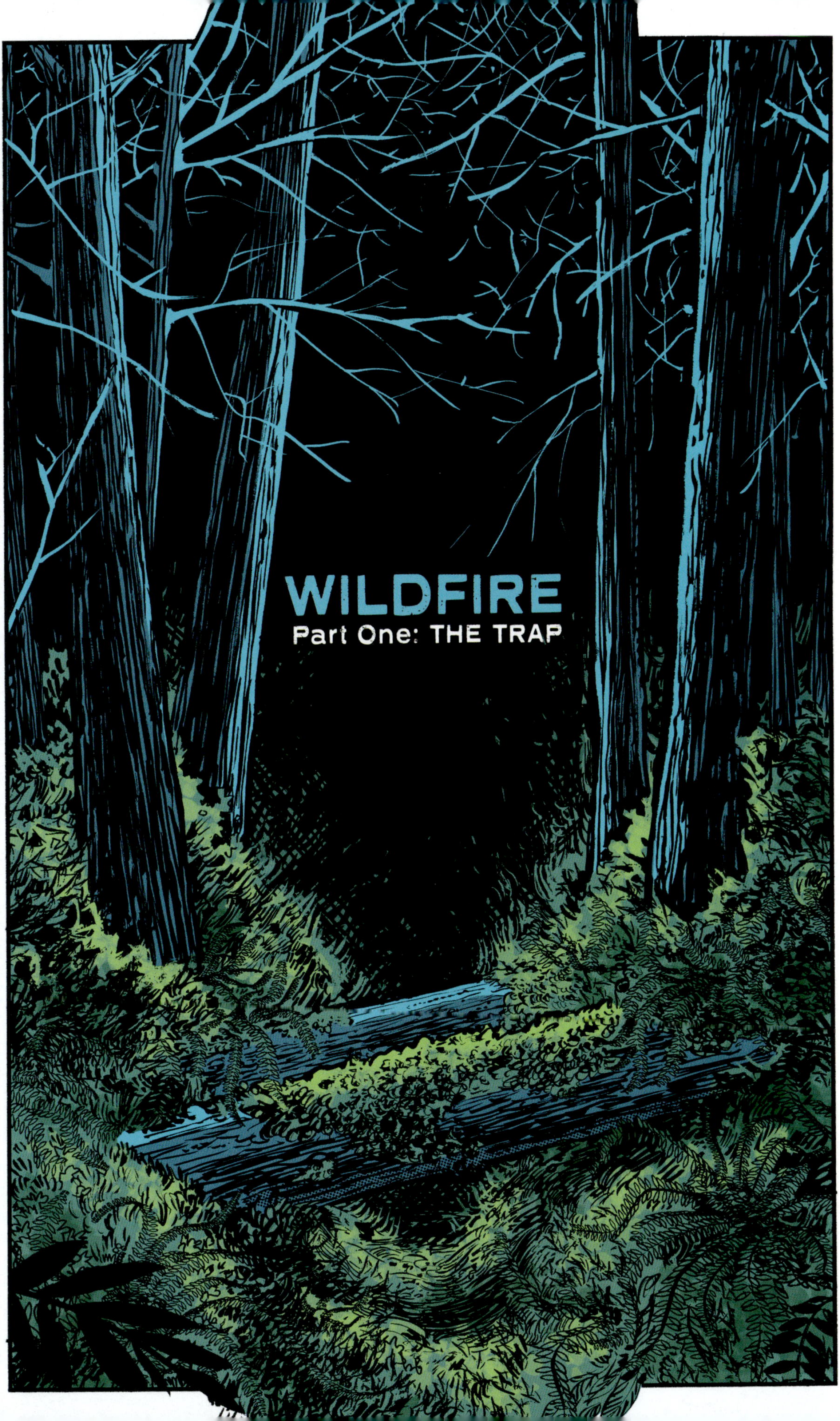
WILDFIRE
Part One: THE TRAP

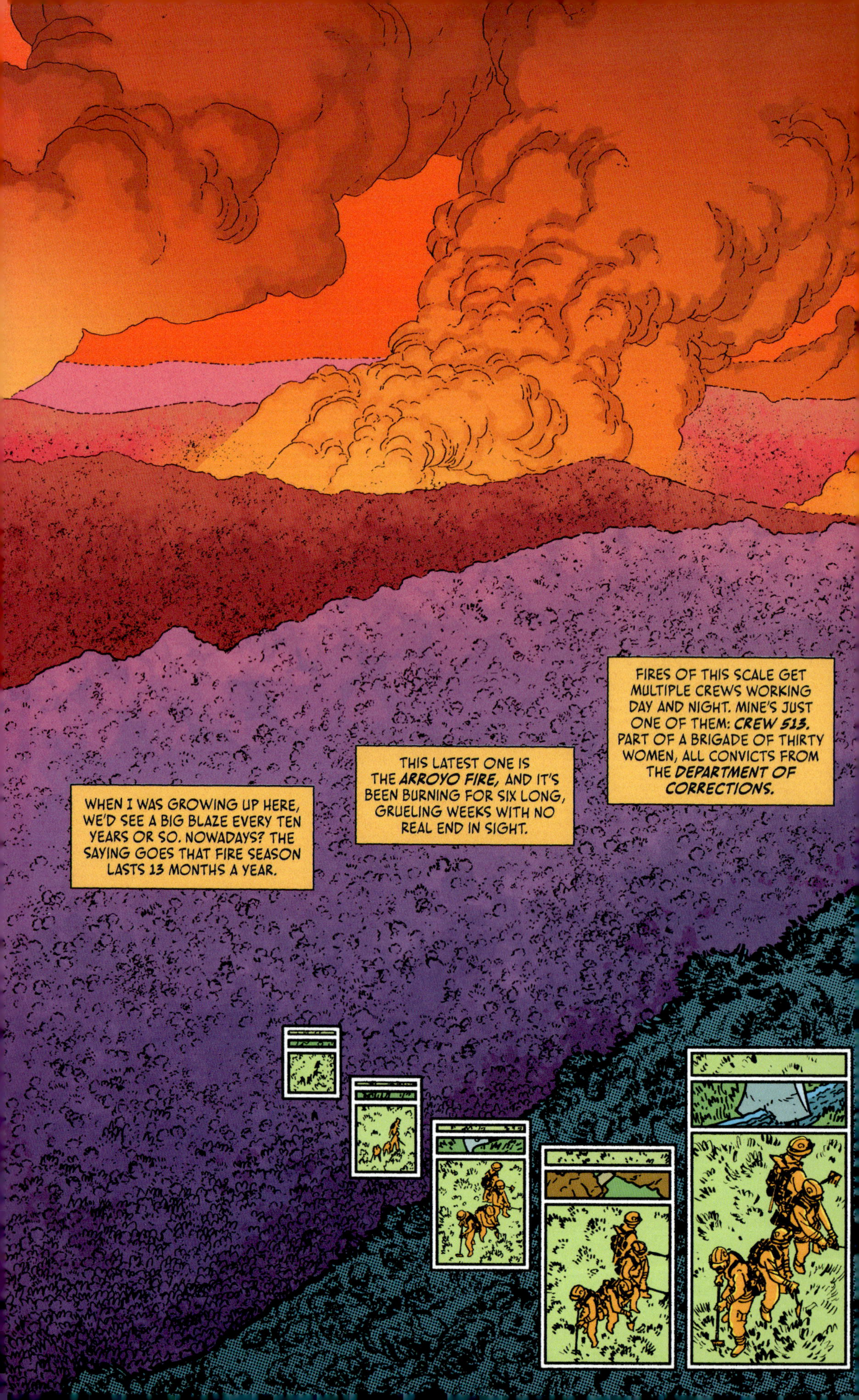
WHEN I WAS GROWING UP HERE, WE'D SEE A BIG BLAZE EVERY TEN YEARS OR SO. NOWADAYS? THE SAYING GOES THAT FIRE SEASON LASTS 13 MONTHS A YEAR.
THIS LATEST ONE IS THE ARROYO FIRE, AND IT'S BEEN BURNING FOR SIX LONG, GRUELING WEEKS WITH NO REAL END IN SIGHT.
FIRES OF THIS SCALE GET MULTIPLE CREWS WORKING DAY AND NIGHT. MINE'S JUST ONE OF THEM: CREW 513. PART OF A BRIGADE OF THIRTY WOMEN, ALL CONVICTS FROM THE DEPARTMENT OF CORRECTIONS.

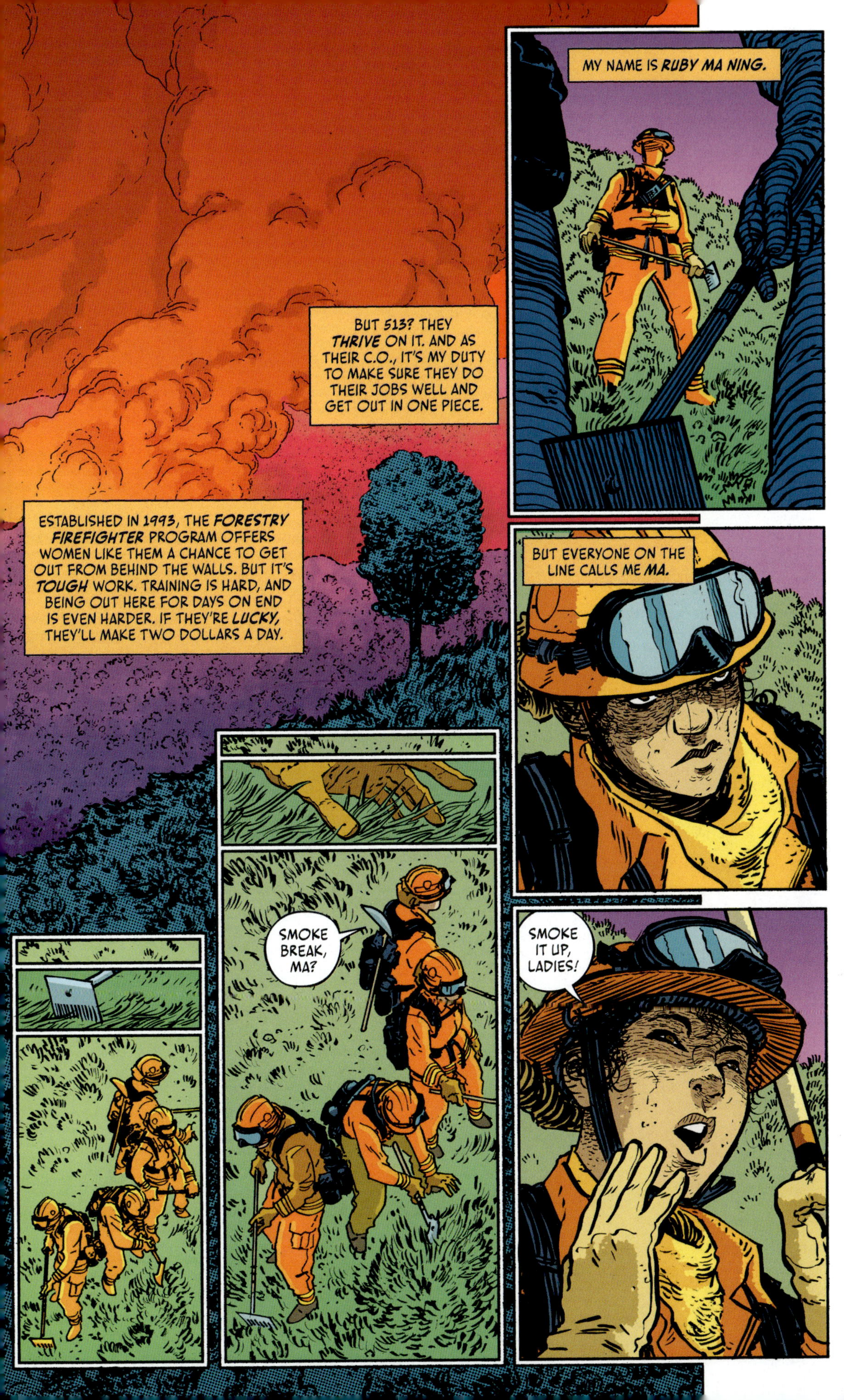
MY NAME IS RUBY MA NING.
BUT 513? THEY THRIVE ON IT. AND AS THEIR C.O., IT'S MY DUTY TO MAKE SURE THEY DO THEIR JOBS WELL AND GET OUT IN ONE PIECE.
ESTABLISHED IN 1993, THE FORESTRY FIREFIGHTER PROGRAM OFFERS WOMEN LIKE THEM A CHANCE TO GET OUT FROM BEHIND THE WALLS. BUT IT'S TOUGH WORK. TRAINING IS HARD, AND BEING OUT HERE FOR DAYS ON END IS EVEN HARDER. IF THEY'RE LUCKY, THEY'LL MAKE TWO DOLLARS A DAY.
BUT EVERYONE ON THE LINE CALLS ME MA.
SMOKE BREAK, MA?
SMOKE IT UP, LADIES!

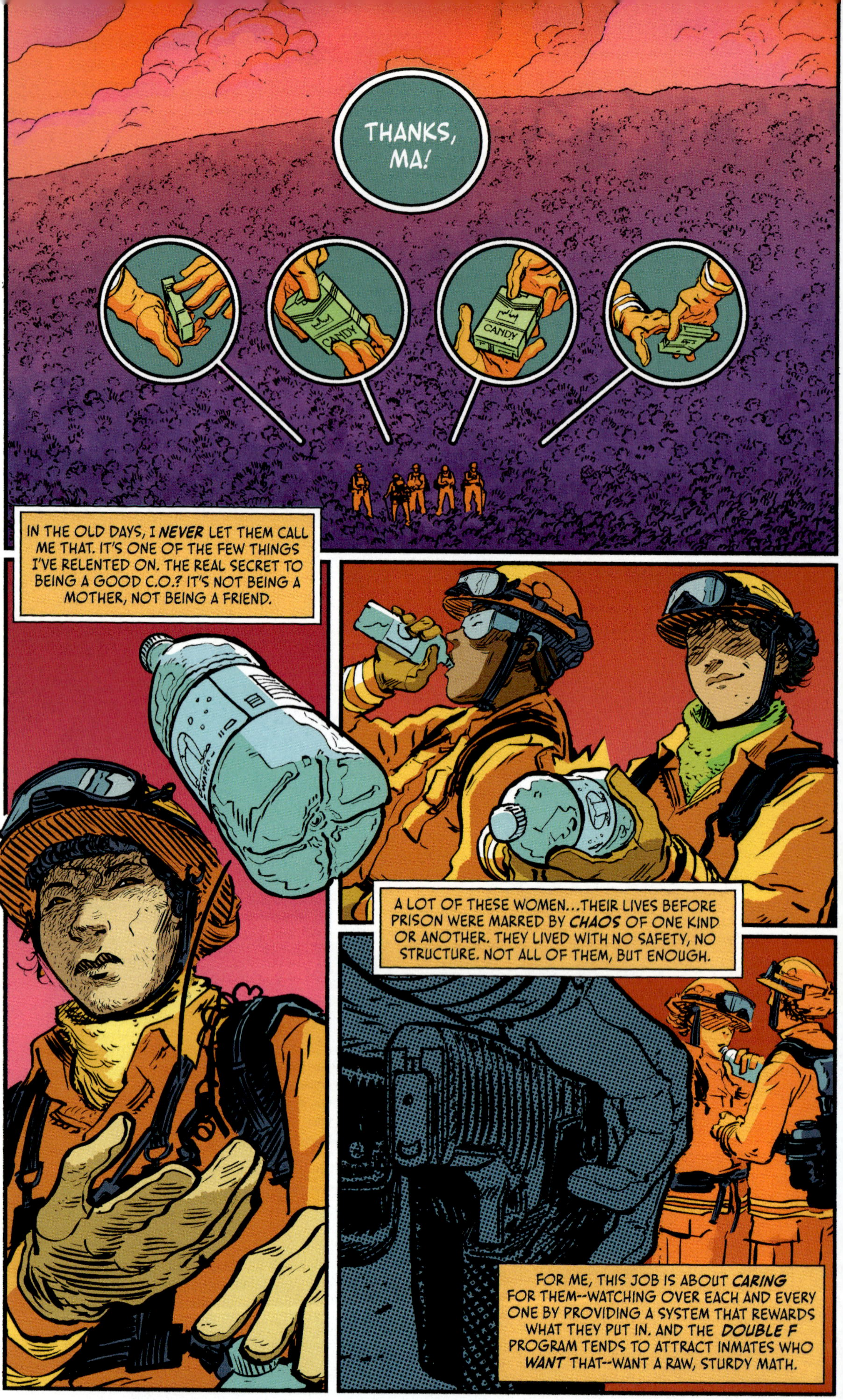
THANKS, MA!
CANDY
CANDY
IN THE OLD DAYS, I NEVER LET THEM CALL ME THAT. IT'S ONE OF THE FEW THINGS I'VE RELENTED ON. THE REAL SECRET TO BEING A GOOD C.O.? IT'S NOT BEING A MOTHER, NOT BEING A FRIEND.
A LOT OF THESE WOMEN...THEIR LIVES BEFORE PRISON WERE MARRED BY CHAOS OF ONE KIND OR ANOTHER. THEY LIVED WITH NO SAFETY, NO STRUCTURE. NOT ALL OF THEM, BUT ENOUGH.
FOR ME, THIS JOB IS ABOUT CARING FOR THEM--WATCHING OVER EACH AND EVERY ONE BY PROVIDING A SYSTEM THAT REWARDS WHAT THEY PUT IN. AND THE DOUBLE F PROGRAM TENDS TO ATTRACT INMATES WHO WANT THAT--WANT A RAW, STURDY MATH.

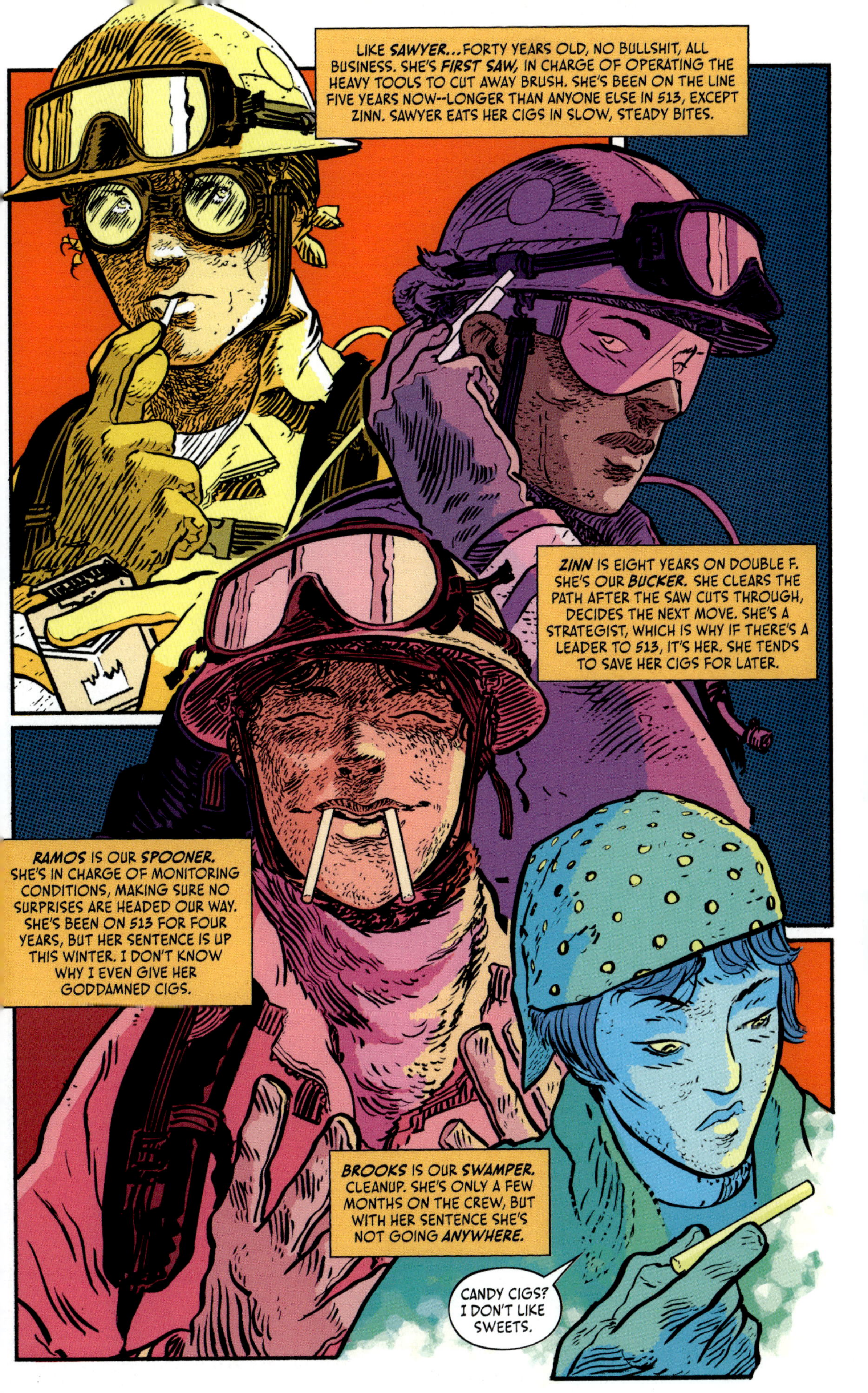
LIKE SAWYER...FORTY YEARS OLD, NO BULLSHIT, ALL BUSINESS. SHE'S FIRST SAW, IN CHARGE OF OPERATING THE HEAVY TOOLS TO CUT AWAY BRUSH. SHE'S BEEN ON THE LINE FIVE YEARS NOW--LONGER THAN ANYONE ELSE IN 513, EXCEPT ZINN. SAWYER EATS HER CIGS IN SLOW, STEADY BITES.
ZINN IS EIGHT YEARS ON DOUBLE F. SHE'S OUR BUCKER. SHE CLEARS THE PATH AFTER THE SAW CUTS THROUGH, DECIDES THE NEXT MOVE. SHE'S A STRATEGIST, WHICH IS WHY IF THERE'S A LEADER TO 513, IT'S HER. SHE TENDS TO SAVE HER CIGS FOR LATER.
RAMOS IS OUR SPOONER. SHE'S IN CHARGE OF MONITORING CONDITIONS, MAKING SURE NO SURPRISES ARE HEADED OUR WAY. SHE'S BEEN ON 513 FOR FOUR YEARS, BUT HER SENTENCE IS UP THIS WINTER. I DON'T KNOW WHY I EVEN GIVE HER GODDAMNED CIGS.
BROOKS IS OUR SWAMPER. CLEANUP. SHE'S ONLY A FEW MONTHS ON THE CREW, BUT WITH HER SENTENCE SHE'S NOT GOING ANYWHERE.
CANDY CIGS? I DON'T LIKE SWEETS.

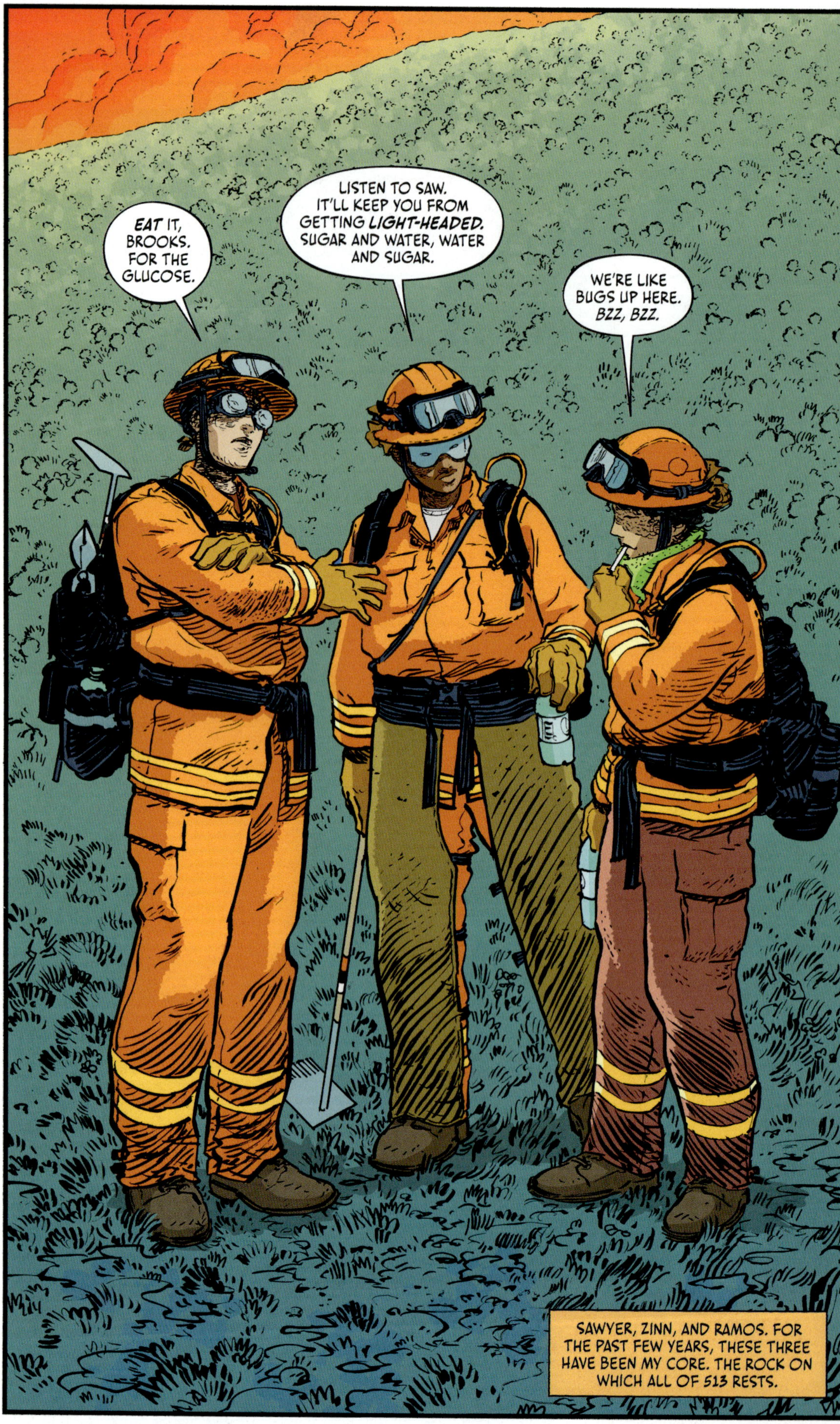
EAT IT, BROOKS. FOR THE GLUCOSE.
LISTEN TO SAW. IT'LL KEEP YOU FROM GETTING LIGHT-HEADED. SUGAR AND WATER, WATER AND SUGAR.
WE'RE LIKE BUGS UP HERE. BZZ, BZZ.
SAWYER, ZINN, AND RAMOS. FOR THE PAST FEW YEARS, THESE THREE HAVE BEEN MY CORE. THE ROCK ON WHICH ALL OF 513 RESTS.

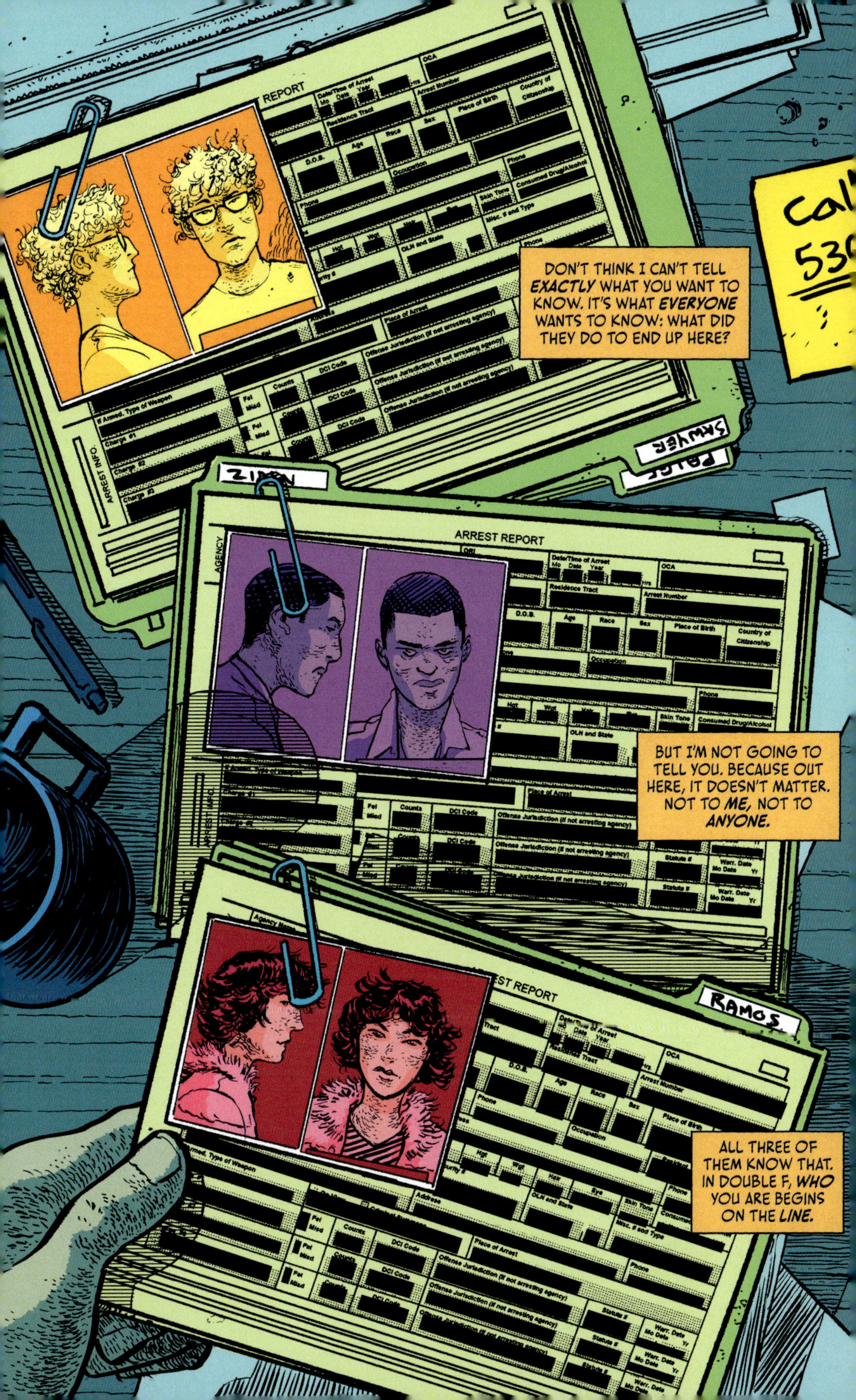
DON'T THINK I CAN'T TELL *EXACTLY* WHAT YOU WANT TO KNOW. IT'S WHAT *EVERYONE* WANTS TO KNOW: WHAT DID THEY DO TO END UP HERE?
ARREST REPORT
BUT I'M NOT GOING TO TELL YOU. BECAUSE OUT HERE, IT DOESN'T MATTER. NOT TO *ME*, NOT TO *ANYONE*.
RAMOS.
ALL THREE OF THEM KNOW THAT. IN DOUBLE F, *WHO* YOU ARE BEGINS ON THE *LINE*.

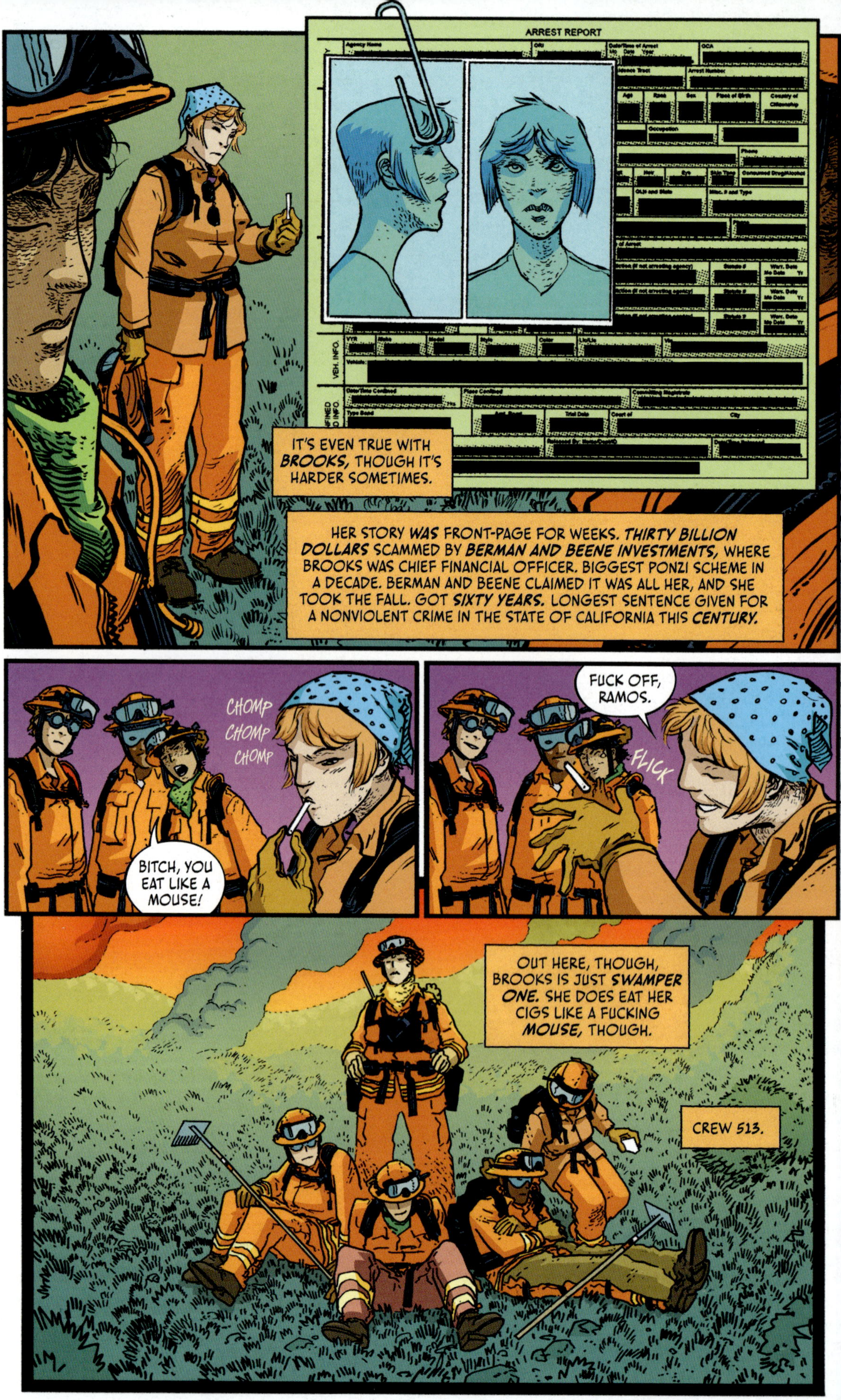
ARREST REPORT
IT'S EVEN TRUE WITH BROOKS, THOUGH IT'S HARDER SOMETIMES.
HER STORY WAS FRONT-PAGE FOR WEEKS. THIRTY BILLION DOLLARS SCAMMED BY BERMAN AND BEENE INVESTMENTS, WHERE BROOKS WAS CHIEF FINANCIAL OFFICER. BIGGEST PONZI SCHEME IN A DECADE. BERMAN AND BEENE CLAIMED IT WAS ALL HER, AND SHE TOOK THE FALL. GOT SIXTY YEARS. LONGEST SENTENCE GIVEN FOR A NONVIOLENT CRIME IN THE STATE OF CALIFORNIA THIS CENTURY.
CHOMP CHOMP CHOMP
BITCH, YOU EAT LIKE A MOUSE!
FUCK OFF, RAMOS.
FLICK
OUT HERE, THOUGH, BROOKS IS JUST SWAMPER ONE. SHE DOES EAT HER CIGS LIKE A FUCKING MOUSE, THOUGH.
CREW 513.

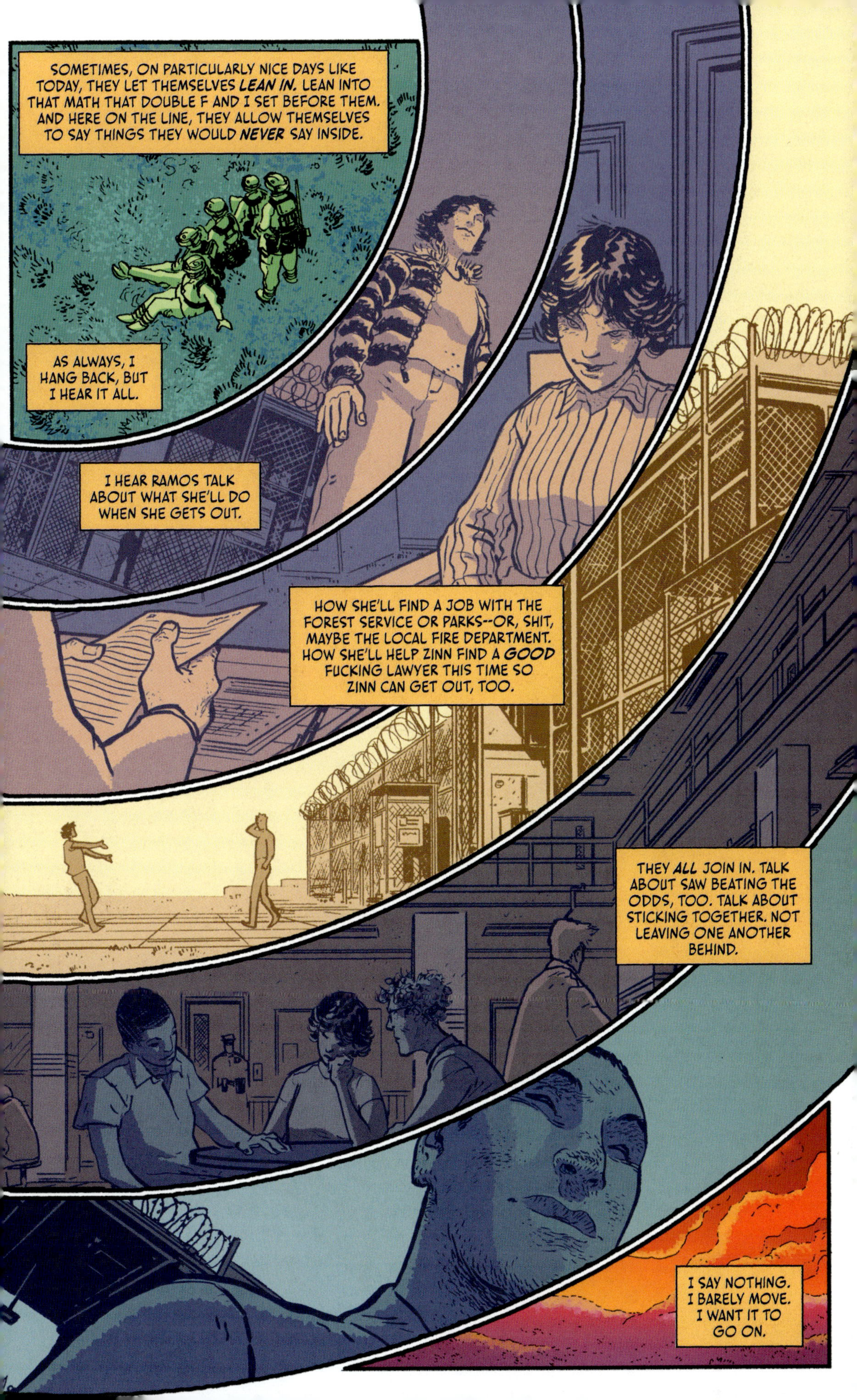
SOMETIMES, ON PARTICULARLY NICE DAYS LIKE TODAY, THEY LET THEMSELVES *LEAN IN.* LEAN INTO THAT MATH THAT DOUBLE F AND I SET BEFORE THEM. AND HERE ON THE LINE, THEY ALLOW THEMSELVES TO SAY THINGS THEY WOULD *NEVER* SAY INSIDE.
AS ALWAYS, I HANG BACK, BUT I HEAR IT ALL.
I HEAR RAMOS TALK ABOUT WHAT SHE'LL DO WHEN SHE GETS OUT.
HOW SHE'LL FIND A JOB WITH THE FOREST SERVICE OR PARKS--OR, SHIT, MAYBE THE LOCAL FIRE DEPARTMENT. HOW SHE'LL HELP ZINN FIND A *GOOD* FUCKING LAWYER THIS TIME SO ZINN CAN GET OUT, TOO.
THEY *ALL* JOIN IN. TALK ABOUT SAW BEATING THE ODDS, TOO. TALK ABOUT STICKING TOGETHER. NOT LEAVING ONE ANOTHER BEHIND.
I SAY NOTHING. I BARELY MOVE. I WANT IT TO GO ON.

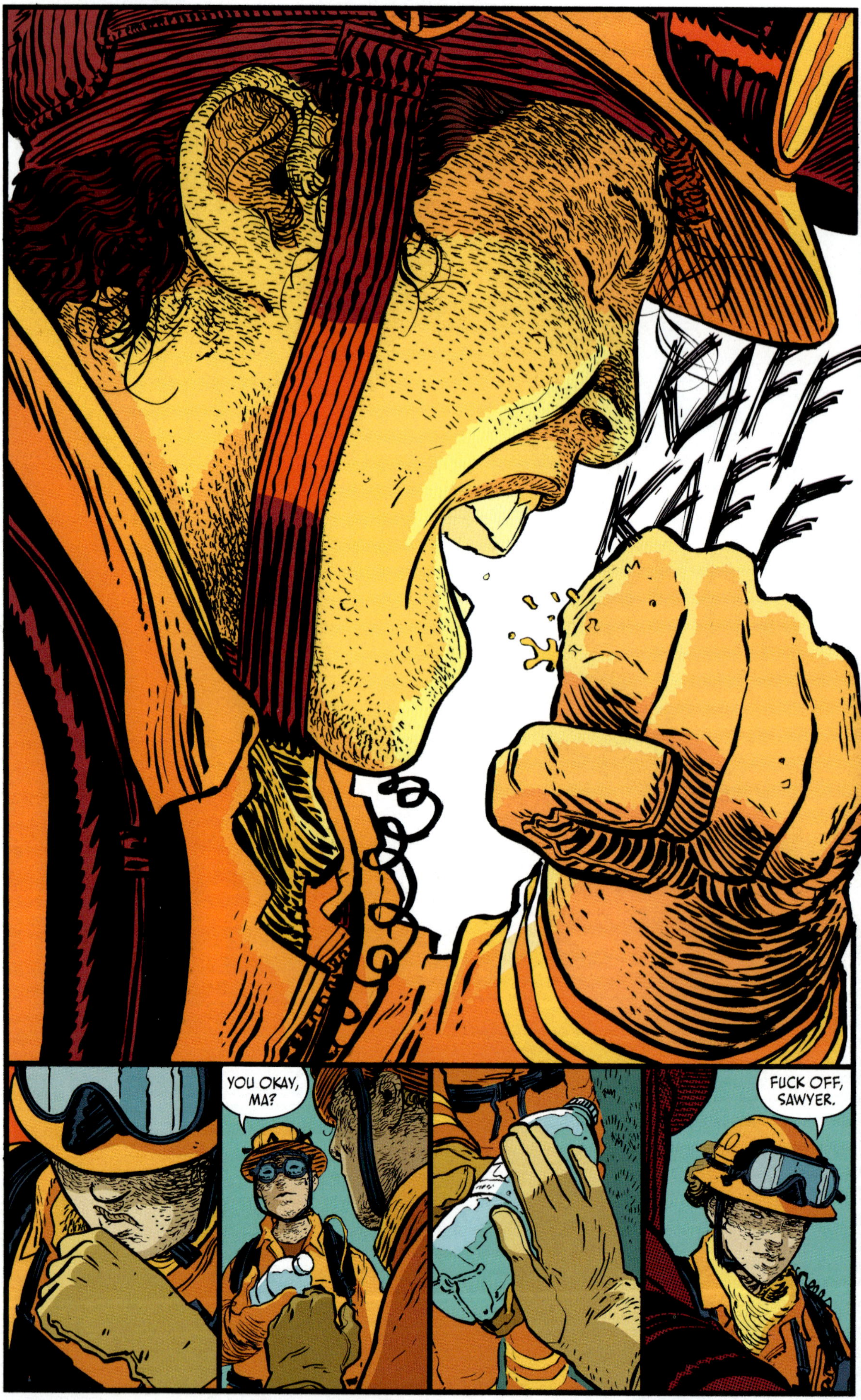
KAFF KAFF
YOU OKAY, MA?
FUCK OFF, SAWYER.

BP-A0373
JUN 10

FEDERAL CORRECTIONAL INSTITUTION

Correctional Officer
Ruby Ma Ning
Gate 2

Ruby Ma Ning

Officer ID Number: 127158976

U.S. DEPARTMENT OF JUSTICE
FEDERAL BUREAU OF PRISONS

...ON CORRECTIONAL OFFICER

RATING PERIOD

ENTER ON DUTY DATE

WHO WE ARE BEGINS ON THE LINE...

	Unacceptable	Marginal	Fully Meets Requirements	Exceeds	Excellent	Unknown

...ecurity and orderly

...in order to

...tems which could be ...effect an escape.

...ntraband.

5. Reports significant instances of disorder, abnormal behavior, and unrest among inmates

6. Responds appropriately to emergency situations.

7. Collects evidence to substantiate institutional or criminal violations by inmates.

8. Controls inmates using the minimum amount of force necessary in order to protect life, property and security of the institution

9. Enforces the rules and regulations of the institution in an impartial manner.

...IT'S SOMETHING I TRY TO LIVE BY, TOO.

WHAT IS THERE TO TELL ABOUT ME *OUTSIDE* CAMP?

NOT MUCH.

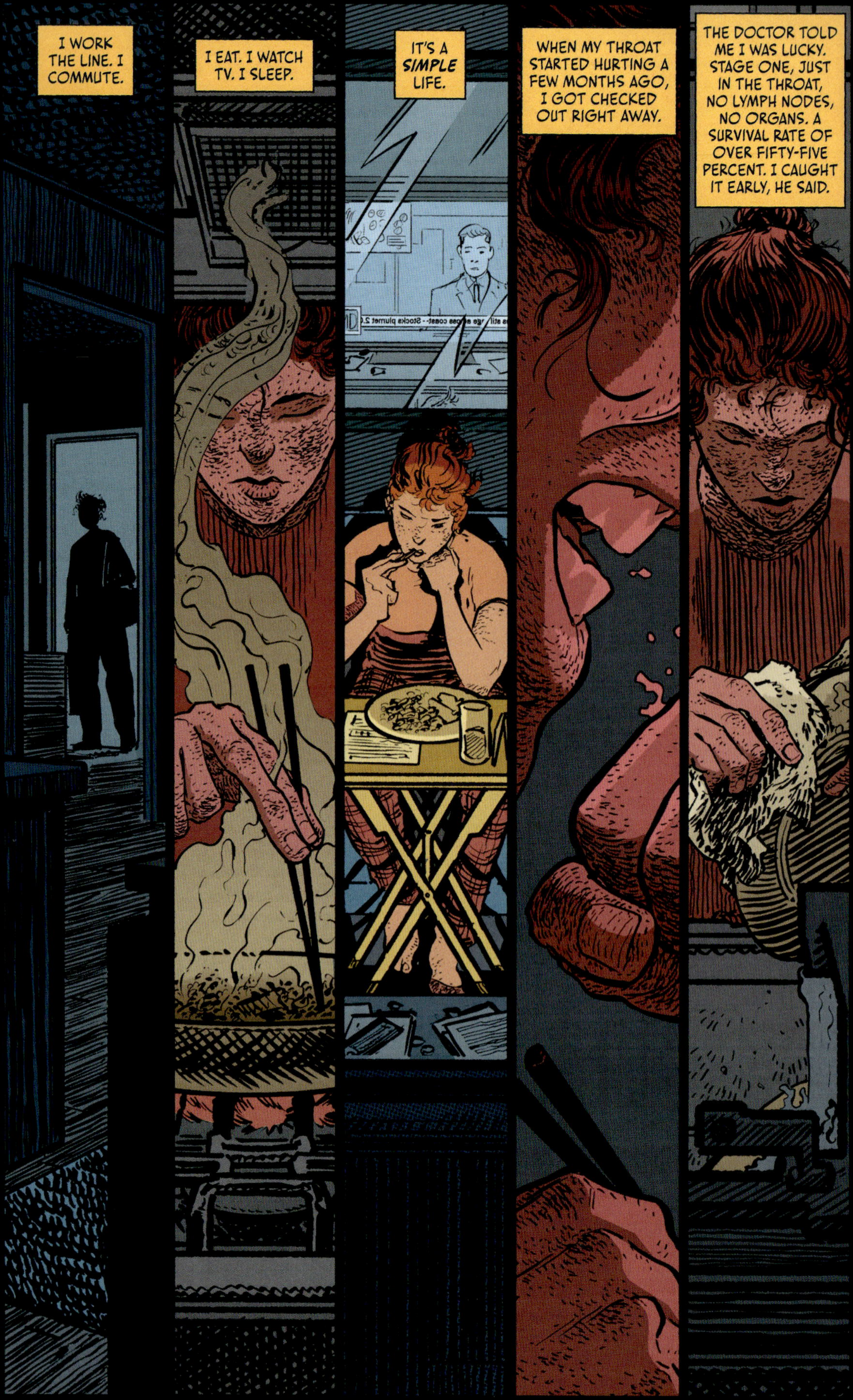
I WORK THE LINE. I COMMUTE.
I EAT. I WATCH TV. I SLEEP.
IT'S A *SIMPLE* LIFE.
WHEN MY THROAT STARTED HURTING A FEW MONTHS AGO, I GOT CHECKED OUT RIGHT AWAY.
THE DOCTOR TOLD ME I WAS LUCKY. STAGE ONE, JUST IN THE THROAT, NO LYMPH NODES, NO ORGANS. A SURVIVAL RATE OF OVER FIFTY-FIVE PERCENT. I CAUGHT IT EARLY, HE SAID.

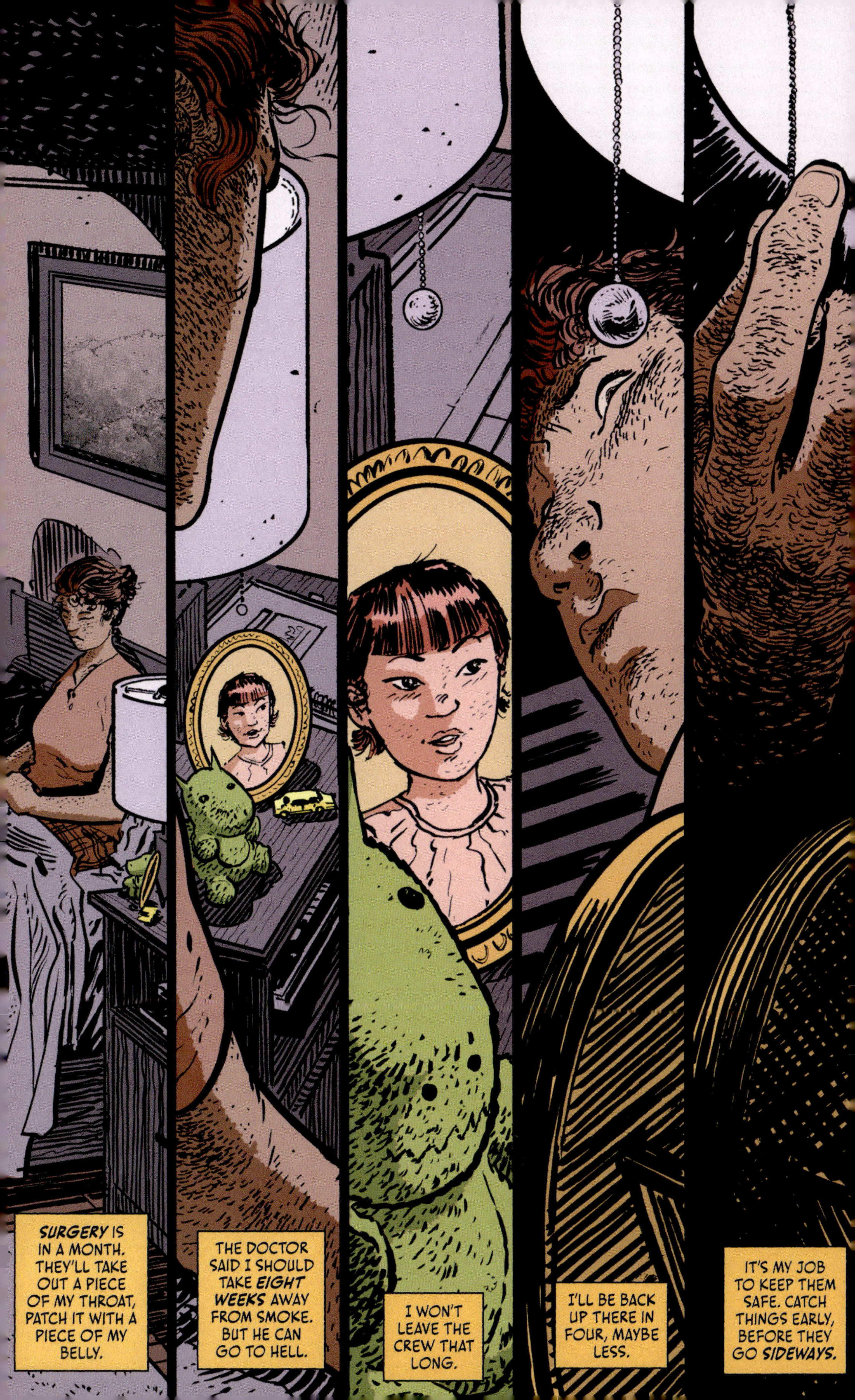
SURGERY IS IN A MONTH. THEY'LL TAKE OUT A PIECE OF MY THROAT, PATCH IT WITH A PIECE OF MY BELLY.
THE DOCTOR SAID I SHOULD TAKE *EIGHT WEEKS* AWAY FROM SMOKE. BUT HE CAN GO TO HELL.
I WON'T LEAVE THE CREW THAT LONG.
I'LL BE BACK UP THERE IN FOUR, MAYBE LESS.
IT'S MY JOB TO KEEP THEM SAFE. CATCH THINGS EARLY, BEFORE THEY GO *SIDEWAYS.*

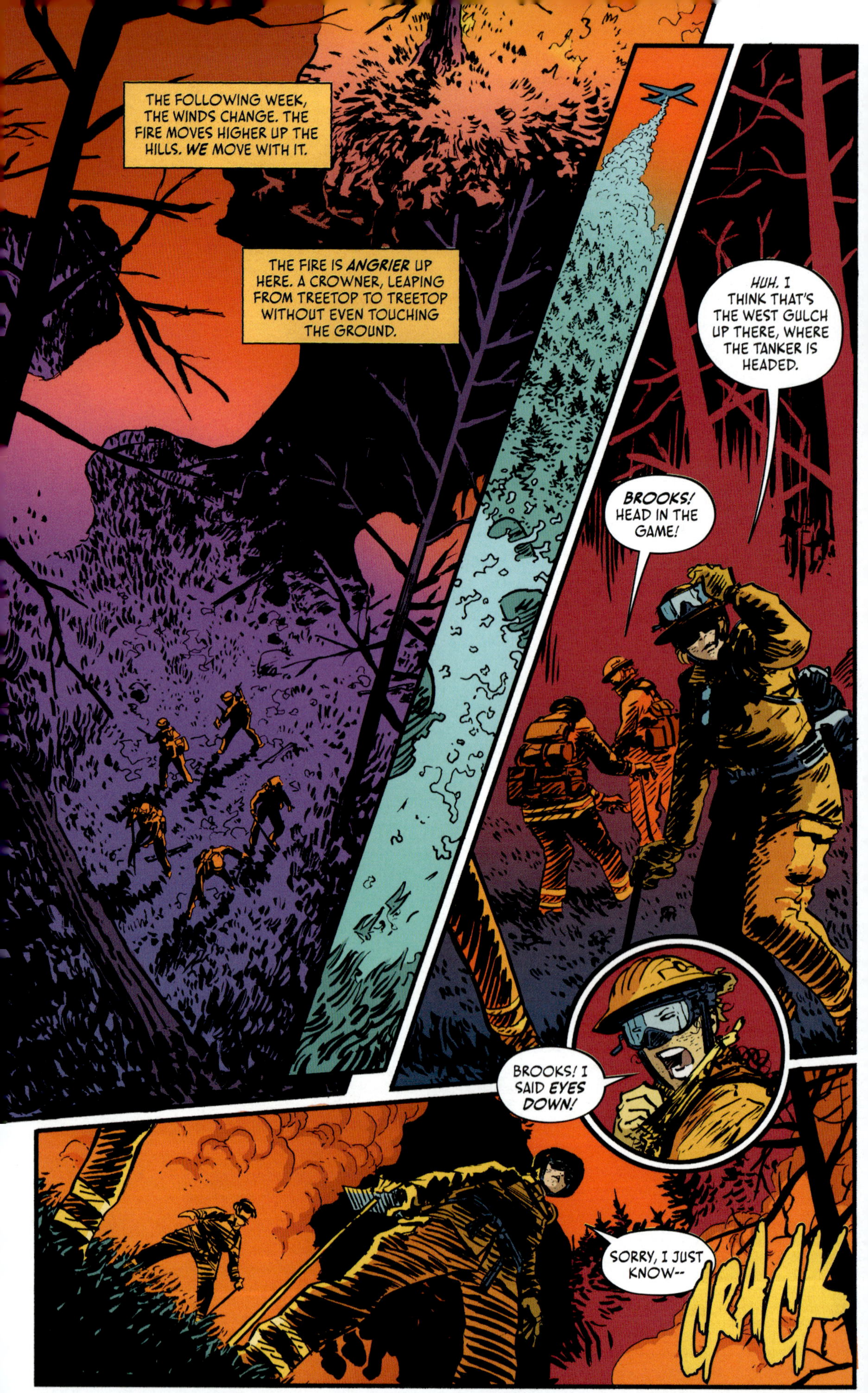
THE FOLLOWING WEEK, THE WINDS CHANGE. THE FIRE MOVES HIGHER UP THE HILLS. *WE* MOVE WITH IT.
THE FIRE IS *ANGRIER* UP HERE. A CROWNER, LEAPING FROM TREETOP TO TREETOP WITHOUT EVEN TOUCHING THE GROUND.
HUH. I THINK THAT'S THE WEST GULCH UP THERE, WHERE THE TANKER IS HEADED.
BROOKS! HEAD IN THE GAME!
BROOKS! I SAID *EYES DOWN!*
SORRY, I JUST KNOW--
CRACK

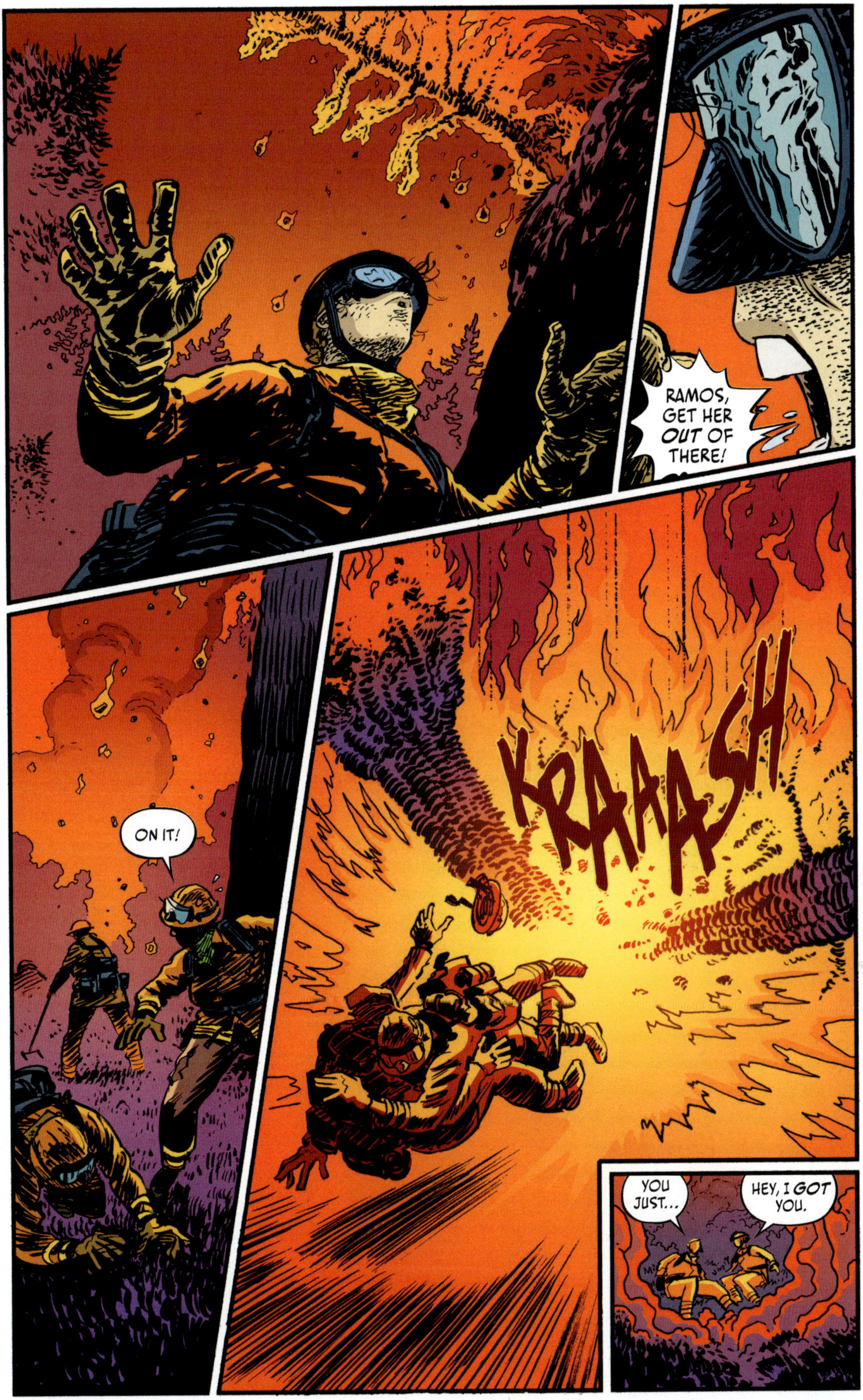
RAMOS, GET HER OUT OF THERE!
ON IT!
KRAAASH
YOU JUST...
HEY, I GOT YOU.

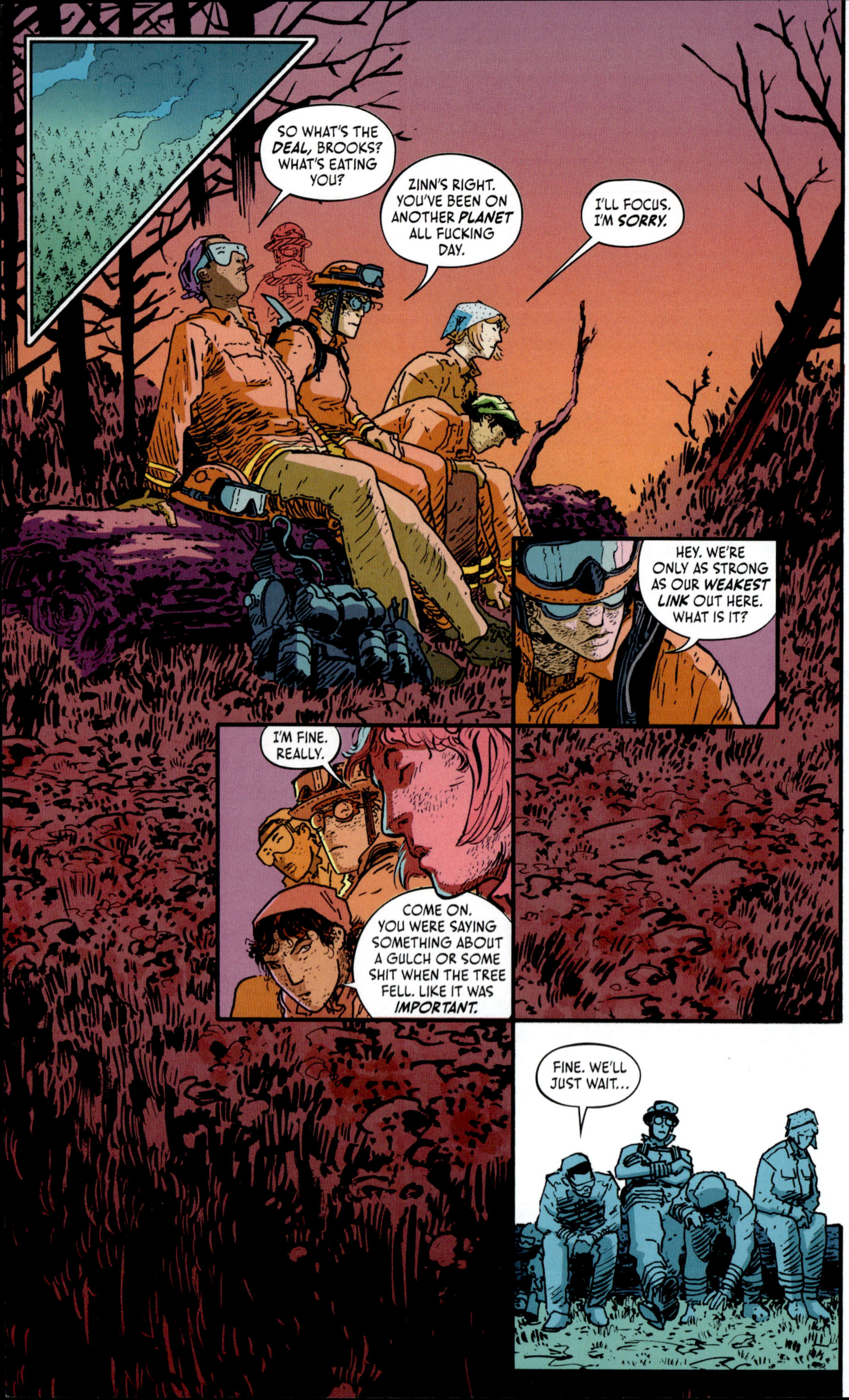
SO WHAT'S THE DEAL, BROOKS? WHAT'S EATING YOU?
ZINN'S RIGHT. YOU'VE BEEN ON ANOTHER PLANET ALL FUCKING DAY.
I'LL FOCUS. I'M SORRY.
HEY. WE'RE ONLY AS STRONG AS OUR WEAKEST LINK OUT HERE. WHAT IS IT?
I'M FINE. REALLY.
COME ON. YOU WERE SAYING SOMETHING ABOUT A GULCH OR SOME SHIT WHEN THE TREE FELL. LIKE IT WAS IMPORTANT.
FINE. WE'LL JUST WAIT...

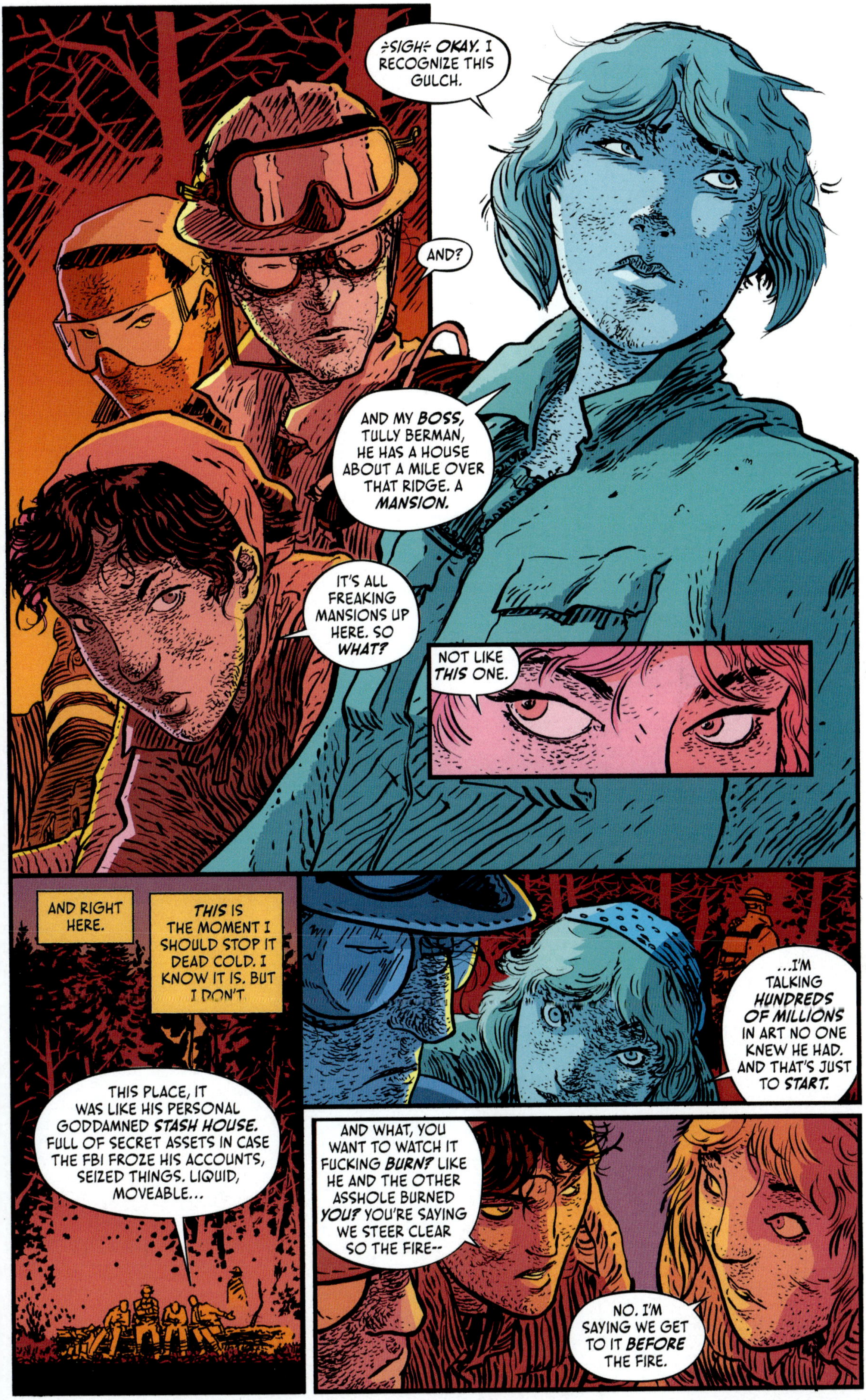

÷SIGH÷ *OKAY.* I RECOGNIZE THIS GULCH.
AND?
AND MY *BOSS,* TULLY BERMAN, HE HAS A HOUSE ABOUT A MILE OVER THAT RIDGE. A *MANSION.*
IT'S ALL FREAKING MANSIONS UP HERE. SO *WHAT?*
NOT LIKE *THIS* ONE.
AND RIGHT HERE.
THIS IS THE MOMENT I SHOULD STOP IT DEAD COLD. I KNOW IT IS. BUT I DON'T.
THIS PLACE, IT WAS LIKE HIS PERSONAL GODDAMNED *STASH HOUSE.* FULL OF SECRET ASSETS IN CASE THE FBI FROZE HIS ACCOUNTS, SEIZED THINGS. LIQUID, MOVEABLE...
...I'M TALKING *HUNDREDS OF MILLIONS* IN ART NO ONE KNEW HE HAD. AND THAT'S JUST TO *START.*
AND WHAT, YOU WANT TO WATCH IT FUCKING *BURN?* LIKE HE AND THE OTHER ASSHOLE BURNED *YOU?* YOU'RE SAYING WE STEER CLEAR SO THE FIRE--
NO. I'M SAYING WE GET TO IT *BEFORE* THE FIRE.

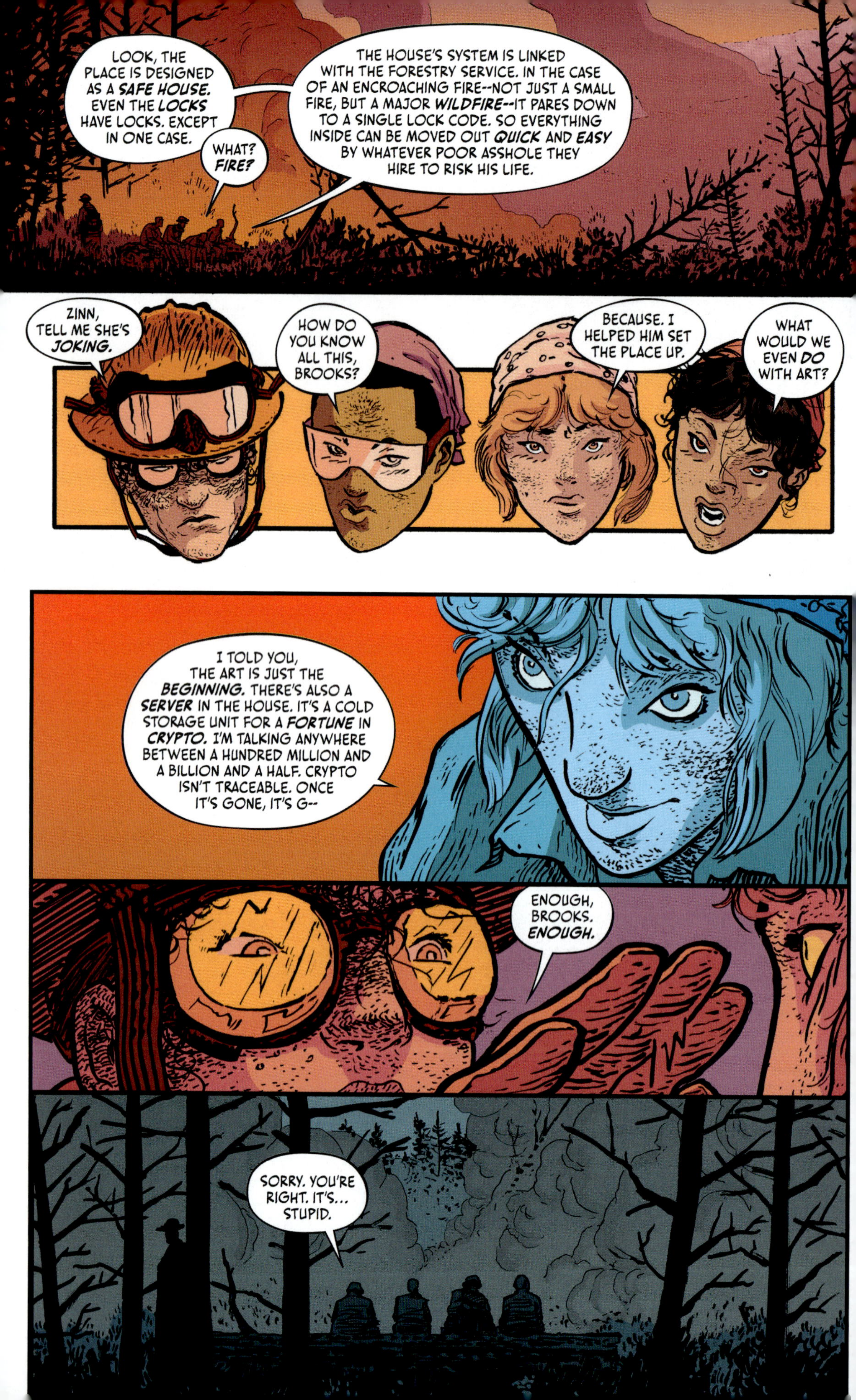
LOOK, THE PLACE IS DESIGNED AS A SAFE HOUSE. EVEN THE LOCKS HAVE LOCKS. EXCEPT IN ONE CASE.
WHAT? FIRE?
THE HOUSE'S SYSTEM IS LINKED WITH THE FORESTRY SERVICE. IN THE CASE OF AN ENCROACHING FIRE--NOT JUST A SMALL FIRE, BUT A MAJOR WILDFIRE--IT PARES DOWN TO A SINGLE LOCK CODE. SO EVERYTHING INSIDE CAN BE MOVED OUT QUICK AND EASY BY WHATEVER POOR ASSHOLE THEY HIRE TO RISK HIS LIFE.
ZINN, TELL ME SHE'S JOKING.
HOW DO YOU KNOW ALL THIS, BROOKS?
BECAUSE. I HELPED HIM SET THE PLACE UP.
WHAT WOULD WE EVEN DO WITH ART?
I TOLD YOU, THE ART IS JUST THE BEGINNING. THERE'S ALSO A SERVER IN THE HOUSE. IT'S A COLD STORAGE UNIT FOR A FORTUNE IN CRYPTO. I'M TALKING ANYWHERE BETWEEN A HUNDRED MILLION AND A BILLION AND A HALF. CRYPTO ISN'T TRACEABLE. ONCE IT'S GONE, IT'S G--
ENOUGH, BROOKS. ENOUGH.
SORRY. YOU'RE RIGHT. IT'S... STUPID.

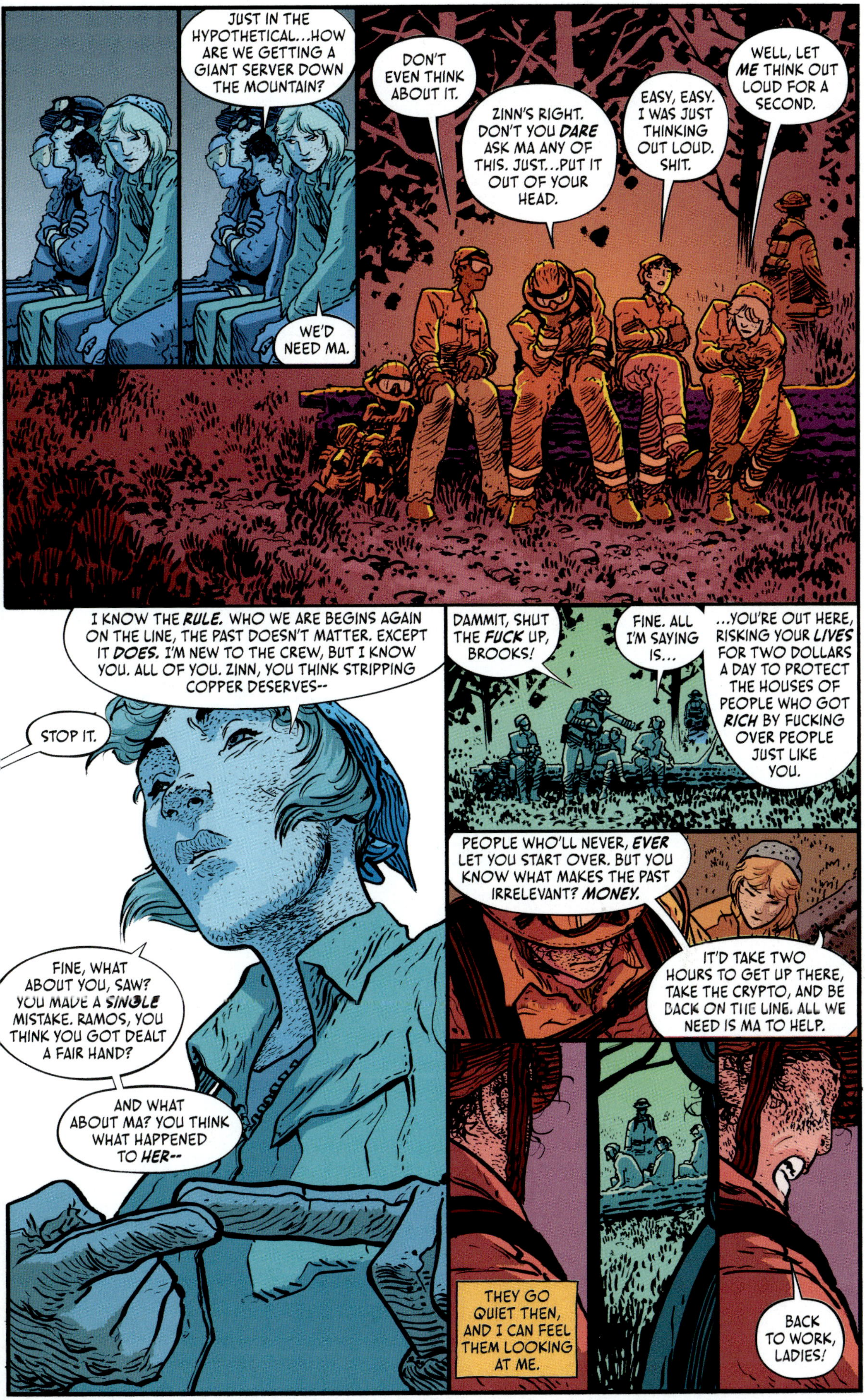
JUST IN THE HYPOTHETICAL...HOW ARE WE GETTING A GIANT SERVER DOWN THE MOUNTAIN?
WE'D NEED MA.
DON'T EVEN THINK ABOUT IT.
ZINN'S RIGHT. DON'T YOU DARE ASK MA ANY OF THIS. JUST...PUT IT OUT OF YOUR HEAD.
EASY, EASY. I WAS JUST THINKING OUT LOUD. SHIT.
WELL, LET ME THINK OUT LOUD FOR A SECOND.
I KNOW THE RULE. WHO WE ARE BEGINS AGAIN ON THE LINE, THE PAST DOESN'T MATTER. EXCEPT IT DOES. I'M NEW TO THE CREW, BUT I KNOW YOU. ALL OF YOU. ZINN, YOU THINK STRIPPING COPPER DESERVES--
STOP IT.
FINE, WHAT ABOUT YOU, SAW? YOU MADE A SINGLE MISTAKE. RAMOS, YOU THINK YOU GOT DEALT A FAIR HAND?
AND WHAT ABOUT MA? YOU THINK WHAT HAPPENED TO HER--
DAMMIT, SHUT THE FUCK UP, BROOKS!
FINE. ALL I'M SAYING IS...
...YOU'RE OUT HERE, RISKING YOUR LIVES FOR TWO DOLLARS A DAY TO PROTECT THE HOUSES OF PEOPLE WHO GOT RICH BY FUCKING OVER PEOPLE JUST LIKE YOU.
PEOPLE WHO'LL NEVER, EVER LET YOU START OVER. BUT YOU KNOW WHAT MAKES THE PAST IRRELEVANT? MONEY.
IT'D TAKE TWO HOURS TO GET UP THERE, TAKE THE CRYPTO, AND BE BACK ON THE LINE. ALL WE NEED IS MA TO HELP.
THEY GO QUIET THEN, AND I CAN FEEL THEM LOOKING AT ME.
BACK TO WORK, LADIES!

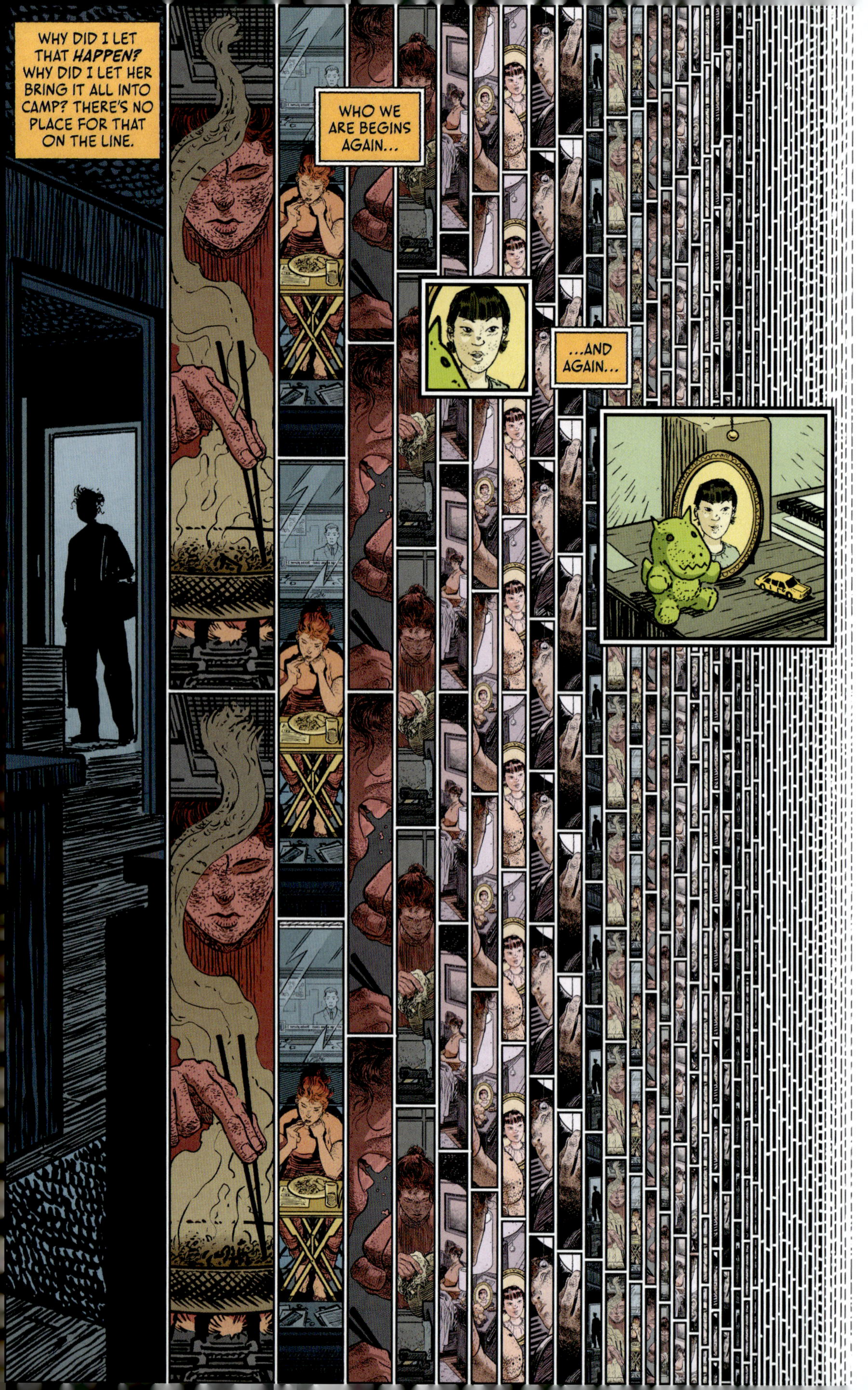
WHY DID I LET THAT *HAPPEN?* WHY DID I LET HER BRING IT ALL INTO CAMP? THERE'S NO PLACE FOR THAT ON THE LINE.
WHO WE ARE BEGINS AGAIN...
...AND AGAIN...

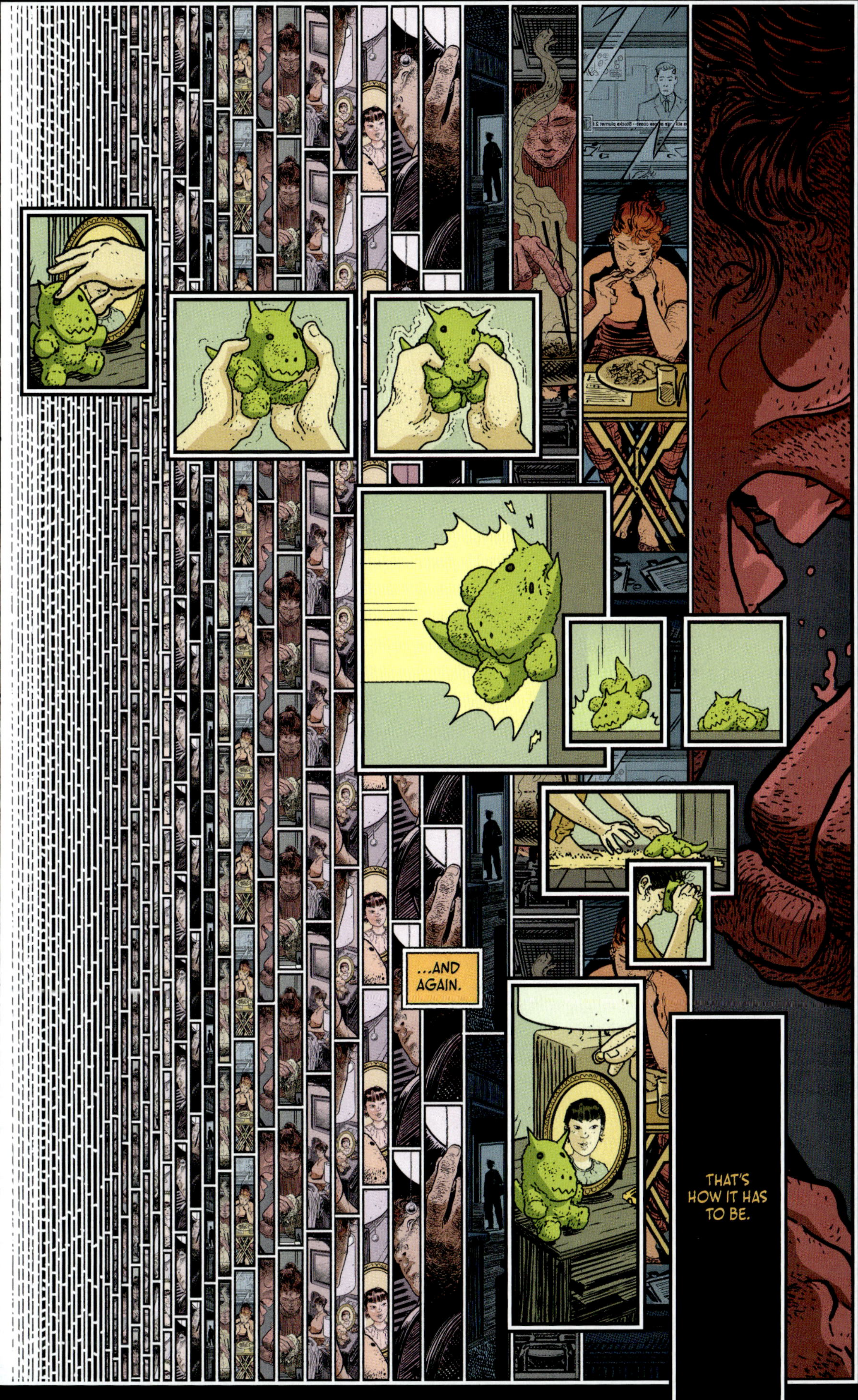
...AND AGAIN.
THAT'S HOW IT HAS TO BE.

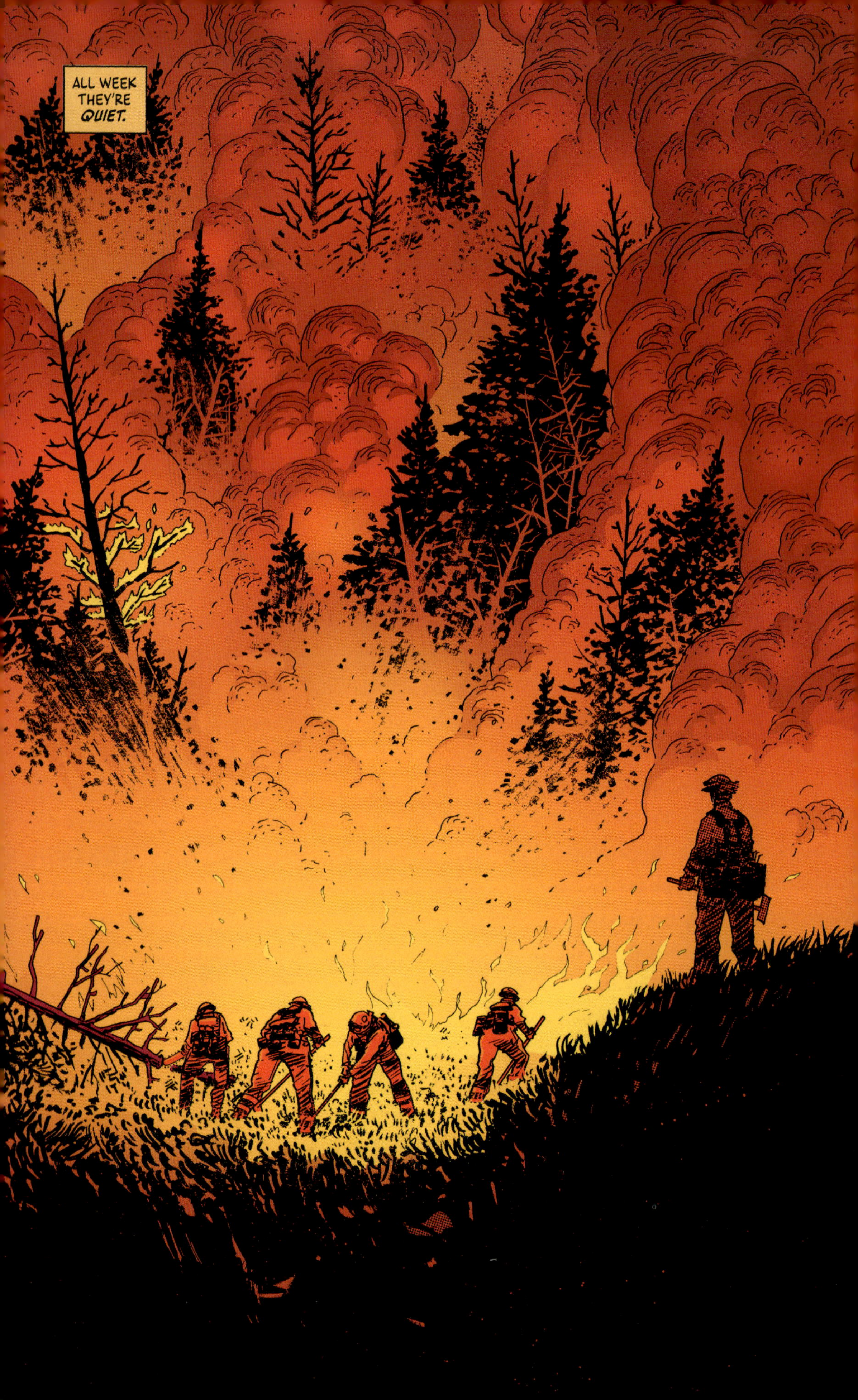
ALL WEEK THEY'RE *QUIET.*

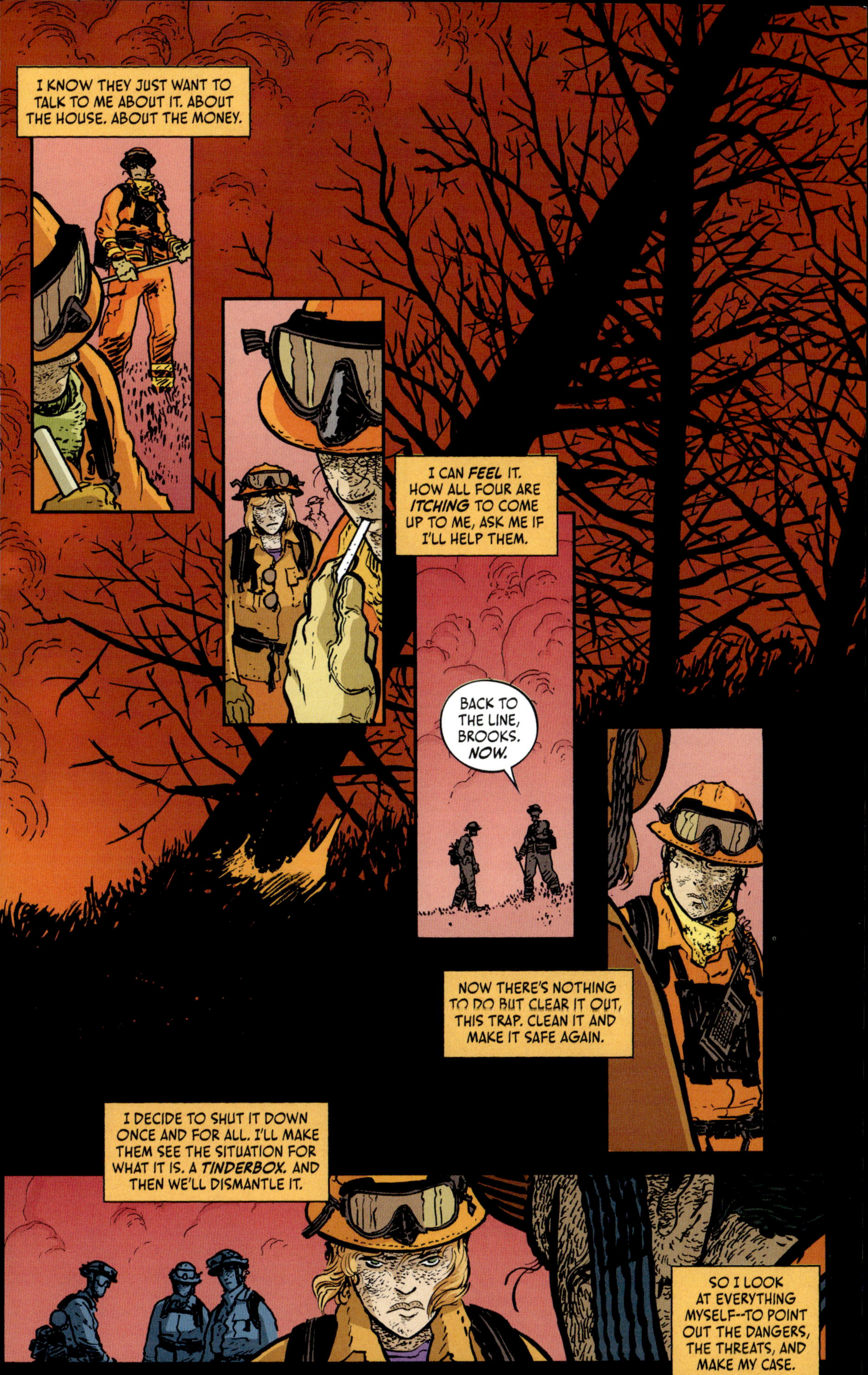
I KNOW THEY JUST WANT TO TALK TO ME ABOUT IT. ABOUT THE HOUSE. ABOUT THE MONEY.
I CAN *FEEL* IT. HOW ALL FOUR ARE *ITCHING* TO COME UP TO ME, ASK ME IF I'LL HELP THEM.
BACK TO THE LINE, BROOKS. *NOW.*
NOW THERE'S NOTHING TO DO BUT CLEAR IT OUT, THIS TRAP. CLEAN IT AND MAKE IT SAFE AGAIN.
I DECIDE TO SHUT IT DOWN ONCE AND FOR ALL. I'LL MAKE THEM SEE THE SITUATION FOR WHAT IT IS. A *TINDERBOX.* AND THEN WE'LL DISMANTLE IT.
SO I LOOK AT EVERYTHING MYSELF--TO POINT OUT THE DANGERS, THE THREATS, AND MAKE MY CASE.

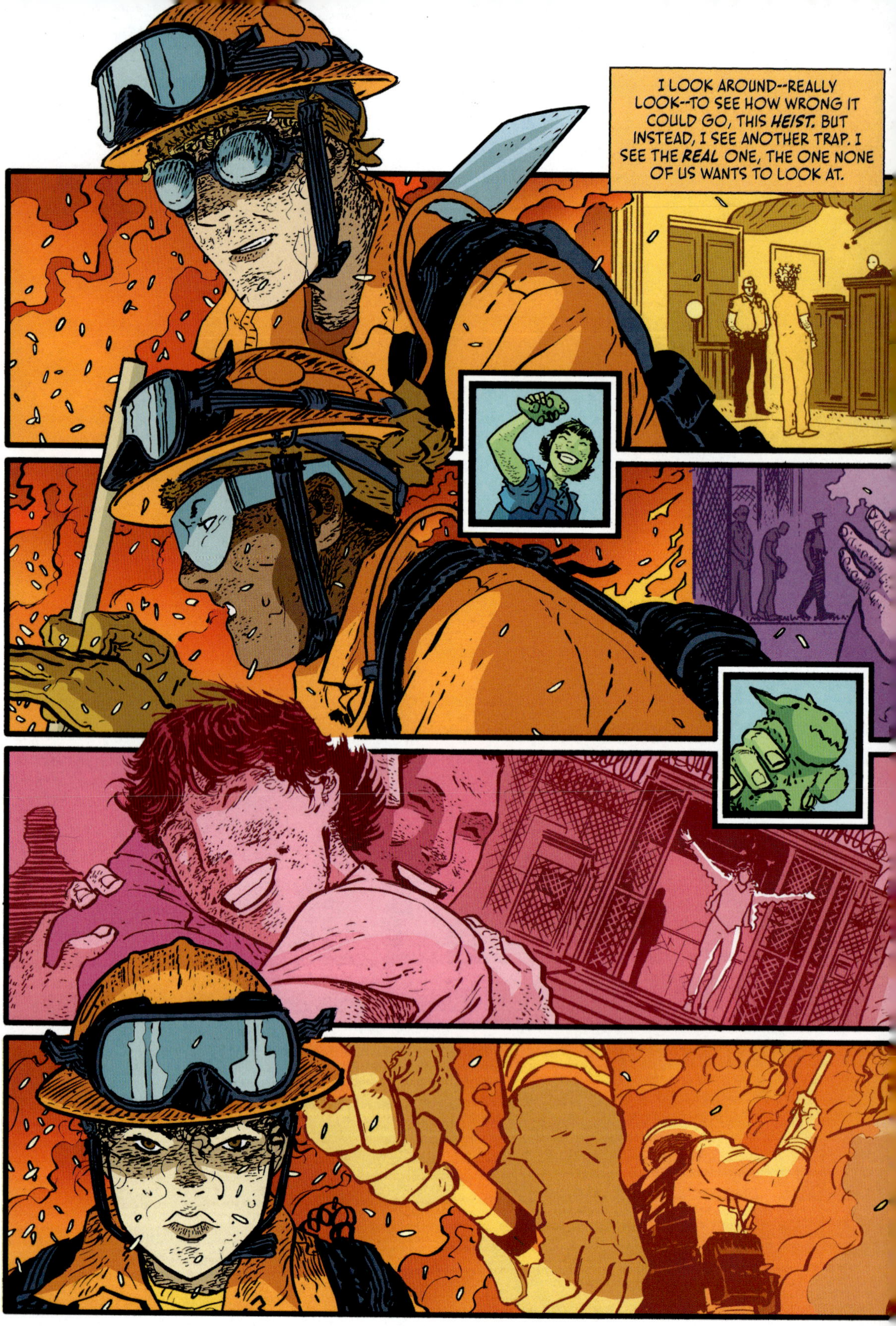
I LOOK AROUND--REALLY LOOK--TO SEE HOW WRONG IT COULD GO, THIS *HEIST.* BUT INSTEAD, I SEE ANOTHER TRAP. I SEE THE *REAL* ONE, THE ONE NONE OF US WANTS TO LOOK AT.

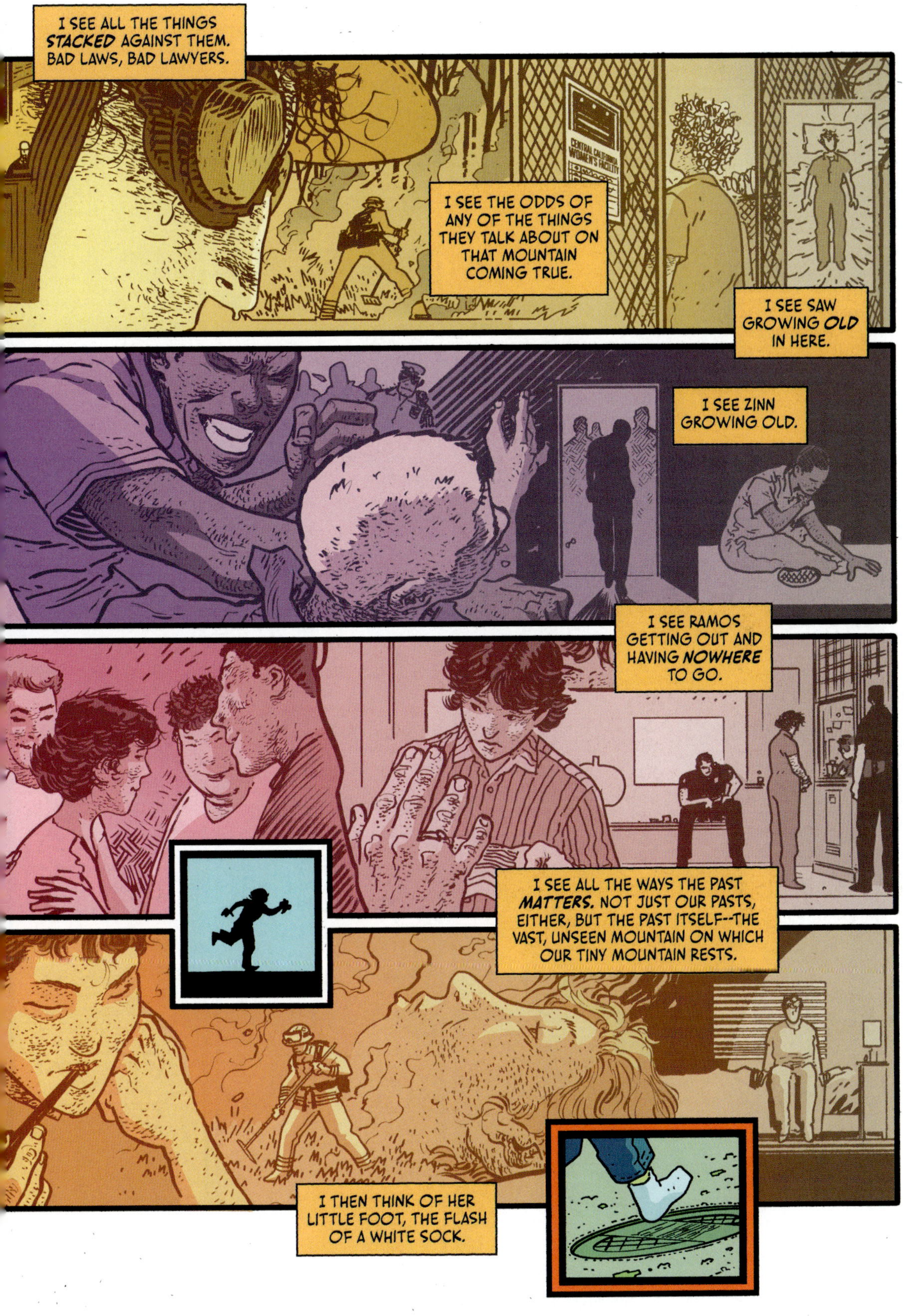

I SEE ALL THE THINGS *STACKED* AGAINST THEM. BAD LAWS, BAD LAWYERS.
I SEE THE ODDS OF ANY OF THE THINGS THEY TALK ABOUT ON THAT MOUNTAIN COMING TRUE.
I SEE SAW GROWING *OLD* IN HERE.
I SEE ZINN GROWING OLD.
I SEE RAMOS GETTING OUT AND HAVING *NOWHERE* TO GO.
I SEE ALL THE WAYS THE PAST *MATTERS.* NOT JUST OUR PASTS, EITHER, BUT THE PAST ITSELF--THE VAST, UNSEEN MOUNTAIN ON WHICH OUR TINY MOUNTAIN RESTS.
I THEN THINK OF HER LITTLE FOOT, THE FLASH OF A WHITE SOCK.

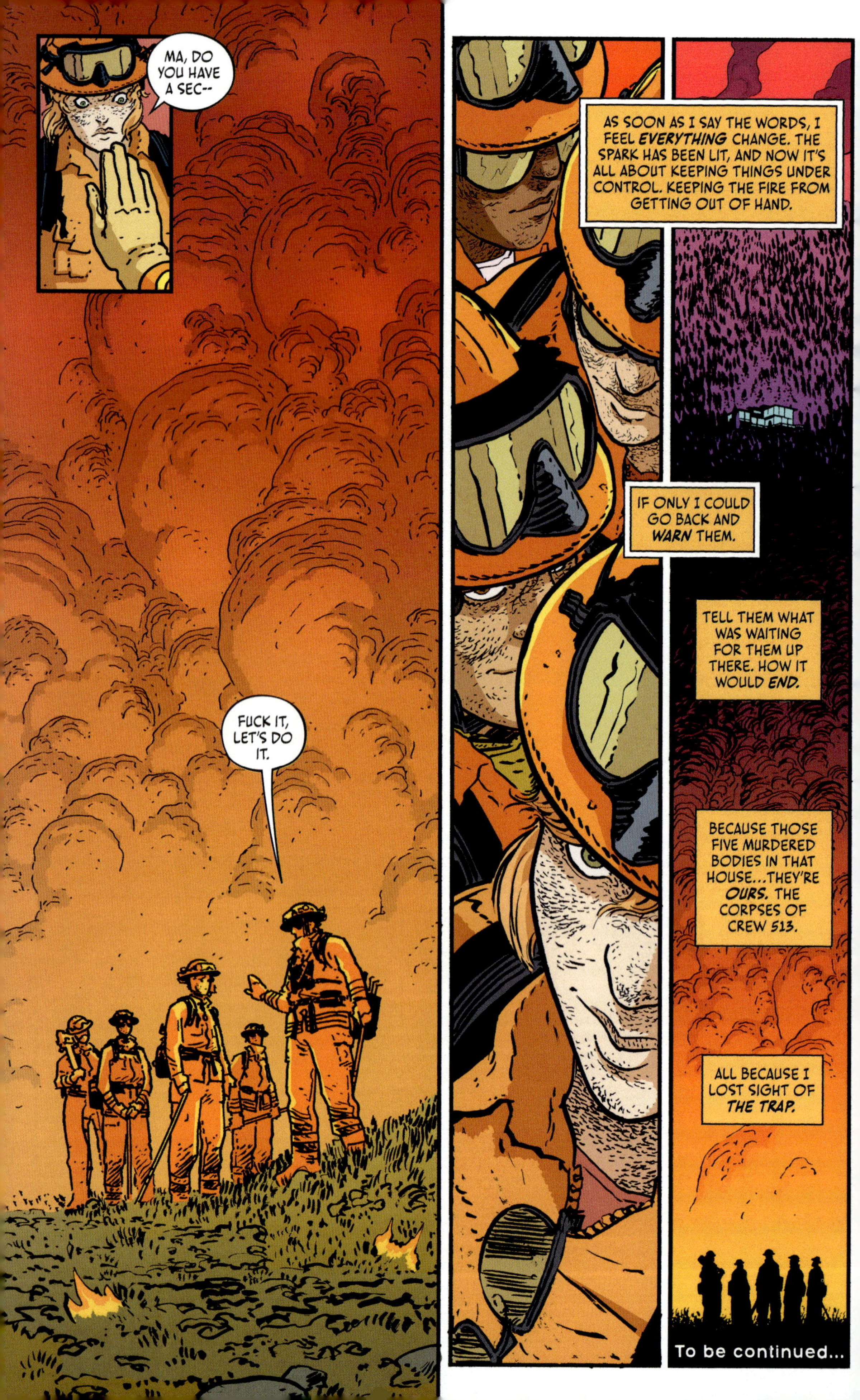
MA, DO YOU HAVE A SEC--
FUCK IT, LET'S DO IT.
AS SOON AS I SAY THE WORDS, I FEEL EVERYTHING CHANGE. THE SPARK HAS BEEN LIT, AND NOW IT'S ALL ABOUT KEEPING THINGS UNDER CONTROL. KEEPING THE FIRE FROM GETTING OUT OF HAND.
IF ONLY I COULD GO BACK AND WARN THEM.
TELL THEM WHAT WAS WAITING FOR THEM UP THERE. HOW IT WOULD END.
BECAUSE THOSE FIVE MURDERED BODIES IN THAT HOUSE...THEY'RE OURS. THE CORPSES OF CREW 513.
ALL BECAUSE I LOST SIGHT OF THE TRAP.
To be continued...

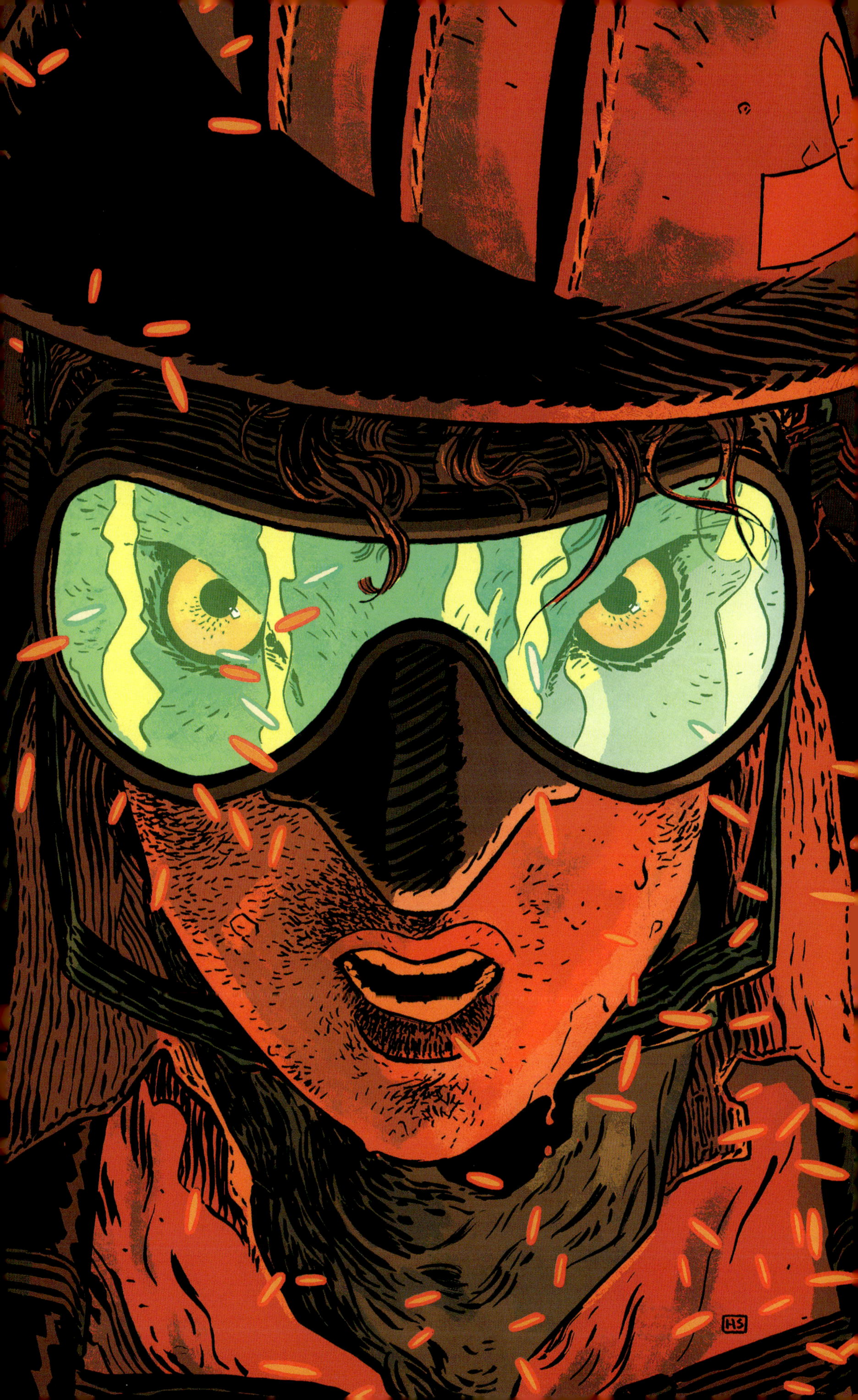

"AND JUST LIKE THAT...
THE SPARK IS LIT."

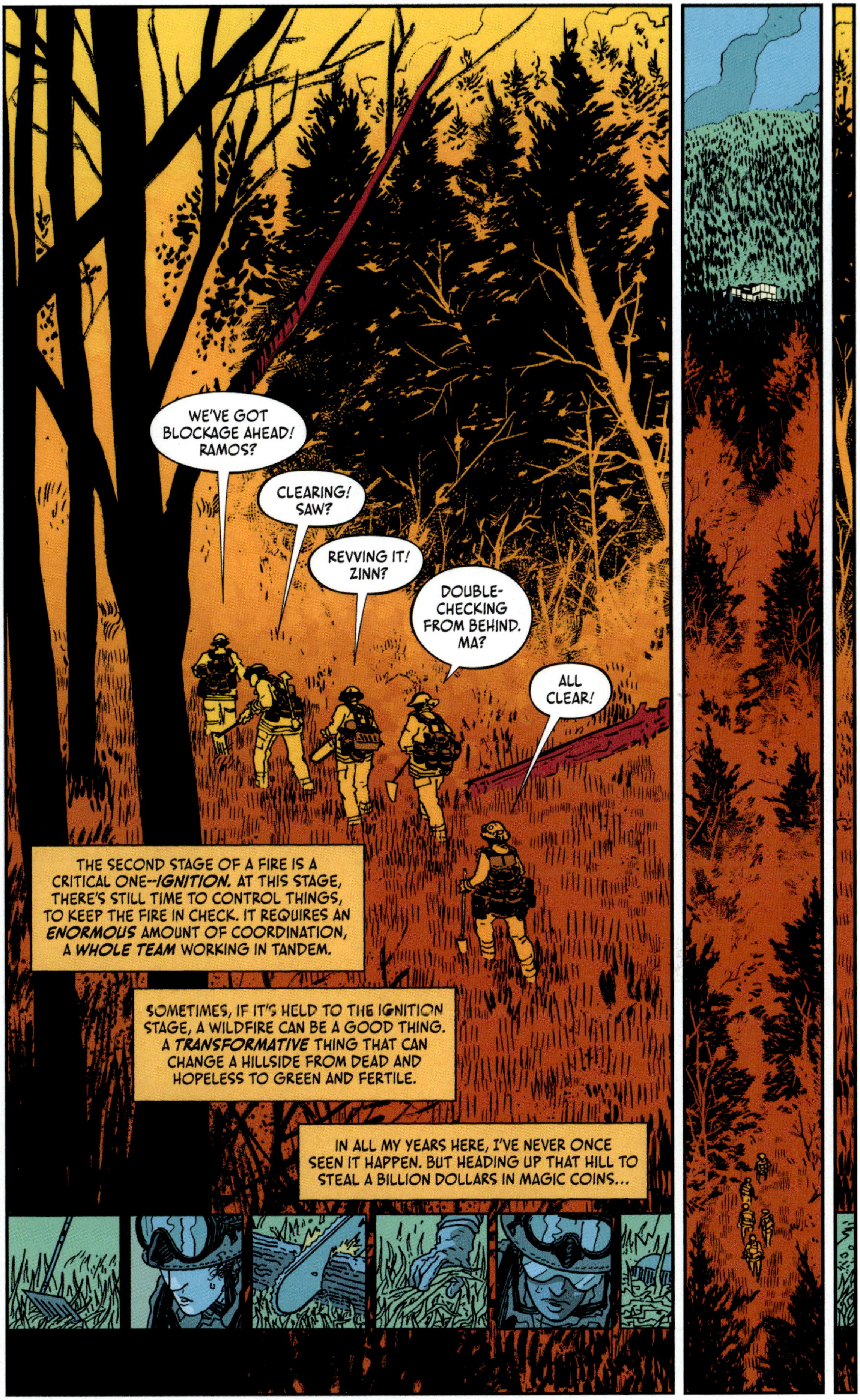
WE'VE GOT BLOCKAGE AHEAD! RAMOS?
CLEARING! SAW?
REVVING IT! ZINN?
DOUBLE-CHECKING FROM BEHIND. MA?
ALL CLEAR!
THE SECOND STAGE OF A FIRE IS A CRITICAL ONE--*IGNITION.* AT THIS STAGE, THERE'S STILL TIME TO CONTROL THINGS, TO KEEP THE FIRE IN CHECK. IT REQUIRES AN *ENORMOUS* AMOUNT OF COORDINATION, A *WHOLE TEAM* WORKING IN TANDEM.
SOMETIMES, IF IT'S HELD TO THE IGNITION STAGE, A WILDFIRE CAN BE A GOOD THING. A *TRANSFORMATIVE* THING THAT CAN CHANGE A HILLSIDE FROM DEAD AND HOPELESS TO GREEN AND FERTILE.
IN ALL MY YEARS HERE, I'VE NEVER ONCE SEEN IT HAPPEN. BUT HEADING UP THAT HILL TO STEAL A BILLION DOLLARS IN MAGIC COINS...

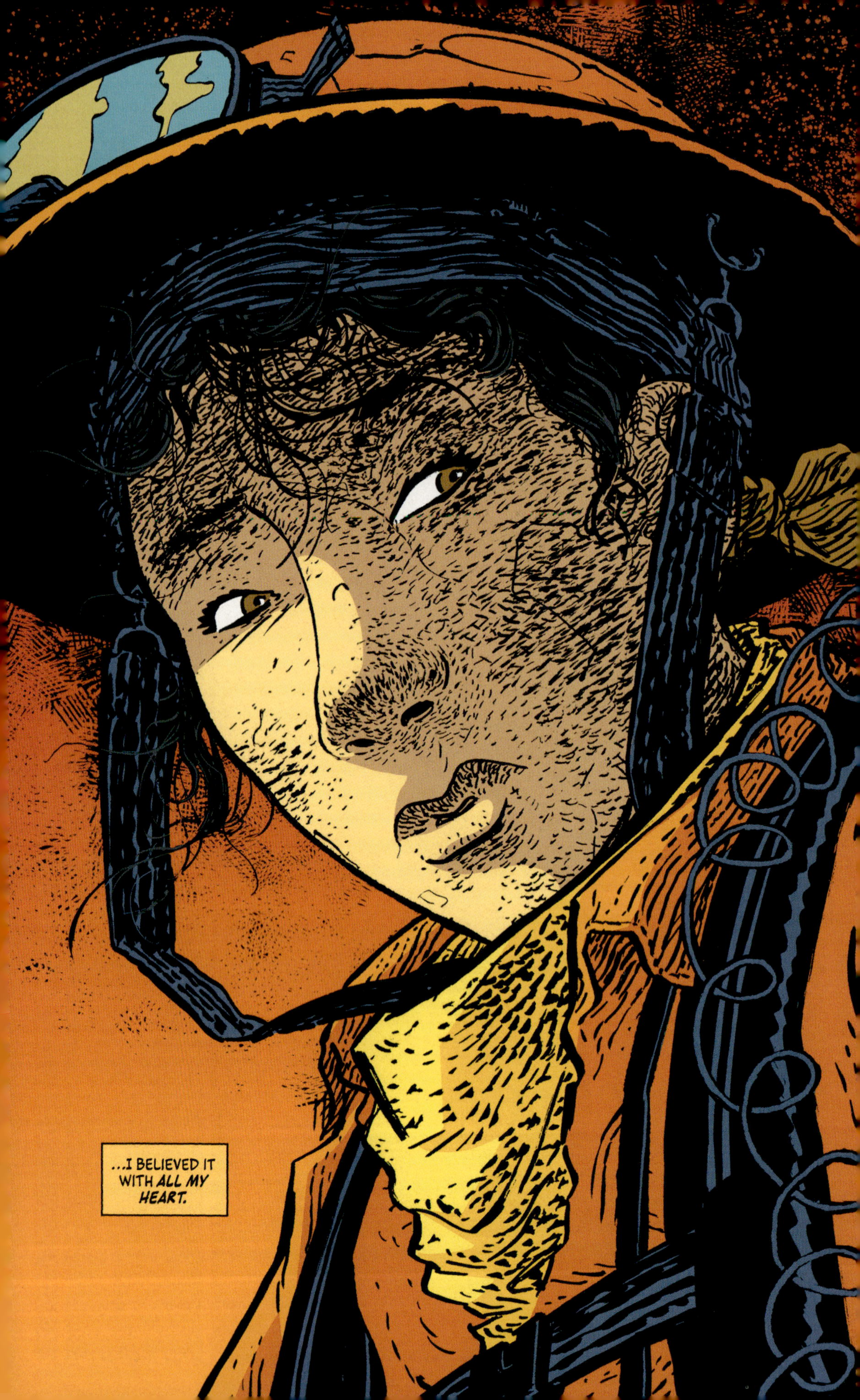
...I BELIEVED IT WITH *ALL MY HEART.*

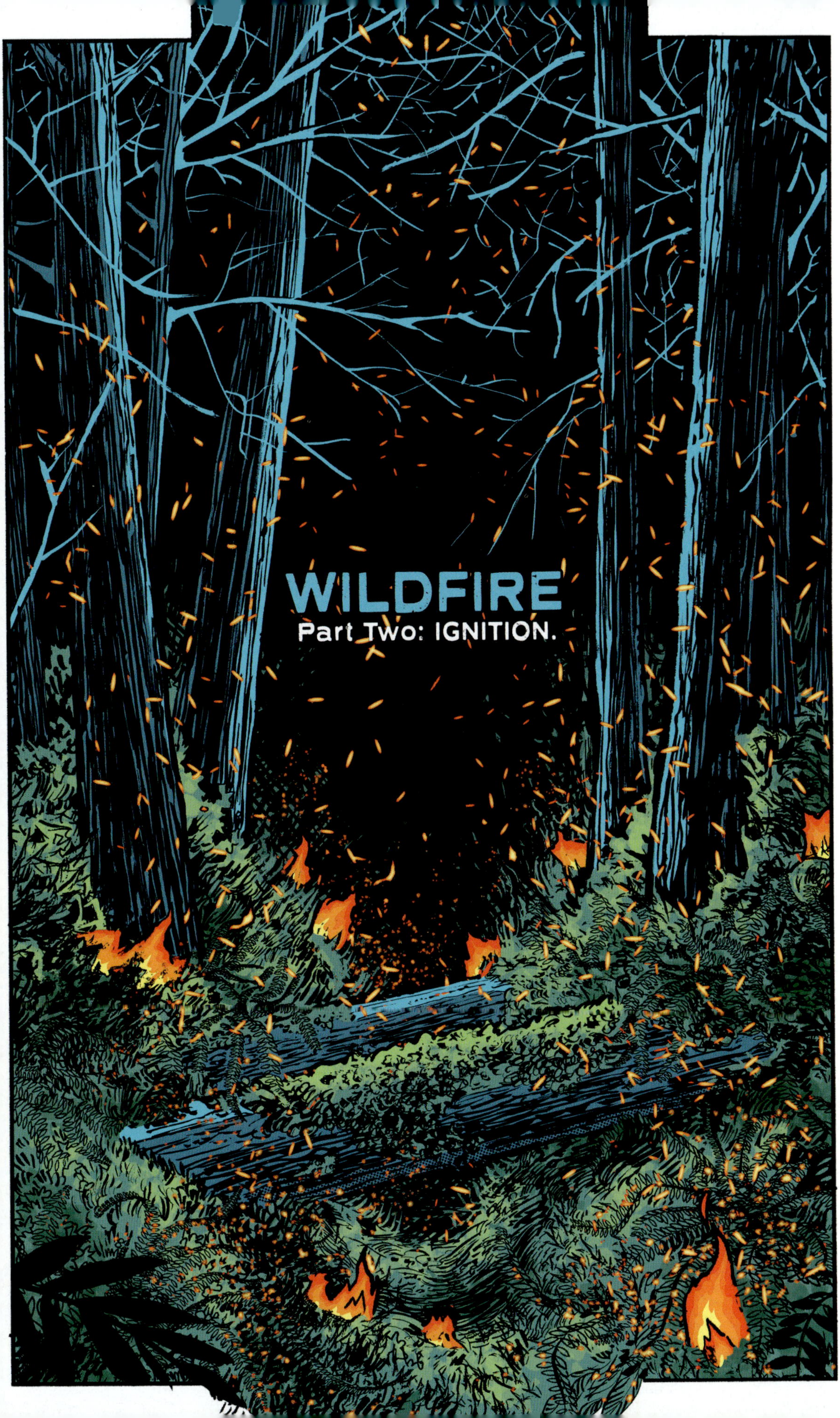
WILDFIRE
Part Two: IGNITION.

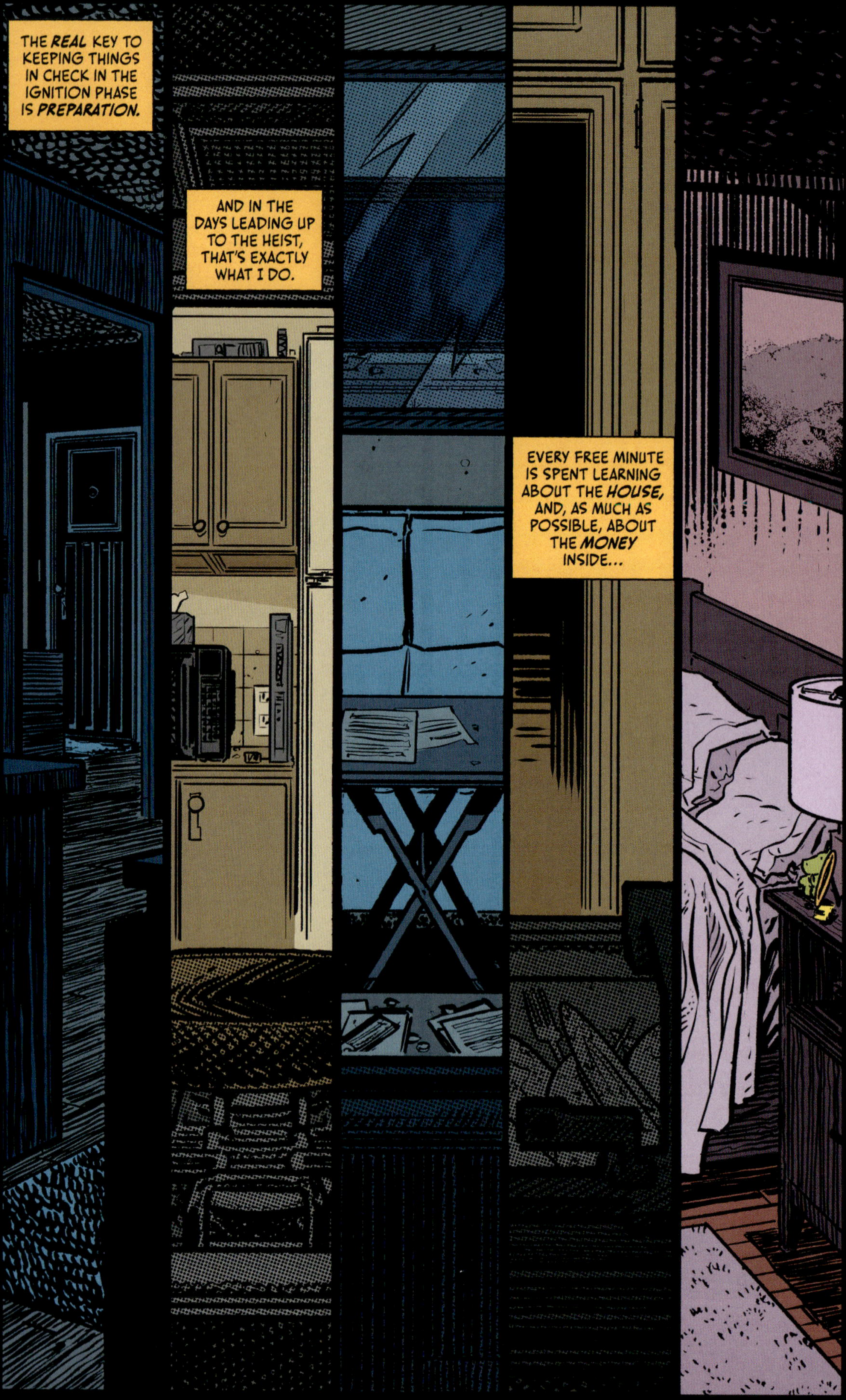
THE *REAL* KEY TO KEEPING THINGS IN CHECK IN THE IGNITION PHASE IS *PREPARATION.*
AND IN THE DAYS LEADING UP TO THE HEIST, THAT'S EXACTLY WHAT I DO.
EVERY FREE MINUTE IS SPENT LEARNING ABOUT THE *HOUSE,* AND, AS MUCH AS POSSIBLE, ABOUT THE *MONEY* INSIDE...

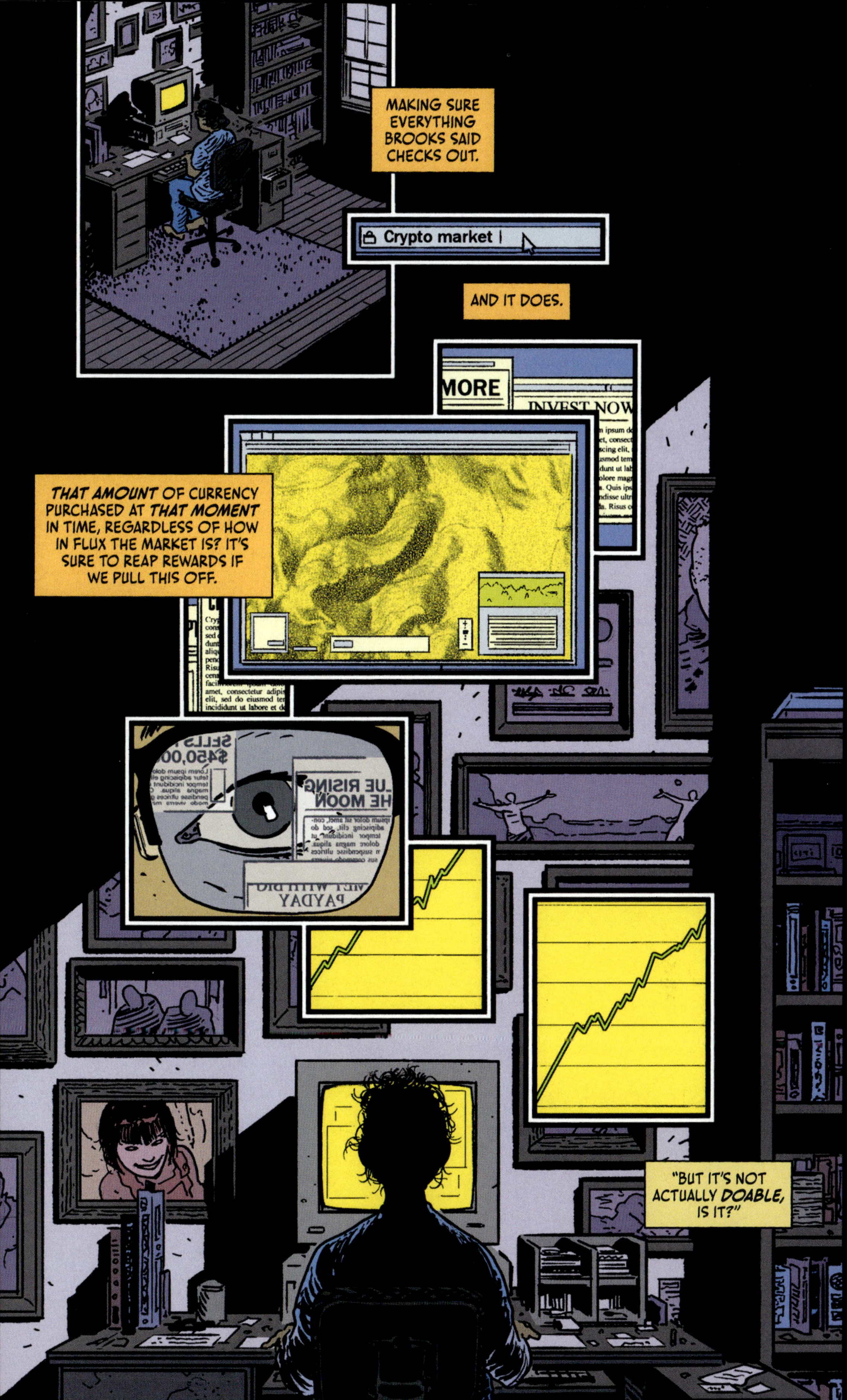
MAKING SURE EVERYTHING BROOKS SAID CHECKS OUT.
Crypto market
AND IT DOES.
MORE
INVEST NOW
THAT AMOUNT OF CURRENCY PURCHASED AT *THAT MOMENT* IN TIME, REGARDLESS OF HOW IN FLUX THE MARKET IS? IT'S SURE TO REAP REWARDS IF WE PULL THIS OFF.
"BUT IT'S NOT ACTUALLY *DOABLE,* IS IT?"

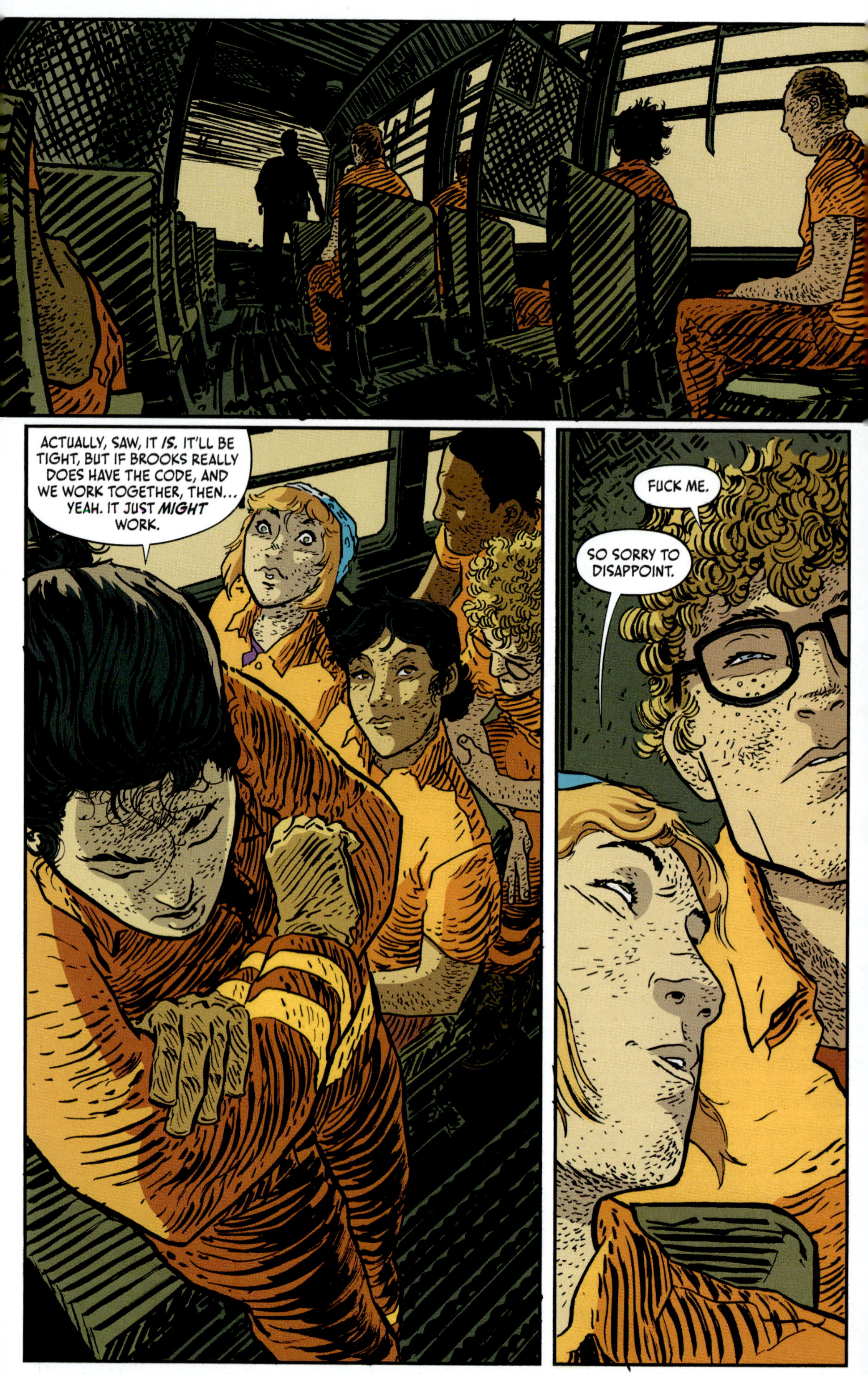
ACTUALLY, SAW, IT *IS.* IT'LL BE TIGHT, BUT IF BROOKS REALLY DOES HAVE THE CODE, AND WE WORK TOGETHER, THEN... YEAH. IT JUST ***MIGHT*** WORK.
FUCK ME.
SO SORRY TO DISAPPOINT.

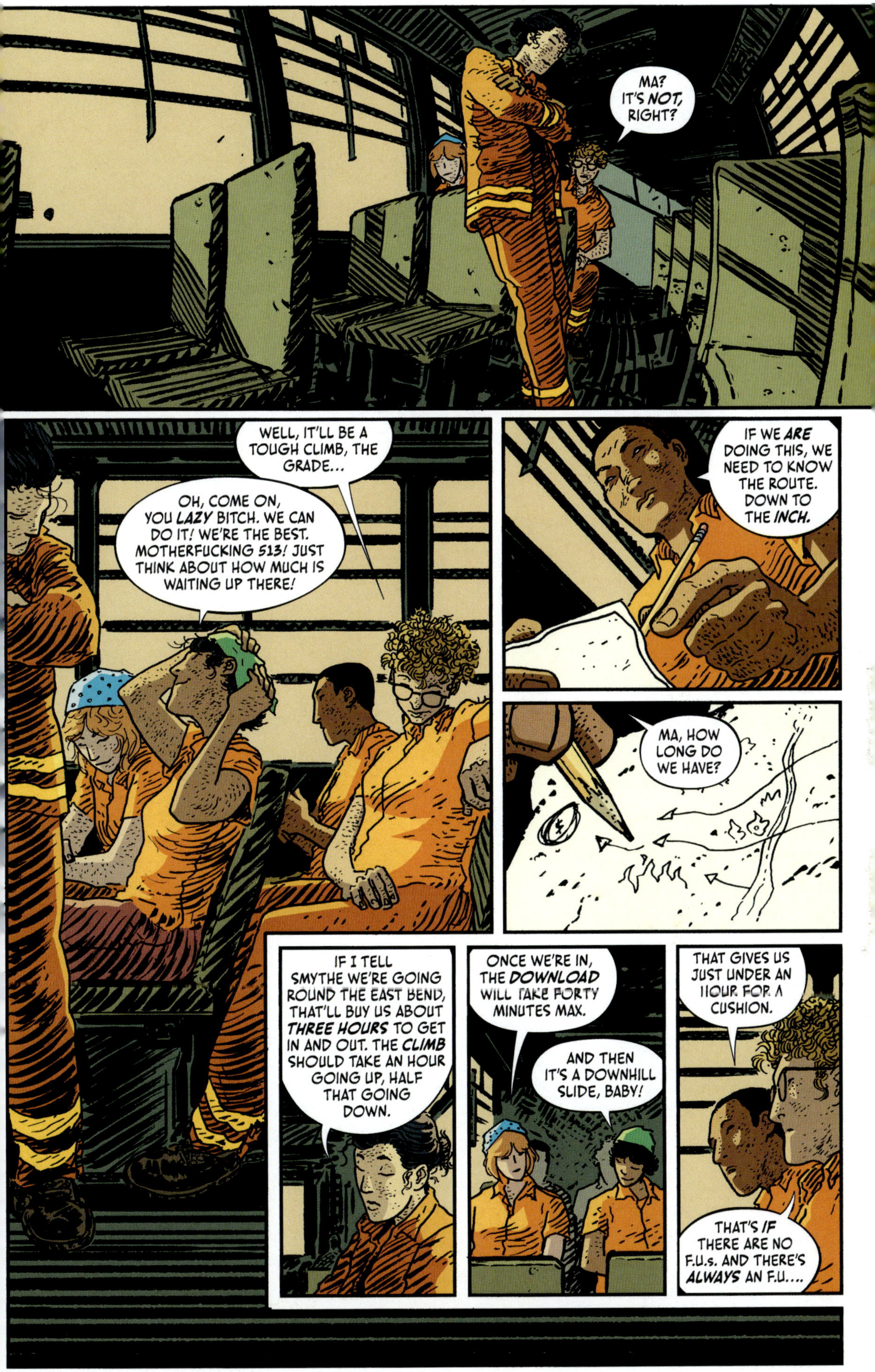
MA? IT'S NOT, RIGHT?
WELL, IT'LL BE A TOUGH CLIMB, THE GRADE...
OH, COME ON, YOU LAZY BITCH. WE CAN DO IT! WE'RE THE BEST. MOTHERFUCKING 513! JUST THINK ABOUT HOW MUCH IS WAITING UP THERE!
IF WE ARE DOING THIS, WE NEED TO KNOW THE ROUTE. DOWN TO THE INCH.
MA, HOW LONG DO WE HAVE?
IF I TELL SMYTHE WE'RE GOING ROUND THE EAST BEND, THAT'LL BUY US ABOUT THREE HOURS TO GET IN AND OUT. THE CLIMB SHOULD TAKE AN HOUR GOING UP, HALF THAT GOING DOWN.
ONCE WE'RE IN, THE DOWNLOAD WILL TAKE FORTY MINUTES MAX.
AND THEN IT'S A DOWNHILL SLIDE, BABY!
THAT GIVES US JUST UNDER AN HOUR FOR A CUSHION.
THAT'S IF THERE ARE NO F.U.s. AND THERE'S ALWAYS AN F.U....

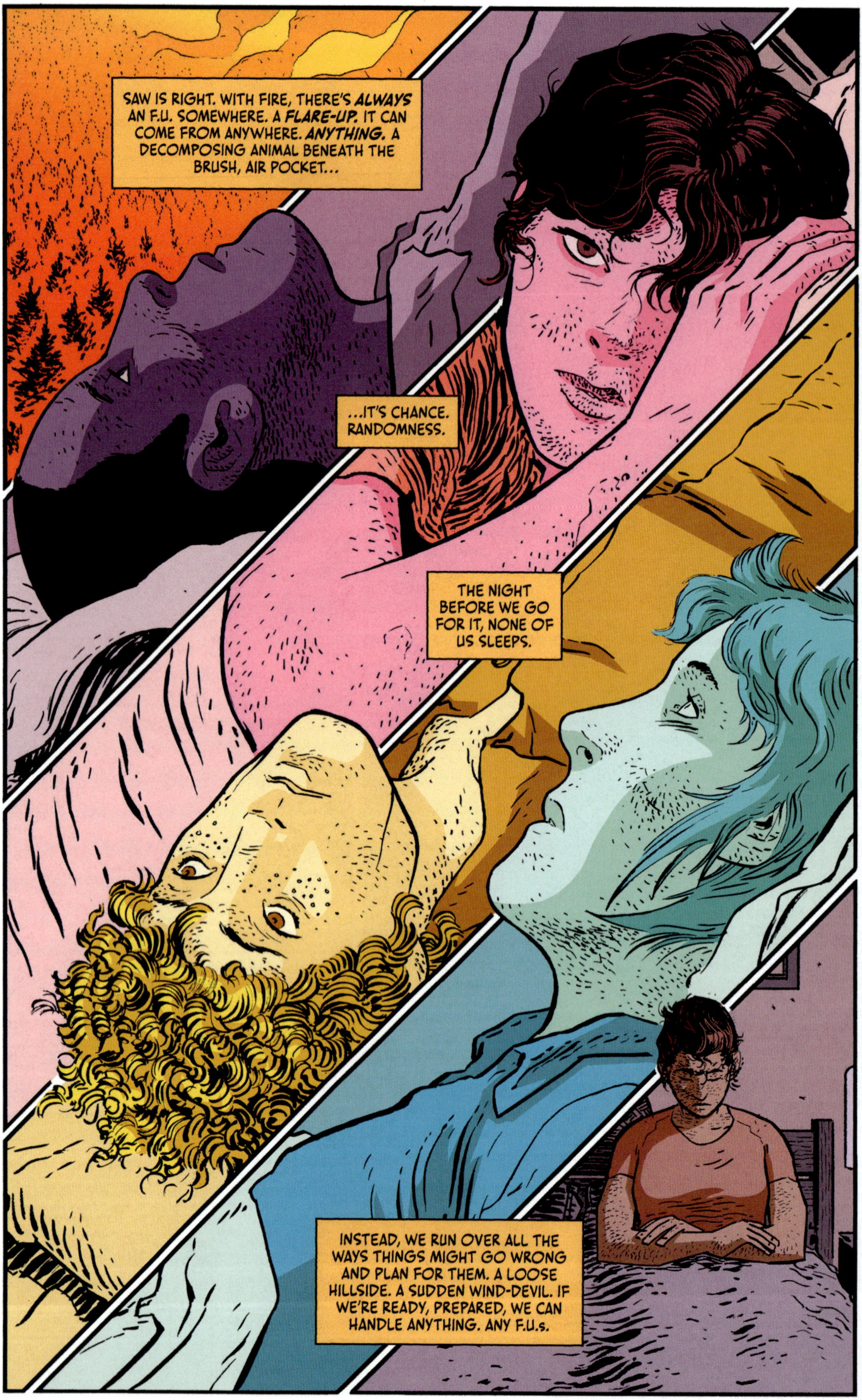
SAW IS RIGHT. WITH FIRE, THERE'S *ALWAYS* AN F.U. SOMEWHERE. A *FLARE-UP.* IT CAN COME FROM ANYWHERE. *ANYTHING.* A DECOMPOSING ANIMAL BENEATH THE BRUSH, AIR POCKET...
...IT'S CHANCE. RANDOMNESS.
THE NIGHT BEFORE WE GO FOR IT, NONE OF US SLEEPS.
INSTEAD, WE RUN OVER ALL THE WAYS THINGS MIGHT GO WRONG AND PLAN FOR THEM. A LOOSE HILLSIDE. A SUDDEN WIND-DEVIL. IF WE'RE READY, PREPARED, WE CAN HANDLE ANYTHING. ANY F.U.s.

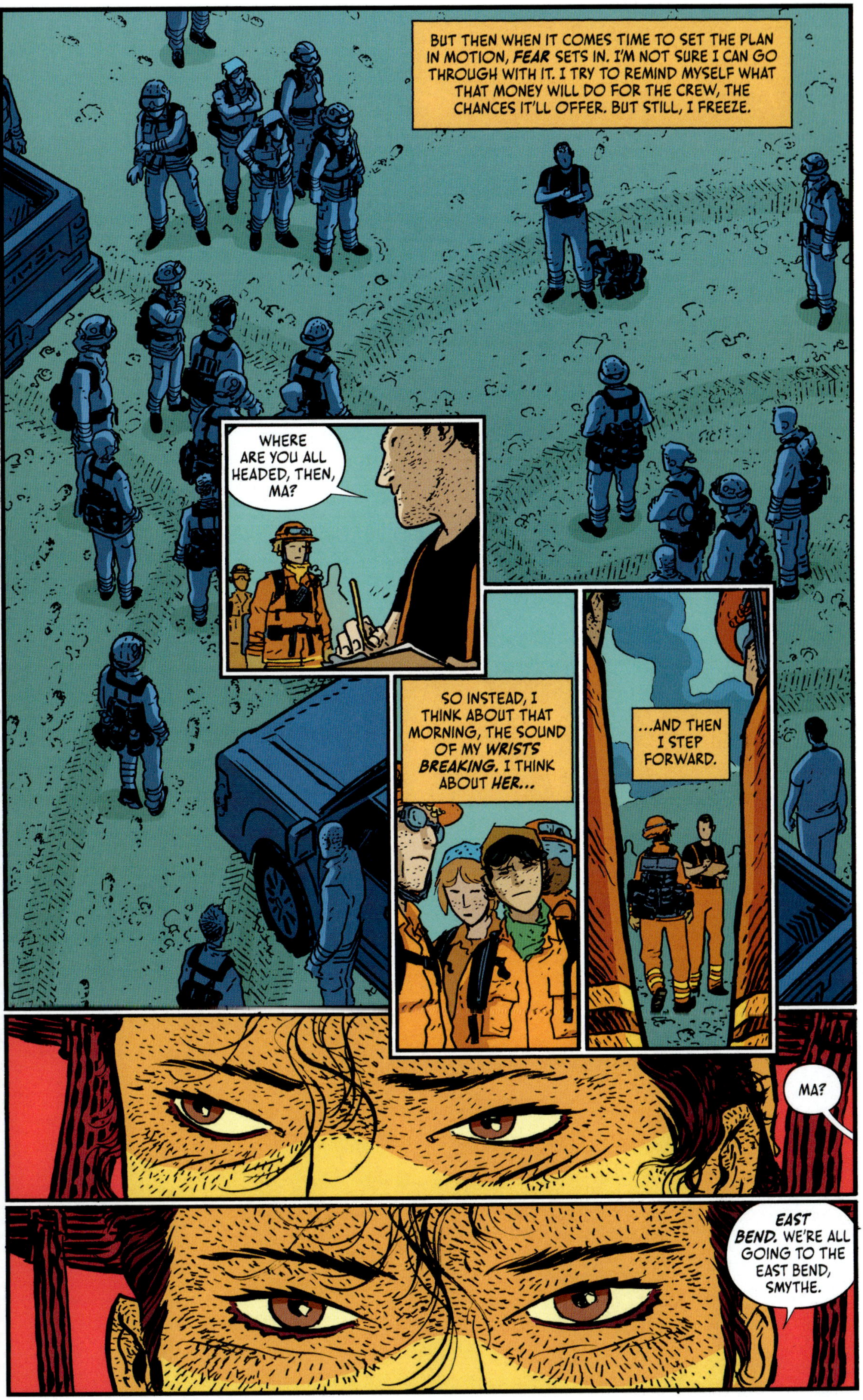
BUT THEN WHEN IT COMES TIME TO SET THE PLAN IN MOTION, *FEAR* SETS IN. I'M NOT SURE I CAN GO THROUGH WITH IT. I TRY TO REMIND MYSELF WHAT THAT MONEY WILL DO FOR THE CREW, THE CHANCES IT'LL OFFER. BUT STILL, I FREEZE.
WHERE ARE YOU ALL HEADED, THEN, MA?
SO INSTEAD, I THINK ABOUT THAT MORNING, THE SOUND OF MY *WRISTS BREAKING.* I THINK ABOUT *HER...*
...AND THEN I STEP FORWARD.
MA?
EAST BEND. WE'RE ALL GOING TO THE EAST BEND, SMYTHE.

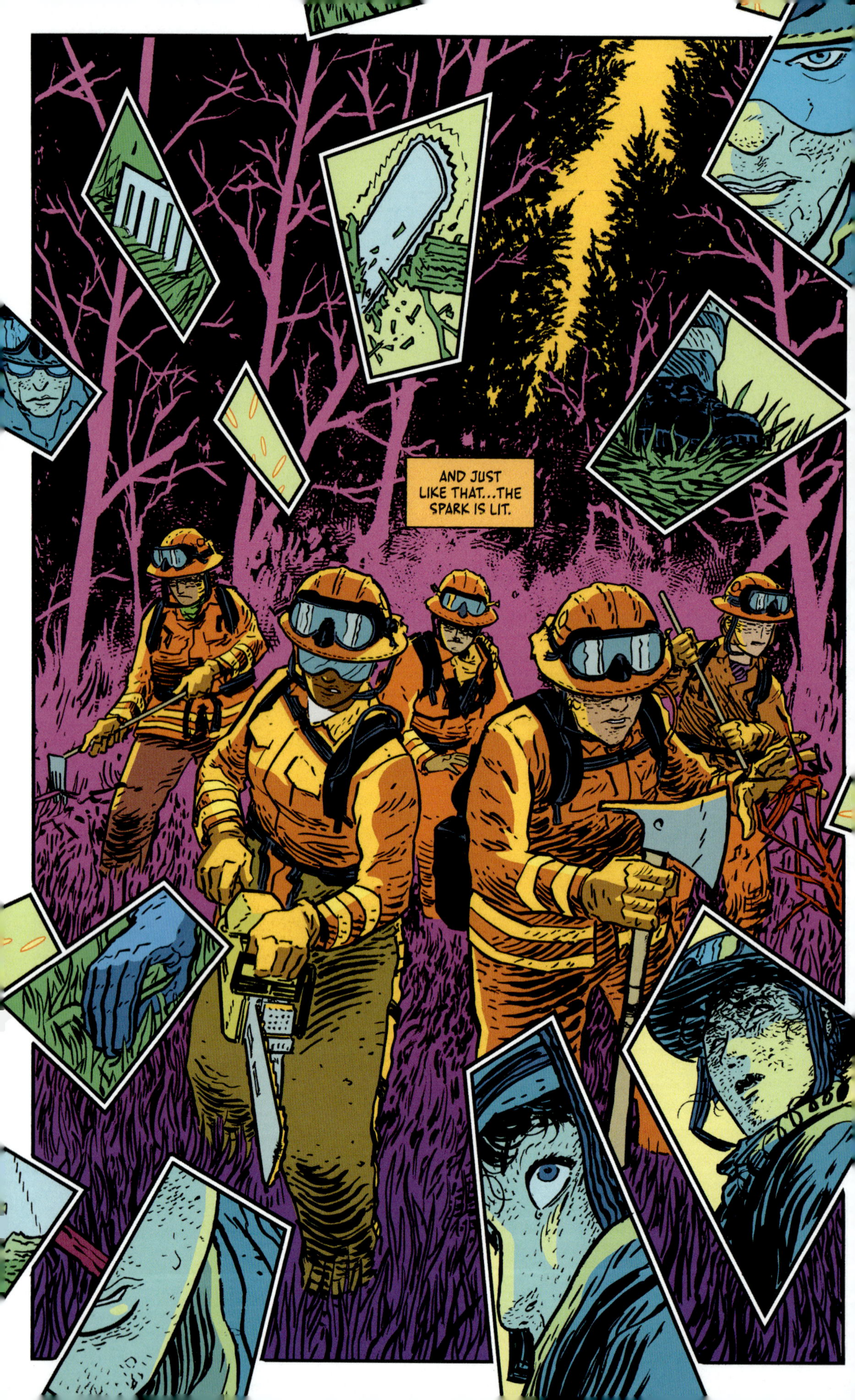
AND JUST LIKE THAT...THE SPARK IS LIT.

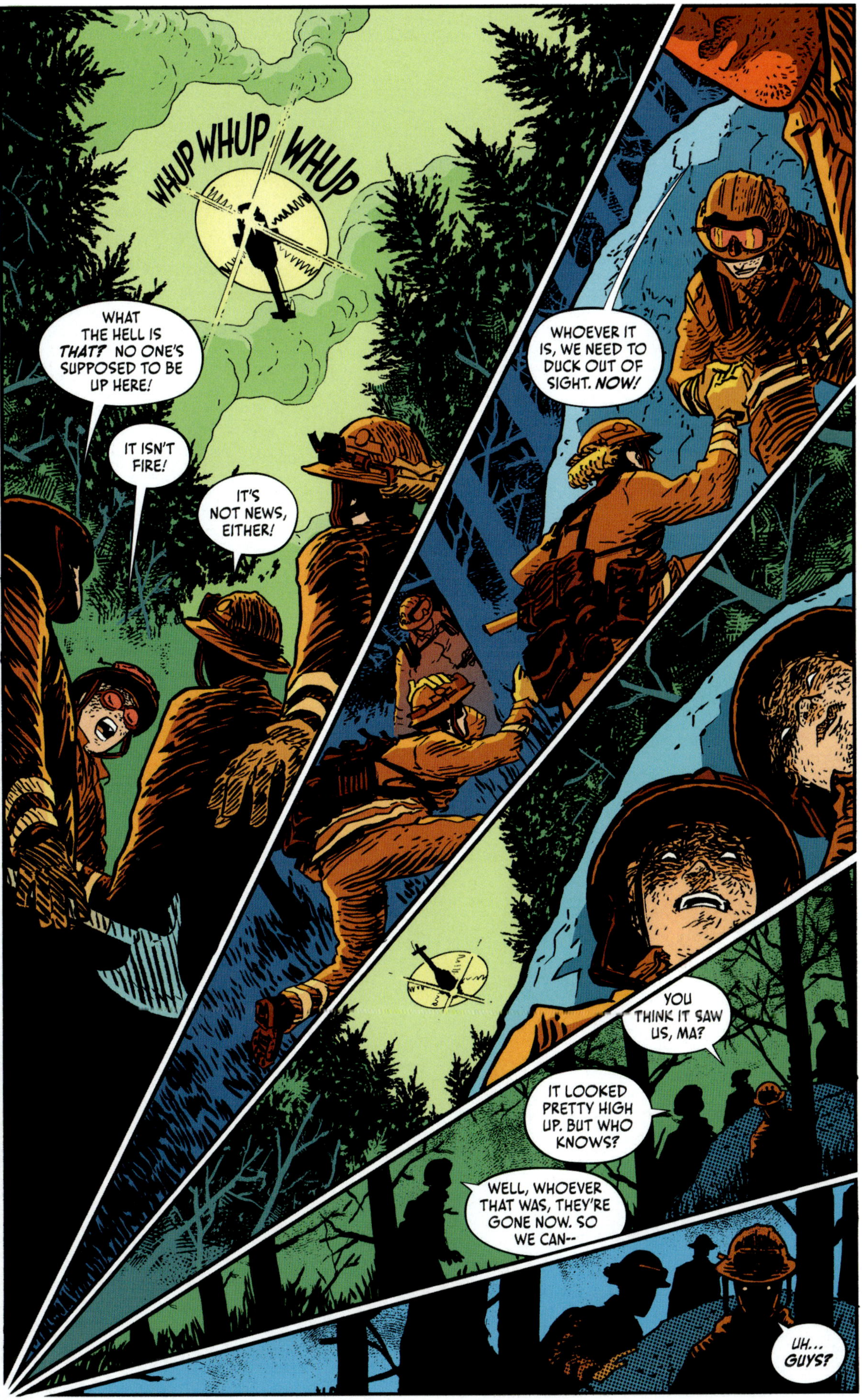
WHUP WHUP WHUP
WHAT THE HELL IS *THAT?* NO ONE'S SUPPOSED TO BE UP HERE!
IT ISN'T FIRE!
IT'S NOT NEWS, EITHER!
WHOEVER IT IS, WE NEED TO DUCK OUT OF SIGHT. *NOW!*
YOU THINK IT SAW US, MA?
IT LOOKED PRETTY HIGH UP. BUT WHO KNOWS?
WELL, WHOEVER THAT WAS, THEY'RE GONE NOW. SO WE CAN--
UH... GUYS?

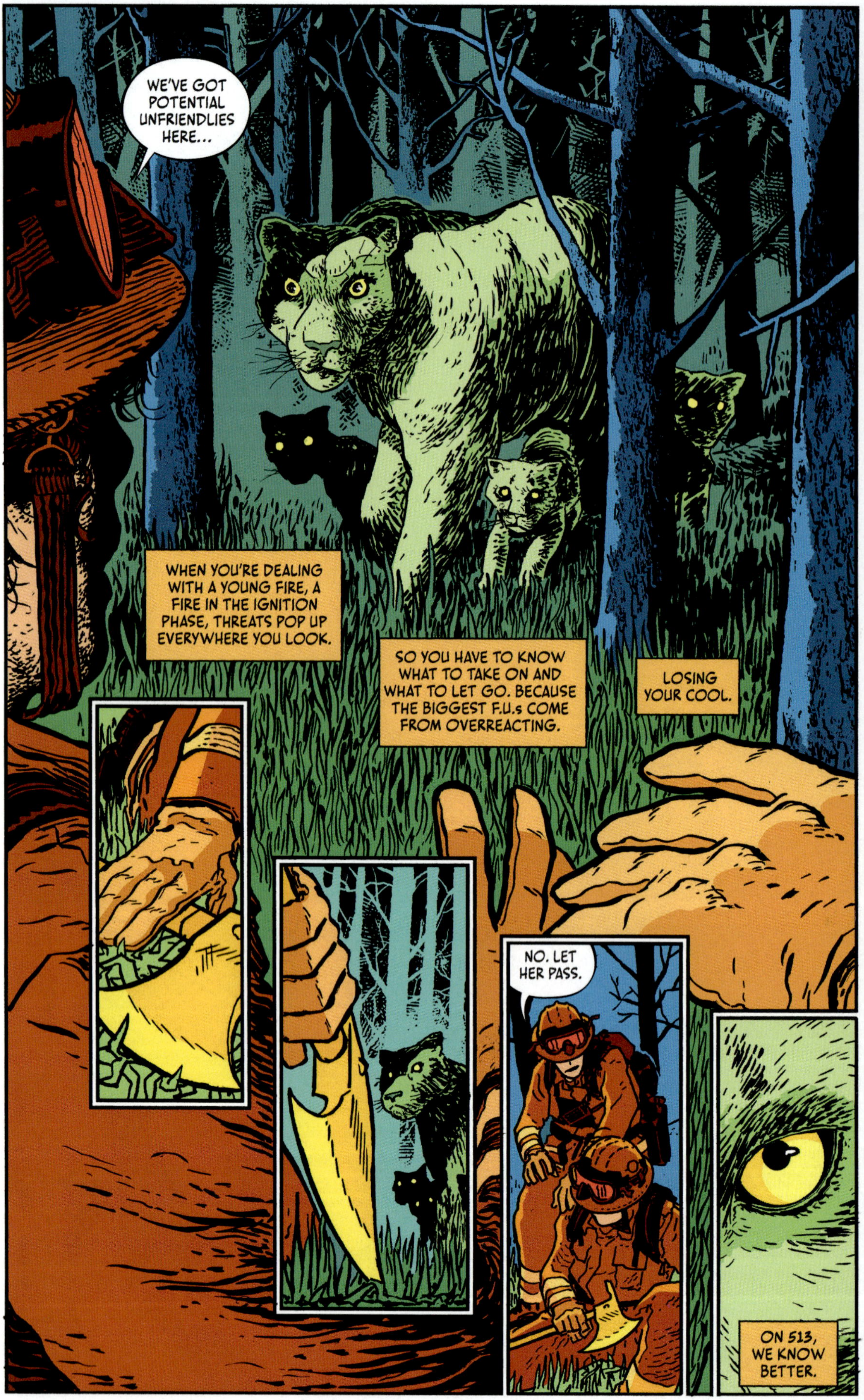
WE'VE GOT POTENTIAL UNFRIENDLIES HERE...
WHEN YOU'RE DEALING WITH A YOUNG FIRE, A FIRE IN THE IGNITION PHASE, THREATS POP UP EVERYWHERE YOU LOOK.
SO YOU HAVE TO KNOW WHAT TO TAKE ON AND WHAT TO LET GO. BECAUSE THE BIGGEST F.U.s COME FROM OVERREACTING.
LOSING YOUR COOL.
NO. LET HER PASS.
ON 513, WE KNOW BETTER.

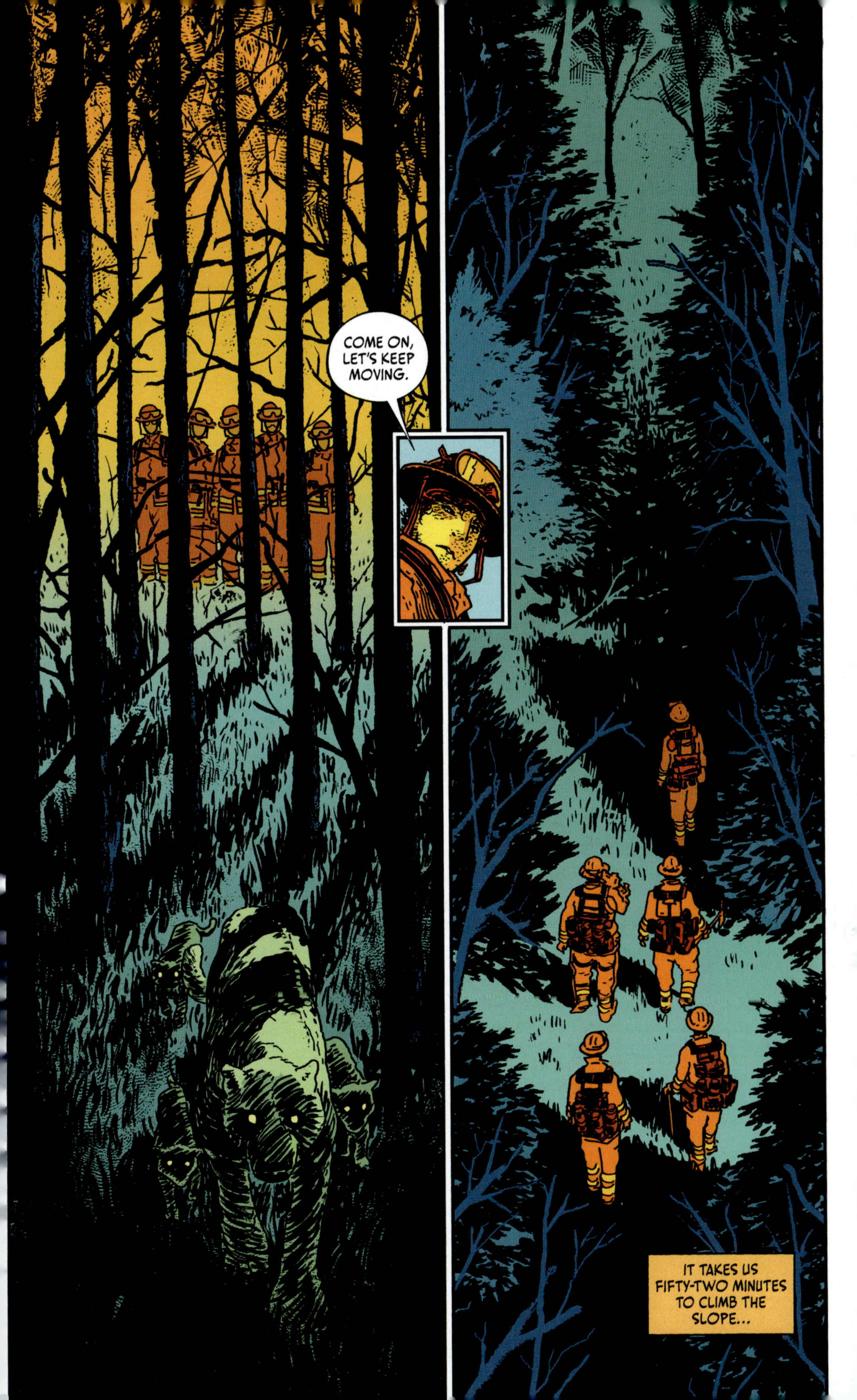
COME ON, LET'S KEEP MOVING.
IT TAKES US FIFTY-TWO MINUTES TO CLIMB THE SLOPE...

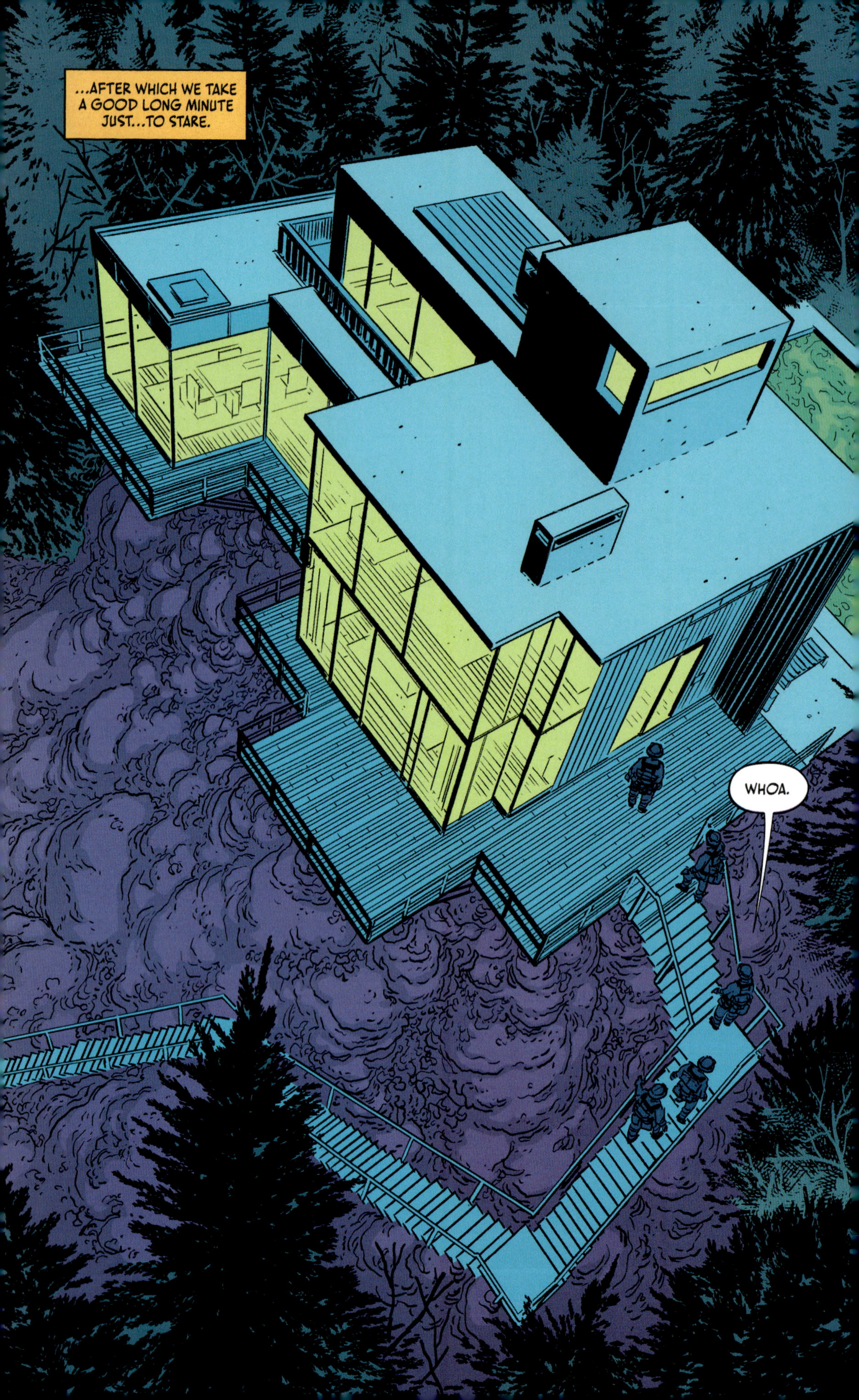
...AFTER WHICH WE TAKE A GOOD LONG MINUTE JUST...TO STARE.
WHOA.

Panel 1: OKAY, GANG...

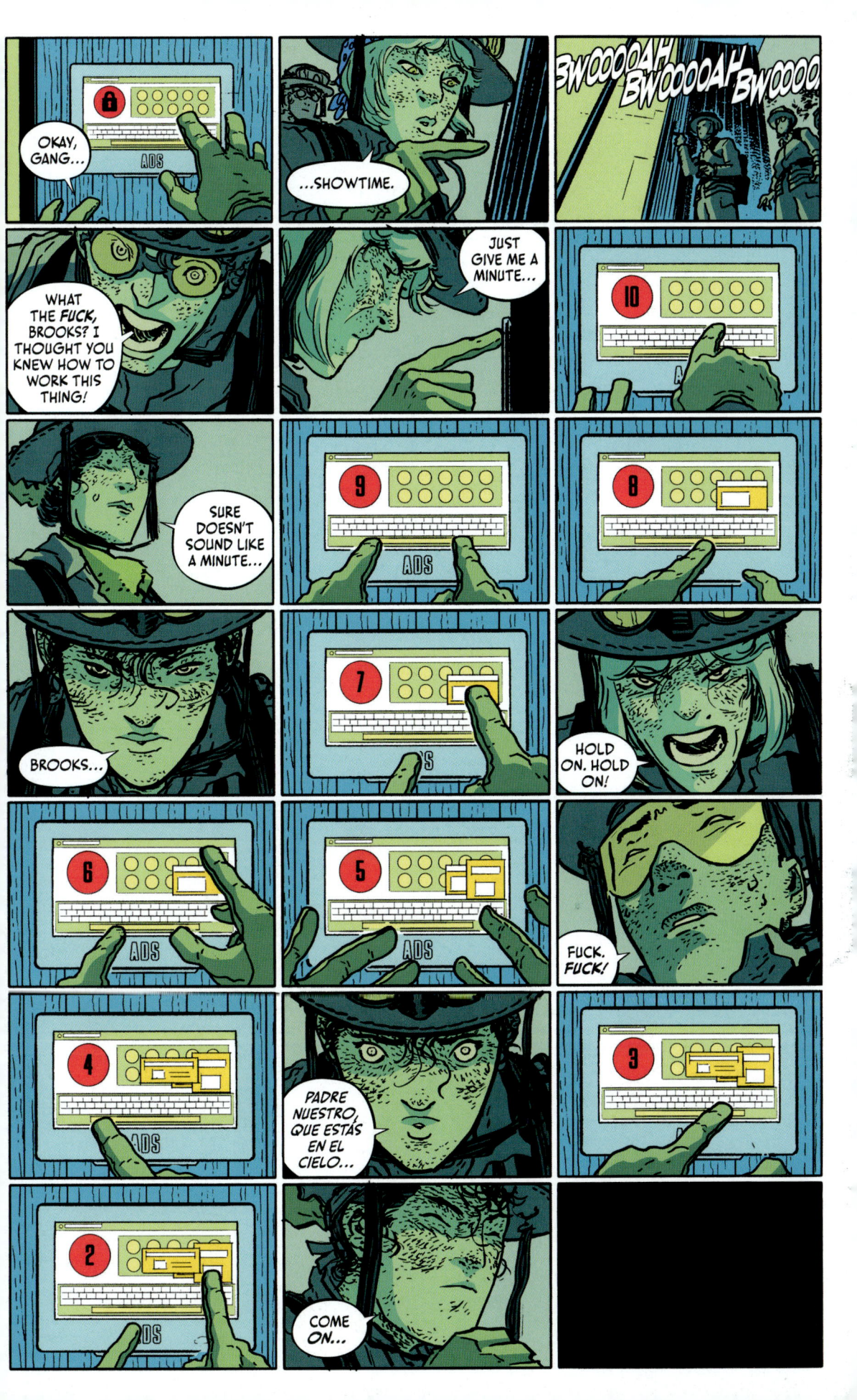

Panel 2: ...SHOWTIME.

Panel 3: BWOOOOAH BWOOOOAH BWOOOO

Panel 4: WHAT THE *FUCK*, BROOKS? I THOUGHT YOU KNEW HOW TO WORK THIS THING!

Panel 5: JUST GIVE ME A MINUTE...

Panel 7: SURE DOESN'T SOUND LIKE A MINUTE...

Panel 10: BROOKS...

Panel 12: HOLD ON. HOLD ON!

Panel 15: FUCK. FUCK!

Panel 17: PADRE NUESTRO, QUE ESTÁS EN EL CIELO...

Panel 19: COME ON...

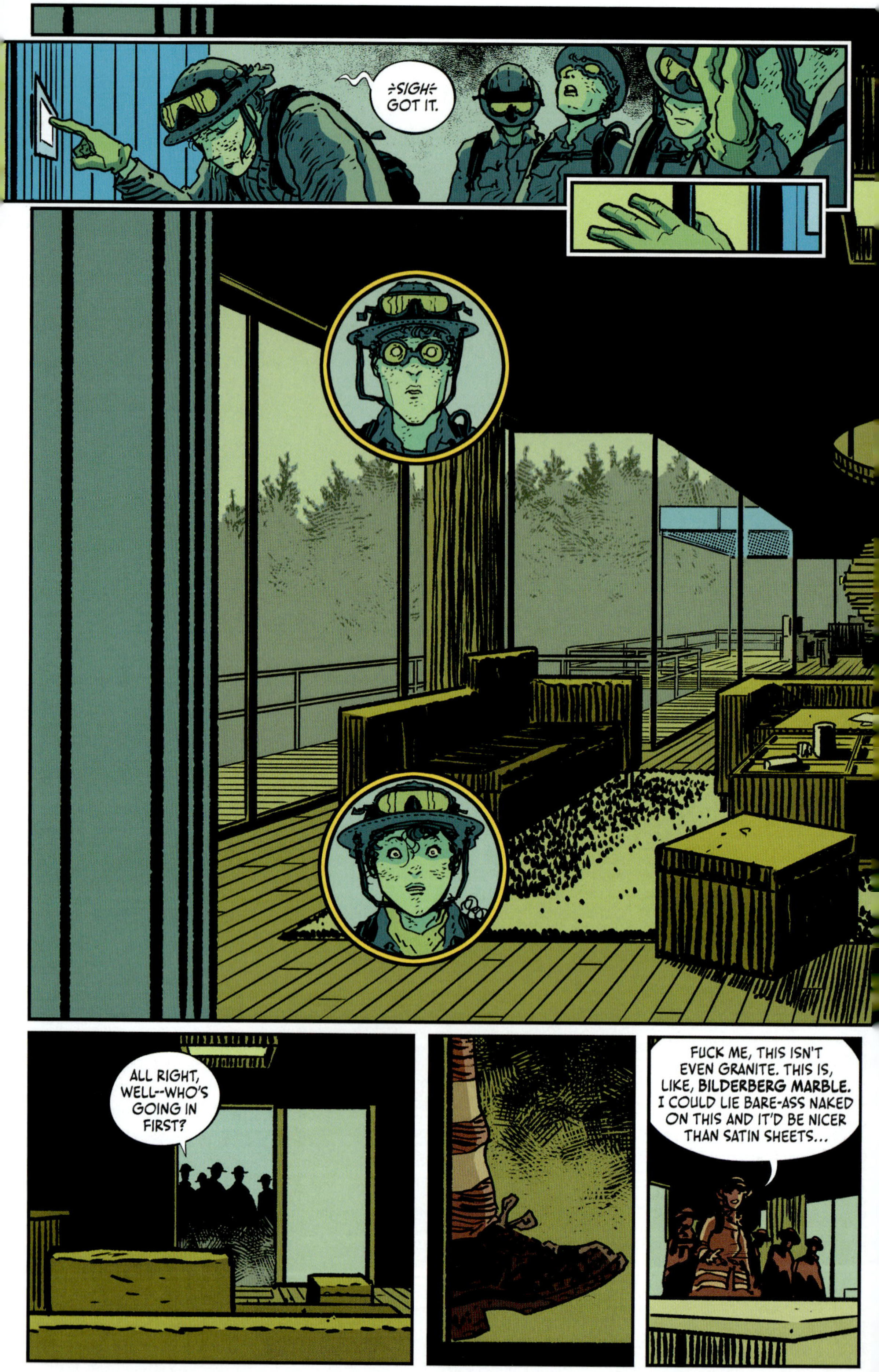

SIGH
GOT IT.
ALL RIGHT, WELL--WHO'S GOING IN FIRST?
FUCK ME, THIS ISN'T EVEN GRANITE. THIS IS, LIKE, **BILDERBERG MARBLE.** I COULD LIE BARE-ASS NAKED ON THIS AND IT'D BE NICER THAN SATIN SHEETS...

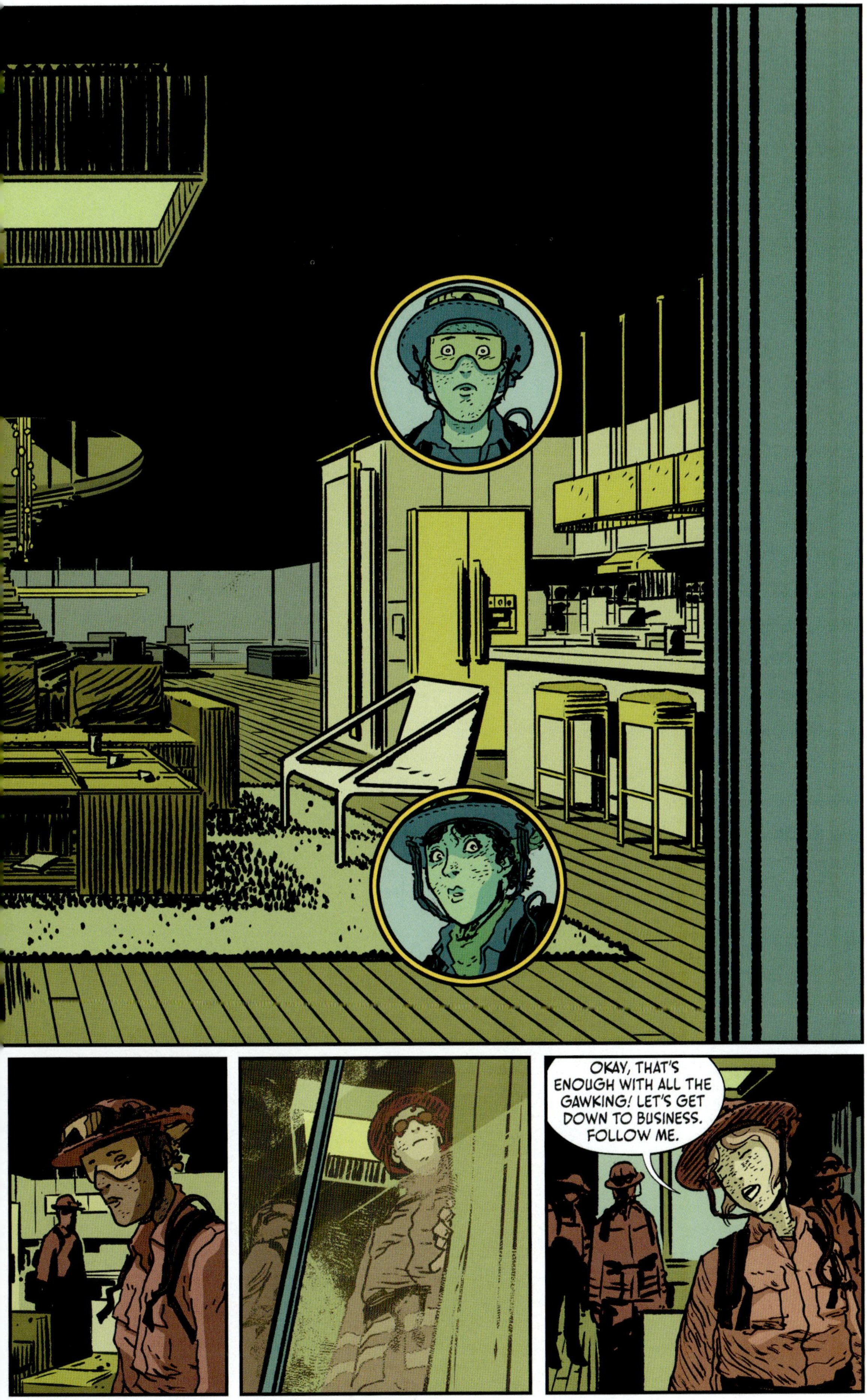
OKAY, THAT'S ENOUGH WITH ALL THE GAWKING! LET'S GET DOWN TO BUSINESS. FOLLOW ME.

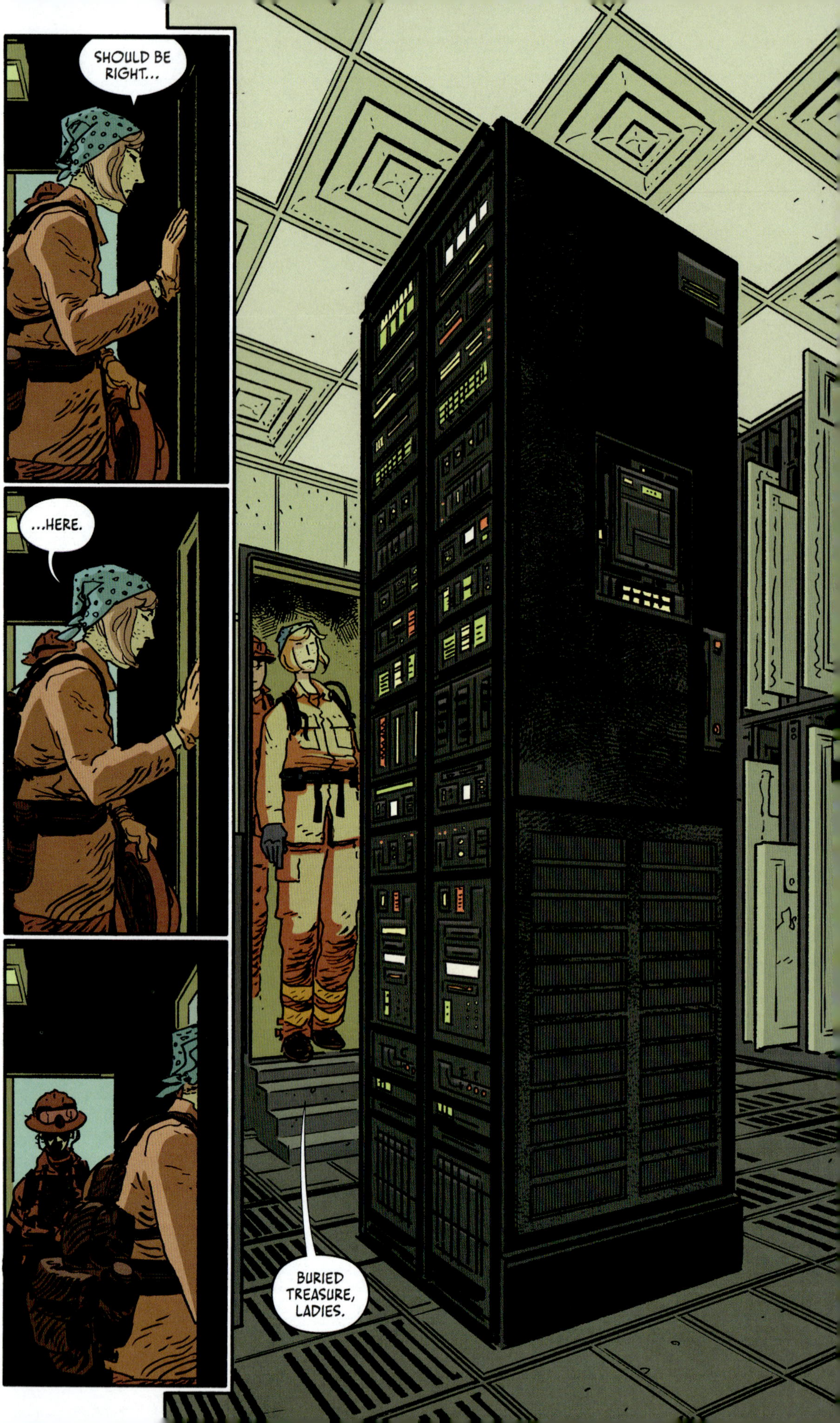
SHOULD BE RIGHT...
...HERE.
BURIED TREASURE, LADIES.

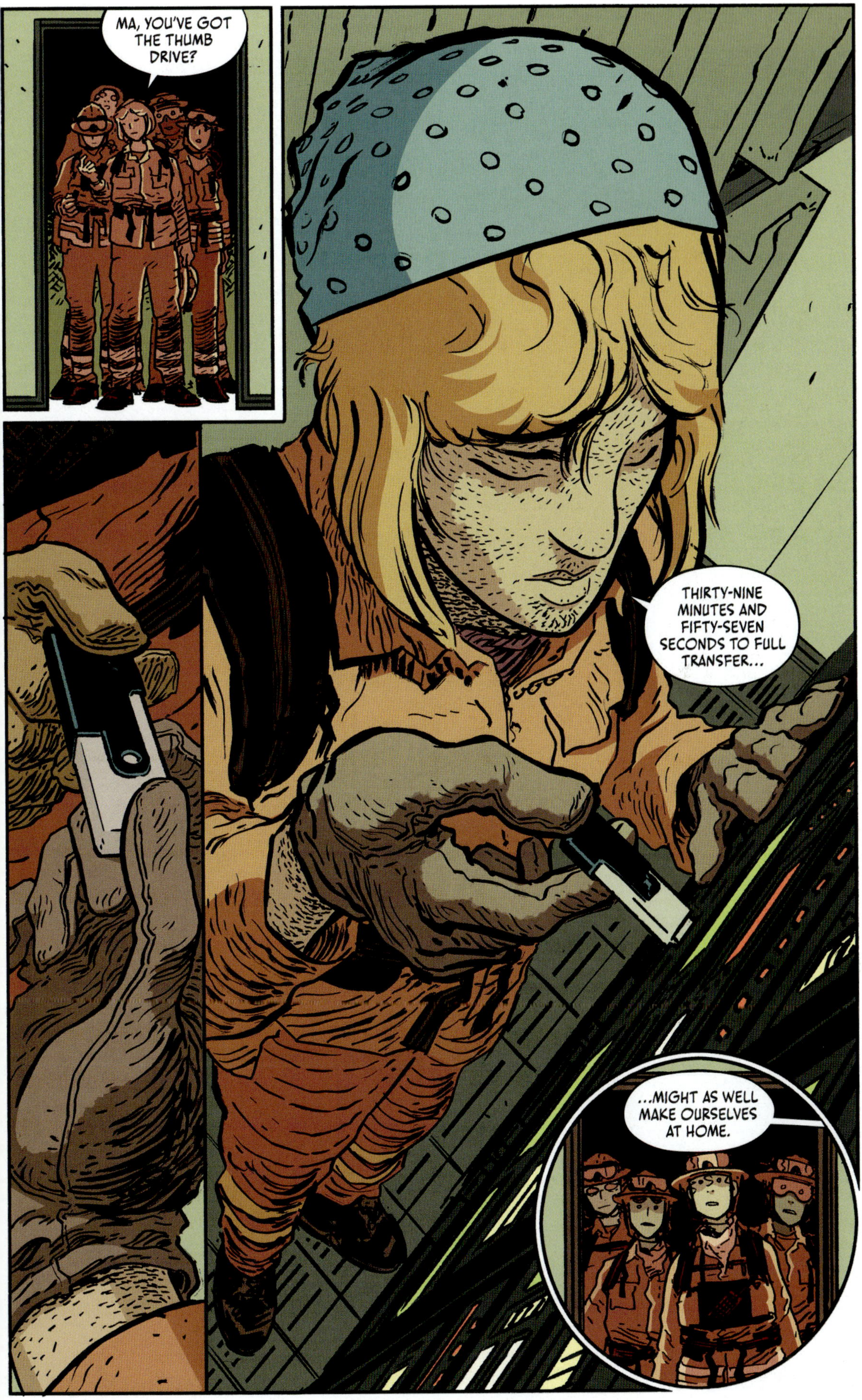
MA, YOU'VE GOT THE THUMB DRIVE?
THIRTY-NINE MINUTES AND FIFTY-SEVEN SECONDS TO FULL TRANSFER...
...MIGHT AS WELL MAKE OURSELVES AT HOME.

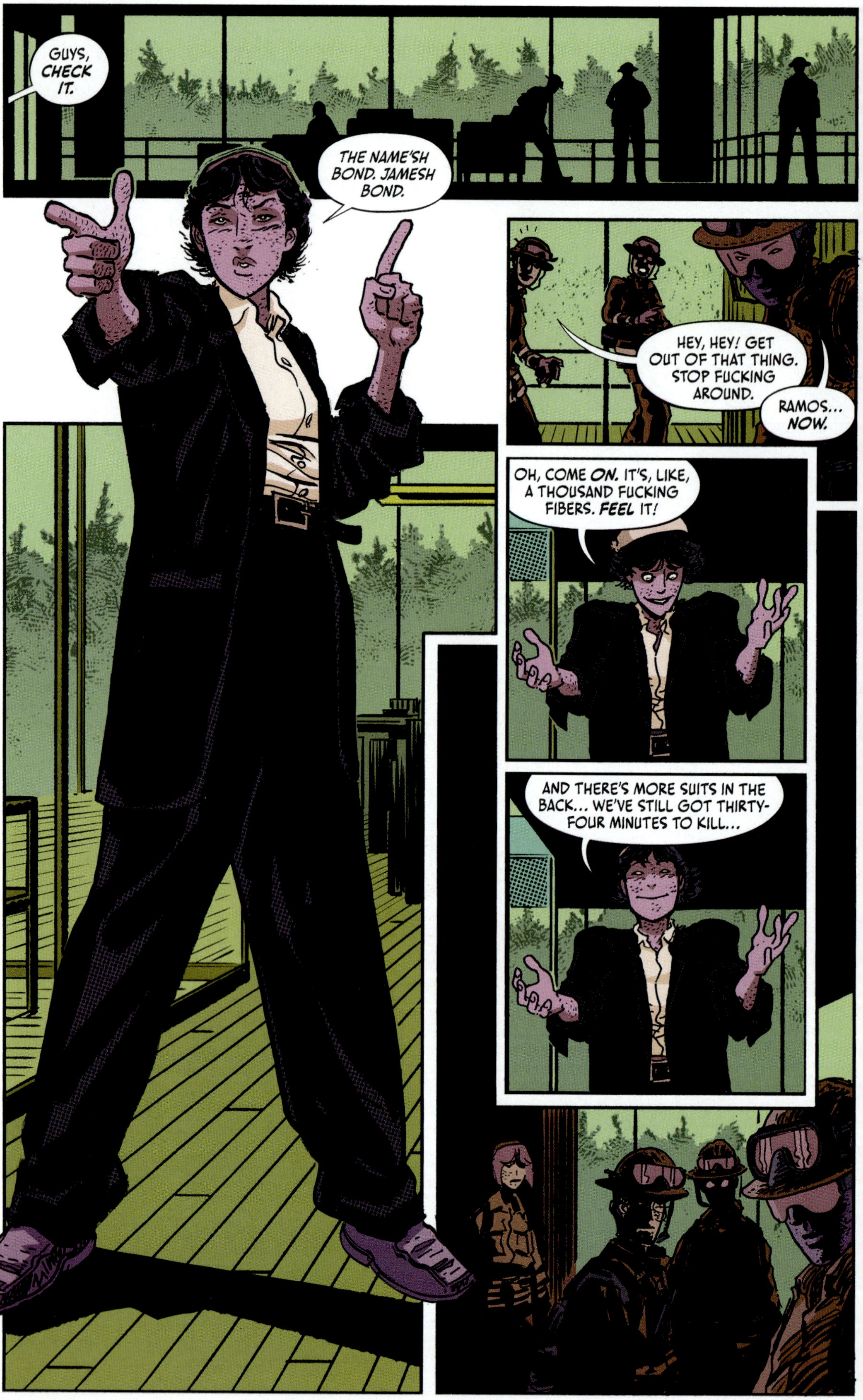
GUYS, CHECK IT.
THE NAME'SH BOND. JAMESH BOND.
HEY, HEY! GET OUT OF THAT THING. STOP FUCKING AROUND.
RAMOS... NOW.
OH, COME ON. IT'S, LIKE, A THOUSAND FUCKING FIBERS. FEEL IT!
AND THERE'S MORE SUITS IN THE BACK... WE'VE STILL GOT THIRTY-FOUR MINUTES TO KILL...

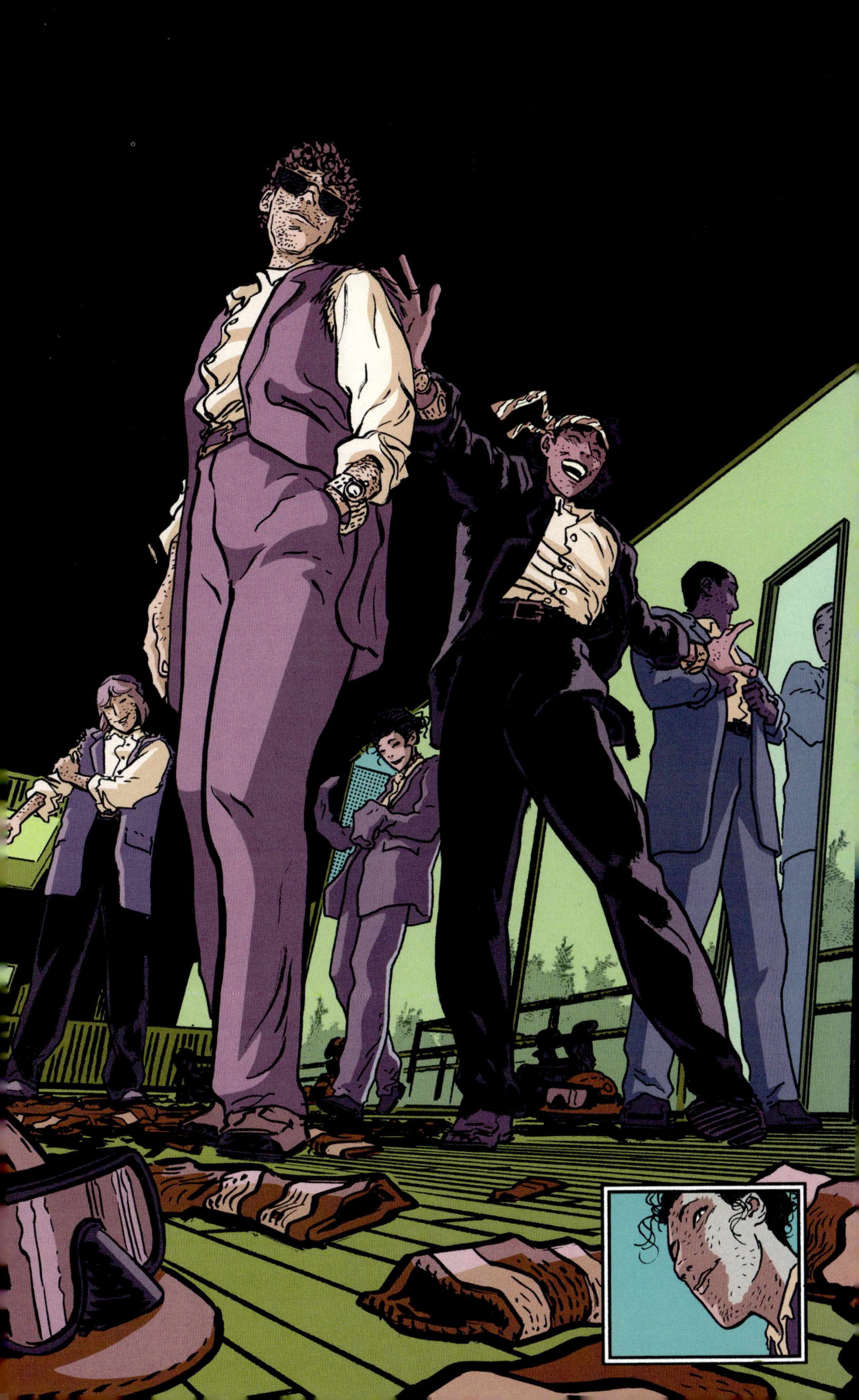

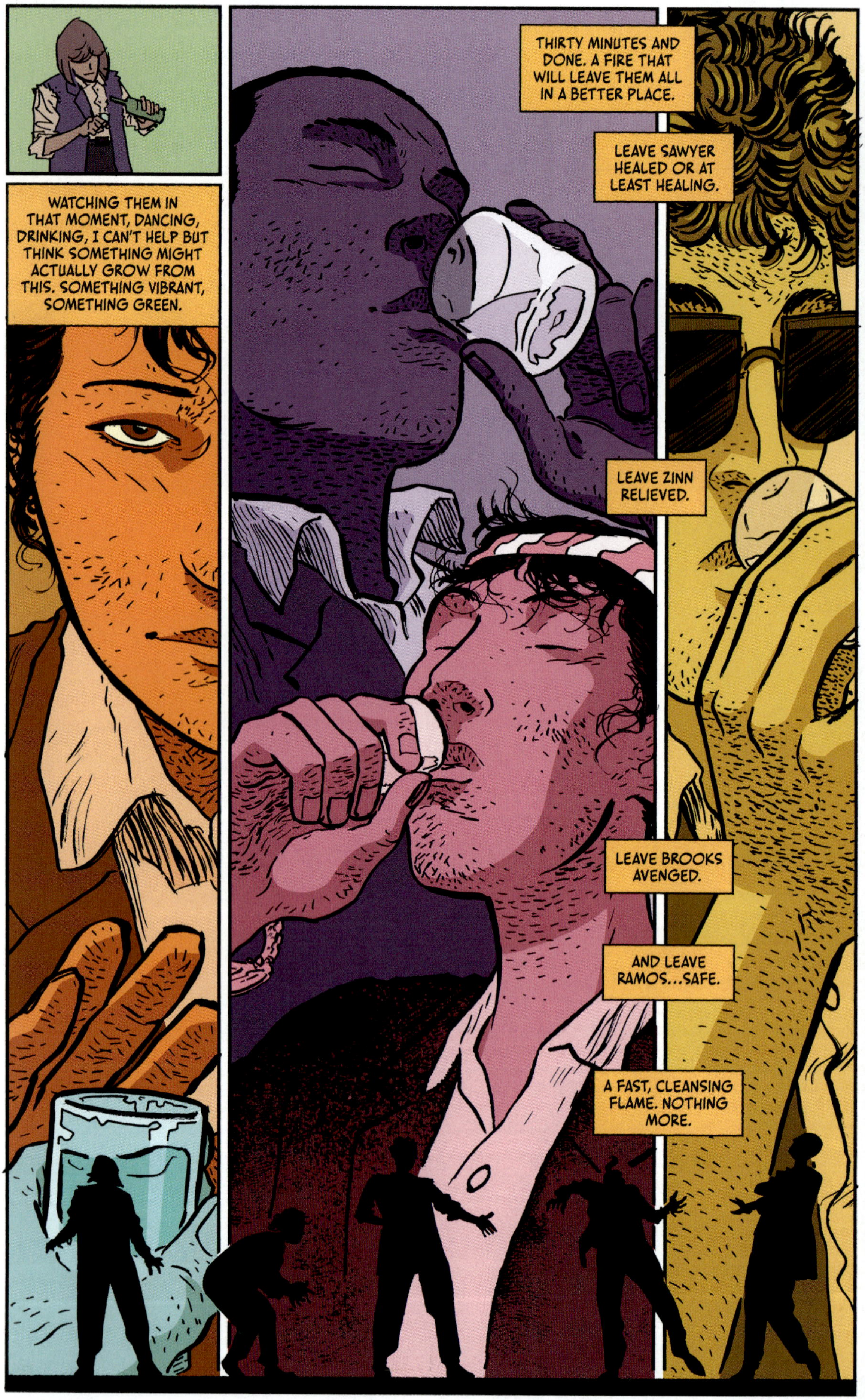
WATCHING THEM IN THAT MOMENT, DANCING, DRINKING, I CAN'T HELP BUT THINK SOMETHING MIGHT ACTUALLY GROW FROM THIS. SOMETHING VIBRANT, SOMETHING GREEN.
THIRTY MINUTES AND DONE. A FIRE THAT WILL LEAVE THEM ALL IN A BETTER PLACE.
LEAVE SAWYER HEALED OR AT LEAST HEALING.
LEAVE ZINN RELIEVED.
LEAVE BROOKS AVENGED.
AND LEAVE RAMOS...SAFE.
A FAST, CLEANSING FLAME. NOTHING MORE.

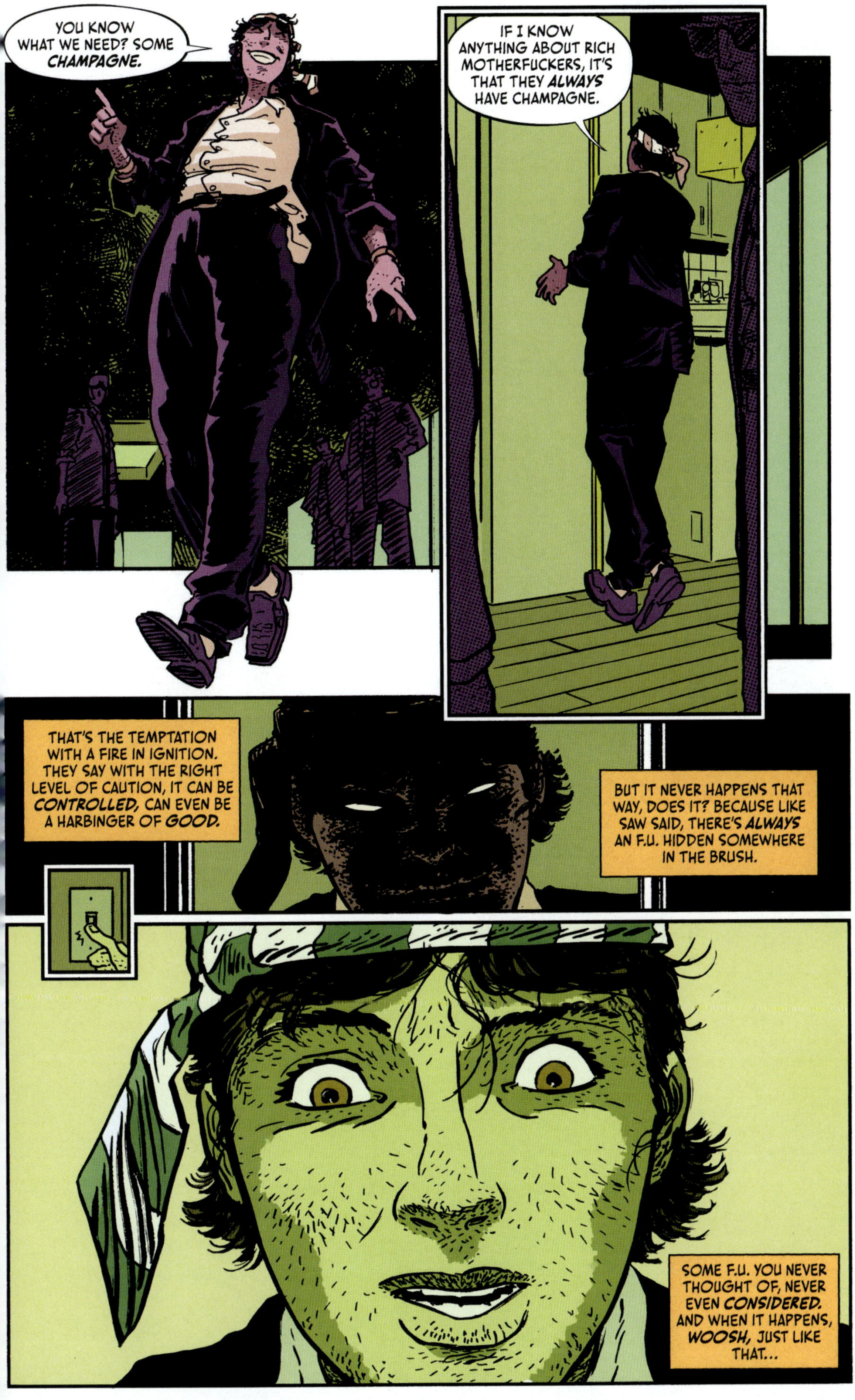
YOU KNOW WHAT WE NEED? SOME CHAMPAGNE.
IF I KNOW ANYTHING ABOUT RICH MOTHERFUCKERS, IT'S THAT THEY ALWAYS HAVE CHAMPAGNE.
THAT'S THE TEMPTATION WITH A FIRE IN IGNITION. THEY SAY WITH THE RIGHT LEVEL OF CAUTION, IT CAN BE CONTROLLED, CAN EVEN BE A HARBINGER OF GOOD.
BUT IT NEVER HAPPENS THAT WAY, DOES IT? BECAUSE LIKE SAW SAID, THERE'S ALWAYS AN F.U. HIDDEN SOMEWHERE IN THE BRUSH.
SOME F.U. YOU NEVER THOUGHT OF, NEVER EVEN CONSIDERED. AND WHEN IT HAPPENS, WOOSH, JUST LIKE THAT...

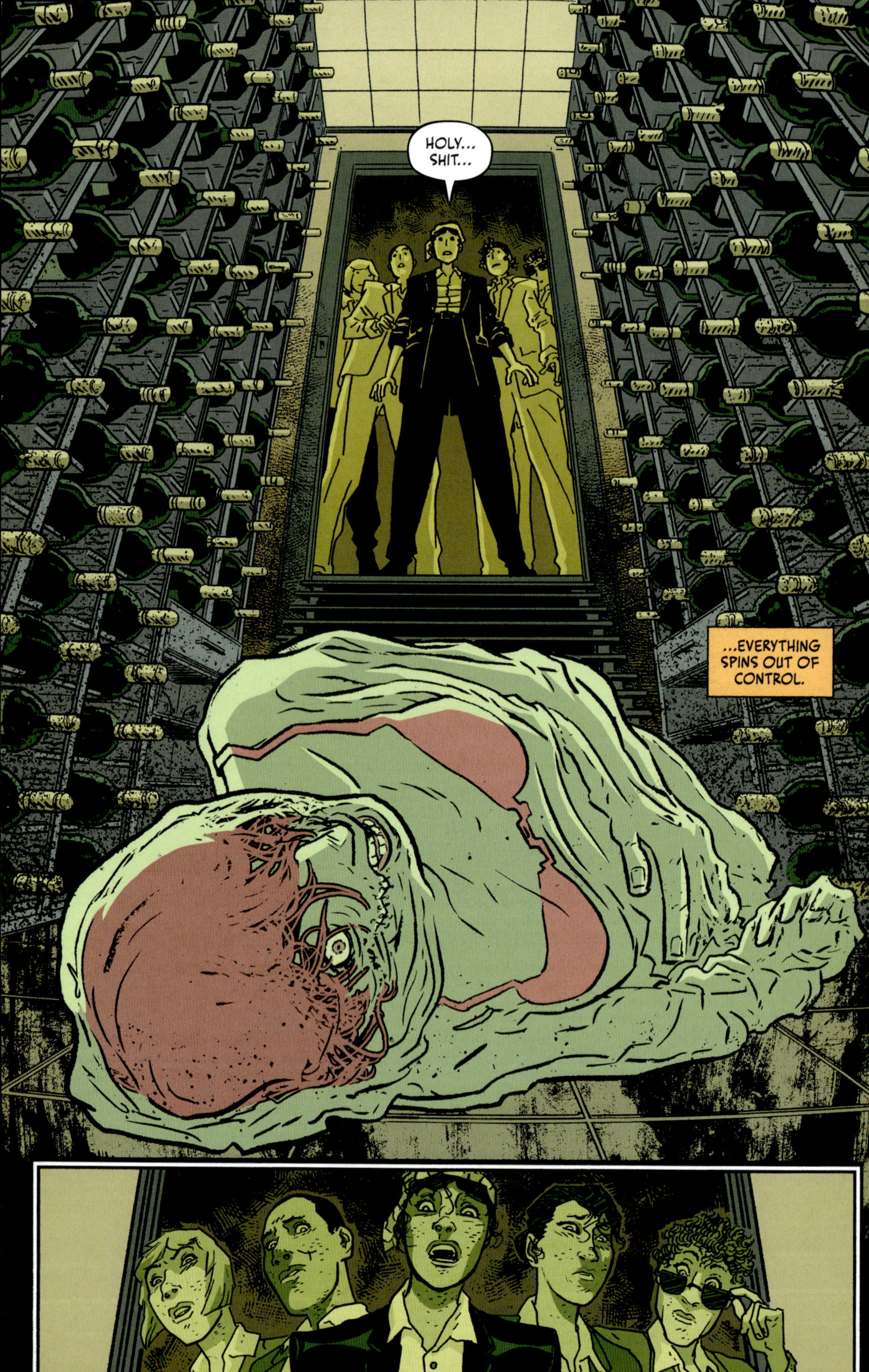
HOLY... SHIT...
...EVERYTHING SPINS OUT OF CONTROL.

TO BE CONTINUED...

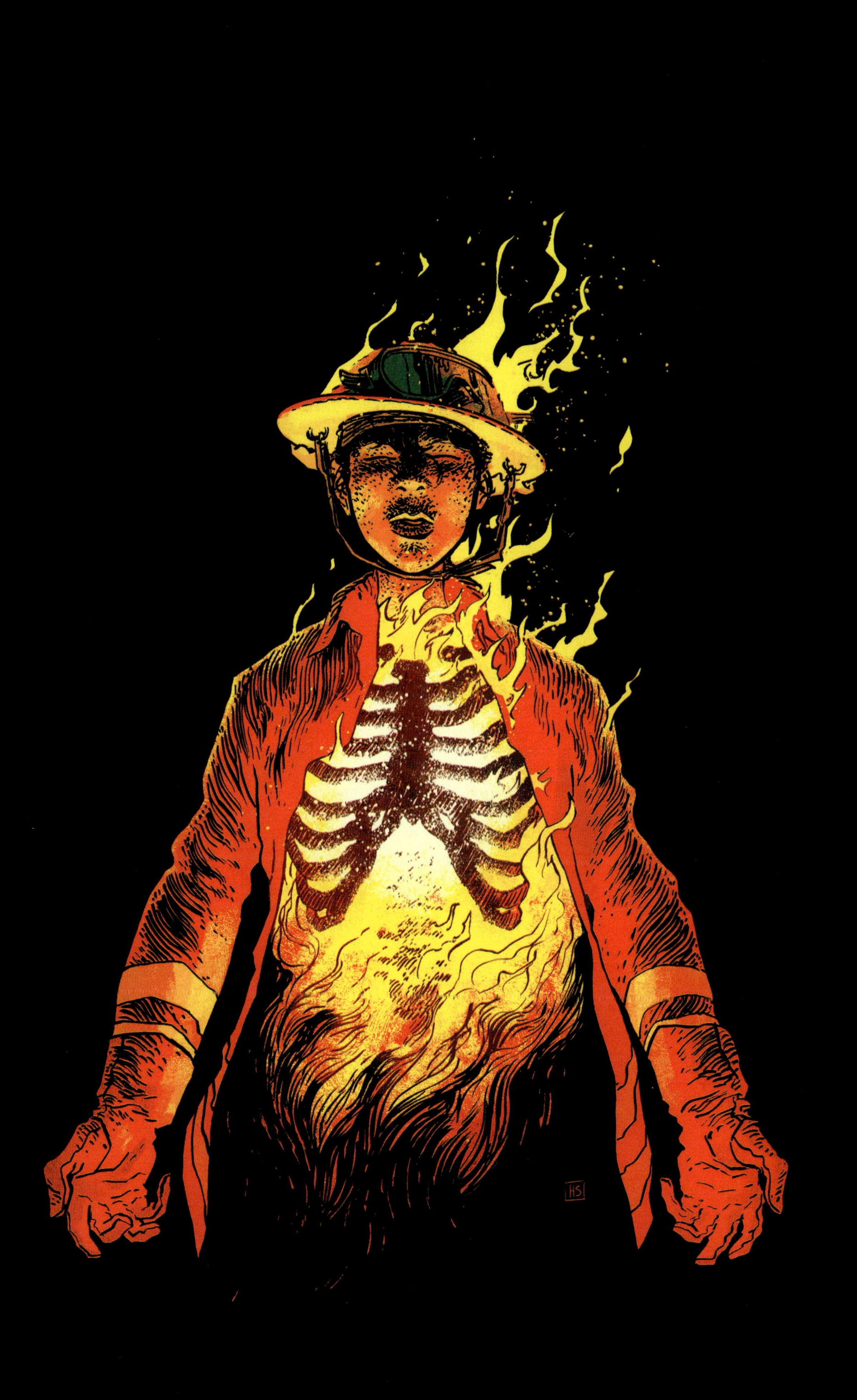

"...AND ALL YOUR PLANS BURN TO ASH RIGHT IN FRONT OF YOUR EYES."

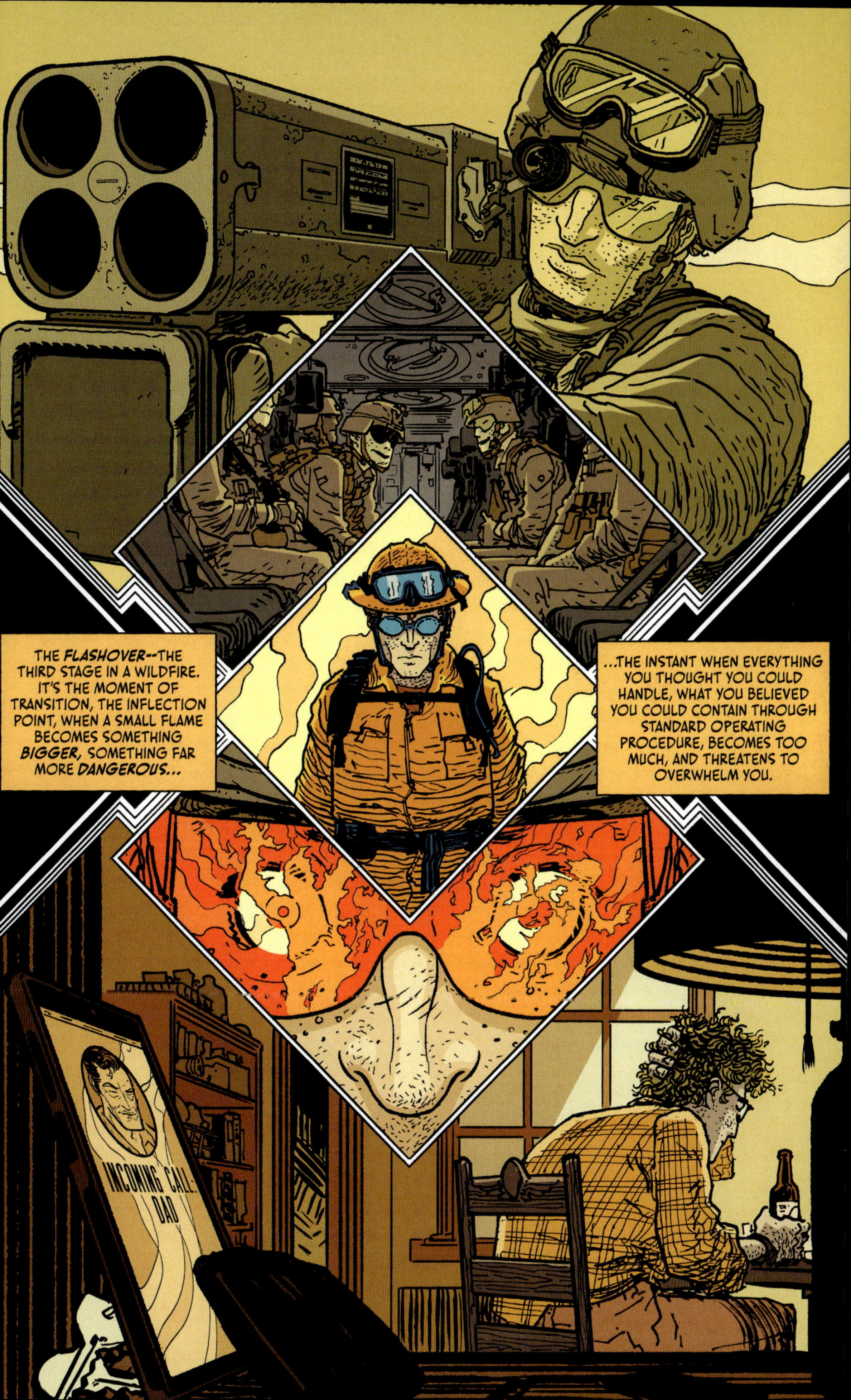
THE *FLASHOVER*--THE THIRD STAGE IN A WILDFIRE. IT'S THE MOMENT OF TRANSITION, THE INFLECTION POINT, WHEN A SMALL FLAME BECOMES SOMETHING *BIGGER*, SOMETHING FAR MORE *DANGEROUS*...
...THE INSTANT WHEN EVERYTHING YOU THOUGHT YOU COULD HANDLE, WHAT YOU BELIEVED YOU COULD CONTAIN THROUGH STANDARD OPERATING PROCEDURE, BECOMES TOO MUCH, AND THREATENS TO OVERWHELM YOU.
INCOMING CALL: DAD

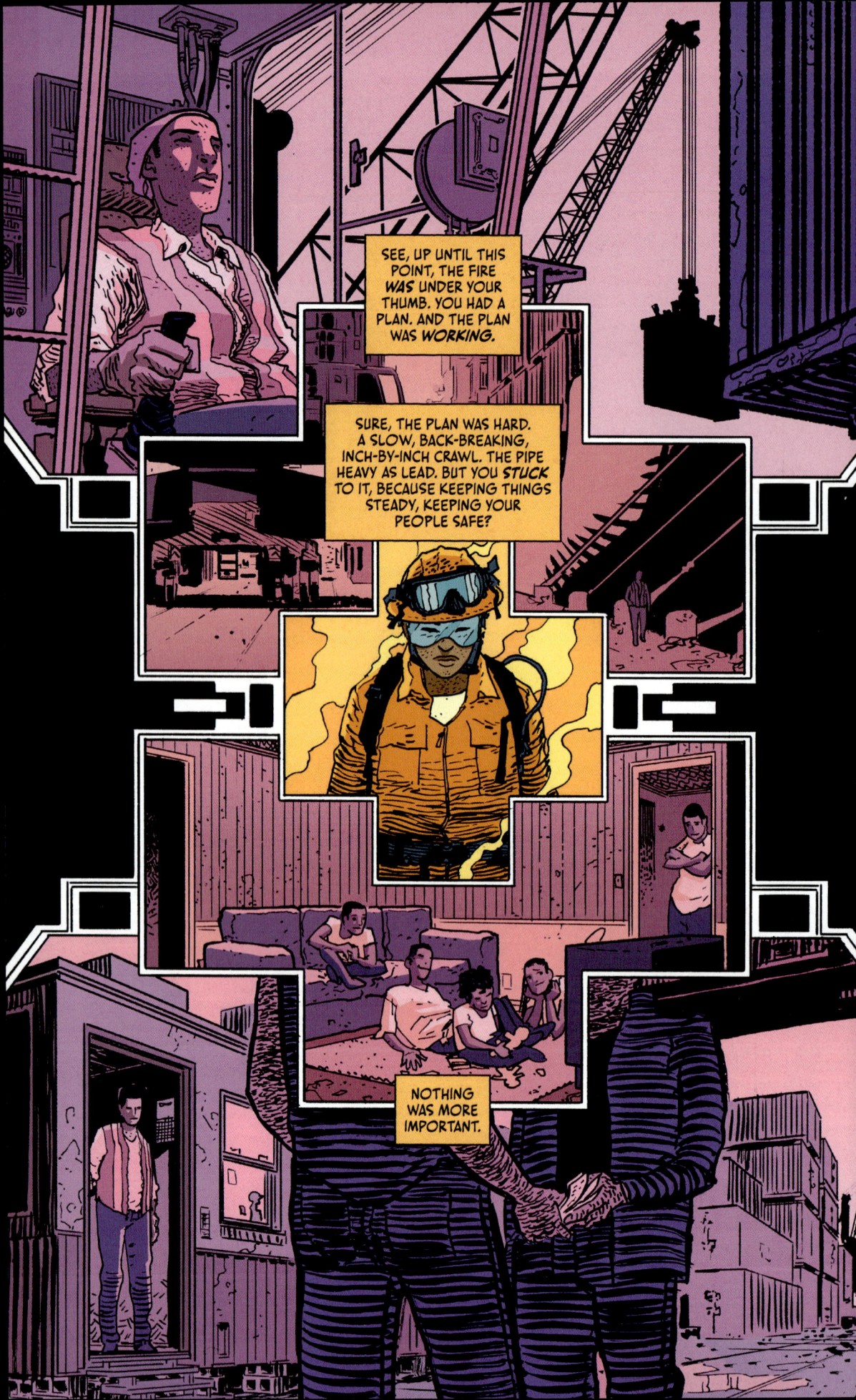

SEE, UP UNTIL THIS POINT, THE FIRE *WAS* UNDER YOUR THUMB. YOU HAD A PLAN. AND THE PLAN WAS *WORKING.*

SURE, THE PLAN WAS HARD. A SLOW, BACK-BREAKING, INCH-BY-INCH CRAWL. THE PIPE HEAVY AS LEAD. BUT YOU *STUCK* TO IT, BECAUSE KEEPING THINGS STEADY, KEEPING YOUR PEOPLE SAFE?

NOTHING WAS MORE IMPORTANT.

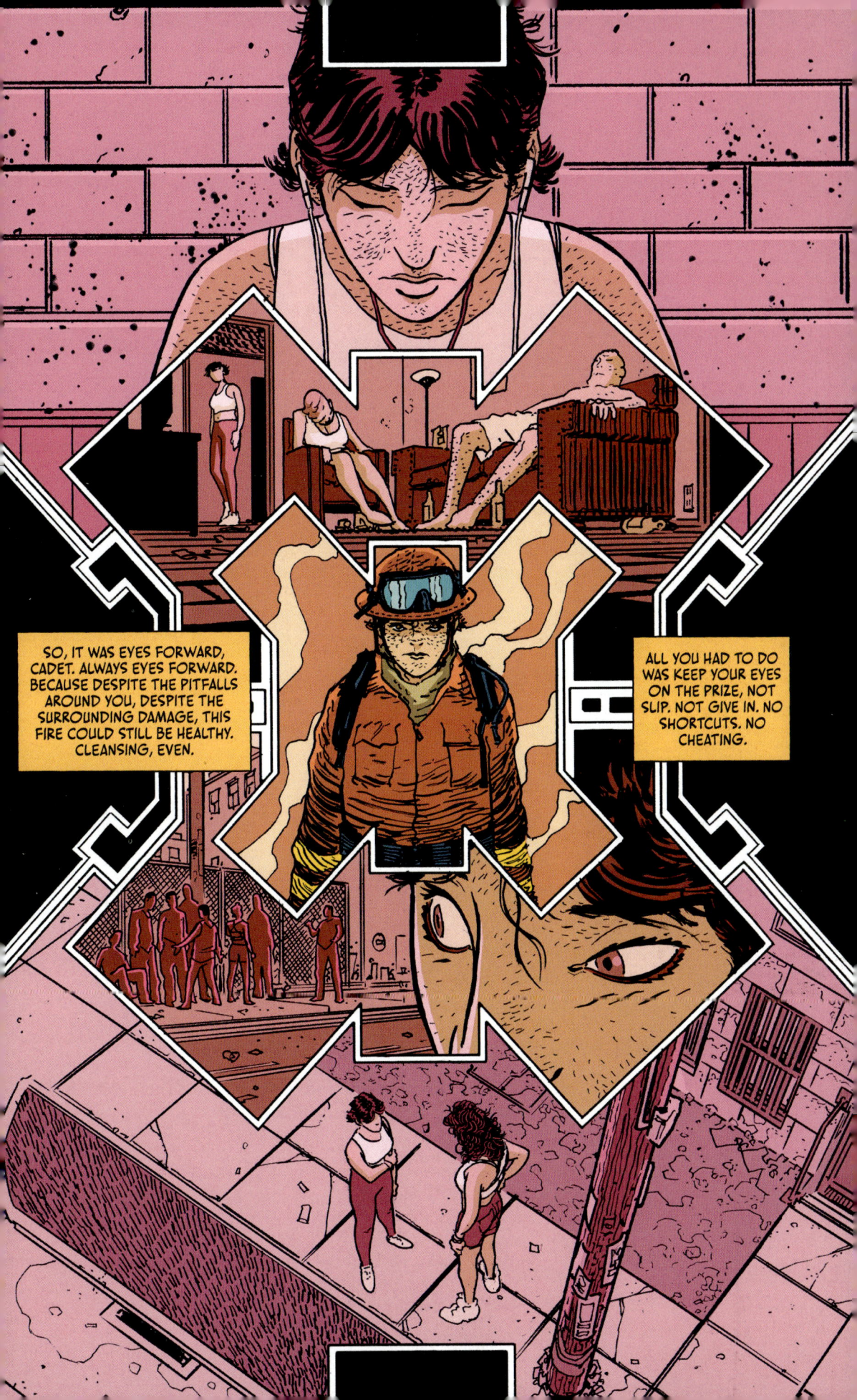

SO, IT WAS EYES FORWARD, CADET. ALWAYS EYES FORWARD. BECAUSE DESPITE THE PITFALLS AROUND YOU, DESPITE THE SURROUNDING DAMAGE, THIS FIRE COULD STILL BE HEALTHY. CLEANSING, EVEN.

ALL YOU HAD TO DO WAS KEEP YOUR EYES ON THE PRIZE, NOT SLIP. NOT GIVE IN. NO SHORTCUTS. NO CHEATING.

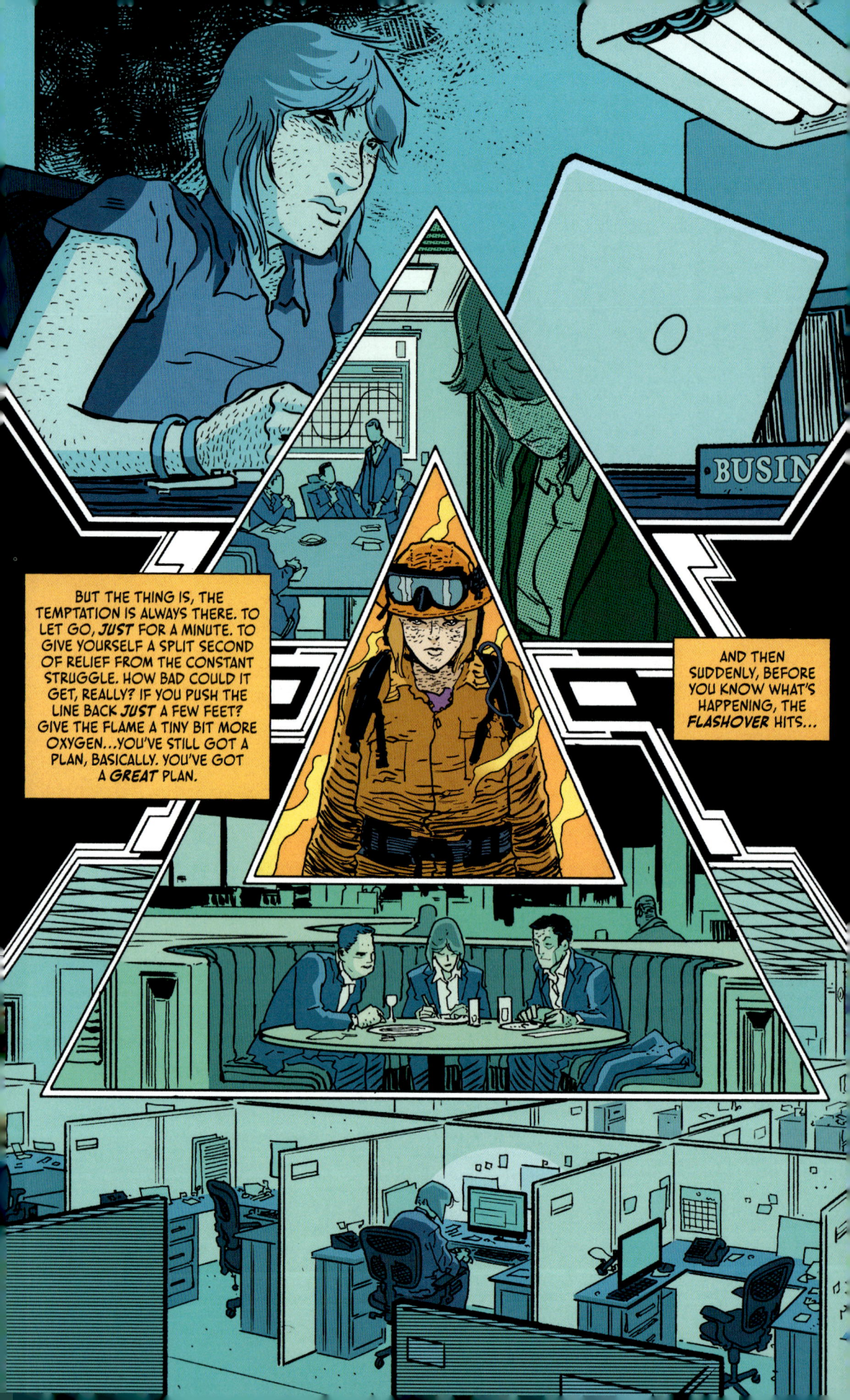

BUT THE THING IS, THE TEMPTATION IS ALWAYS THERE. TO LET GO, *JUST* FOR A MINUTE. TO GIVE YOURSELF A SPLIT SECOND OF RELIEF FROM THE CONSTANT STRUGGLE. HOW BAD COULD IT GET, REALLY? IF YOU PUSH THE LINE BACK *JUST* A FEW FEET? GIVE THE FLAME A TINY BIT MORE OXYGEN...YOU'VE STILL GOT A PLAN, BASICALLY. YOU'VE GOT A *GREAT* PLAN.

AND THEN SUDDENLY, BEFORE YOU KNOW WHAT'S HAPPENING, THE *FLASHOVER* HITS...

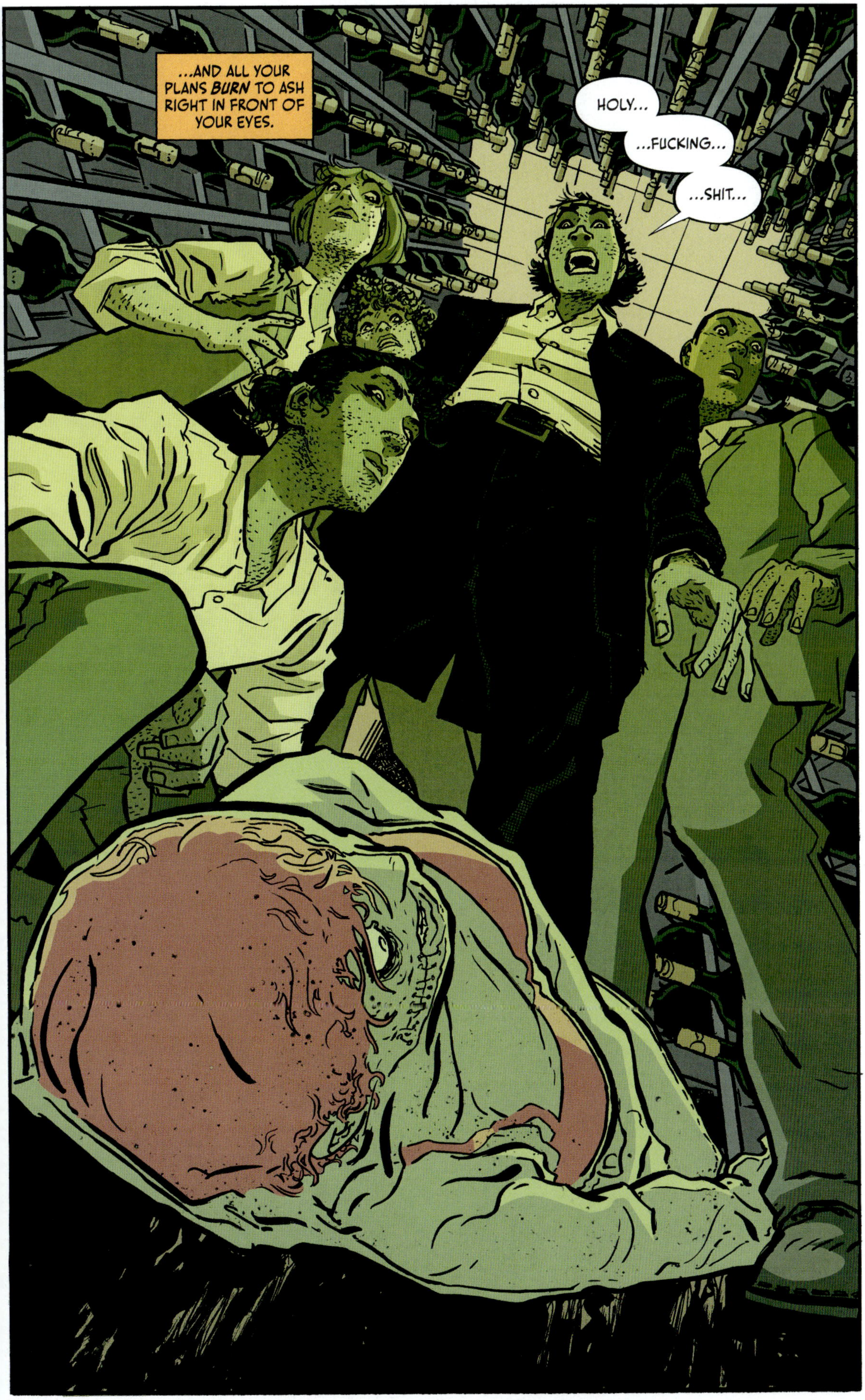
...AND ALL YOUR PLANS *BURN* TO ASH RIGHT IN FRONT OF YOUR EYES.
HOLY...
...FUCKING...
...SHIT...

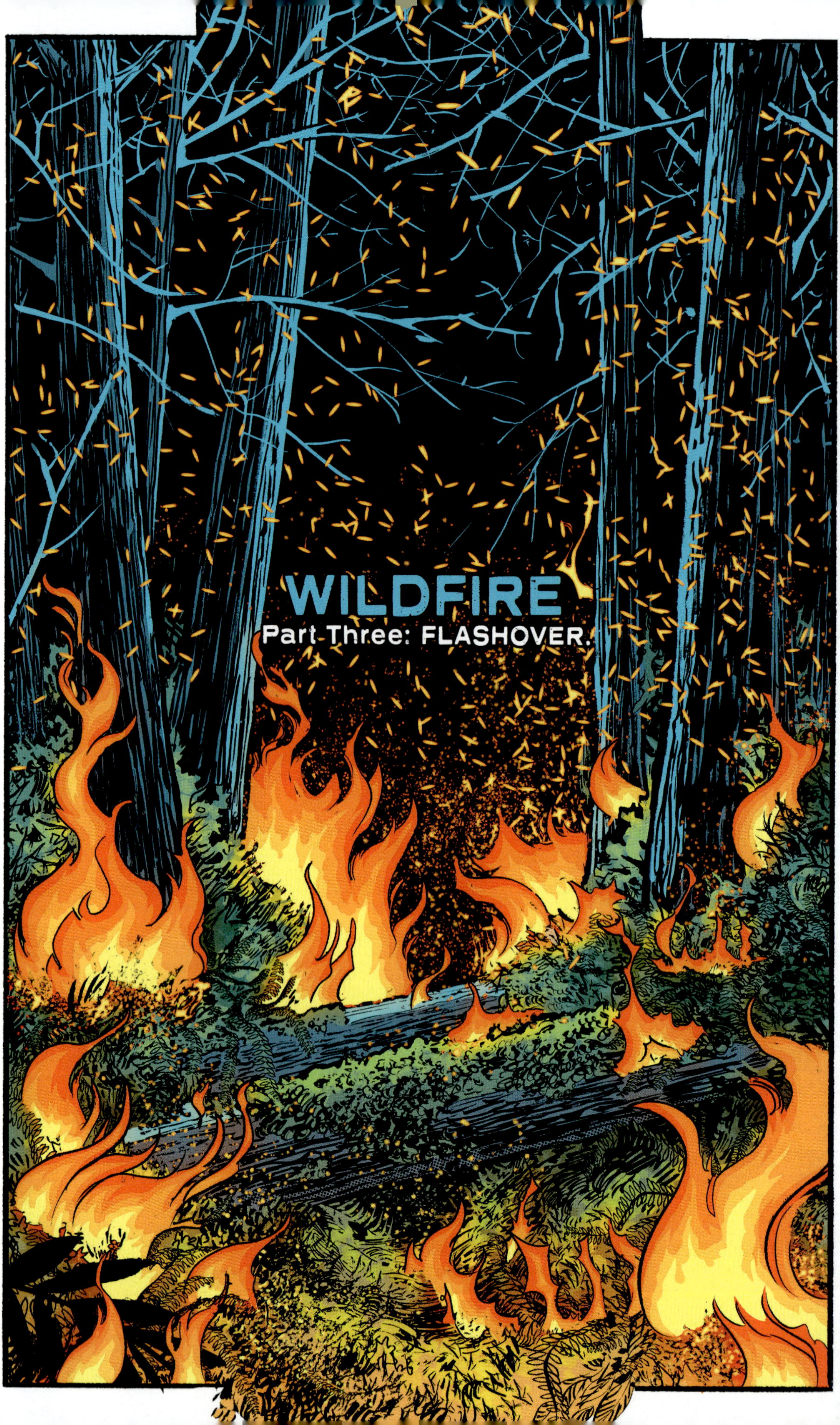
WILDFIRE
Part Three: FLASHOVER.

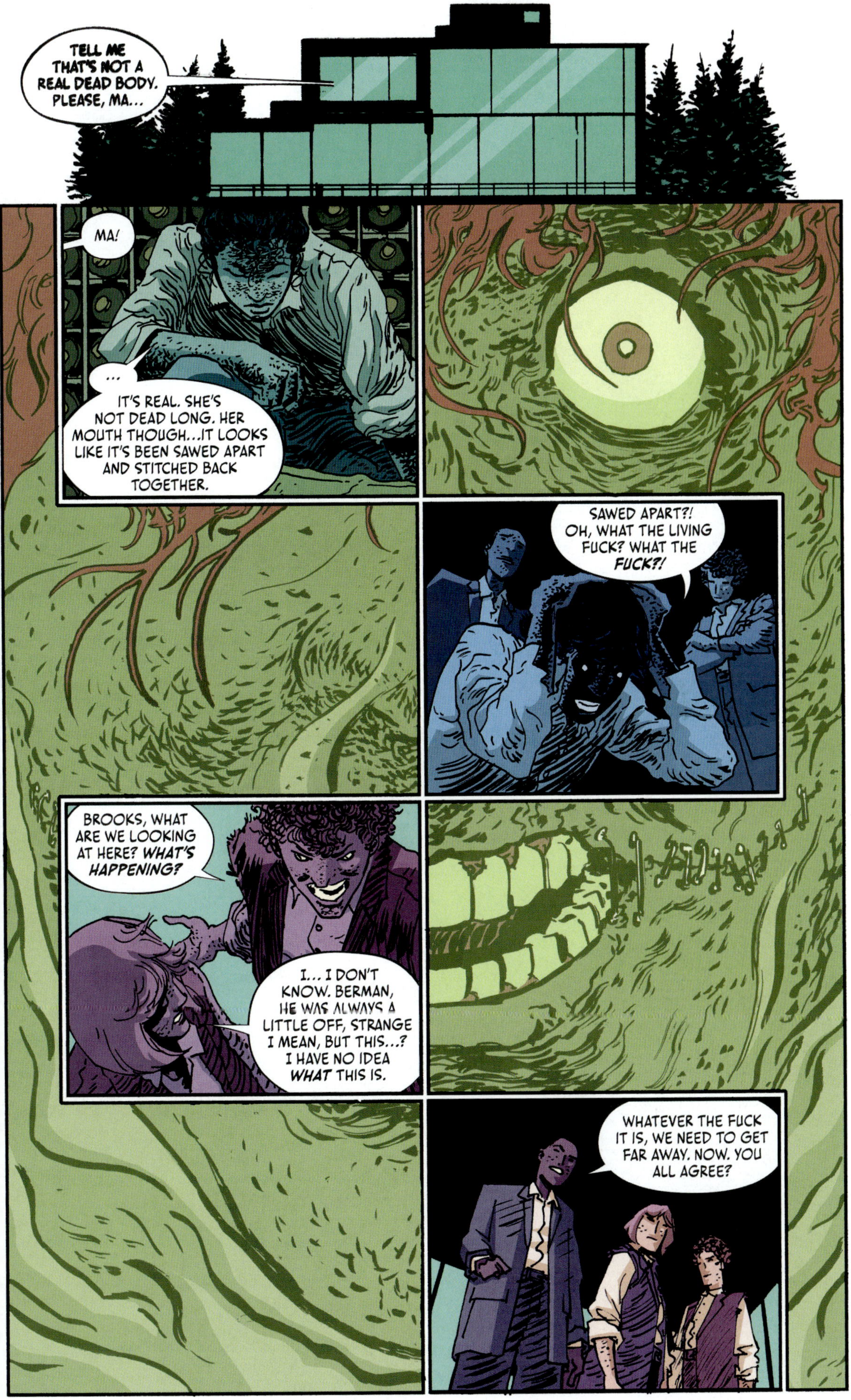

TELL ME THAT'S NOT A REAL DEAD BODY. PLEASE, MA...
MA!
...
IT'S REAL. SHE'S NOT DEAD LONG. HER MOUTH THOUGH...IT LOOKS LIKE IT'S BEEN SAWED APART AND STITCHED BACK TOGETHER.
SAWED APART?! OH, WHAT THE LIVING FUCK? WHAT THE *FUCK?!*
BROOKS, WHAT ARE WE LOOKING AT HERE? *WHAT'S HAPPENING?*
I... I DON'T KNOW. BERMAN, HE WAS ALWAYS A LITTLE OFF, STRANGE I MEAN, BUT THIS...? I HAVE NO IDEA *WHAT* THIS IS.
WHATEVER THE FUCK IT IS, WE NEED TO GET FAR AWAY. NOW. YOU ALL AGREE?

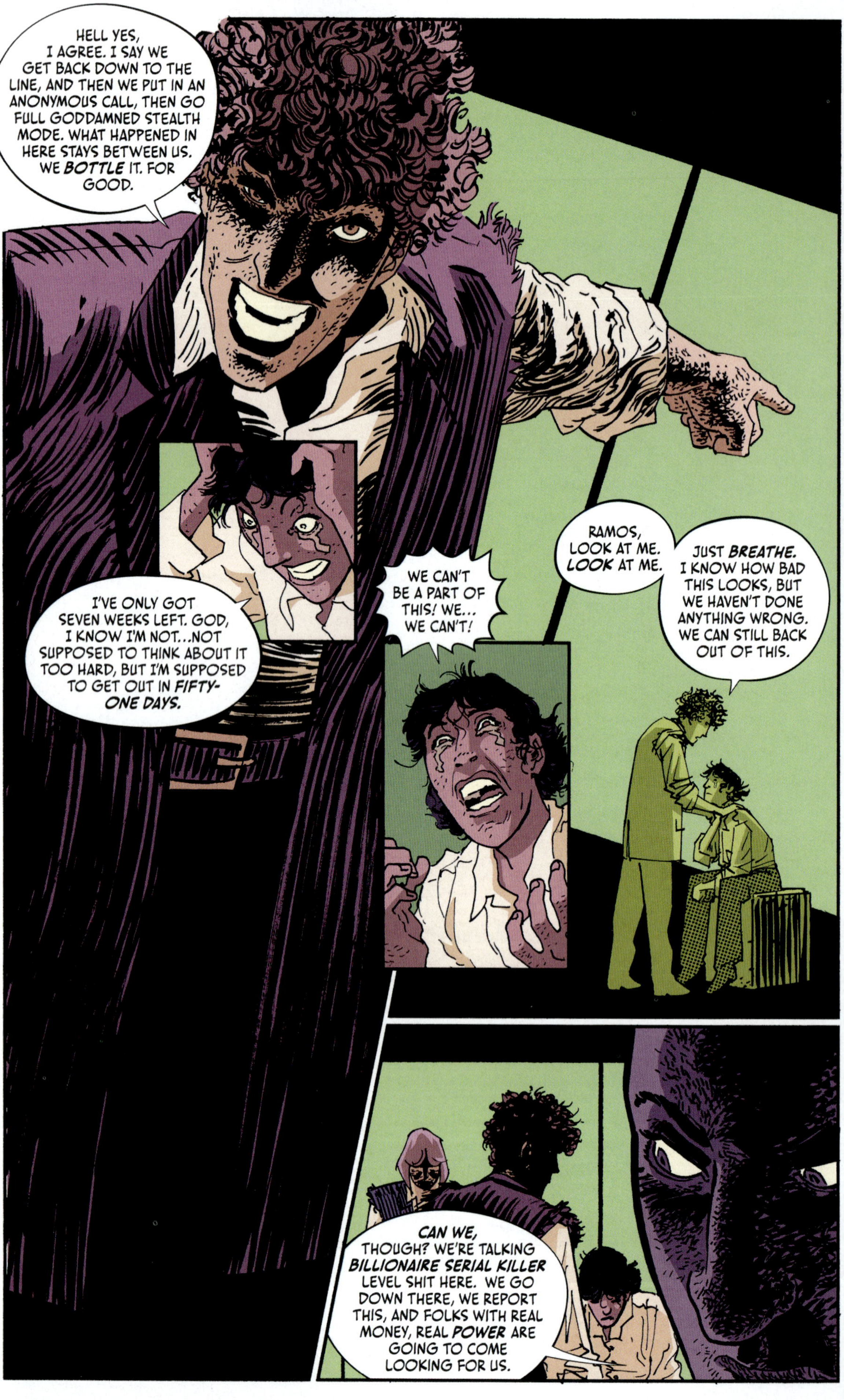
HELL YES, I AGREE. I SAY WE GET BACK DOWN TO THE LINE, AND THEN WE PUT IN AN ANONYMOUS CALL, THEN GO FULL GODDAMNED STEALTH MODE. WHAT HAPPENED IN HERE STAYS BETWEEN US. WE BOTTLE IT. FOR GOOD.
I'VE ONLY GOT SEVEN WEEKS LEFT. GOD, I KNOW I'M NOT...NOT SUPPOSED TO THINK ABOUT IT TOO HARD, BUT I'M SUPPOSED TO GET OUT IN FIFTY-ONE DAYS.
WE CAN'T BE A PART OF THIS! WE... WE CAN'T!
RAMOS, LOOK AT ME. LOOK AT ME.
JUST BREATHE. I KNOW HOW BAD THIS LOOKS, BUT WE HAVEN'T DONE ANYTHING WRONG. WE CAN STILL BACK OUT OF THIS.
CAN WE, THOUGH? WE'RE TALKING BILLIONAIRE SERIAL KILLER LEVEL SHIT HERE. WE GO DOWN THERE, WE REPORT THIS, AND FOLKS WITH REAL MONEY, REAL POWER ARE GOING TO COME LOOKING FOR US.

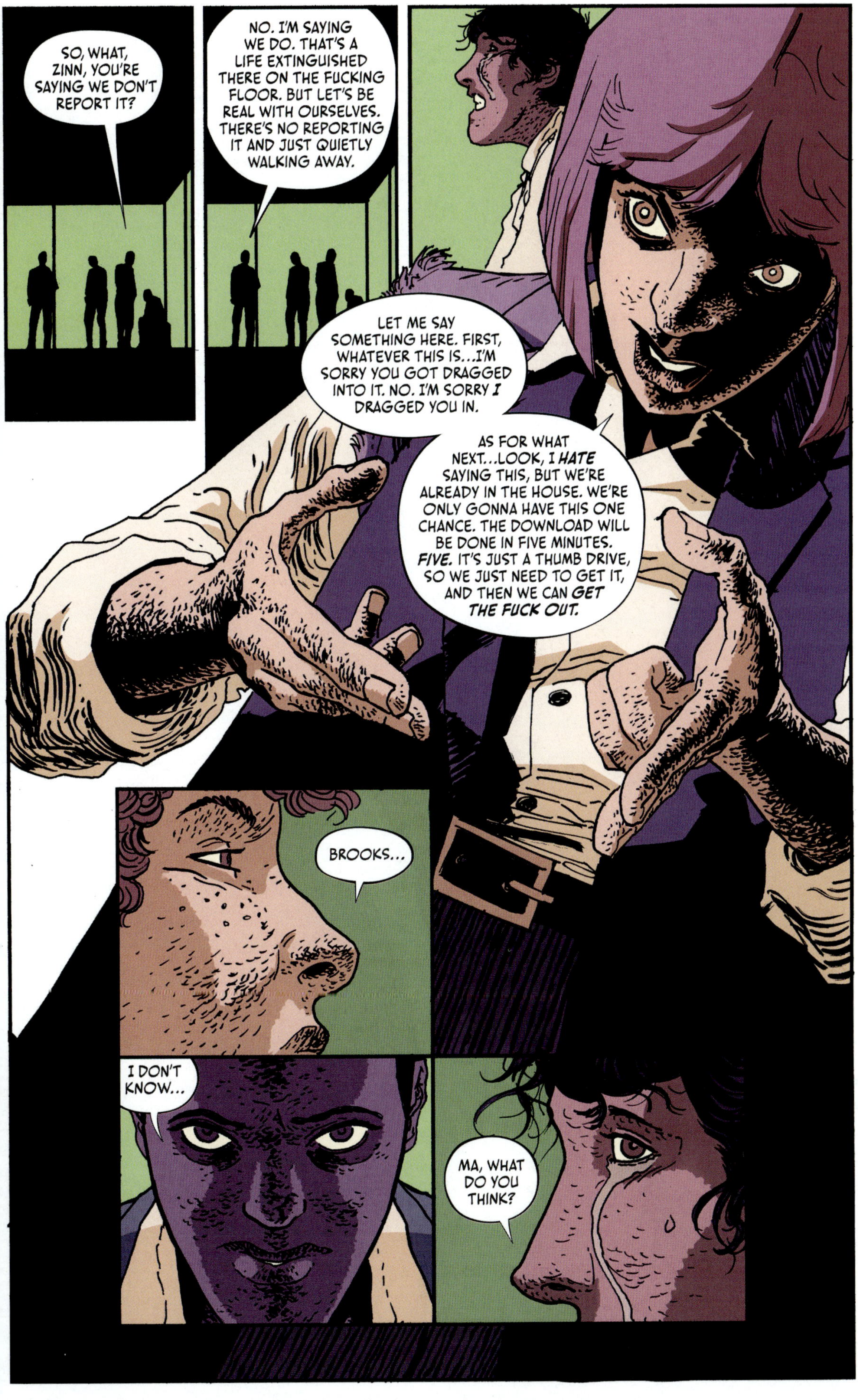
SO, WHAT, ZINN, YOU'RE SAYING WE DON'T REPORT IT?
NO. I'M SAYING WE DO. THAT'S A LIFE EXTINGUISHED THERE ON THE FUCKING FLOOR. BUT LET'S BE REAL WITH OURSELVES. THERE'S NO REPORTING IT AND JUST QUIETLY WALKING AWAY.
LET ME SAY SOMETHING HERE. FIRST, WHATEVER THIS IS...I'M SORRY YOU GOT DRAGGED INTO IT. NO. I'M SORRY *I* DRAGGED YOU IN.
AS FOR WHAT NEXT...LOOK, I *HATE* SAYING THIS, BUT WE'RE ALREADY IN THE HOUSE. WE'RE ONLY GONNA HAVE THIS ONE CHANCE. THE DOWNLOAD WILL BE DONE IN FIVE MINUTES. *FIVE.* IT'S JUST A THUMB DRIVE, SO WE JUST NEED TO GET IT, AND THEN WE CAN *GET THE FUCK OUT.*
BROOKS...
I DON'T KNOW...
MA, WHAT DO YOU THINK?

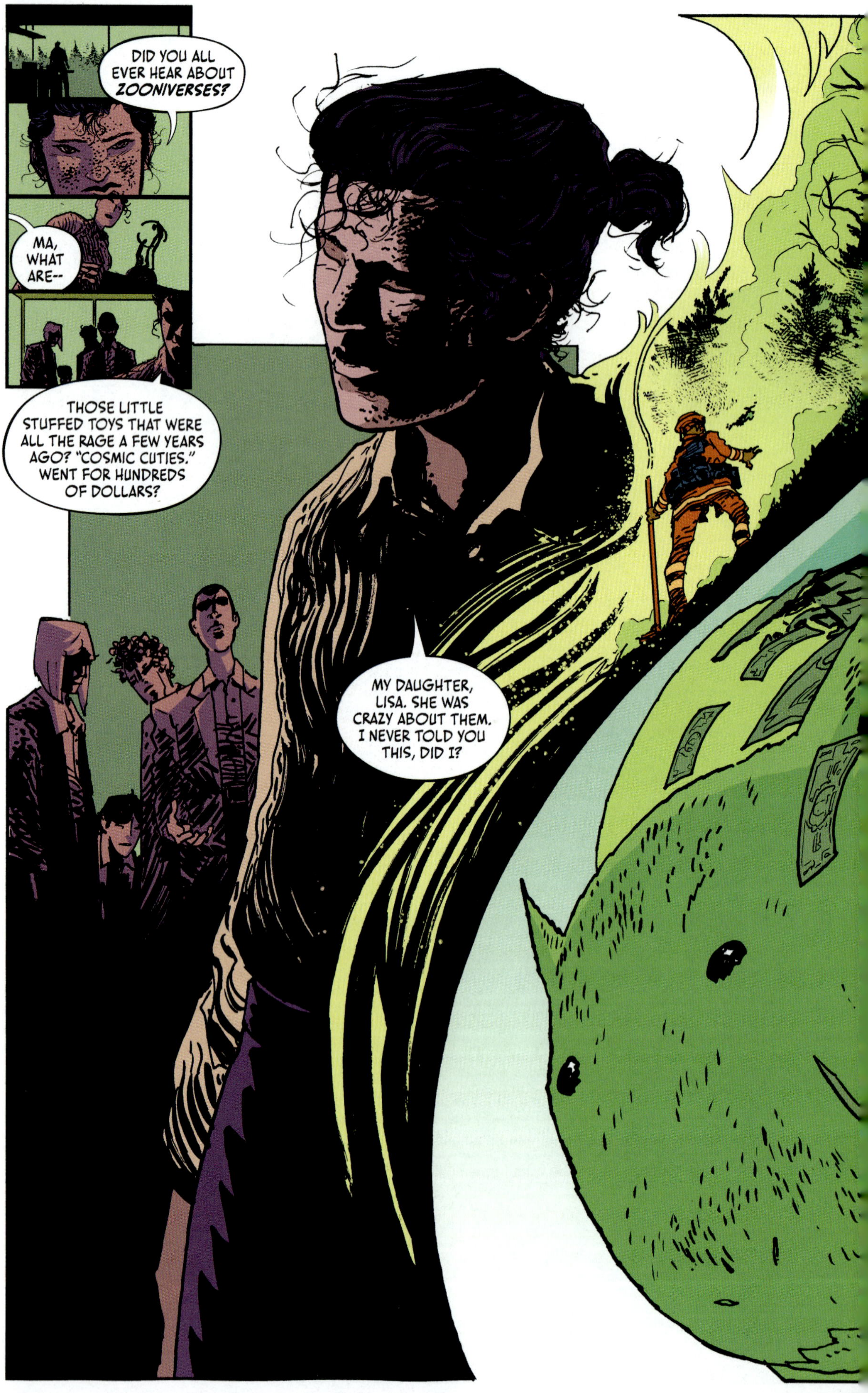
DID YOU ALL EVER HEAR ABOUT ZOONIVERSES?
MA, WHAT ARE--
THOSE LITTLE STUFFED TOYS THAT WERE ALL THE RAGE A FEW YEARS AGO? "COSMIC CUTIES." WENT FOR HUNDREDS OF DOLLARS?
MY DAUGHTER, LISA. SHE WAS CRAZY ABOUT THEM. I NEVER TOLD YOU THIS, DID I?

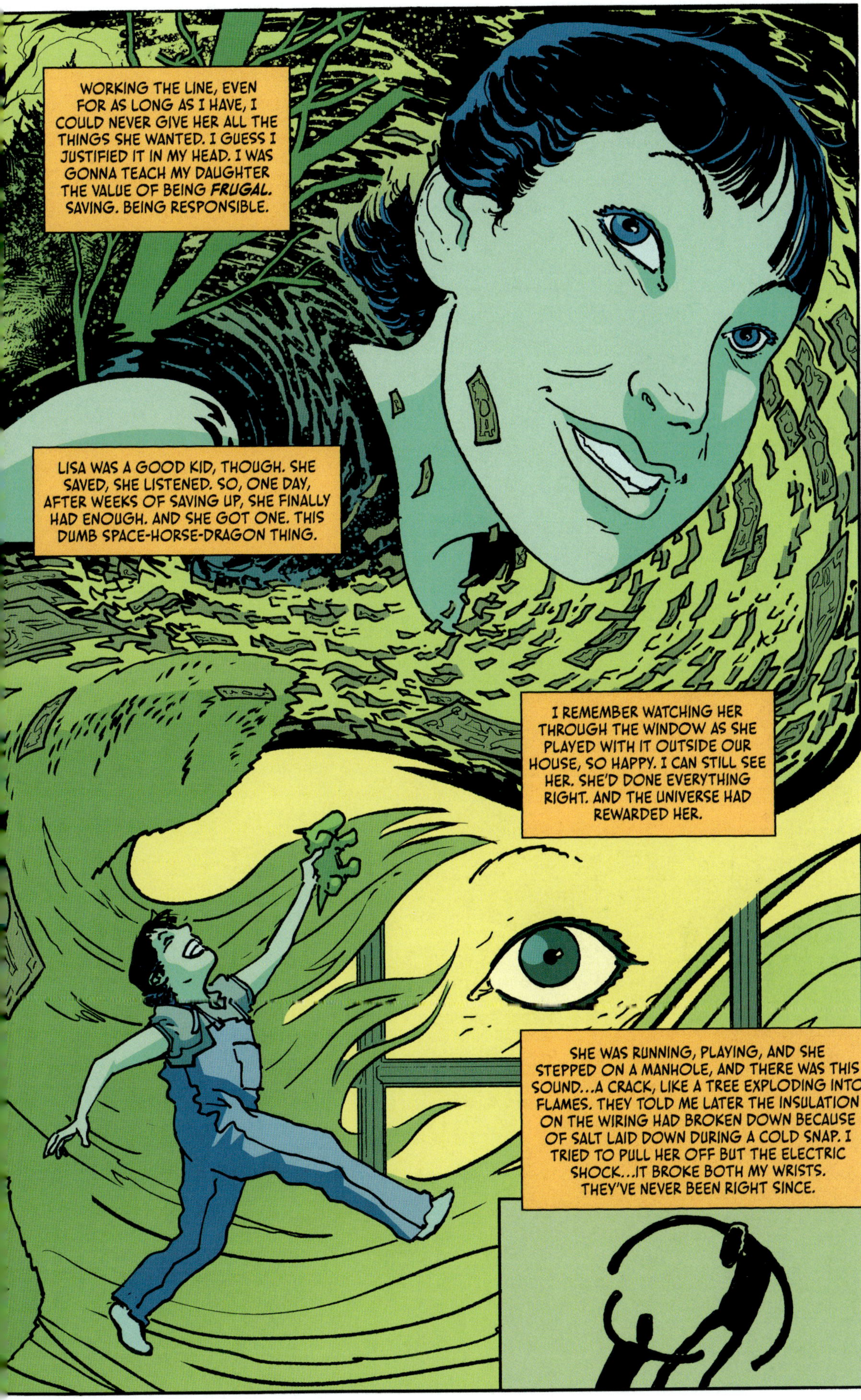
WORKING THE LINE, EVEN FOR AS LONG AS I HAVE, I COULD NEVER GIVE HER ALL THE THINGS SHE WANTED. I GUESS I JUSTIFIED IT IN MY HEAD. I WAS GONNA TEACH MY DAUGHTER THE VALUE OF BEING *FRUGAL.* SAVING. BEING RESPONSIBLE.
LISA WAS A GOOD KID, THOUGH. SHE SAVED, SHE LISTENED. SO, ONE DAY, AFTER WEEKS OF SAVING UP, SHE FINALLY HAD ENOUGH. AND SHE GOT ONE. THIS DUMB SPACE-HORSE-DRAGON THING.
I REMEMBER WATCHING HER THROUGH THE WINDOW AS SHE PLAYED WITH IT OUTSIDE OUR HOUSE, SO HAPPY. I CAN STILL SEE HER. SHE'D DONE EVERYTHING RIGHT. AND THE UNIVERSE HAD REWARDED HER.
SHE WAS RUNNING, PLAYING, AND SHE STEPPED ON A MANHOLE, AND THERE WAS THIS SOUND...A CRACK, LIKE A TREE EXPLODING INTO FLAMES. THEY TOLD ME LATER THE INSULATION ON THE WIRING HAD BROKEN DOWN BECAUSE OF SALT LAID DOWN DURING A COLD SNAP. I TRIED TO PULL HER OFF BUT THE ELECTRIC SHOCK...IT BROKE BOTH MY WRISTS. THEY'VE NEVER BEEN RIGHT SINCE.

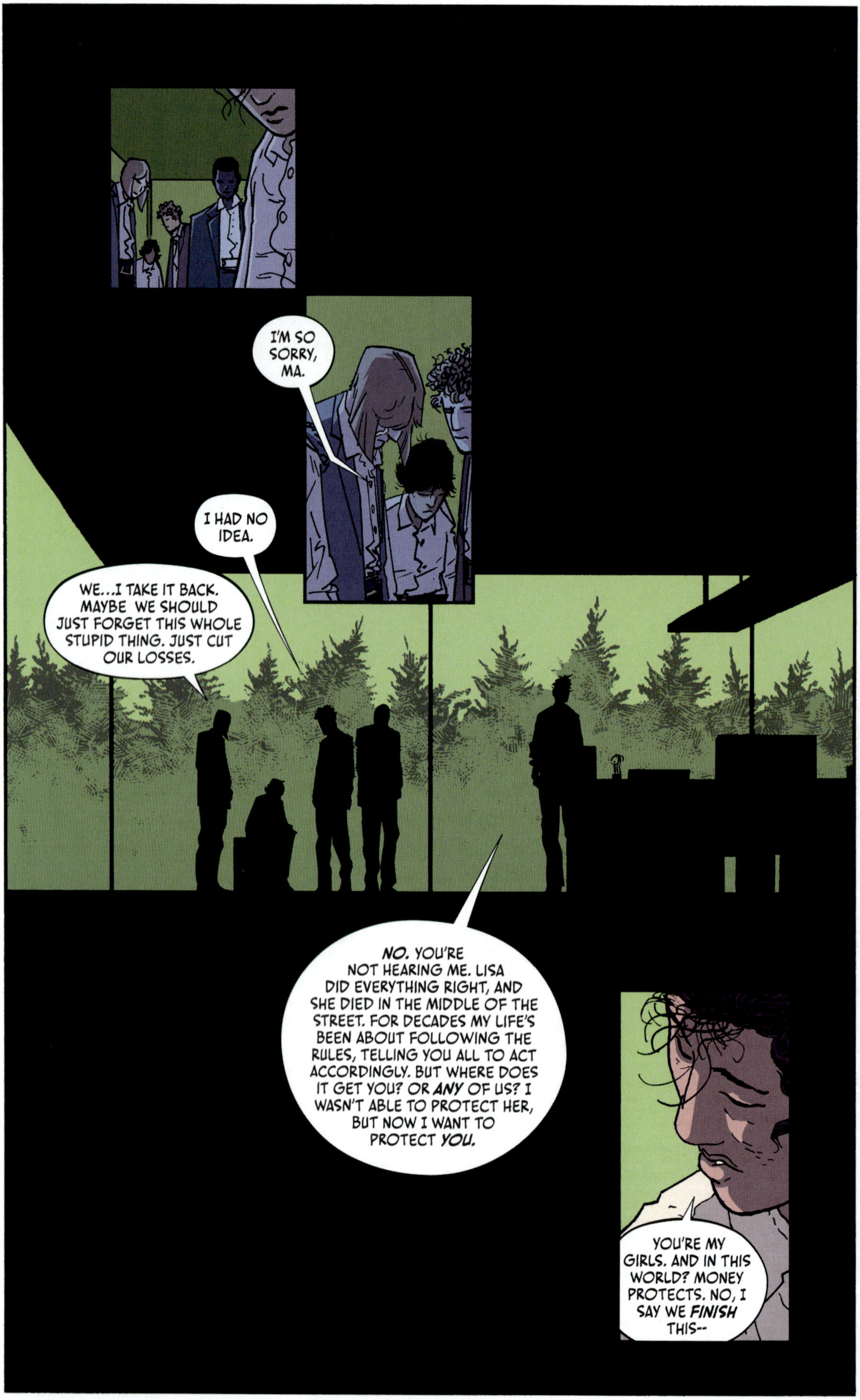
I'M SO SORRY, MA.
I HAD NO IDEA.
WE...I TAKE IT BACK. MAYBE WE SHOULD JUST FORGET THIS WHOLE STUPID THING. JUST CUT OUR LOSSES.
NO. YOU'RE NOT HEARING ME. LISA DID EVERYTHING RIGHT, AND SHE DIED IN THE MIDDLE OF THE STREET. FOR DECADES MY LIFE'S BEEN ABOUT FOLLOWING THE RULES, TELLING YOU ALL TO ACT ACCORDINGLY. BUT WHERE DOES IT GET YOU? OR ANY OF US? I WASN'T ABLE TO PROTECT HER, BUT NOW I WANT TO PROTECT YOU.
YOU'RE MY GIRLS. AND IN THIS WORLD? MONEY PROTECTS. NO, I SAY WE FINISH THIS--

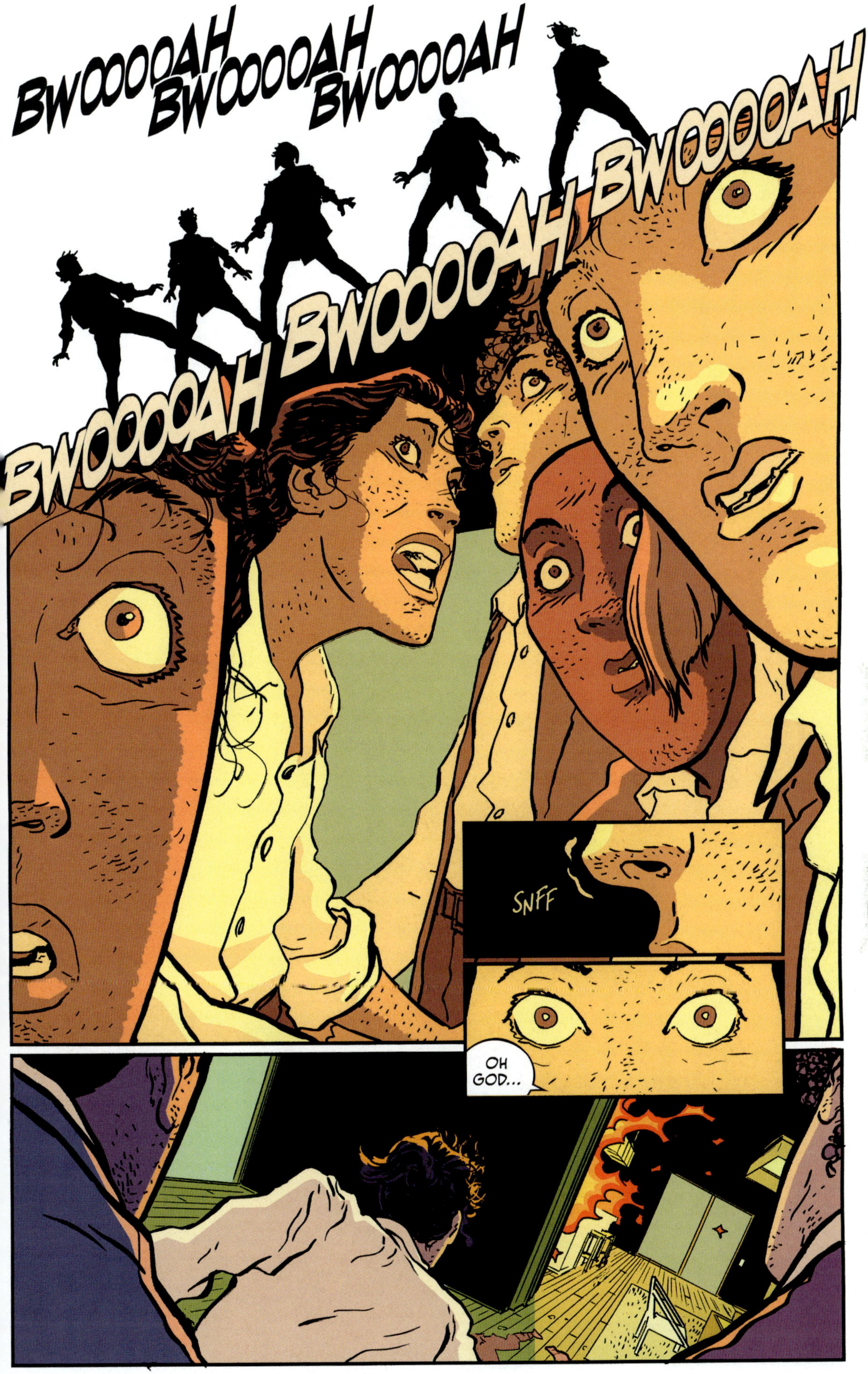
BWOOOOAH
BWOOOOAH
BWOOOOAH
BWOOOOAH BWOOOOAH BWOOOOAH BWOOOOAH
SNFF
OH GOD...

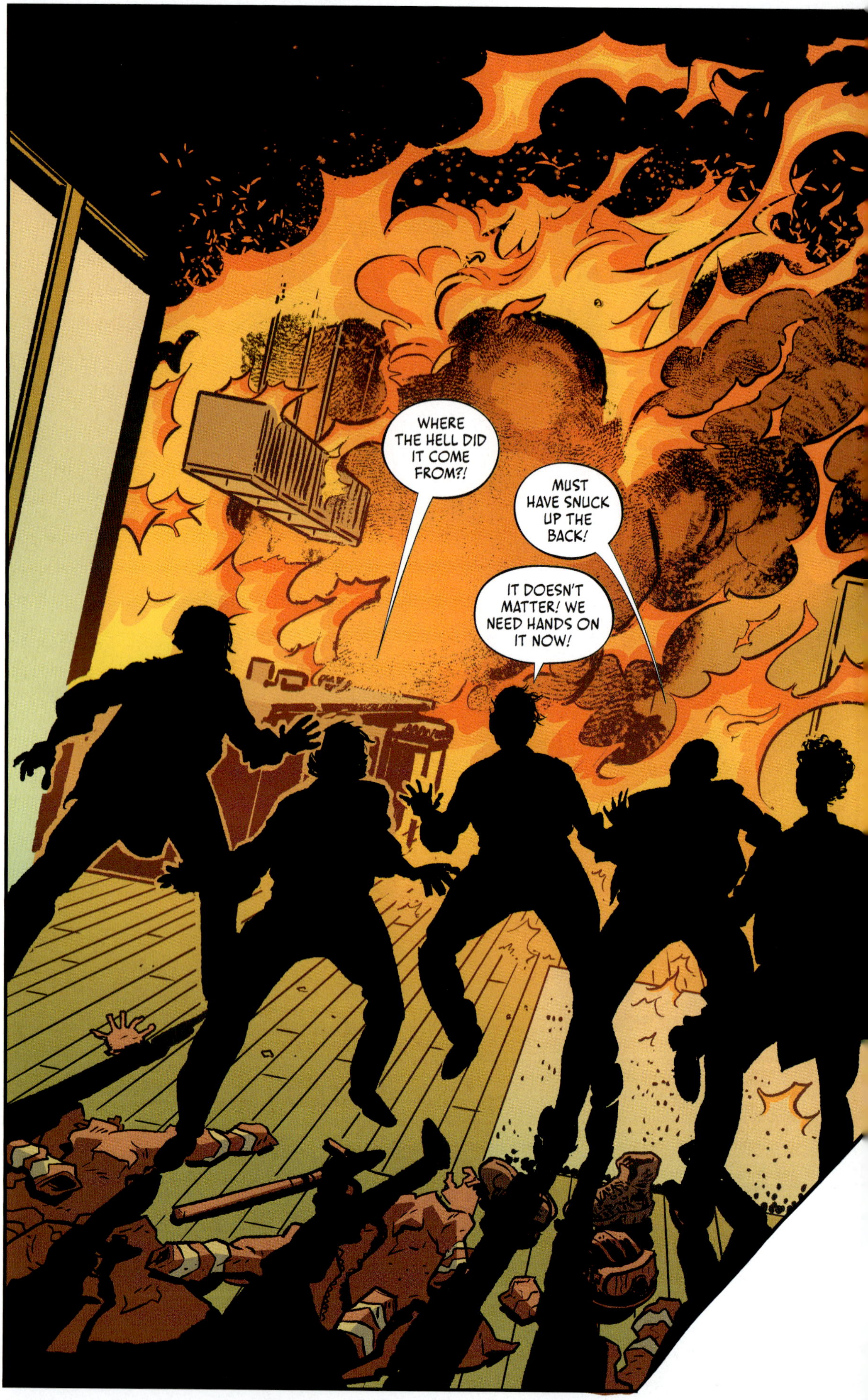
WHERE THE HELL DID IT COME FROM?!
MUST HAVE SNUCK UP THE BACK!
IT DOESN'T MATTER! WE NEED HANDS ON IT NOW!

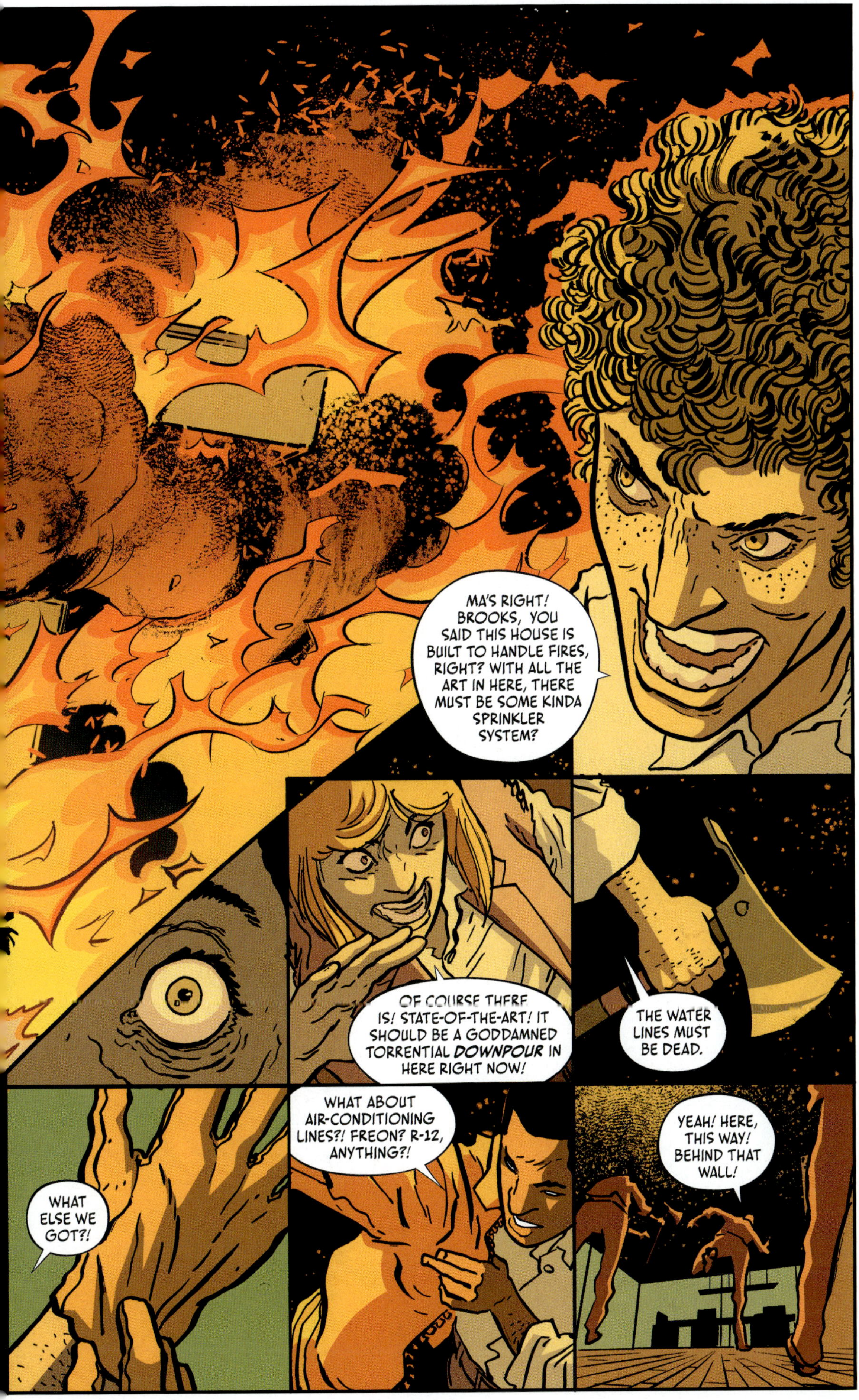
MA'S RIGHT! BROOKS, YOU SAID THIS HOUSE IS BUILT TO HANDLE FIRES, RIGHT? WITH ALL THE ART IN HERE, THERE MUST BE SOME KINDA SPRINKLER SYSTEM?
OF COURSE THERE IS! STATE-OF-THE-ART! IT SHOULD BE A GODDAMNED TORRENTIAL *DOWNPOUR* IN HERE RIGHT NOW!
THE WATER LINES MUST BE DEAD.
WHAT ELSE WE GOT?!
WHAT ABOUT AIR-CONDITIONING LINES?! FREON? R-12, ANYTHING?!
YEAH! HERE, THIS WAY! BEHIND THAT WALL!

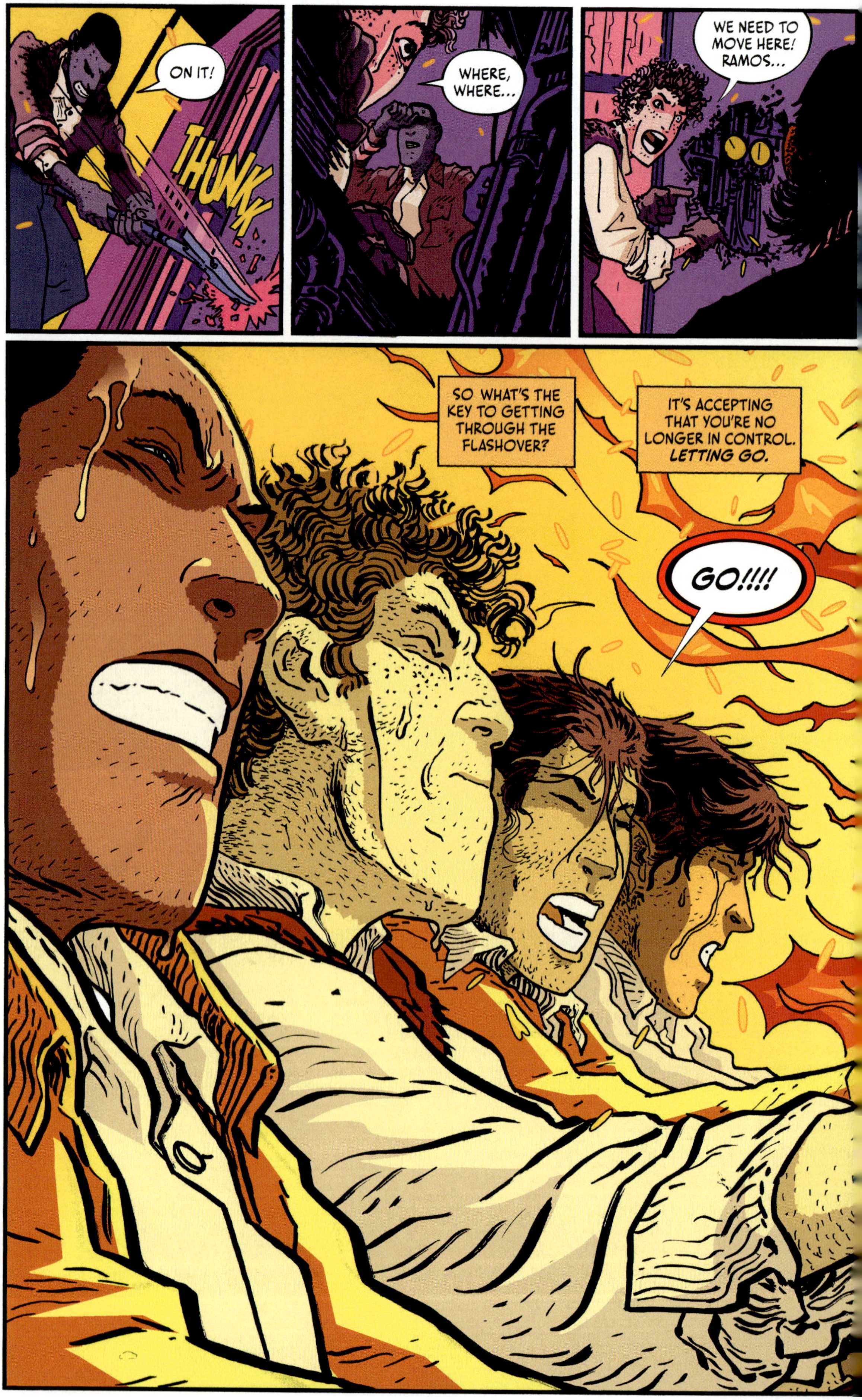
ON IT!
THUNKK
WHERE, WHERE...
WE NEED TO MOVE HERE! RAMOS...
SO WHAT'S THE KEY TO GETTING THROUGH THE FLASHOVER?
IT'S ACCEPTING THAT YOU'RE NO LONGER IN CONTROL. *LETTING GO.*
GO!!!!

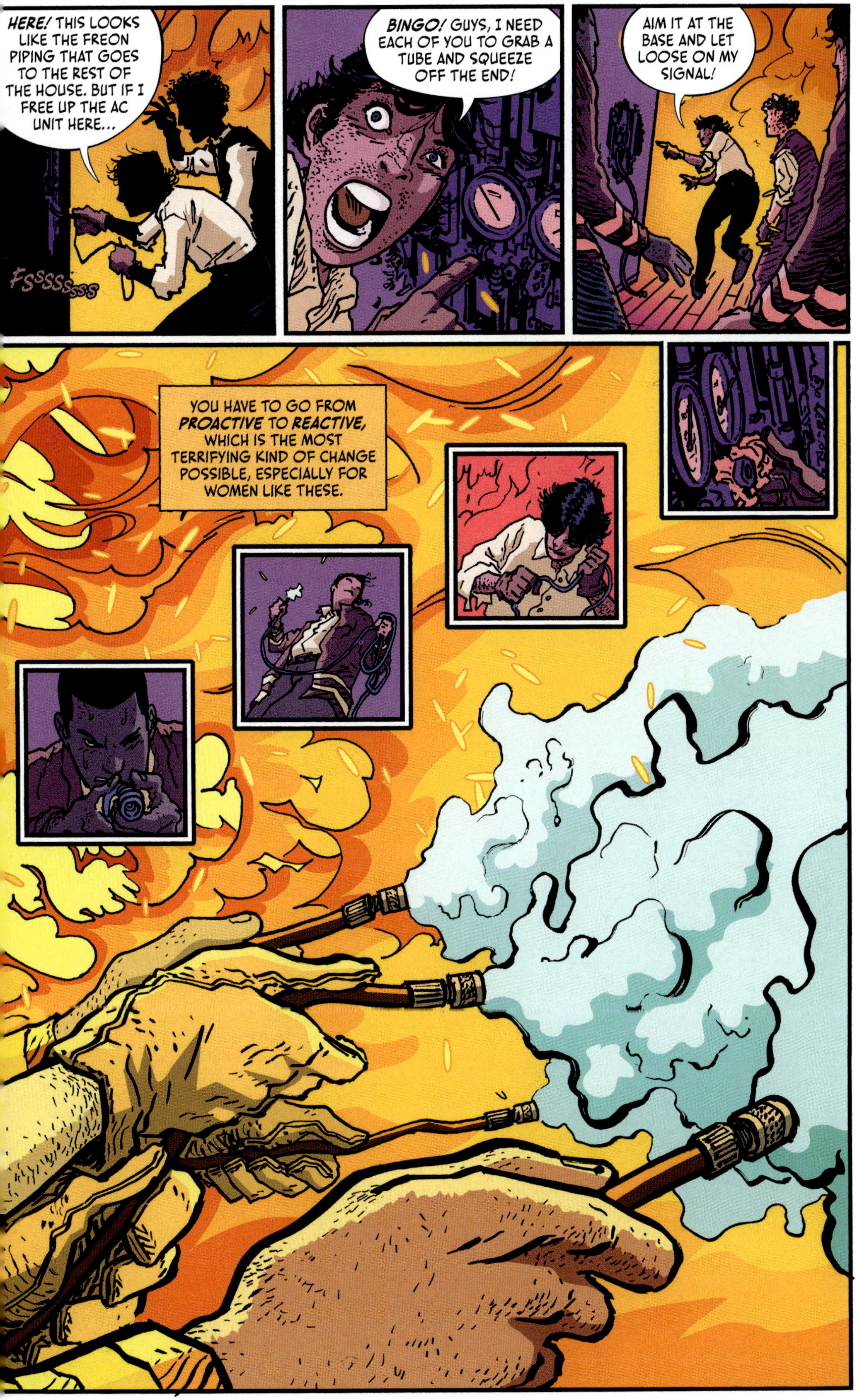

HERE! THIS LOOKS LIKE THE FREON PIPING THAT GOES TO THE REST OF THE HOUSE. BUT IF I FREE UP THE AC UNIT HERE...
FSSSSSSSS
BINGO! GUYS, I NEED EACH OF YOU TO GRAB A TUBE AND SQUEEZE OFF THE END!
AIM IT AT THE BASE AND LET LOOSE ON MY SIGNAL!
YOU HAVE TO GO FROM PROACTIVE TO REACTIVE, WHICH IS THE MOST TERRIFYING KIND OF CHANGE POSSIBLE, ESPECIALLY FOR WOMEN LIKE THESE.

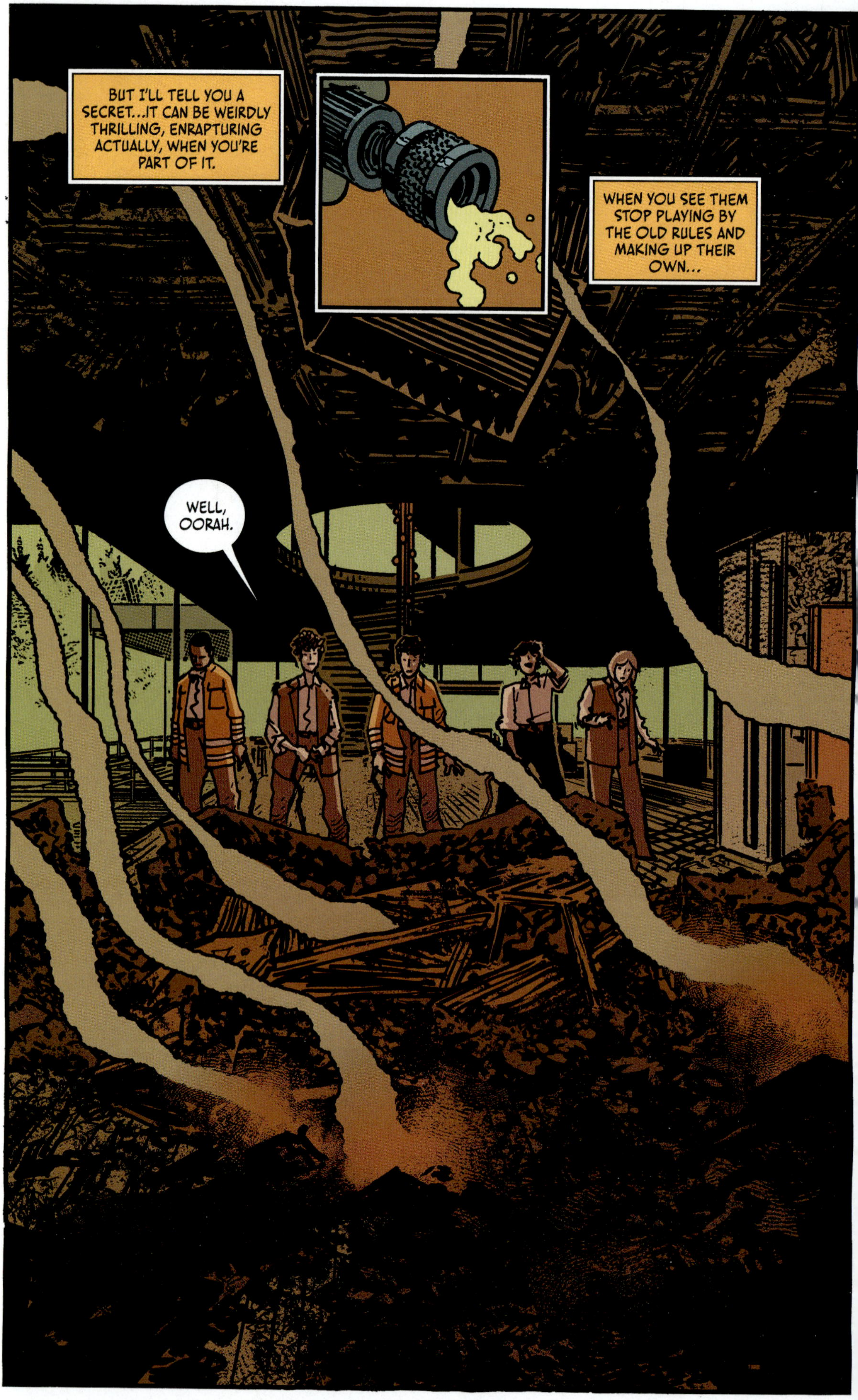
BUT I'LL TELL YOU A SECRET...IT CAN BE WEIRDLY THRILLING, ENRAPTURING ACTUALLY, WHEN YOU'RE PART OF IT.
WHEN YOU SEE THEM STOP PLAYING BY THE OLD RULES AND MAKING UP THEIR OWN...
WELL, OORAH.

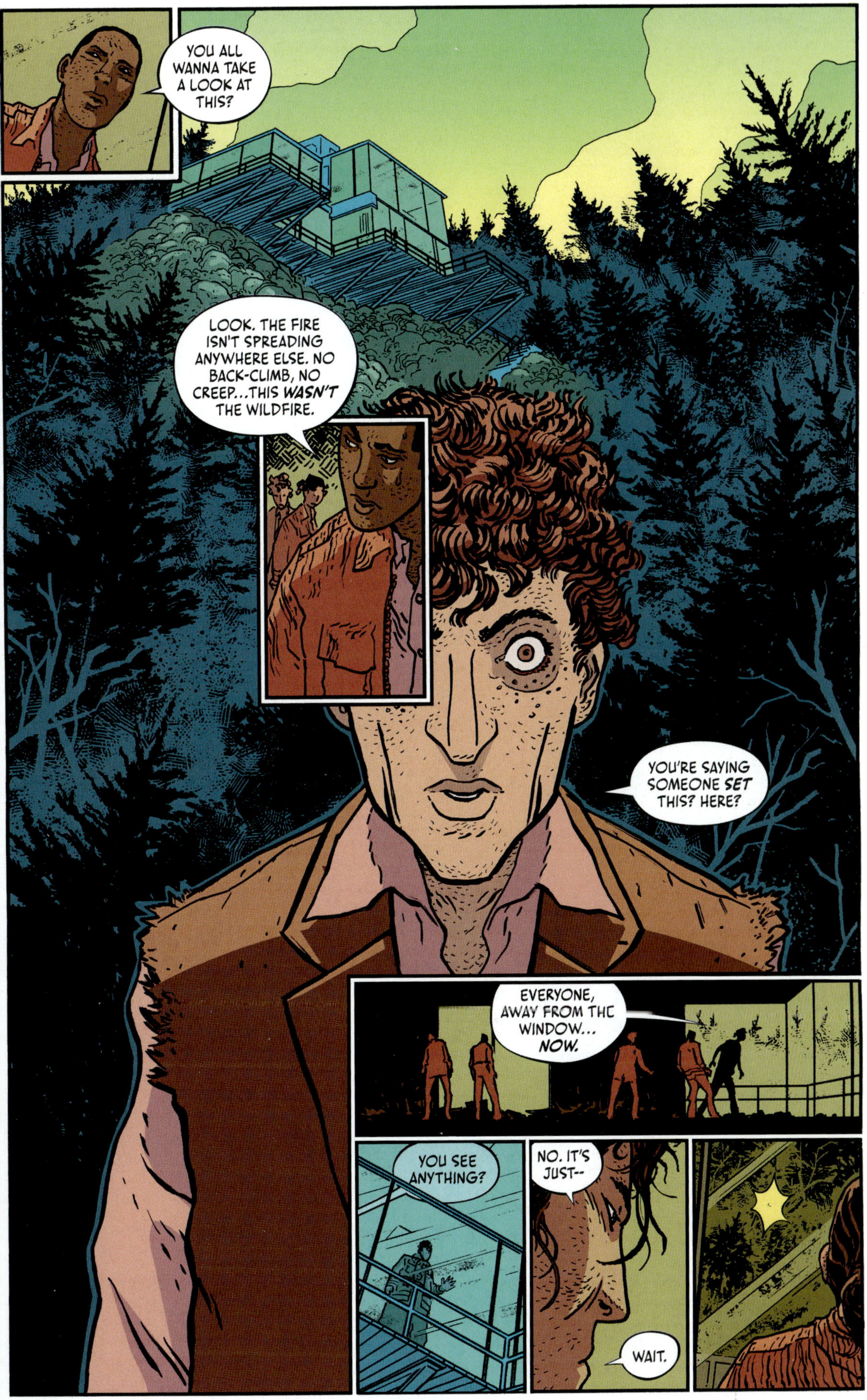
YOU ALL WANNA TAKE A LOOK AT THIS?
LOOK. THE FIRE ISN'T SPREADING ANYWHERE ELSE. NO BACK-CLIMB, NO CREEP...THIS *WASN'T* THE WILDFIRE.
YOU'RE SAYING SOMEONE *SET* THIS? HERE?
EVERYONE, AWAY FROM THE WINDOW... *NOW.*
YOU SEE ANYTHING?
NO. IT'S JUST--
WAIT.

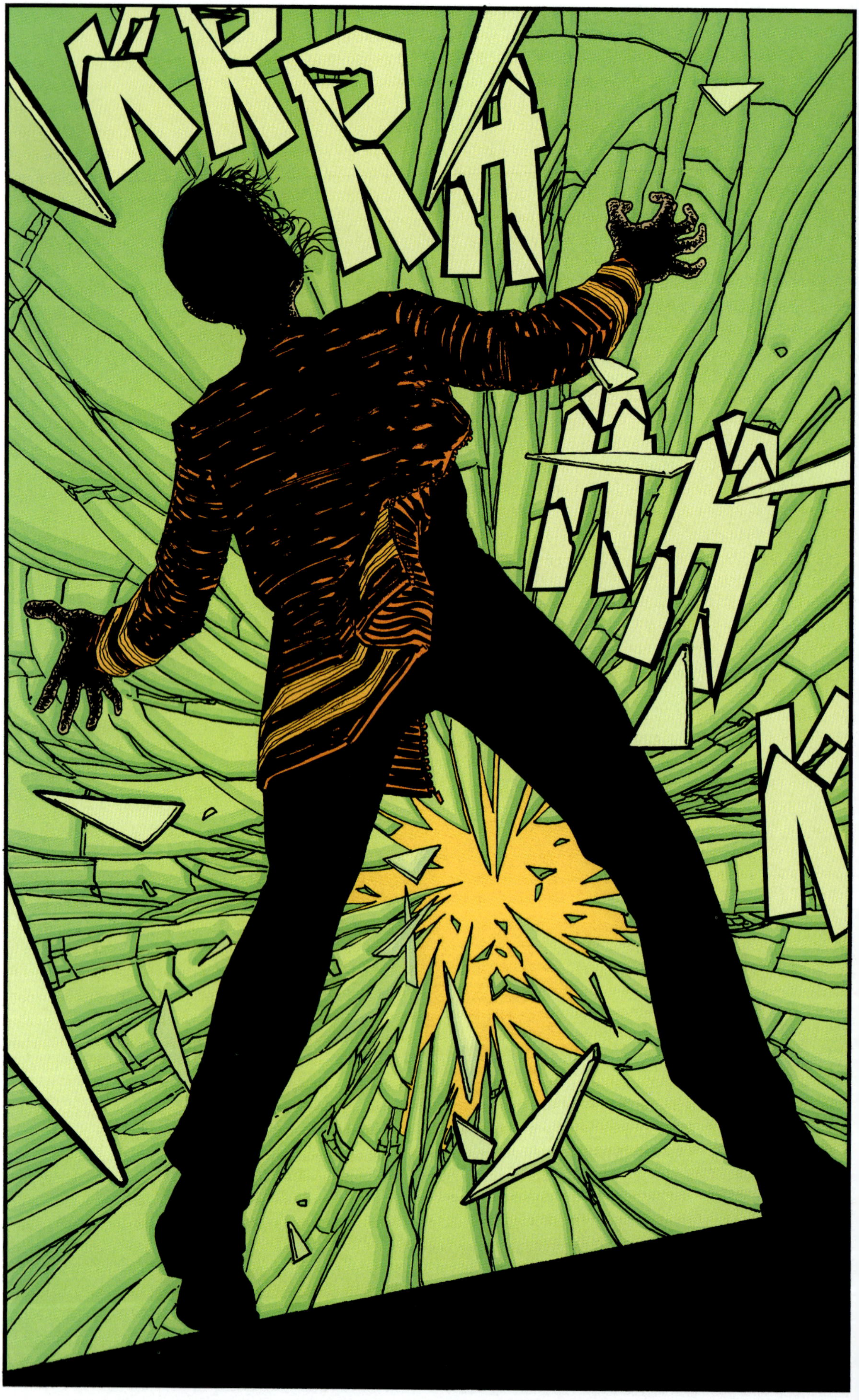
KRRAAAK

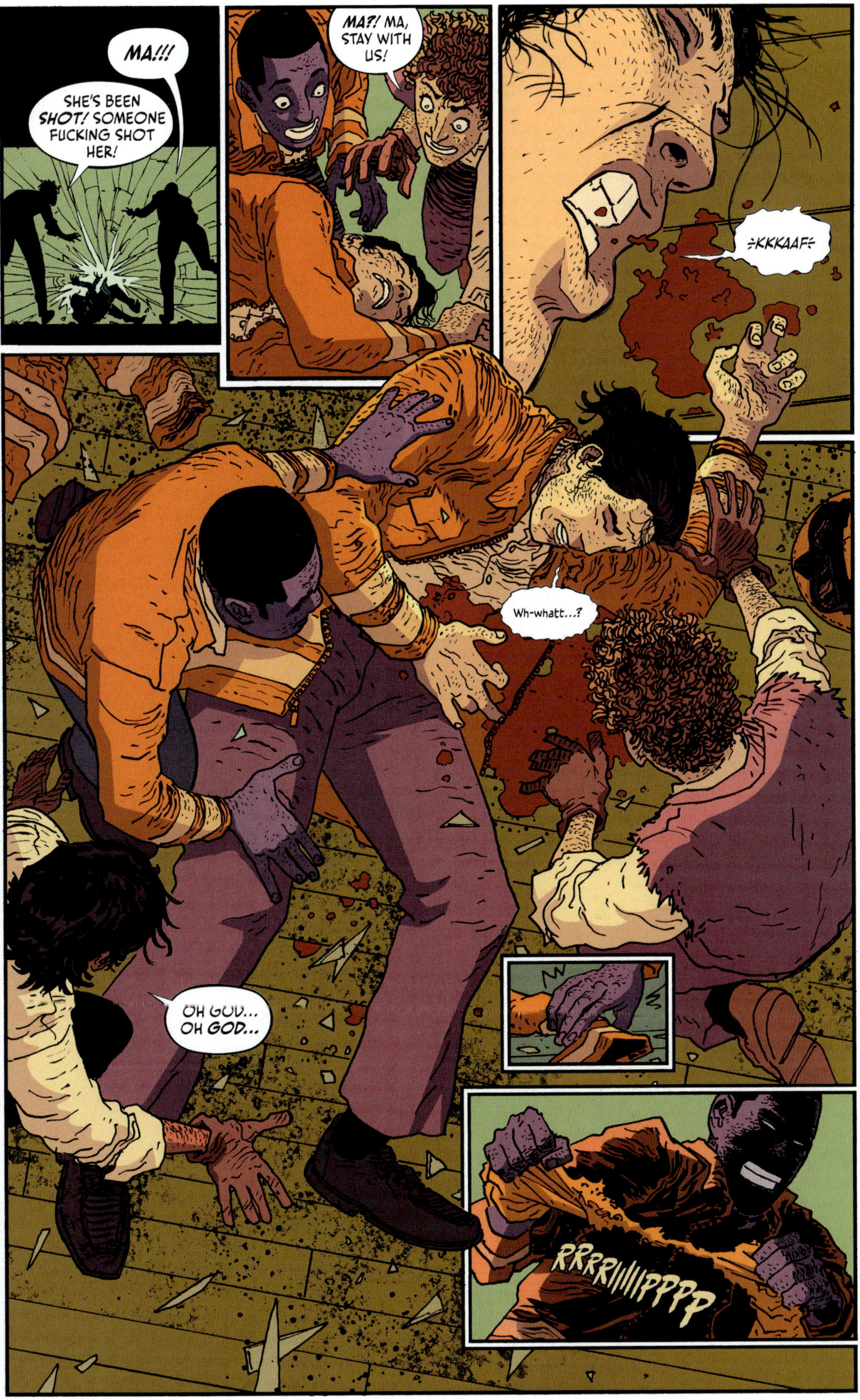
MA!!!
SHE'S BEEN SHOT! SOMEONE FUCKING SHOT HER!
MA?! MA, STAY WITH US!
KKKAAF
Wh-whatt...?
OH GOD... OH GOD...
RRRRIIIIIPPPP

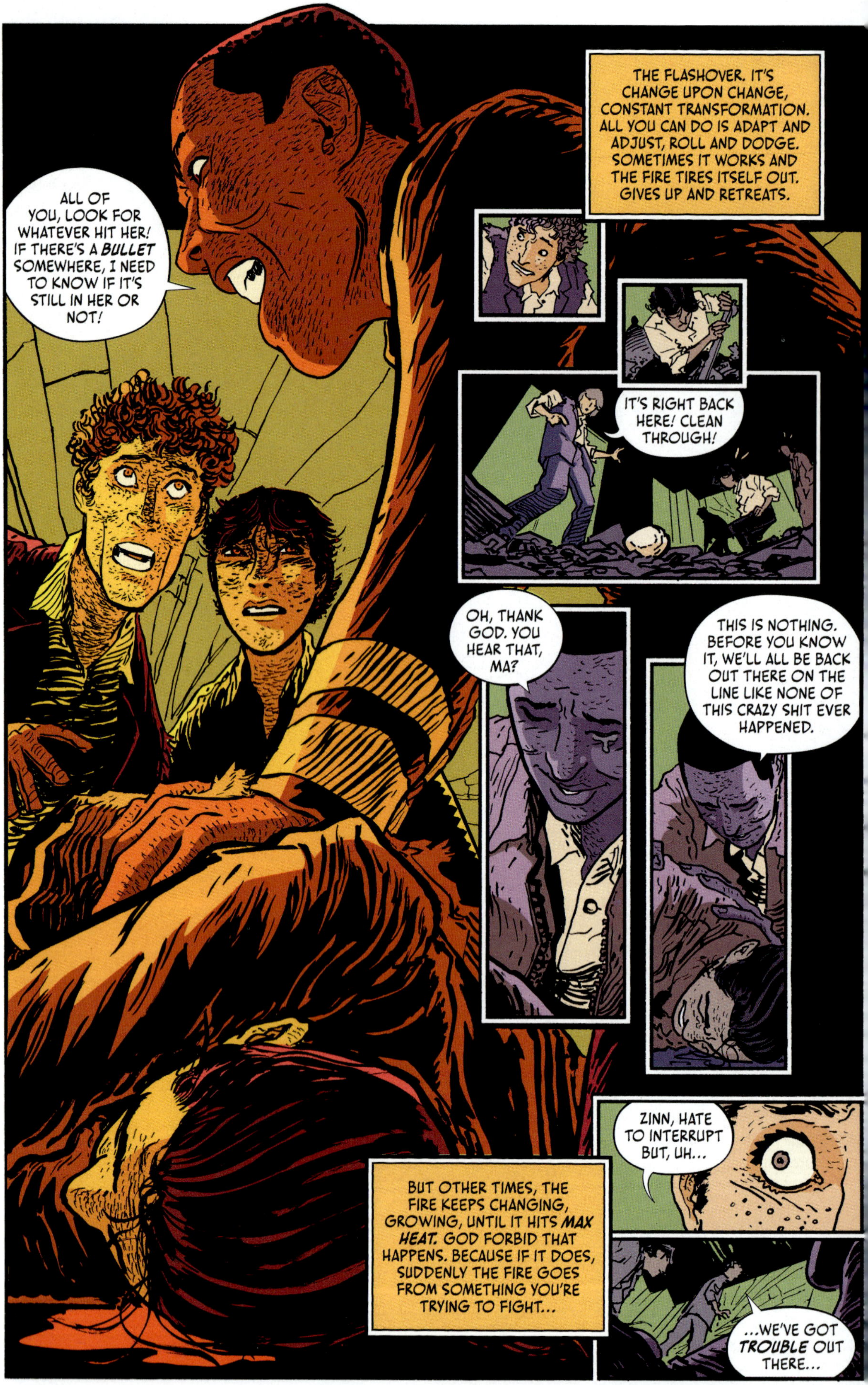
THE FLASHOVER. IT'S CHANGE UPON CHANGE, CONSTANT TRANSFORMATION. ALL YOU CAN DO IS ADAPT AND ADJUST, ROLL AND DODGE. SOMETIMES IT WORKS AND THE FIRE TIRES ITSELF OUT. GIVES UP AND RETREATS.
ALL OF YOU, LOOK FOR WHATEVER HIT HER! IF THERE'S A ***BULLET*** SOMEWHERE, I NEED TO KNOW IF IT'S STILL IN HER OR NOT!
IT'S RIGHT BACK HERE! CLEAN THROUGH!
OH, THANK GOD. YOU HEAR THAT, MA?
THIS IS NOTHING. BEFORE YOU KNOW IT, WE'LL ALL BE BACK OUT THERE ON THE LINE LIKE NONE OF THIS CRAZY SHIT EVER HAPPENED.
BUT OTHER TIMES, THE FIRE KEEPS CHANGING, GROWING, UNTIL IT HITS ***MAX HEAT.*** GOD FORBID THAT HAPPENS. BECAUSE IF IT DOES, SUDDENLY THE FIRE GOES FROM SOMETHING YOU'RE TRYING TO FIGHT...
ZINN, HATE TO INTERRUPT BUT, UH...
...WE'VE GOT ***TROUBLE*** OUT THERE...

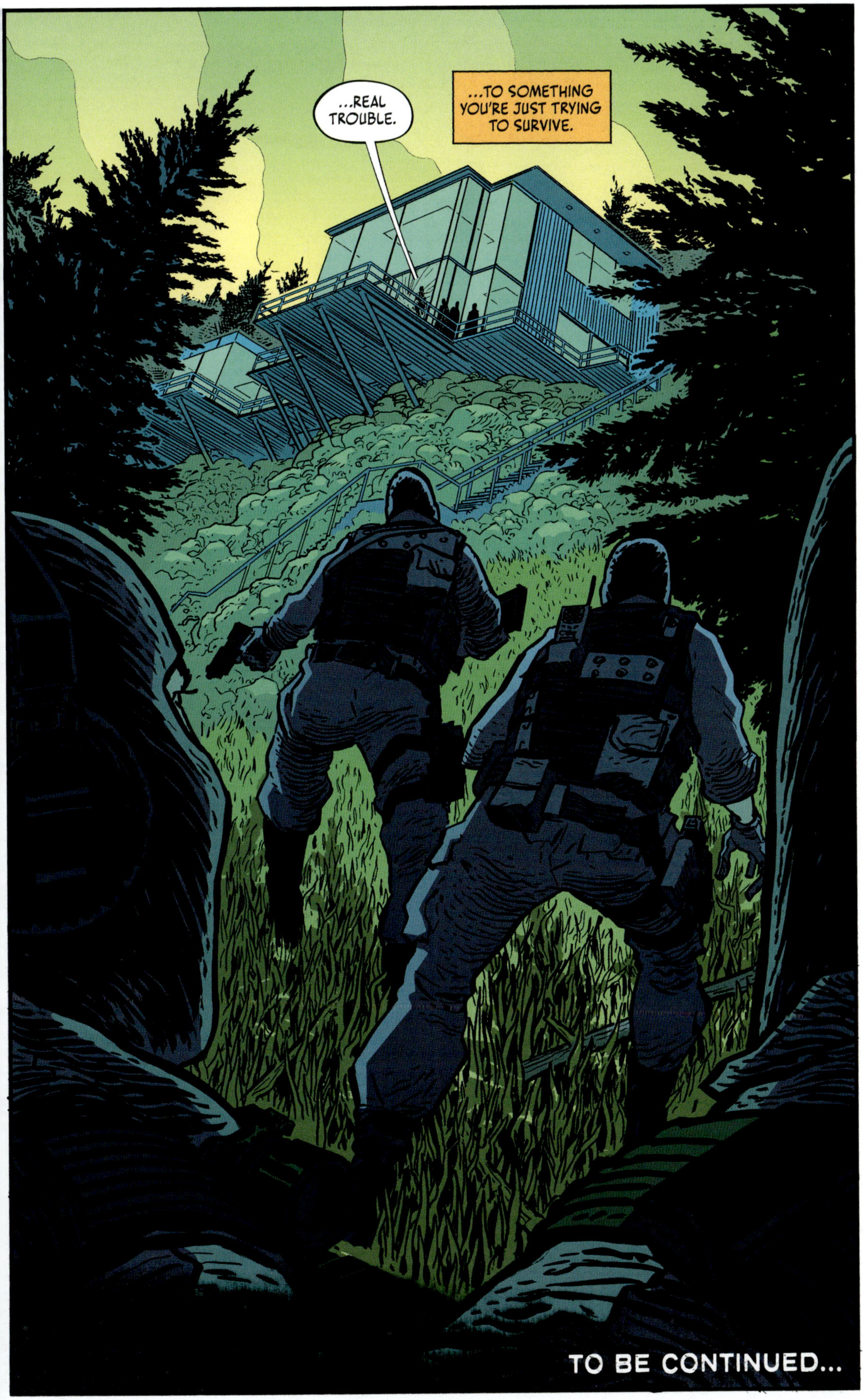
...TO SOMETHING YOU'RE JUST TRYING TO SURVIVE.
...REAL TROUBLE.
TO BE CONTINUED...

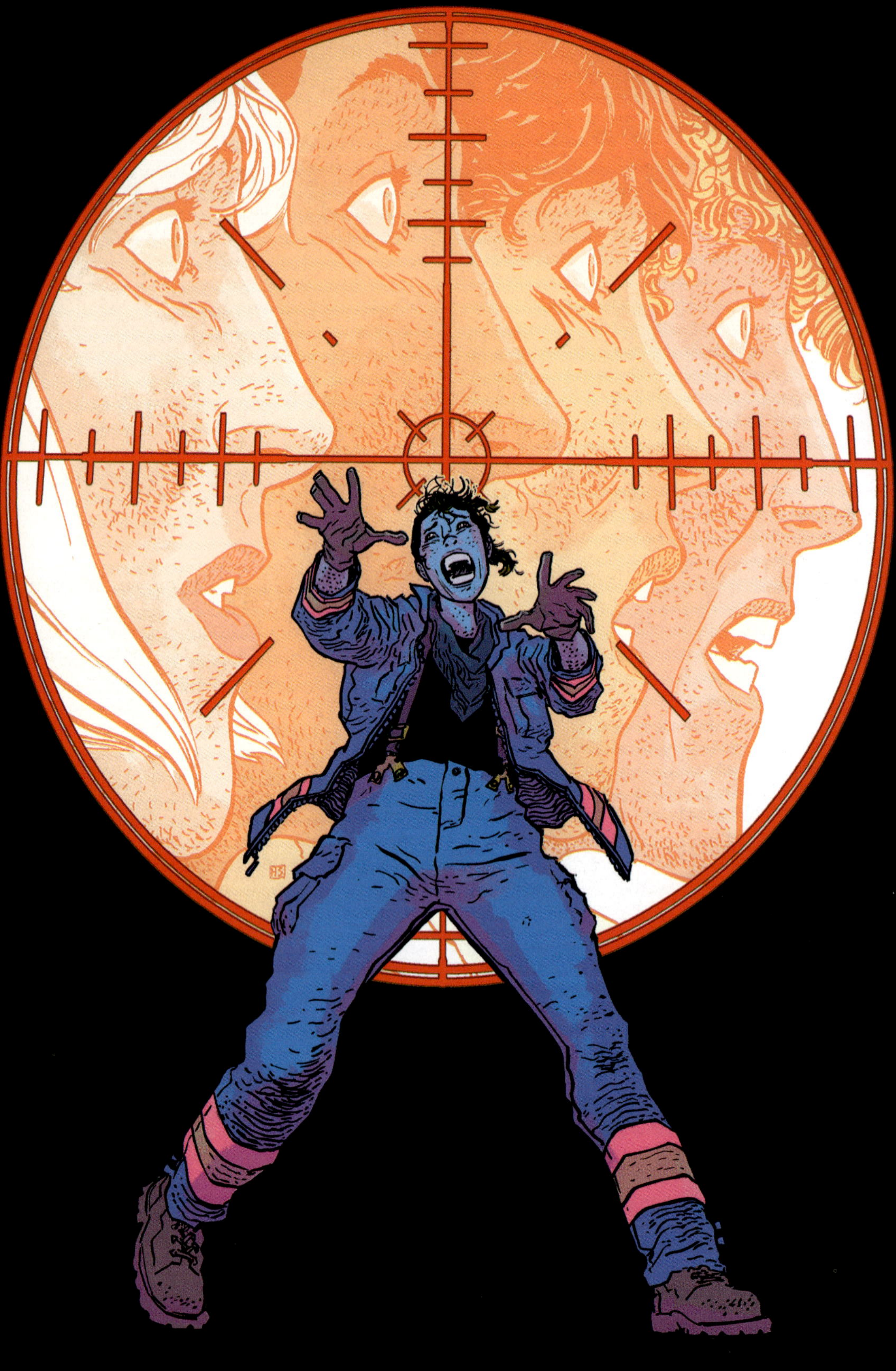

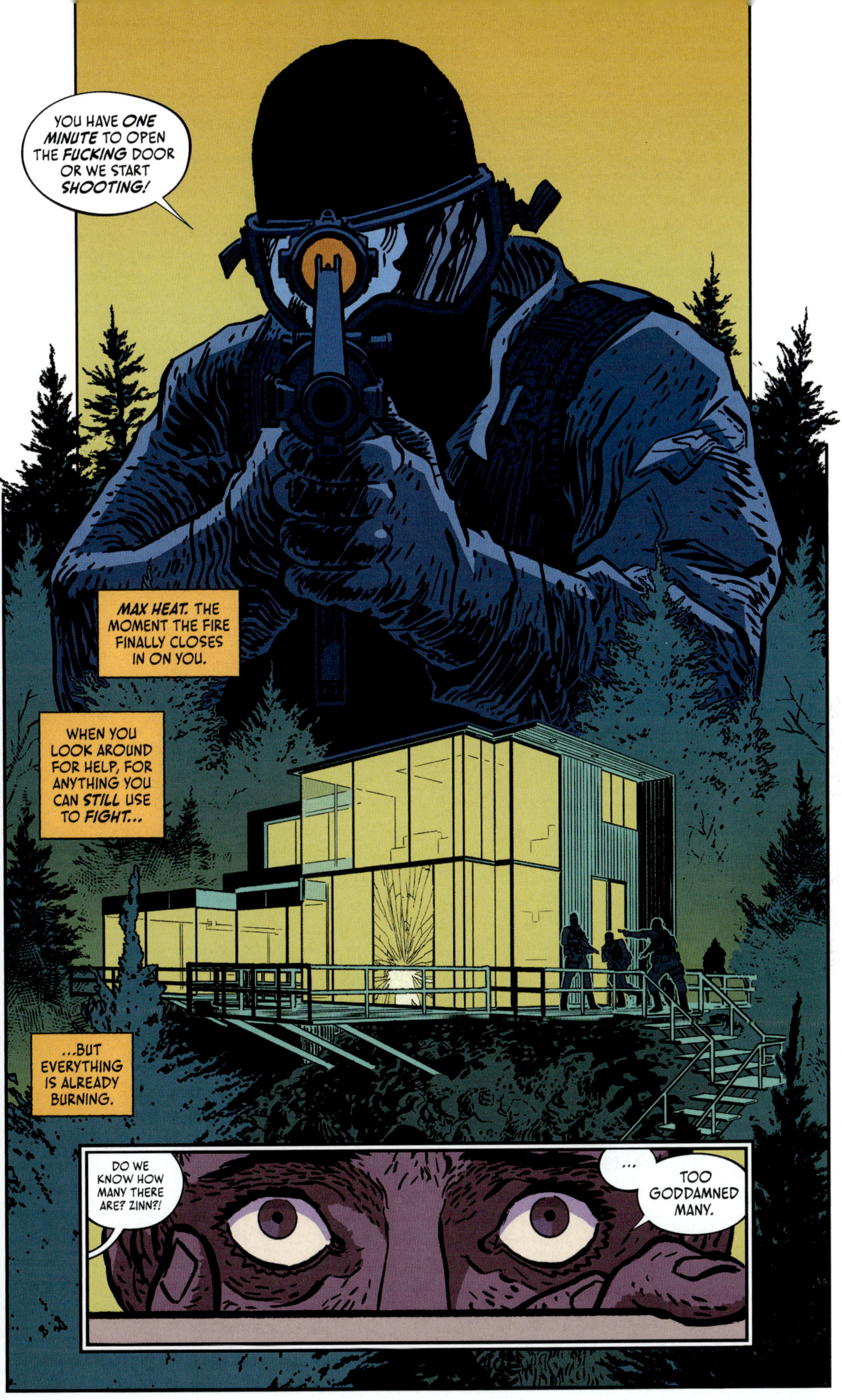
YOU HAVE ONE MINUTE TO OPEN THE FUCKING DOOR OR WE START SHOOTING!
MAX HEAT. THE MOMENT THE FIRE FINALLY CLOSES IN ON YOU.
WHEN YOU LOOK AROUND FOR HELP, FOR ANYTHING YOU CAN STILL USE TO FIGHT...
...BUT EVERYTHING IS ALREADY BURNING.
DO WE KNOW HOW MANY THERE ARE? ZINN?!
...
TOO GODDAMNED MANY.

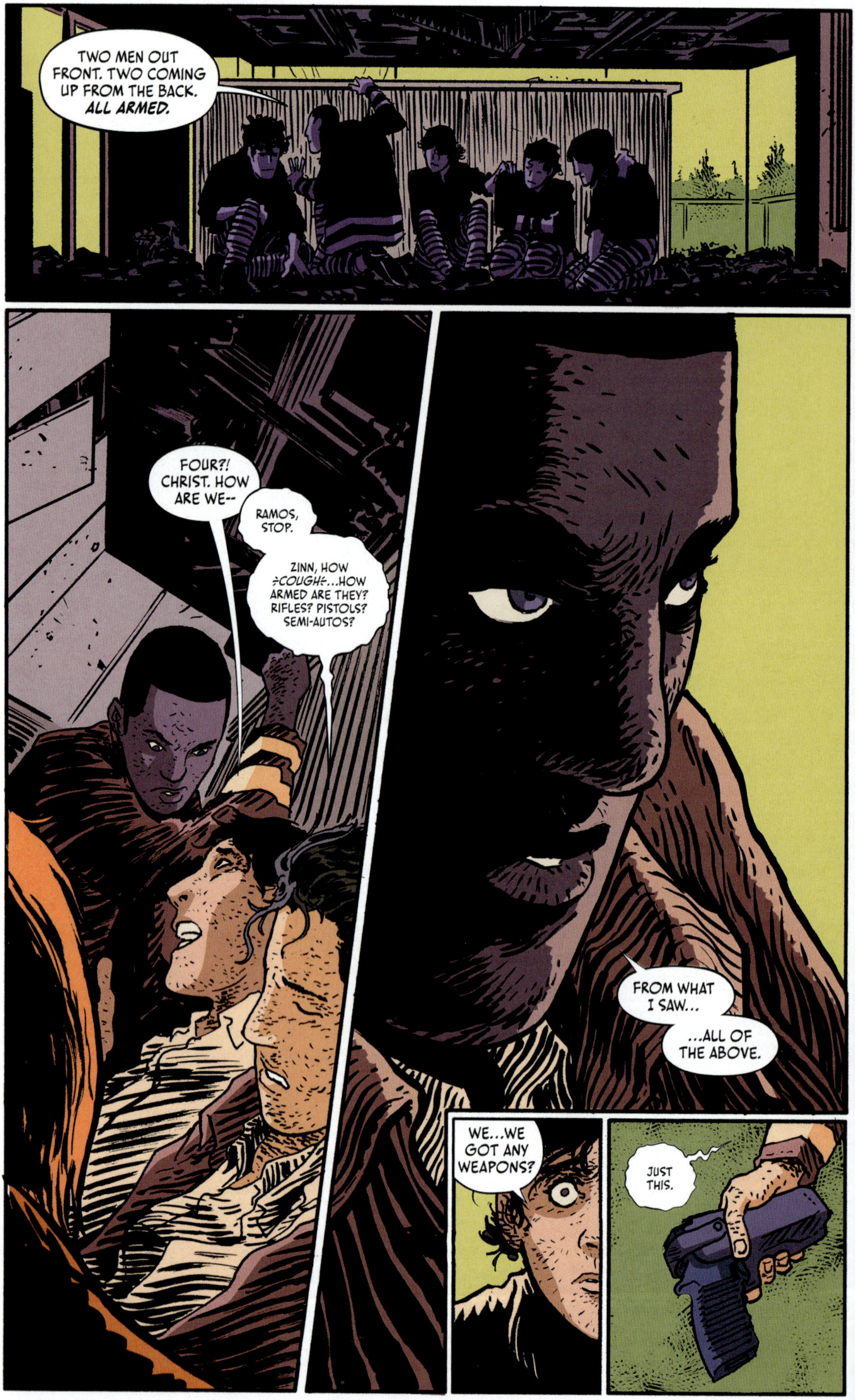
TWO MEN OUT FRONT. TWO COMING UP FROM THE BACK. ***ALL ARMED.***
FOUR?! CHRIST. HOW ARE WE--
RAMOS, STOP.
ZINN, HOW *COUGH*...HOW ARMED ARE THEY? RIFLES? PISTOLS? SEMI-AUTOS?
FROM WHAT I SAW...
...ALL OF THE ABOVE.
WE...WE GOT ANY WEAPONS?
JUST THIS.

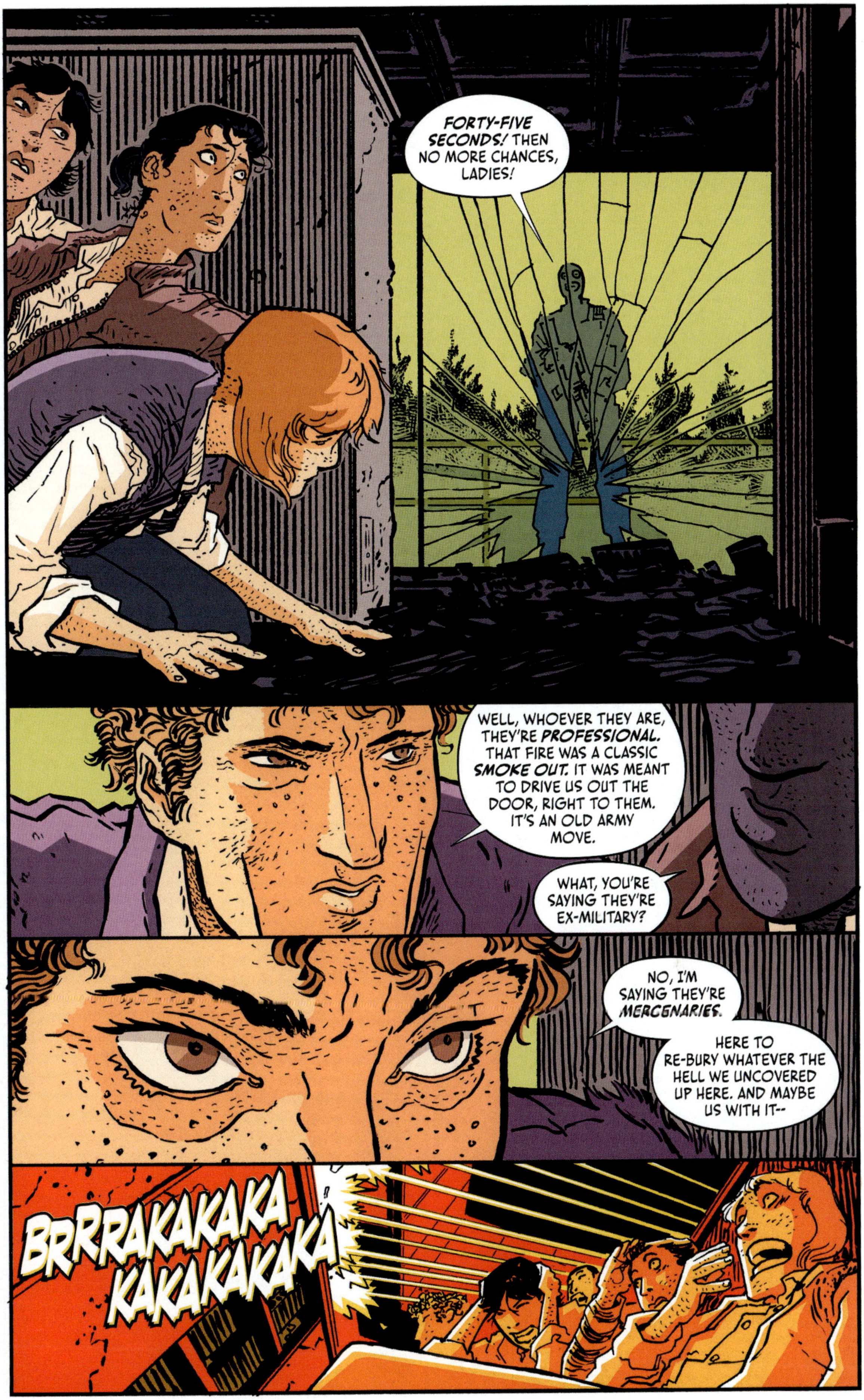
FORTY-FIVE SECONDS! THEN NO MORE CHANCES, LADIES!
WELL, WHOEVER THEY ARE, THEY'RE PROFESSIONAL. THAT FIRE WAS A CLASSIC SMOKE OUT. IT WAS MEANT TO DRIVE US OUT THE DOOR, RIGHT TO THEM. IT'S AN OLD ARMY MOVE.
WHAT, YOU'RE SAYING THEY'RE EX-MILITARY?
NO, I'M SAYING THEY'RE MERCENARIES.
HERE TO RE-BURY WHATEVER THE HELL WE UNCOVERED UP HERE. AND MAYBE US WITH IT--
BRRRAKAKAKA KAKAKAKAKA

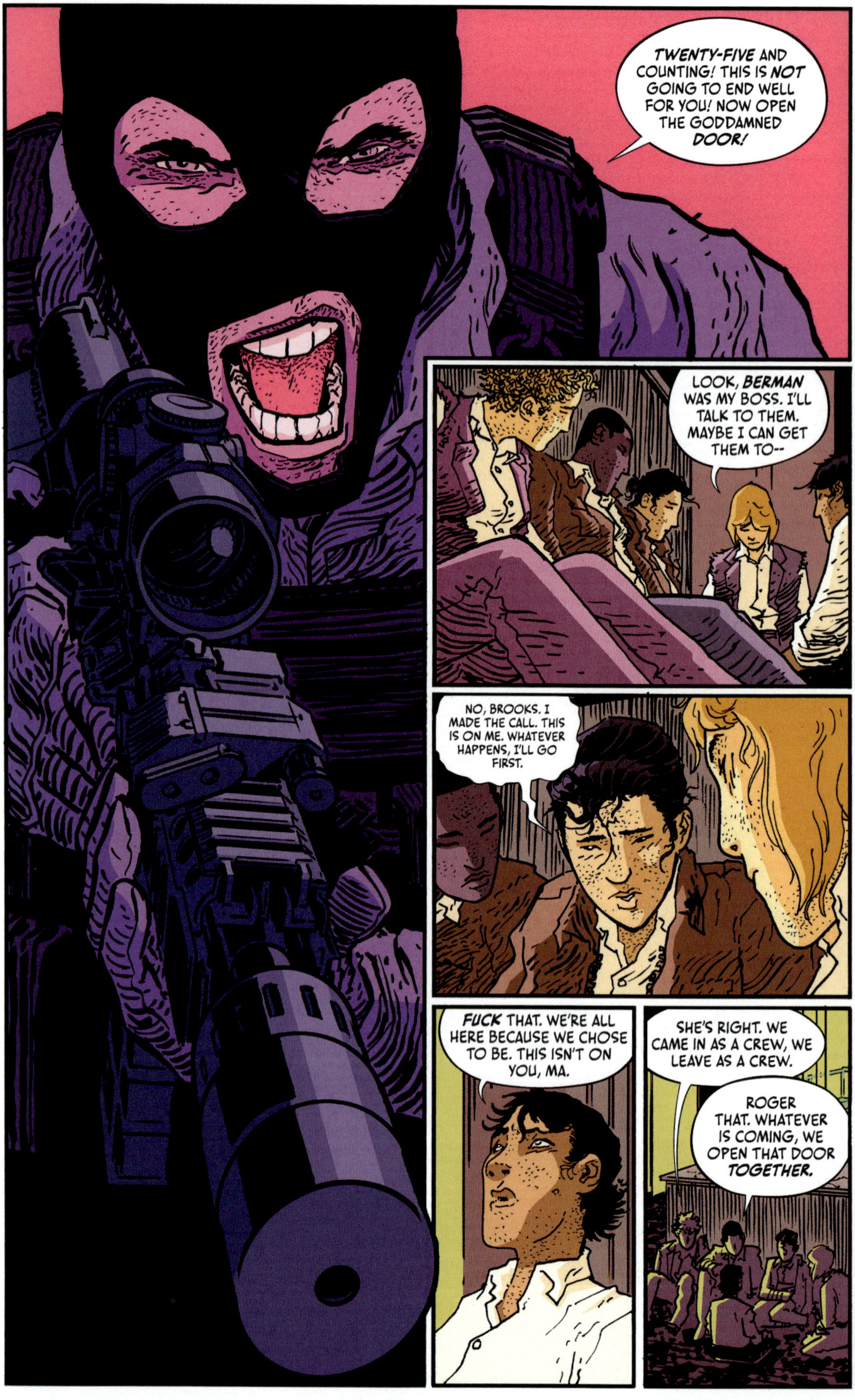
TWENTY-FIVE AND COUNTING! THIS IS NOT GOING TO END WELL FOR YOU! NOW OPEN THE GODDAMNED DOOR!
LOOK, BERMAN WAS MY BOSS. I'LL TALK TO THEM. MAYBE I CAN GET THEM TO--
NO, BROOKS. I MADE THE CALL. THIS IS ON ME. WHATEVER HAPPENS, I'LL GO FIRST.
FUCK THAT. WE'RE ALL HERE BECAUSE WE CHOSE TO BE. THIS ISN'T ON YOU, MA.
SHE'S RIGHT. WE CAME IN AS A CREW, WE LEAVE AS A CREW.
ROGER THAT. WHATEVER IS COMING, WE OPEN THAT DOOR TOGETHER.

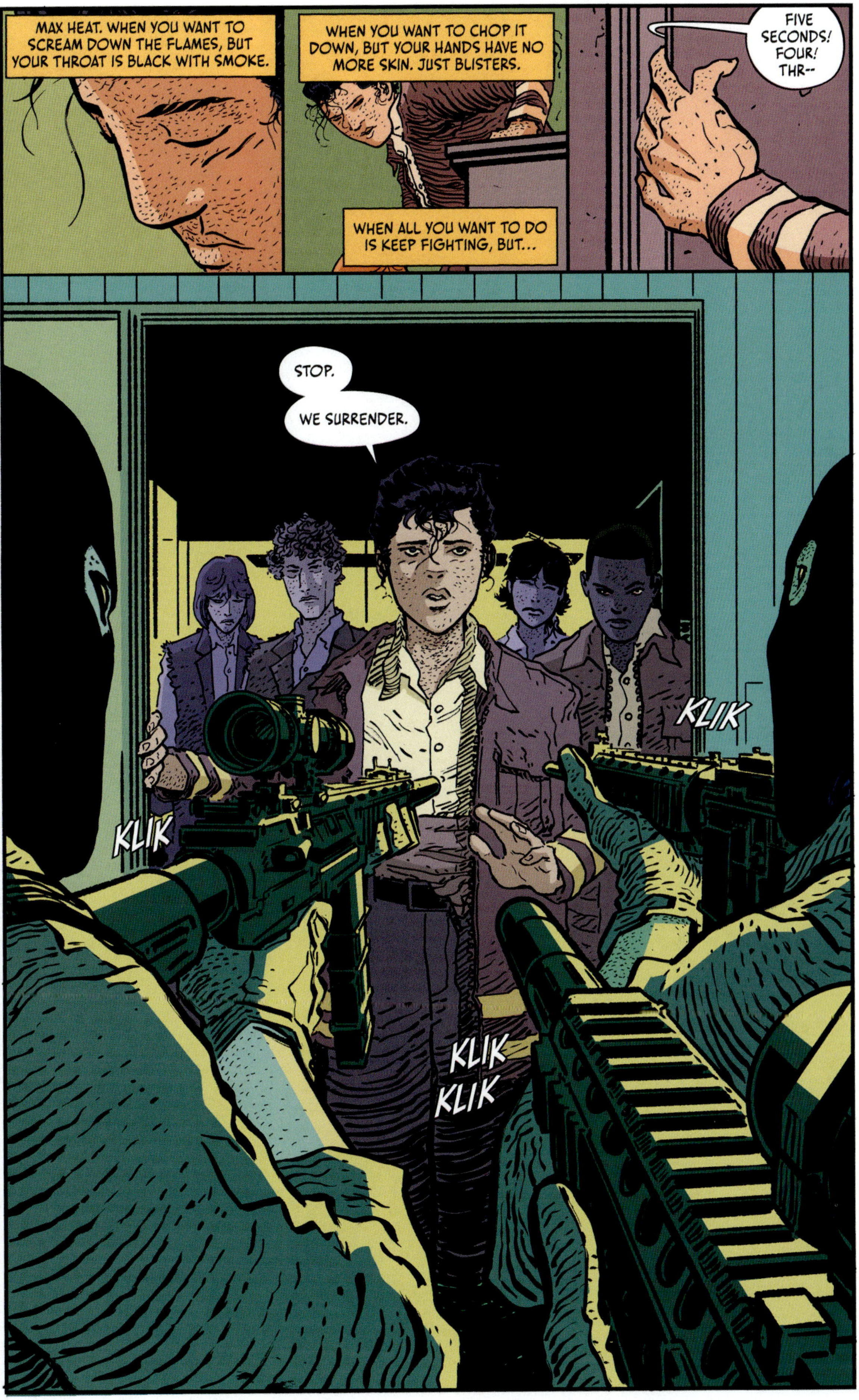
MAX HEAT. WHEN YOU WANT TO SCREAM DOWN THE FLAMES, BUT YOUR THROAT IS BLACK WITH SMOKE.
WHEN YOU WANT TO CHOP IT DOWN, BUT YOUR HANDS HAVE NO MORE SKIN. JUST BLISTERS.
WHEN ALL YOU WANT TO DO IS KEEP FIGHTING, BUT...
FIVE SECONDS! FOUR! THR--
STOP.
WE SURRENDER.
KLIK
KLIK
KLIK
KLIK

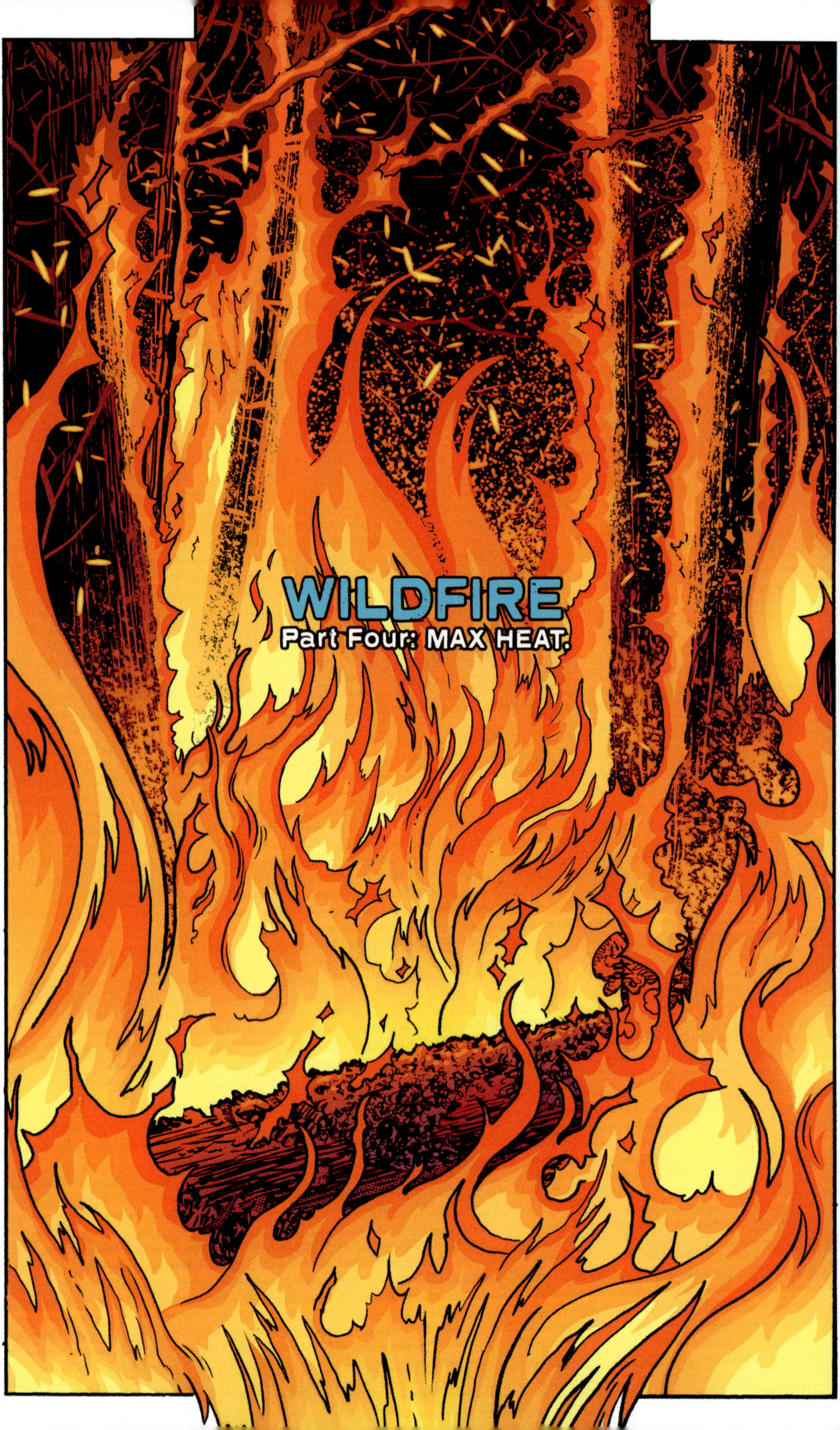
WILDFIRE
Part Four: MAX HEAT.

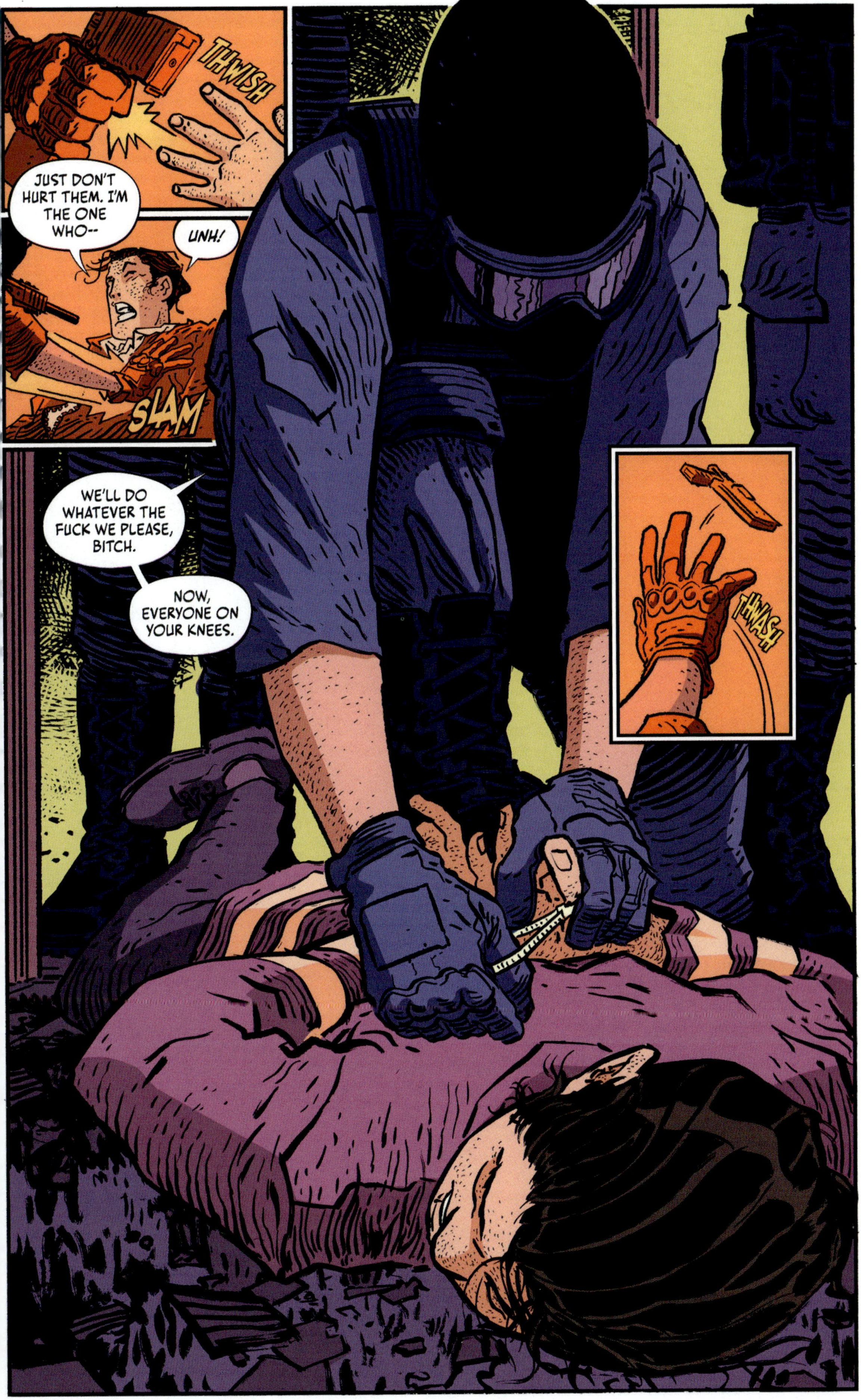
THWISH
JUST DON'T HURT THEM. I'M THE ONE WHO--
UNH!
SLAM
WE'LL DO WHATEVER THE FUCK WE PLEASE, BITCH.
NOW, EVERYONE ON YOUR KNEES.
THWASH

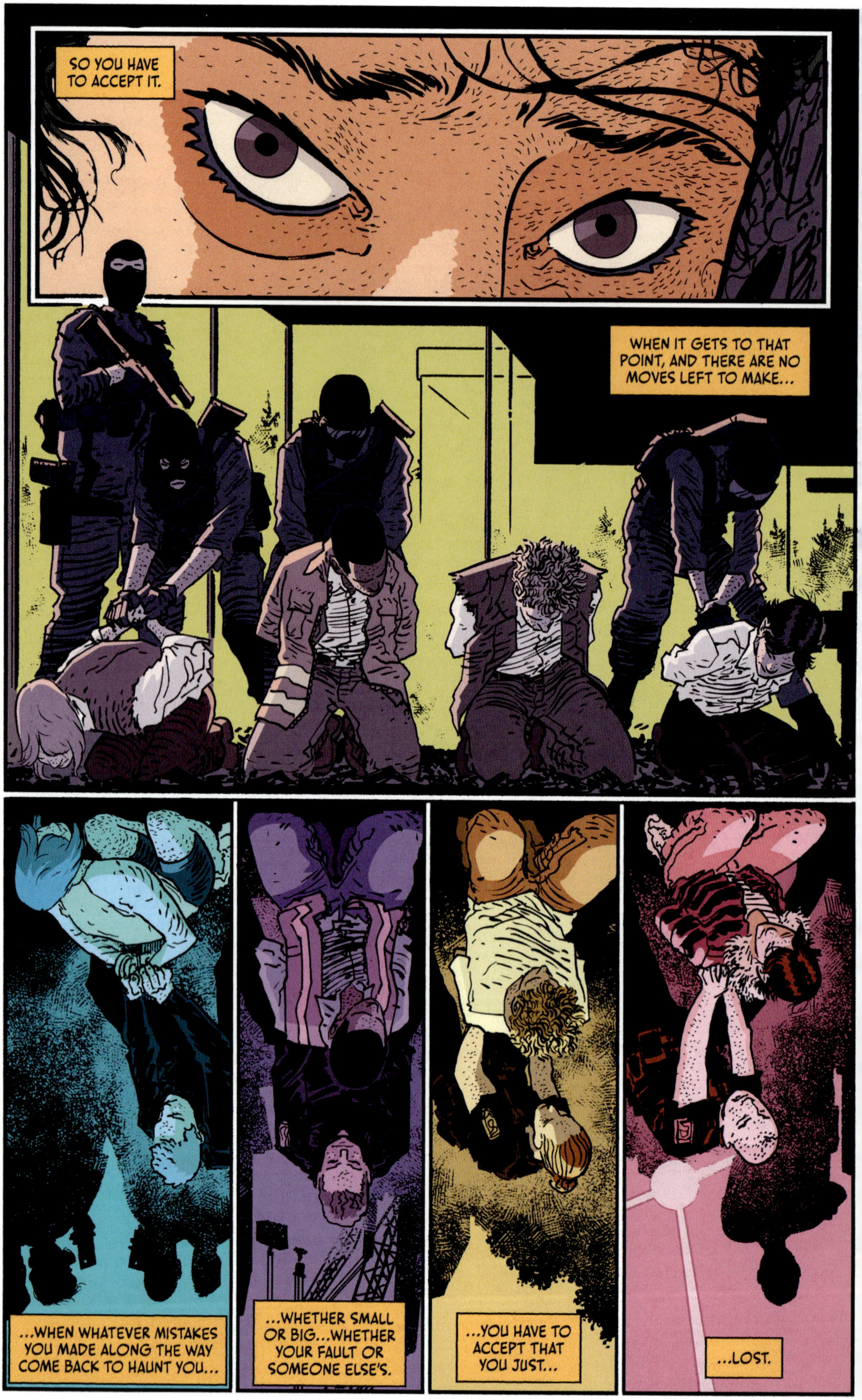
SO YOU HAVE TO ACCEPT IT.
WHEN IT GETS TO THAT POINT, AND THERE ARE NO MOVES LEFT TO MAKE...
...WHEN WHATEVER MISTAKES YOU MADE ALONG THE WAY COME BACK TO HAUNT YOU...
...WHETHER SMALL OR BIG...WHETHER YOUR FAULT OR SOMEONE ELSE'S.
...YOU HAVE TO ACCEPT THAT YOU JUST...
...LOST.

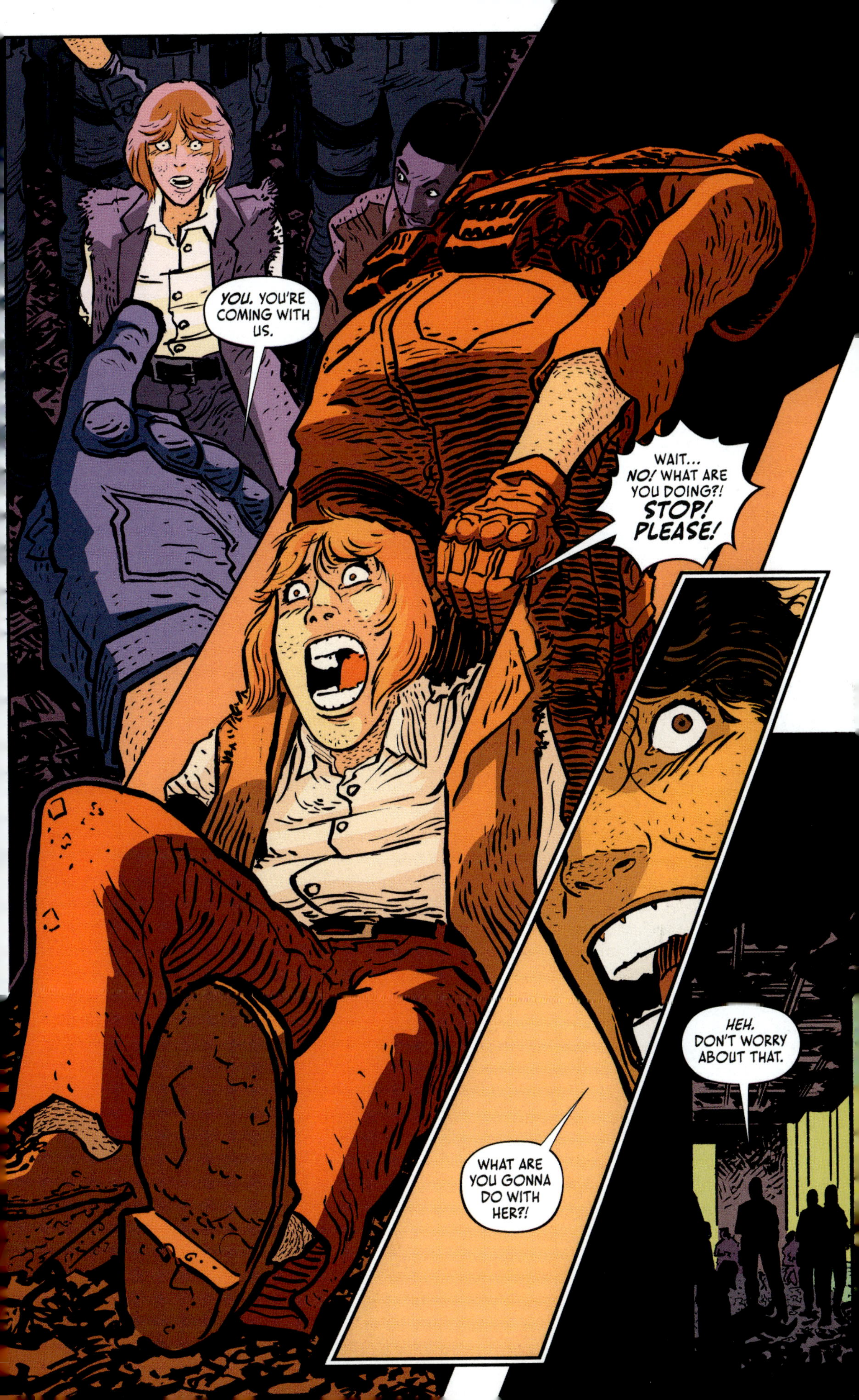
YOU. YOU'RE COMING WITH US.
WAIT... NO! WHAT ARE YOU DOING?! STOP! PLEASE!
WHAT ARE YOU GONNA DO WITH HER?!
HEH. DON'T WORRY ABOUT THAT.

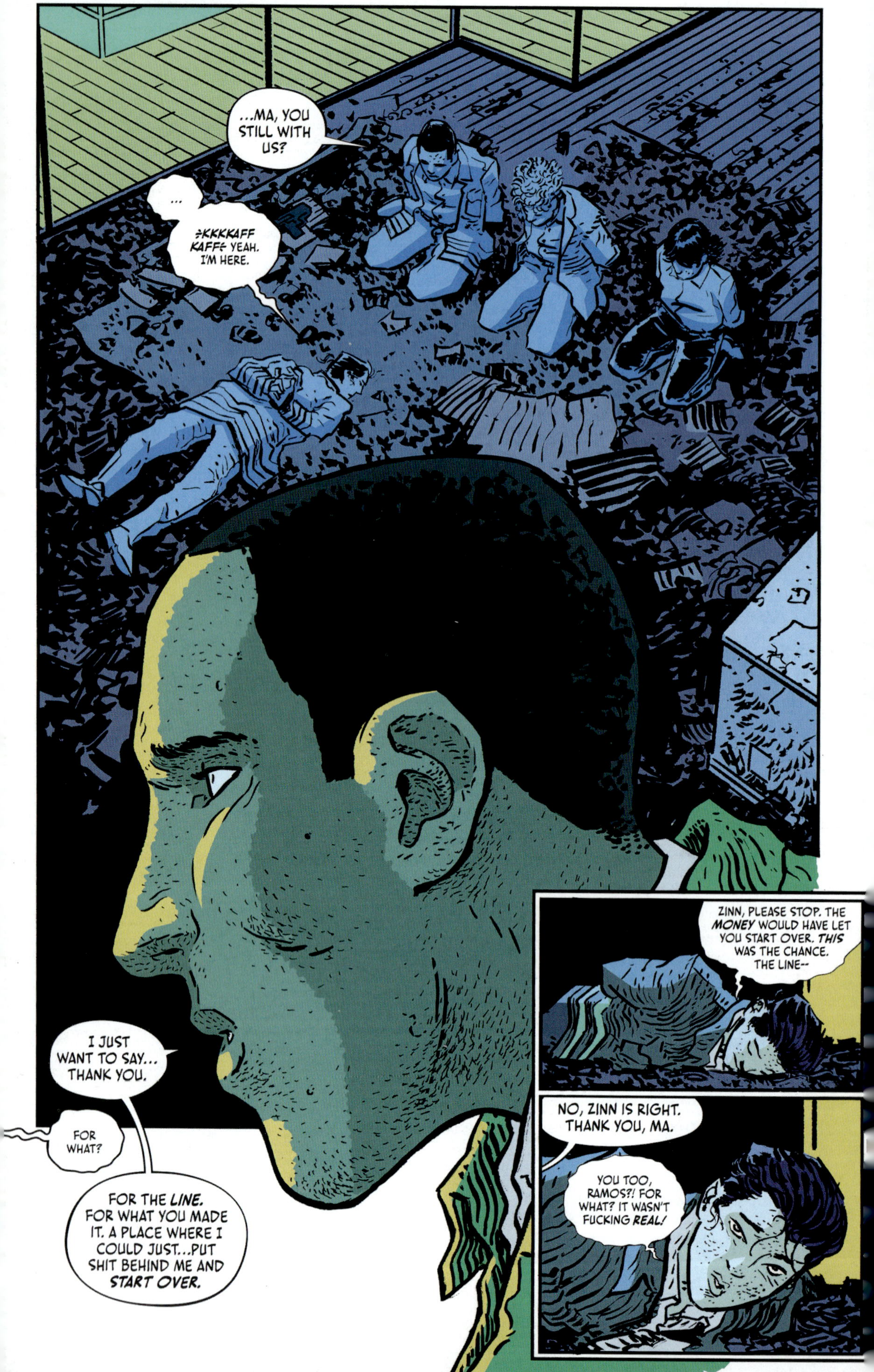
...MA, YOU STILL WITH US?
...
≠KKKKAFF KAFF≠ YEAH. I'M HERE.
I JUST WANT TO SAY... THANK YOU.
FOR WHAT?
FOR THE *LINE.* FOR WHAT YOU MADE IT. A PLACE WHERE I COULD JUST...PUT SHIT BEHIND ME AND *START OVER.*
ZINN, PLEASE STOP. THE *MONEY* WOULD HAVE LET YOU START OVER. *THIS* WAS THE CHANCE. THE LINE--
NO, ZINN IS RIGHT. THANK YOU, MA.
YOU TOO, RAMOS?! FOR WHAT? IT WASN'T FUCKING *REAL!*

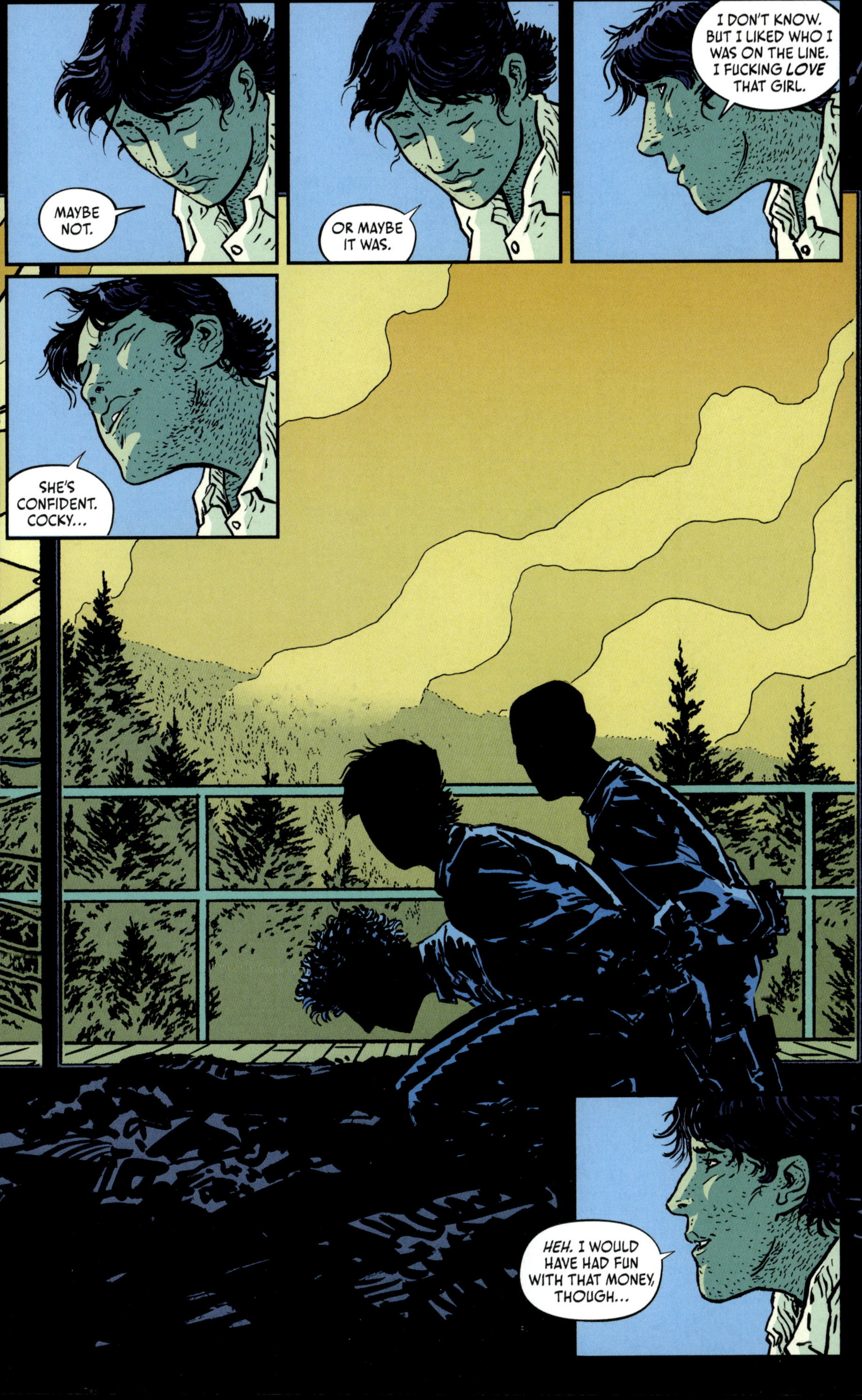
MAYBE NOT.
OR MAYBE IT WAS.
I DON'T KNOW. BUT I LIKED WHO I WAS ON THE LINE. I FUCKING *LOVE* THAT GIRL.
SHE'S CONFIDENT. COCKY...
HEH. I WOULD HAVE HAD FUN WITH THAT MONEY, THOUGH...

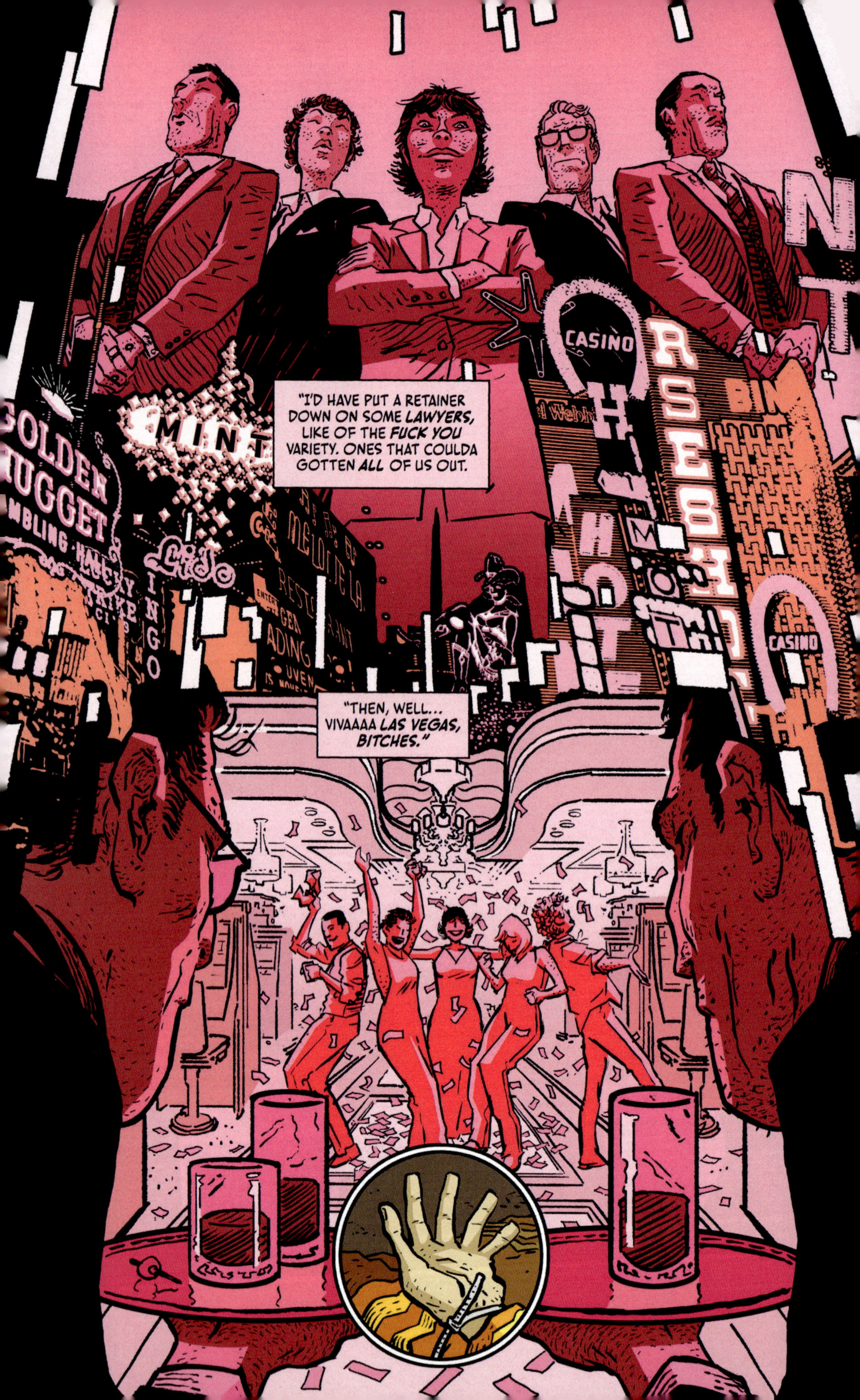
"I'D HAVE PUT A RETAINER DOWN ON SOME *LAWYERS*, LIKE OF THE *FUCK YOU* VARIETY. ONES THAT COULDA GOTTEN *ALL* OF US OUT.
"THEN, WELL... VIVAAAA *LAS VEGAS, BITCHES.*"

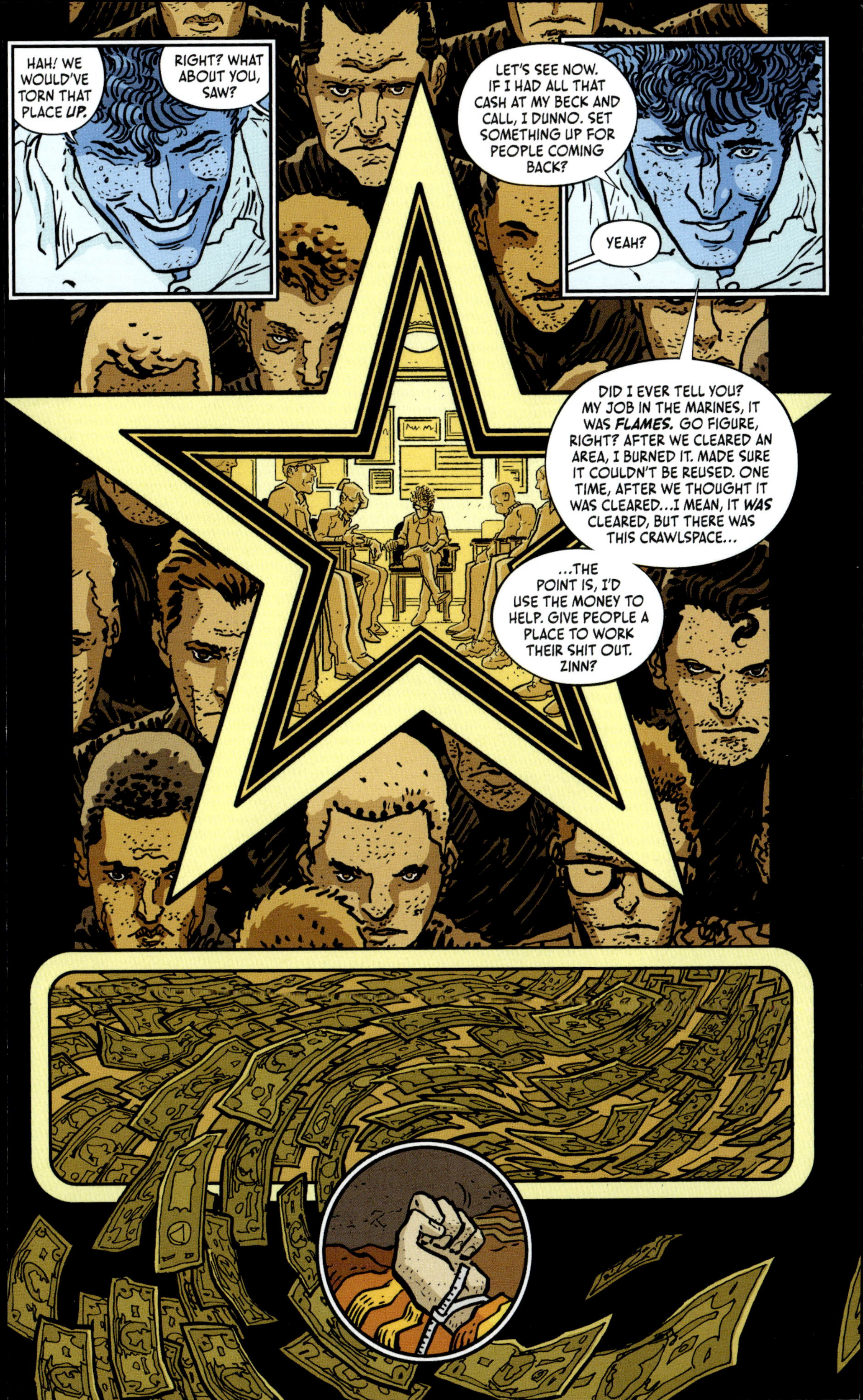

HAH! WE WOULD'VE TORN THAT PLACE *UP*.
RIGHT? WHAT ABOUT YOU, SAW?
LET'S SEE NOW. IF I HAD ALL THAT CASH AT MY BECK AND CALL, I DUNNO. SET SOMETHING UP FOR PEOPLE COMING BACK?
YEAH?
DID I EVER TELL YOU? MY JOB IN THE MARINES, IT WAS ***FLAMES.*** GO FIGURE, RIGHT? AFTER WE CLEARED AN AREA, I BURNED IT. MADE SURE IT COULDN'T BE REUSED. ONE TIME, AFTER WE THOUGHT IT WAS CLEARED...I MEAN, IT ***WAS*** CLEARED, BUT THERE WAS THIS CRAWLSPACE...
...THE POINT IS, I'D USE THE MONEY TO HELP. GIVE PEOPLE A PLACE TO WORK THEIR SHIT OUT. ZINN?

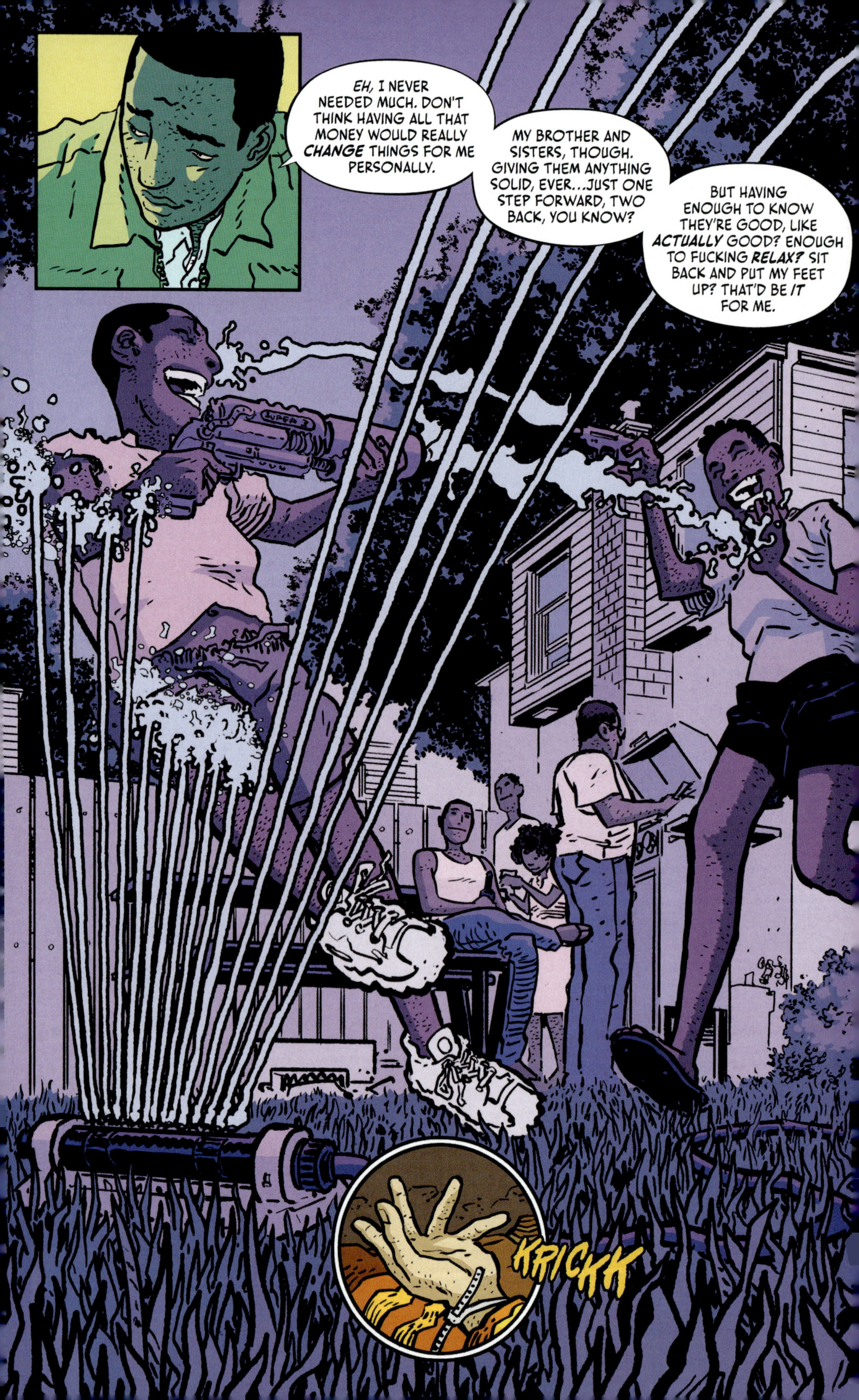
EH, I NEVER NEEDED MUCH. DON'T THINK HAVING ALL THAT MONEY WOULD REALLY CHANGE THINGS FOR ME PERSONALLY.
MY BROTHER AND SISTERS, THOUGH. GIVING THEM ANYTHING SOLID, EVER...JUST ONE STEP FORWARD, TWO BACK, YOU KNOW?
BUT HAVING ENOUGH TO KNOW THEY'RE GOOD, LIKE ACTUALLY GOOD? ENOUGH TO FUCKING RELAX? SIT BACK AND PUT MY FEET UP? THAT'D BE IT FOR ME.
KRICKK

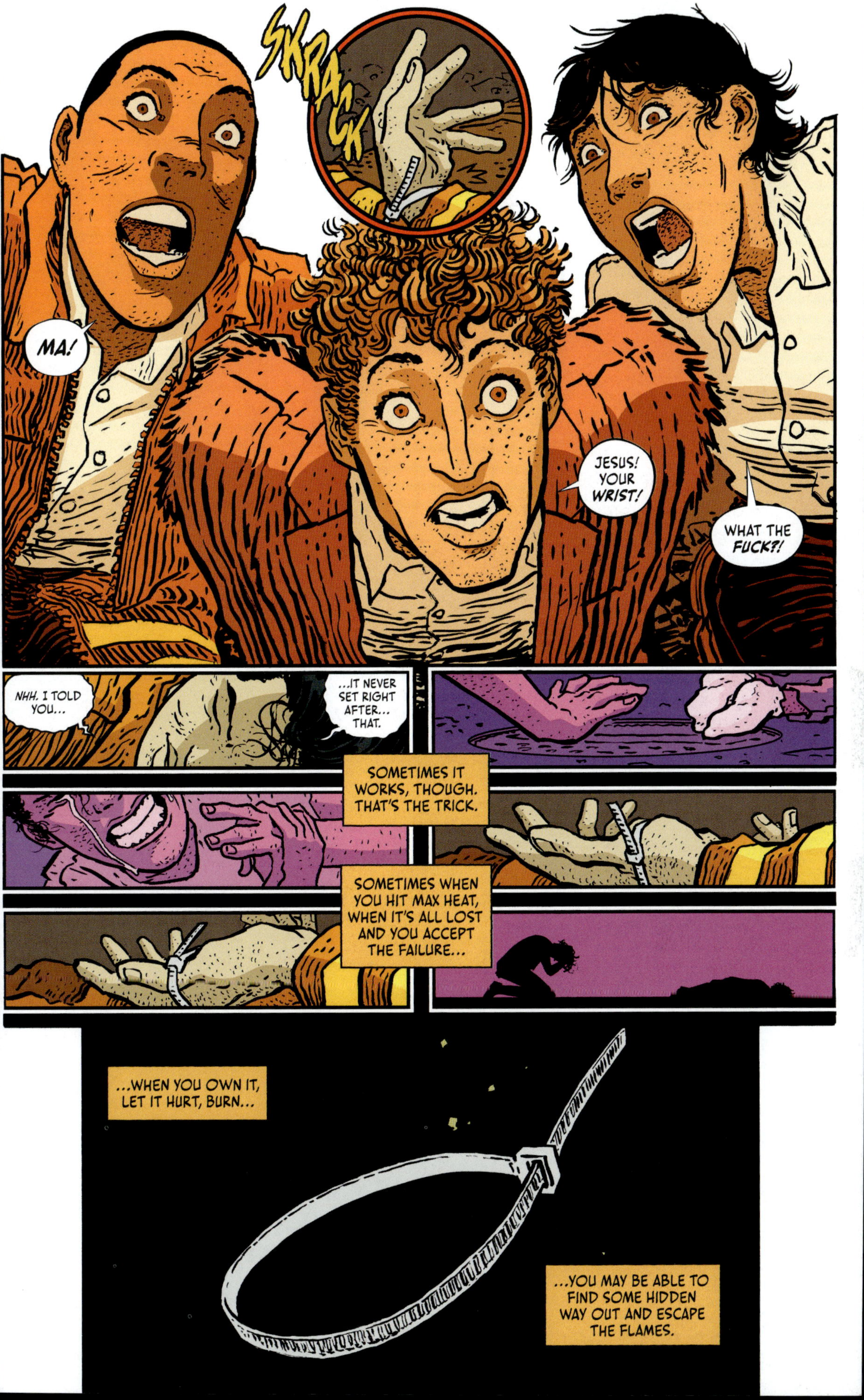
SKRACK
MA!
JESUS! YOUR WRIST!
WHAT THE FUCK?!
NHH. I TOLD YOU...
...IT NEVER SET RIGHT AFTER... THAT.
SOMETIMES IT WORKS, THOUGH. THAT'S THE TRICK.
SOMETIMES WHEN YOU HIT MAX HEAT, WHEN IT'S ALL LOST AND YOU ACCEPT THE FAILURE...
...WHEN YOU OWN IT, LET IT HURT, BURN...
...YOU MAY BE ABLE TO FIND SOME HIDDEN WAY OUT AND ESCAPE THE FLAMES.

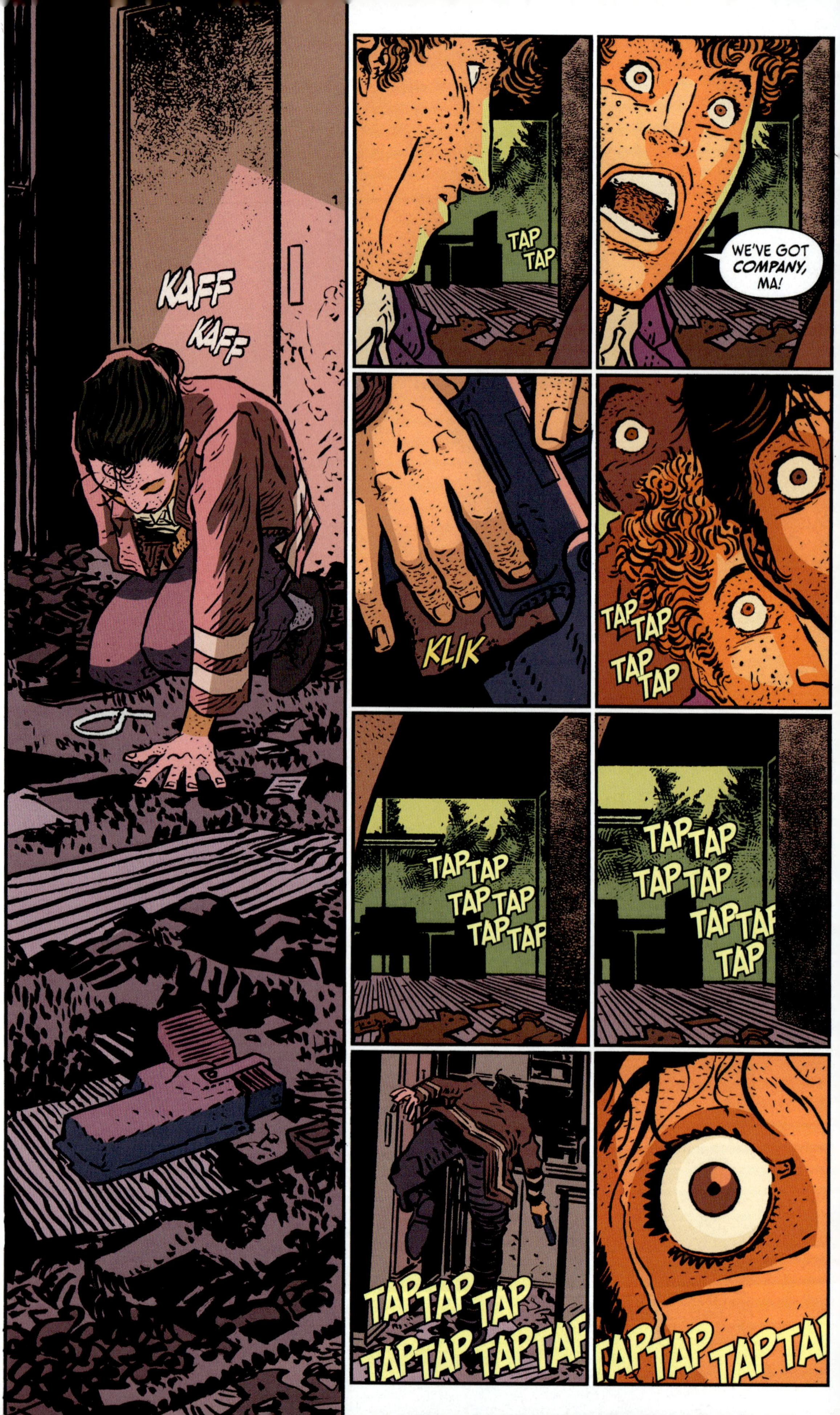
KAFF KAFF
TAP TAP
WE'VE GOT COMPANY, MA!
KLIK
TAP TAP TAP TAP
TAP TAP TAP TAP TAP TAP
TAP TAP TAP TAP TAP
TAP TAP TAP TAPTAP TAPTAP
TAP TAP TAP

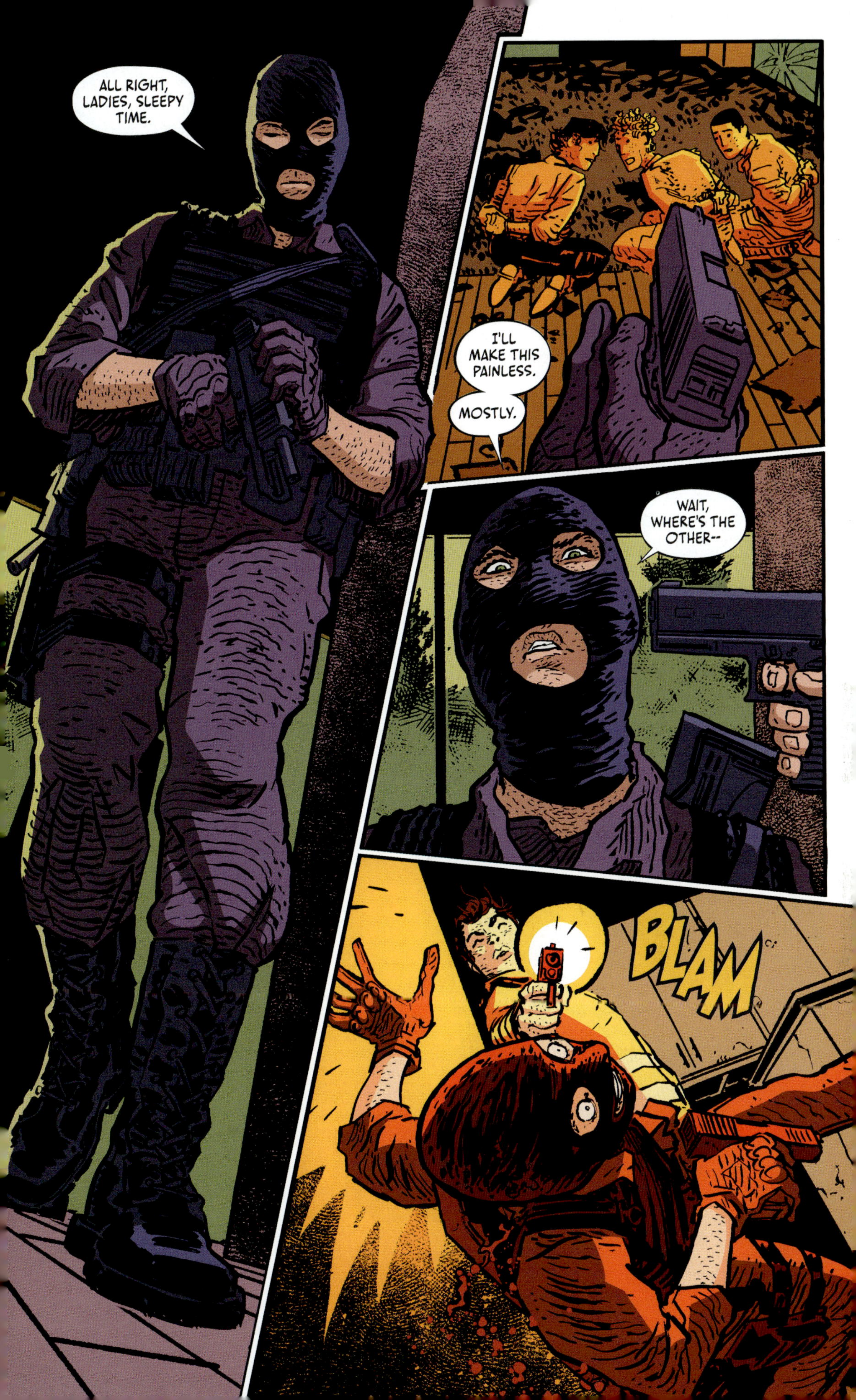
ALL RIGHT, LADIES, SLEEPY TIME.
I'LL MAKE THIS PAINLESS.
MOSTLY.
WAIT, WHERE'S THE OTHER--
BLAM

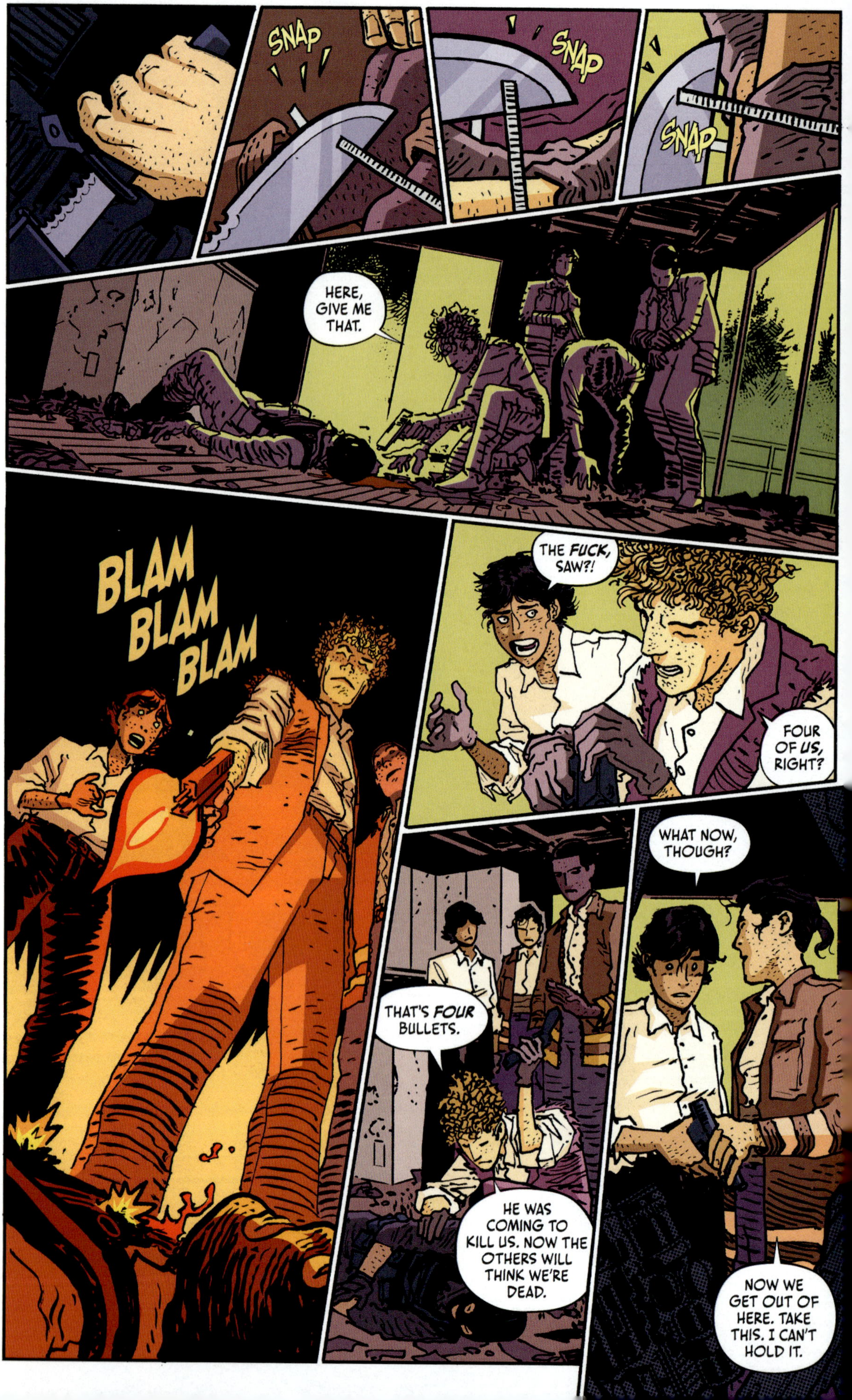
SNAP
SNAP
SNAP
HERE, GIVE ME THAT.
BLAM BLAM BLAM
THE FUCK, SAW?!
FOUR OF US, RIGHT?
THAT'S FOUR BULLETS.
HE WAS COMING TO KILL US. NOW THE OTHERS WILL THINK WE'RE DEAD.
WHAT NOW, THOUGH?
NOW WE GET OUT OF HERE. TAKE THIS. I CAN'T HOLD IT.

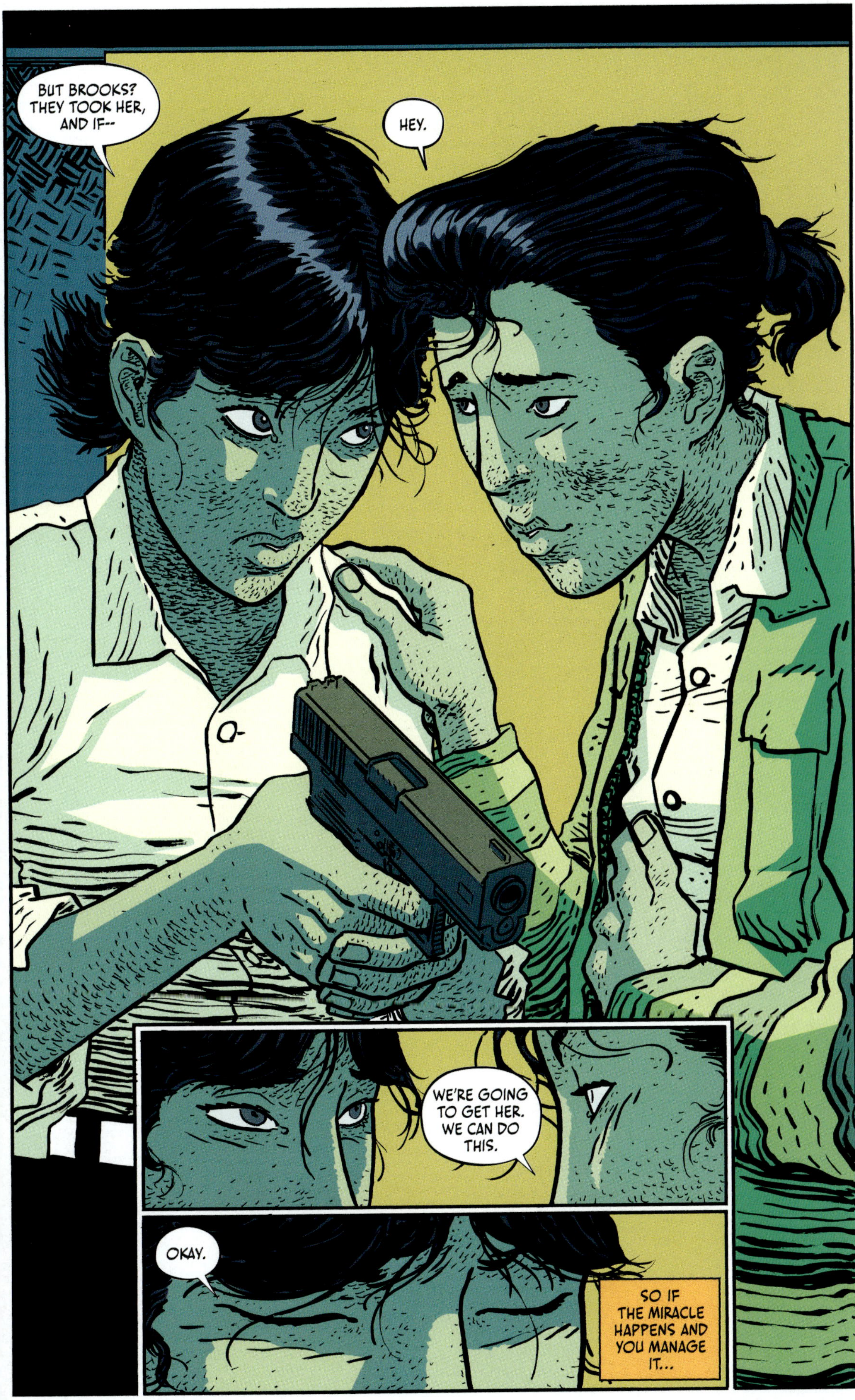
BUT BROOKS? THEY TOOK HER, AND IF--
HEY.
WE'RE GOING TO GET HER. WE CAN DO THIS.
OKAY.
SO IF THE MIRACLE HAPPENS AND YOU MANAGE IT...

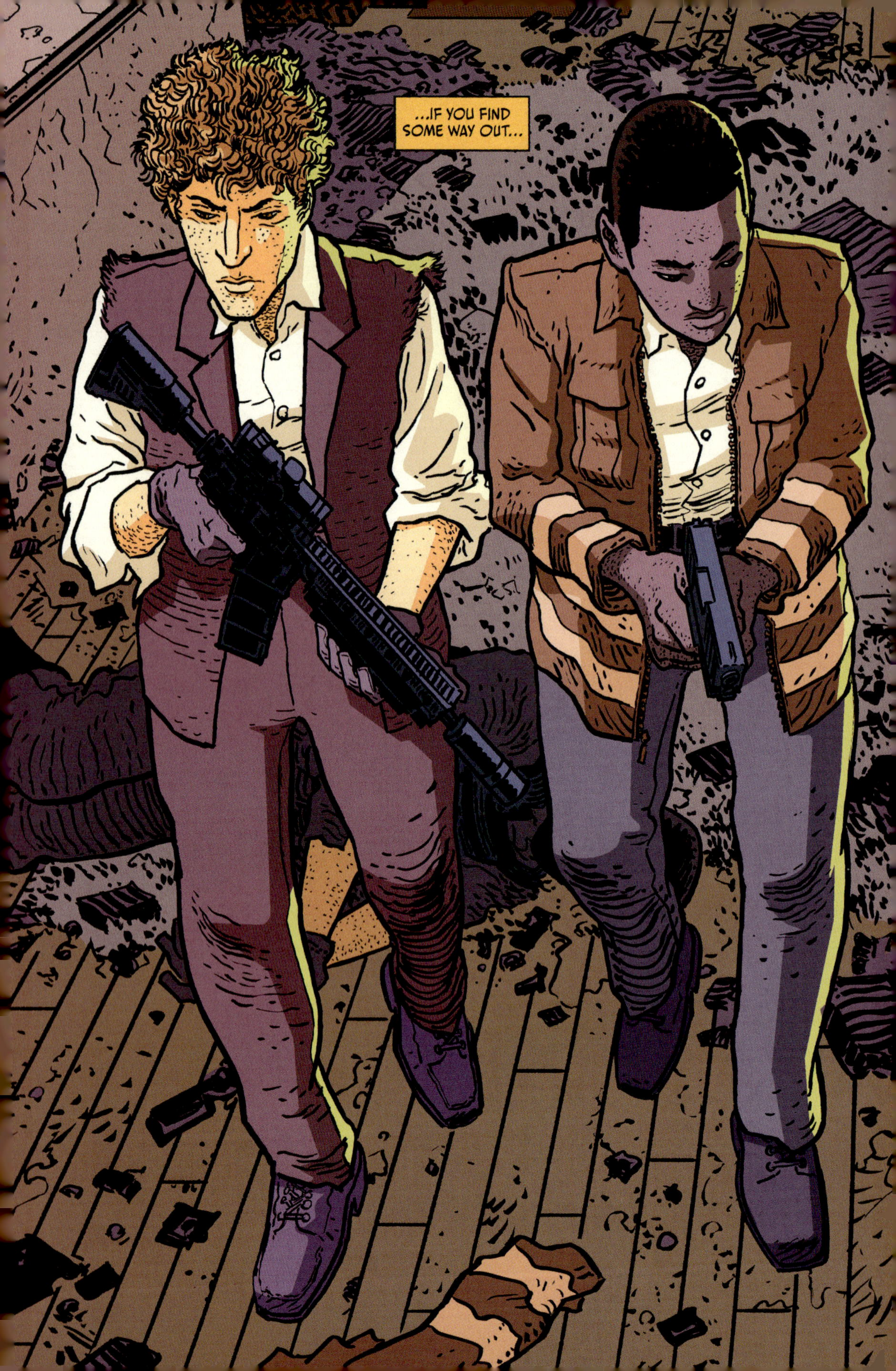
...IF YOU FIND SOME WAY OUT...

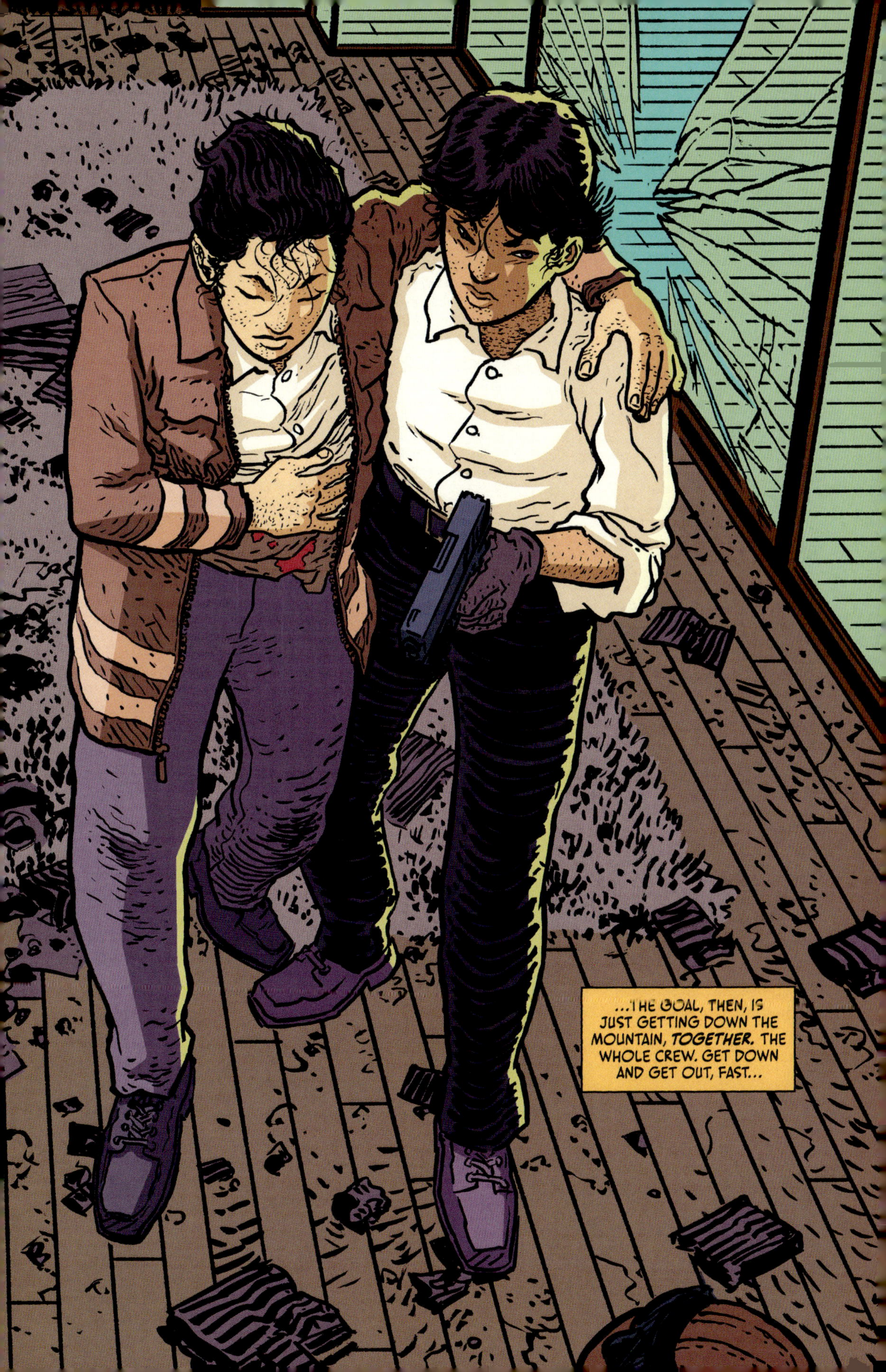
...THE GOAL, THEN, IS JUST GETTING DOWN THE MOUNTAIN, *TOGETHER.* THE WHOLE CREW. GET DOWN AND GET OUT, FAST...

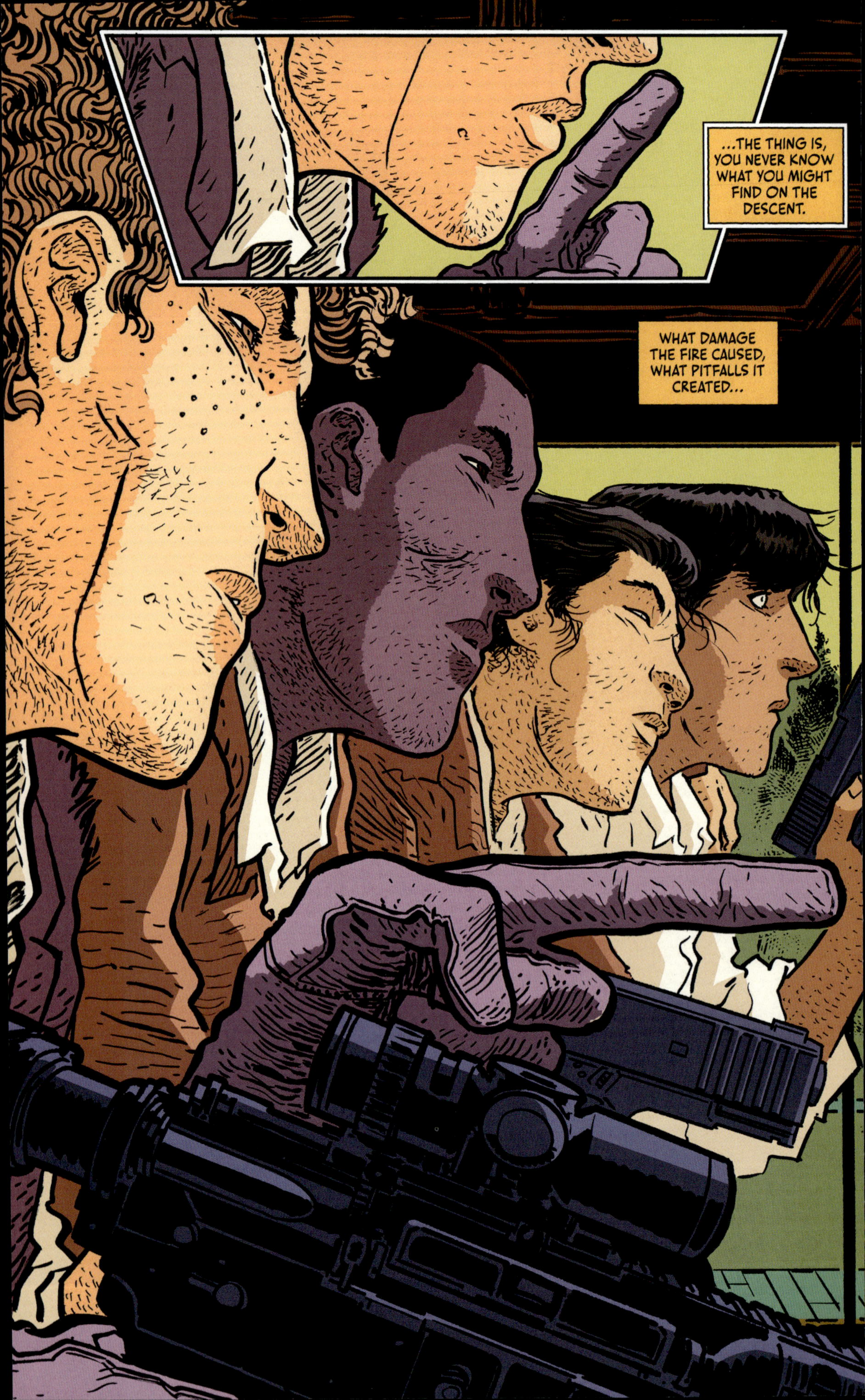
...THE THING IS, YOU NEVER KNOW WHAT YOU MIGHT FIND ON THE DESCENT.
WHAT DAMAGE THE FIRE CAUSED, WHAT PITFALLS IT CREATED...

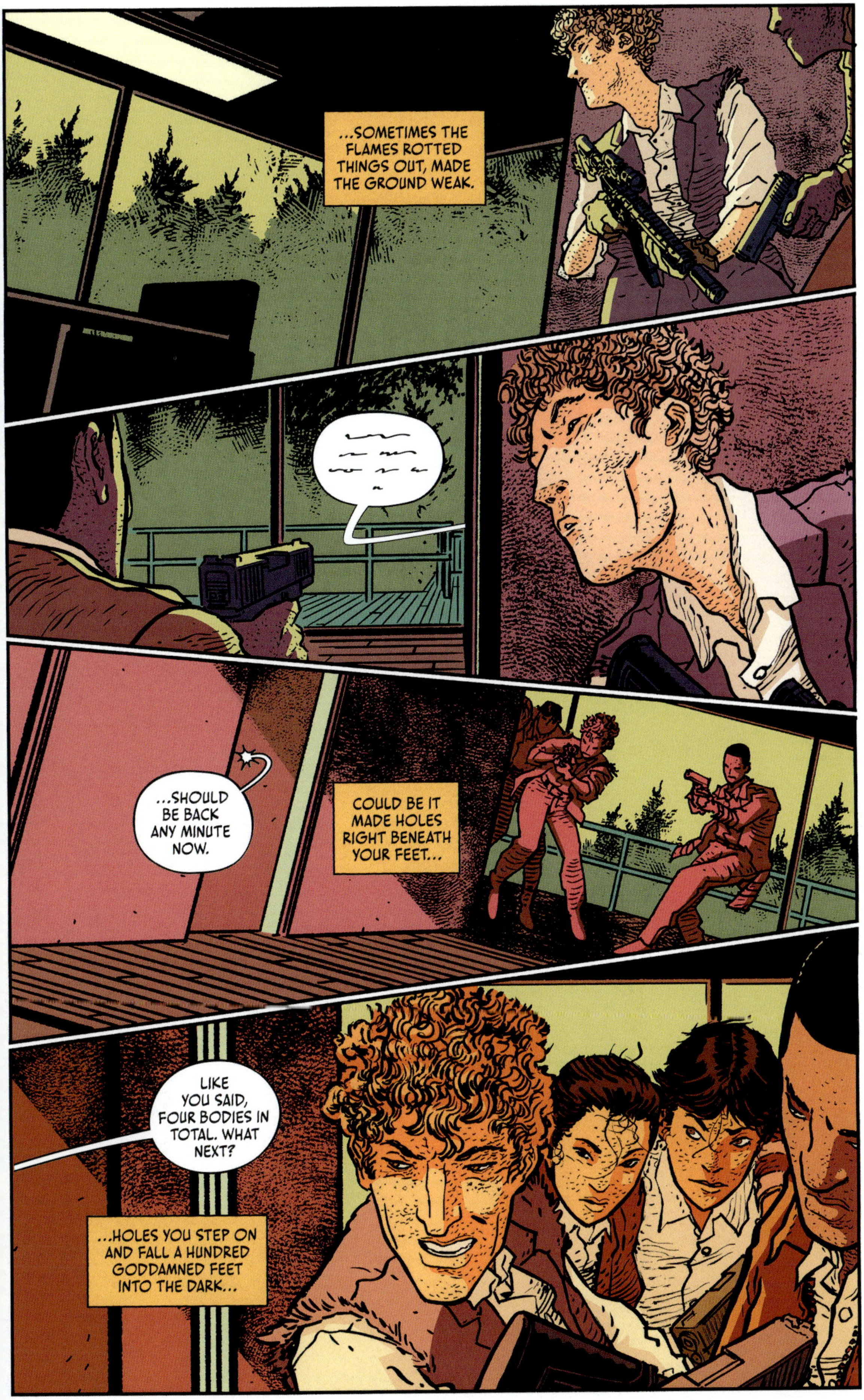
...SOMETIMES THE FLAMES ROTTED THINGS OUT, MADE THE GROUND WEAK.
...SHOULD BE BACK ANY MINUTE NOW.
COULD BE IT MADE HOLES RIGHT BENEATH YOUR FEET...
LIKE YOU SAID, FOUR BODIES IN TOTAL. WHAT NEXT?
...HOLES YOU STEP ON AND FALL A HUNDRED GODDAMNED FEET INTO THE DARK...

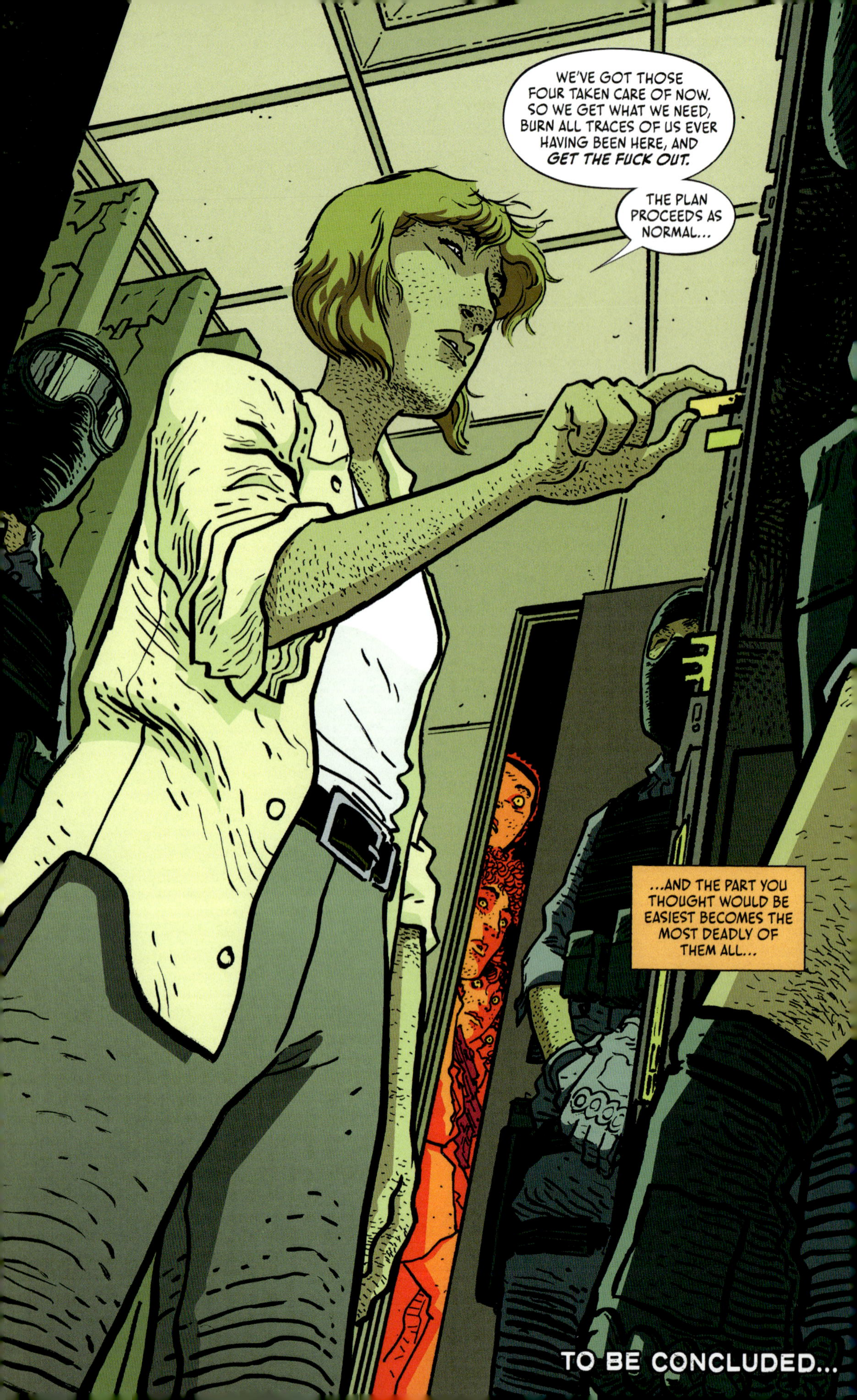
WE'VE GOT THOSE FOUR TAKEN CARE OF NOW. SO WE GET WHAT WE NEED, BURN ALL TRACES OF US EVER HAVING BEEN HERE, AND *GET THE FUCK OUT.*
THE PLAN PROCEEDS AS NORMAL...
...AND THE PART YOU THOUGHT WOULD BE EASIEST BECOMES THE MOST DEADLY OF THEM ALL...
TO BE CONCLUDED...

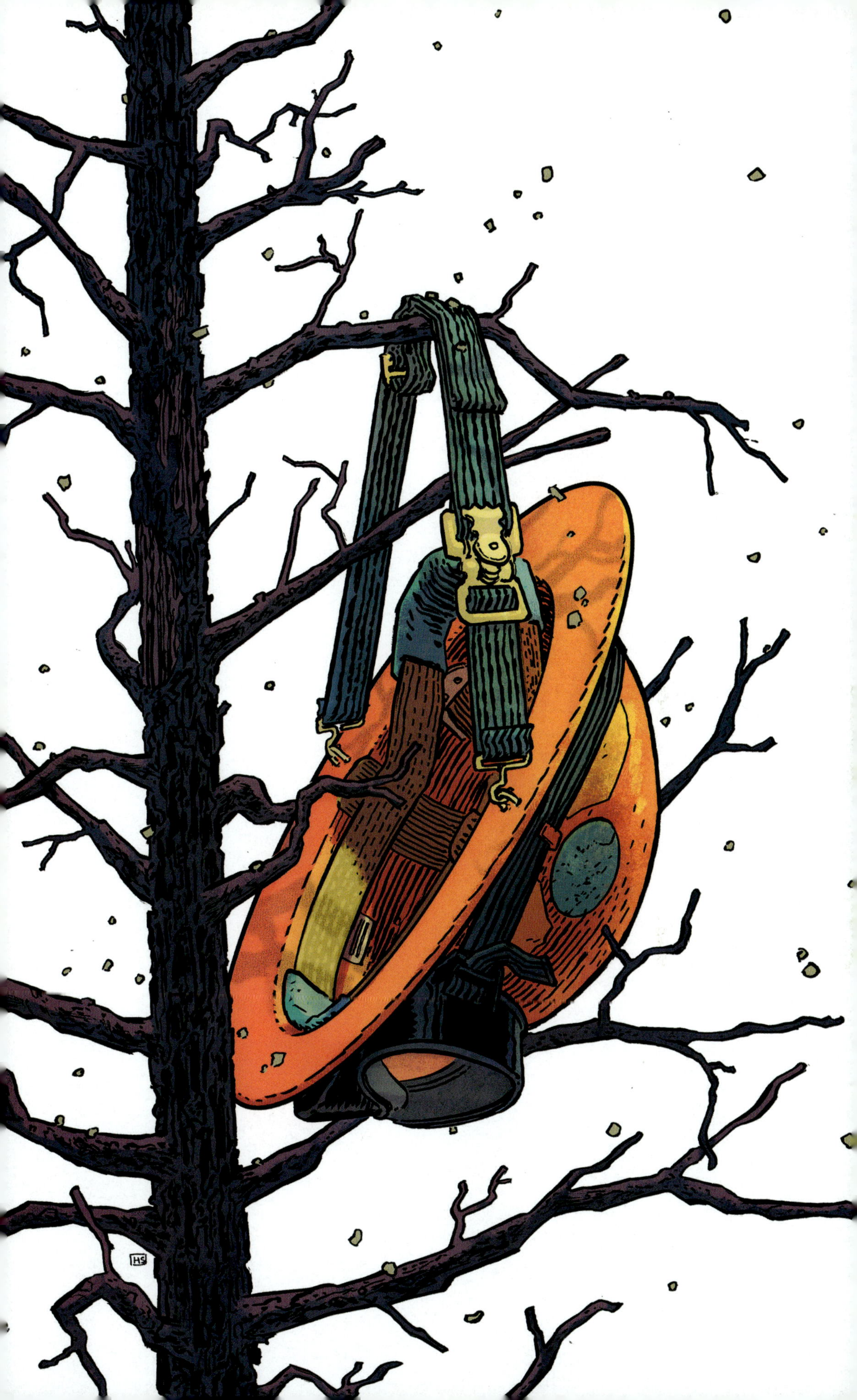

"WE LEAVE IT
ALL BEHIND."

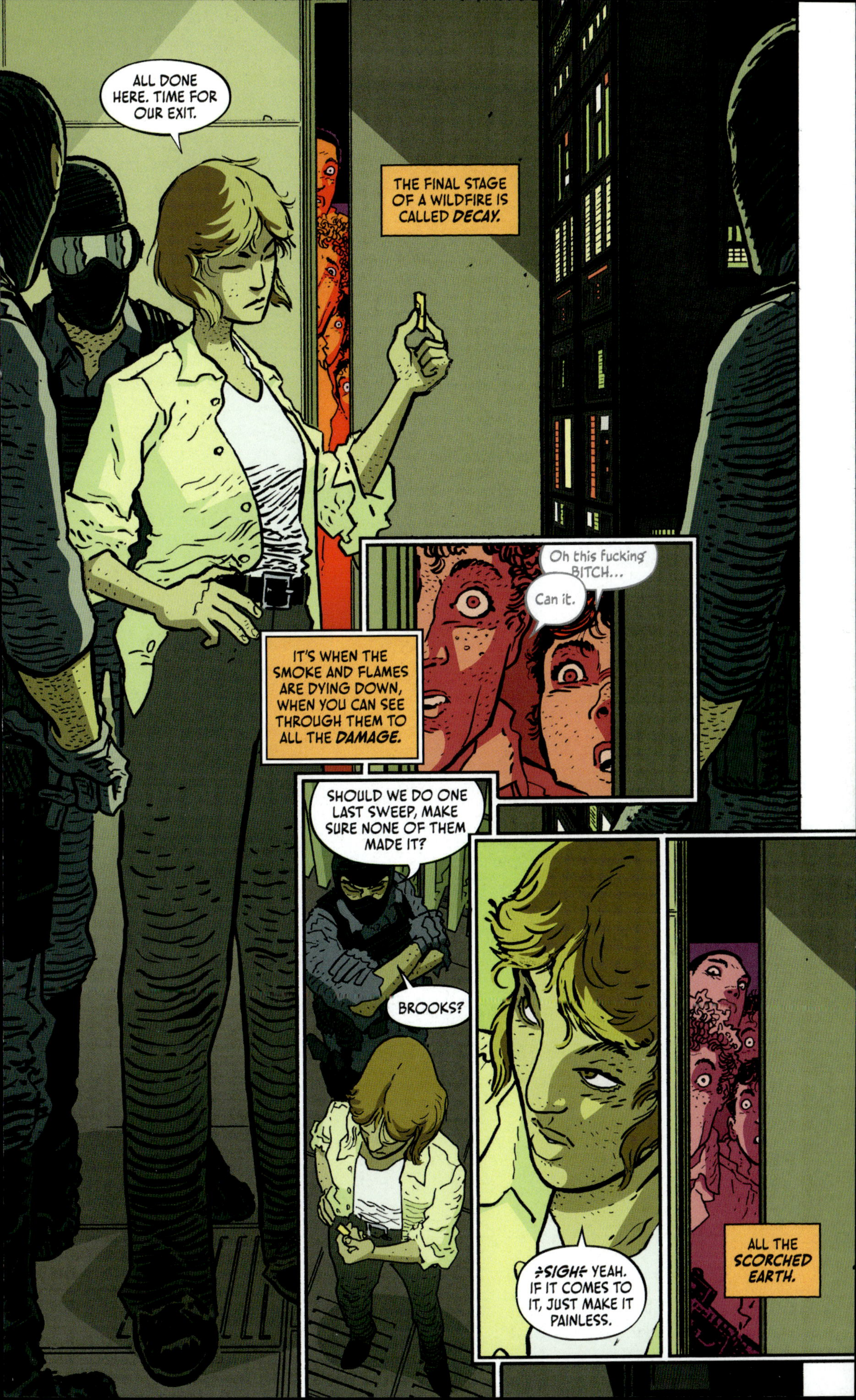
ALL DONE HERE. TIME FOR OUR EXIT.
THE FINAL STAGE OF A WILDFIRE IS CALLED DECAY.
Oh this fucking BITCH...
Can it.
IT'S WHEN THE SMOKE AND FLAMES ARE DYING DOWN, WHEN YOU CAN SEE THROUGH THEM TO ALL THE DAMAGE.
SHOULD WE DO ONE LAST SWEEP, MAKE SURE NONE OF THEM MADE IT?
BROOKS?
SIGH YEAH. IF IT COMES TO IT, JUST MAKE IT PAINLESS.
ALL THE SCORCHED EARTH.

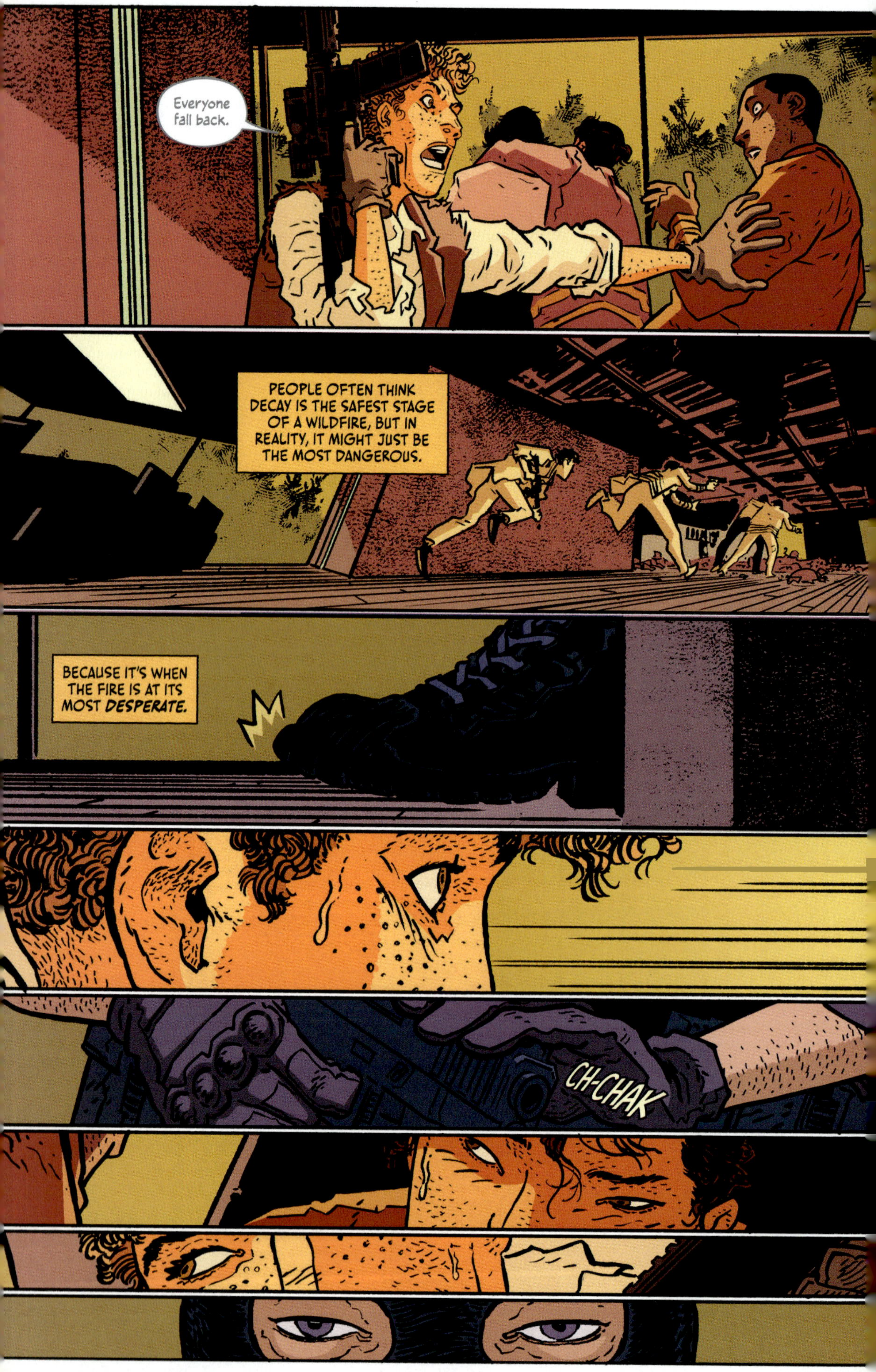
Everyone fall back.
PEOPLE OFTEN THINK DECAY IS THE SAFEST STAGE OF A WILDFIRE, BUT IN REALITY, IT MIGHT JUST BE THE MOST DANGEROUS.
BECAUSE IT'S WHEN THE FIRE IS AT ITS MOST *DESPERATE.*
CH-CHAK

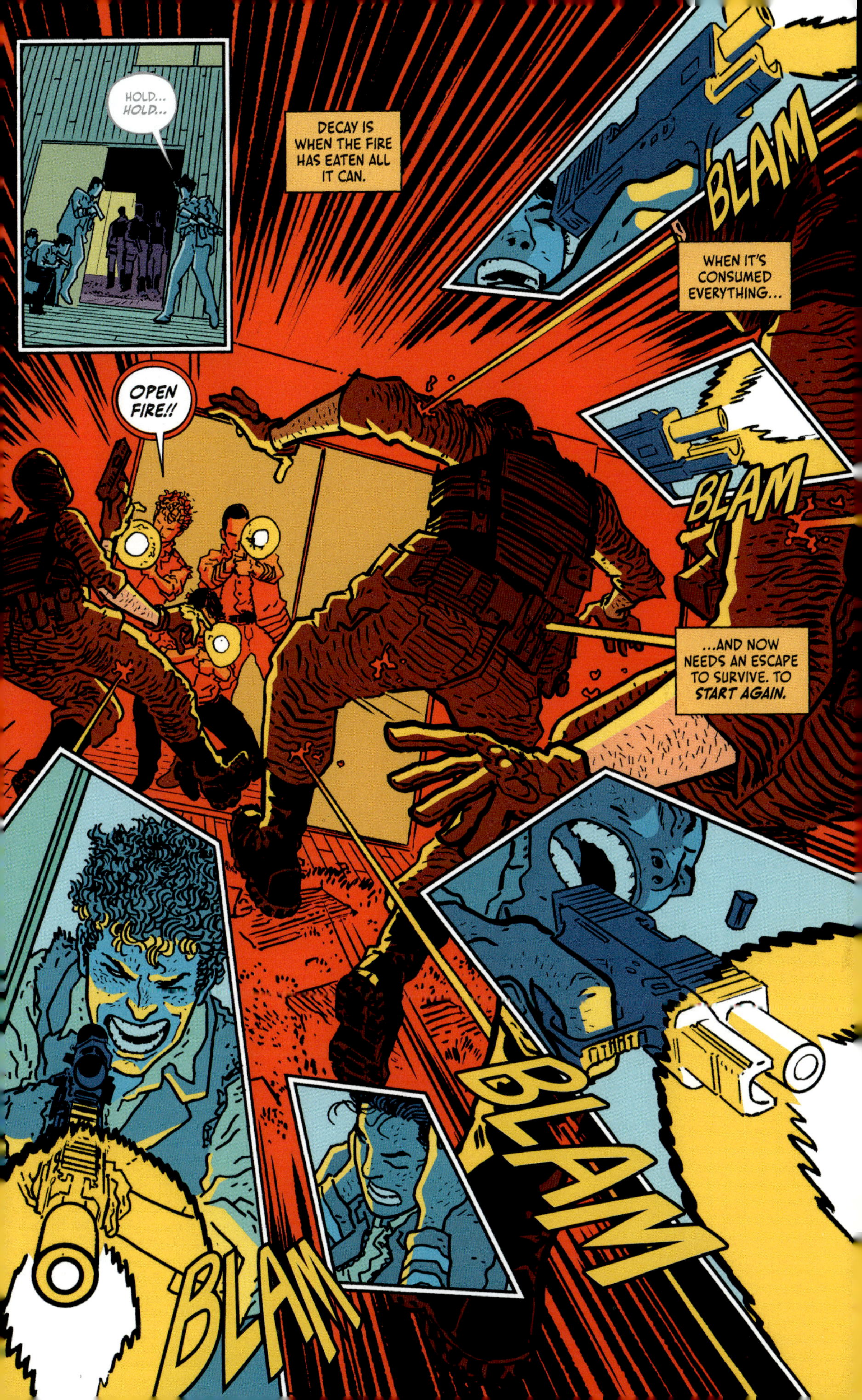
HOLD... HOLD...
DECAY IS WHEN THE FIRE HAS EATEN ALL IT CAN.
BLAM
WHEN IT'S CONSUMED EVERYTHING...
OPEN FIRE!!
BLAM
...AND NOW NEEDS AN ESCAPE TO SURVIVE. TO *START AGAIN.*
BLAM
BLAM

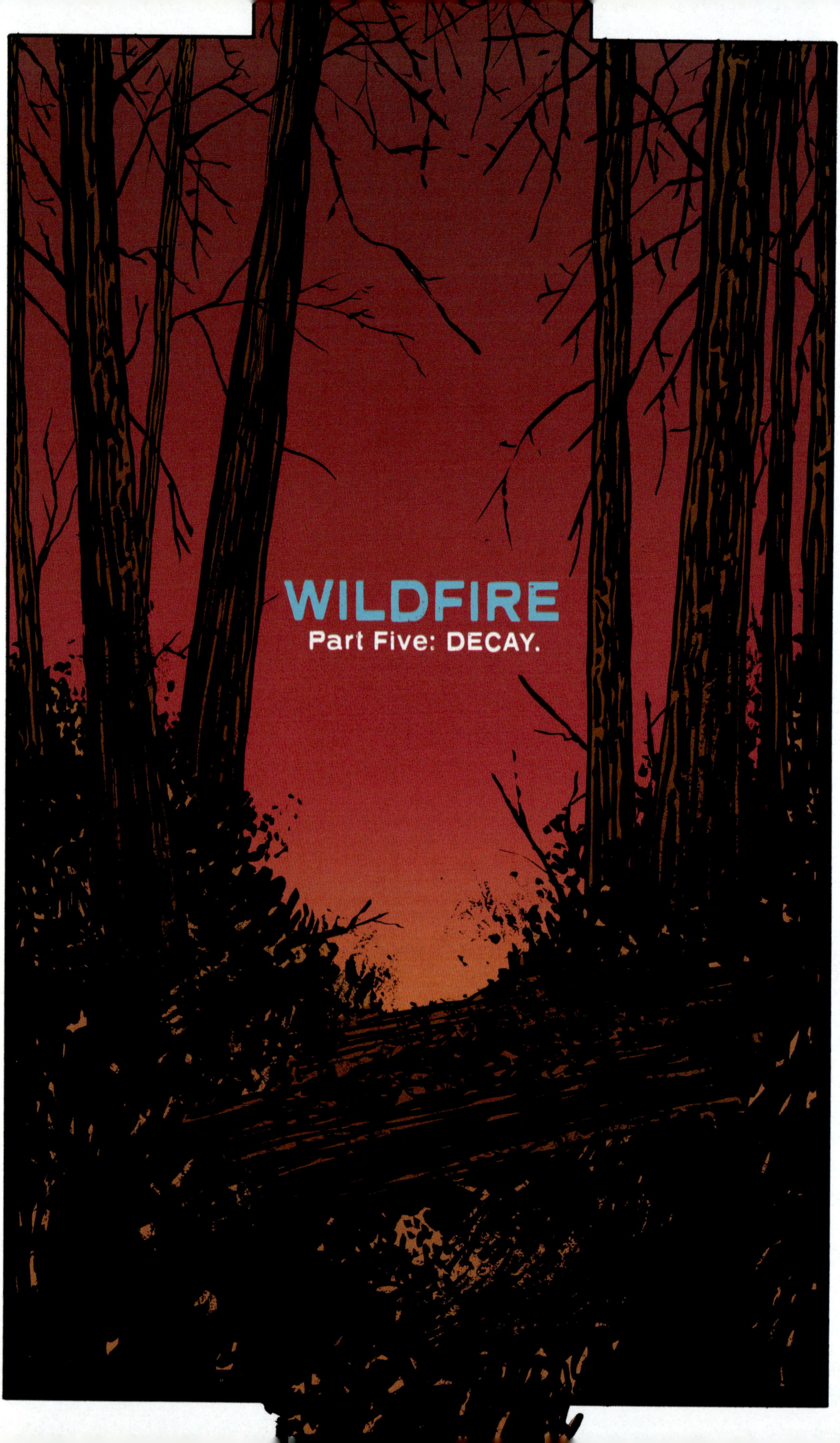
WILDFIRE
Part Five: DECAY.

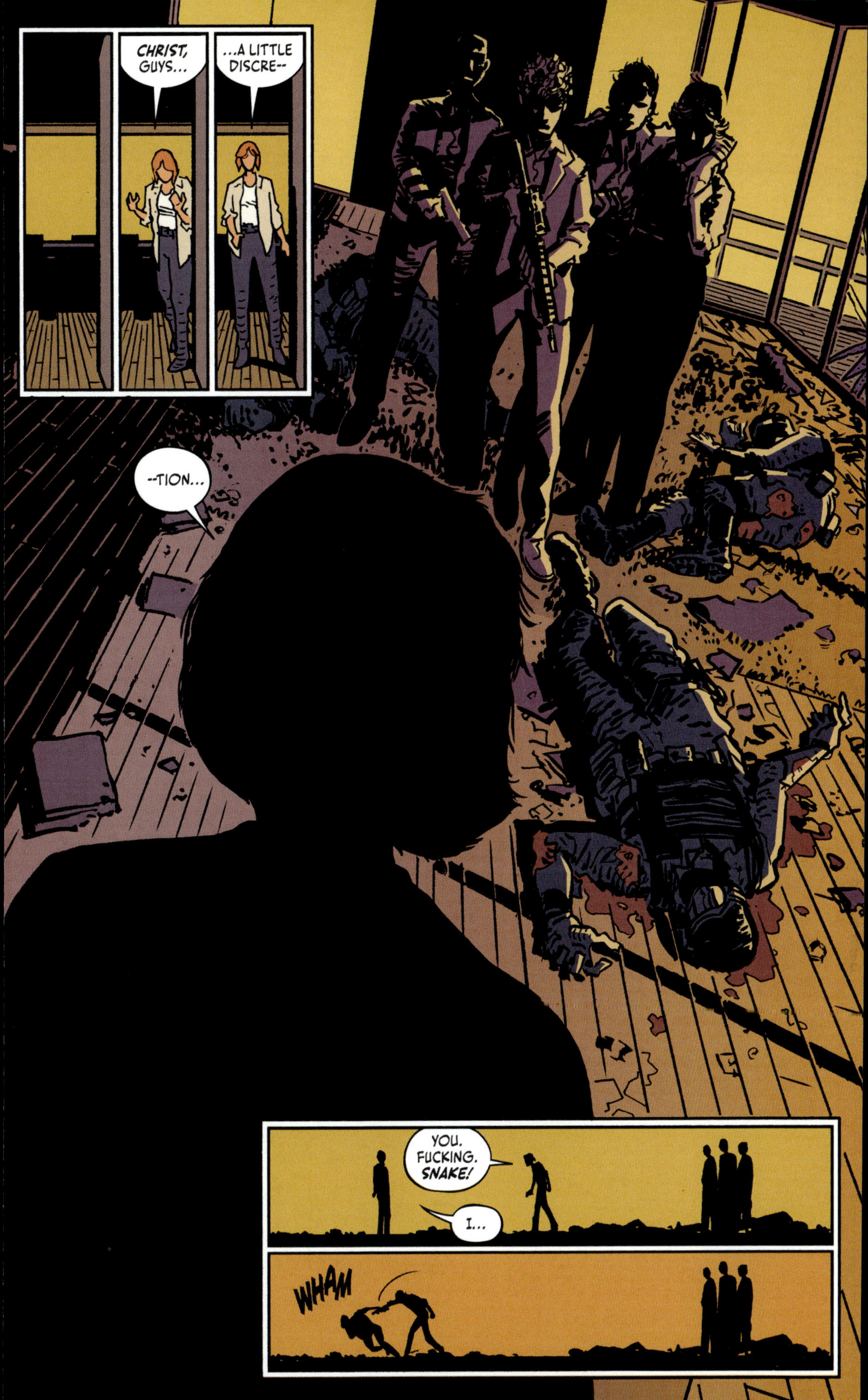
CHRIST, GUYS...
...A LITTLE DISCRE--
--TION...
YOU. FUCKING. SNAKE!
I...
WHAM

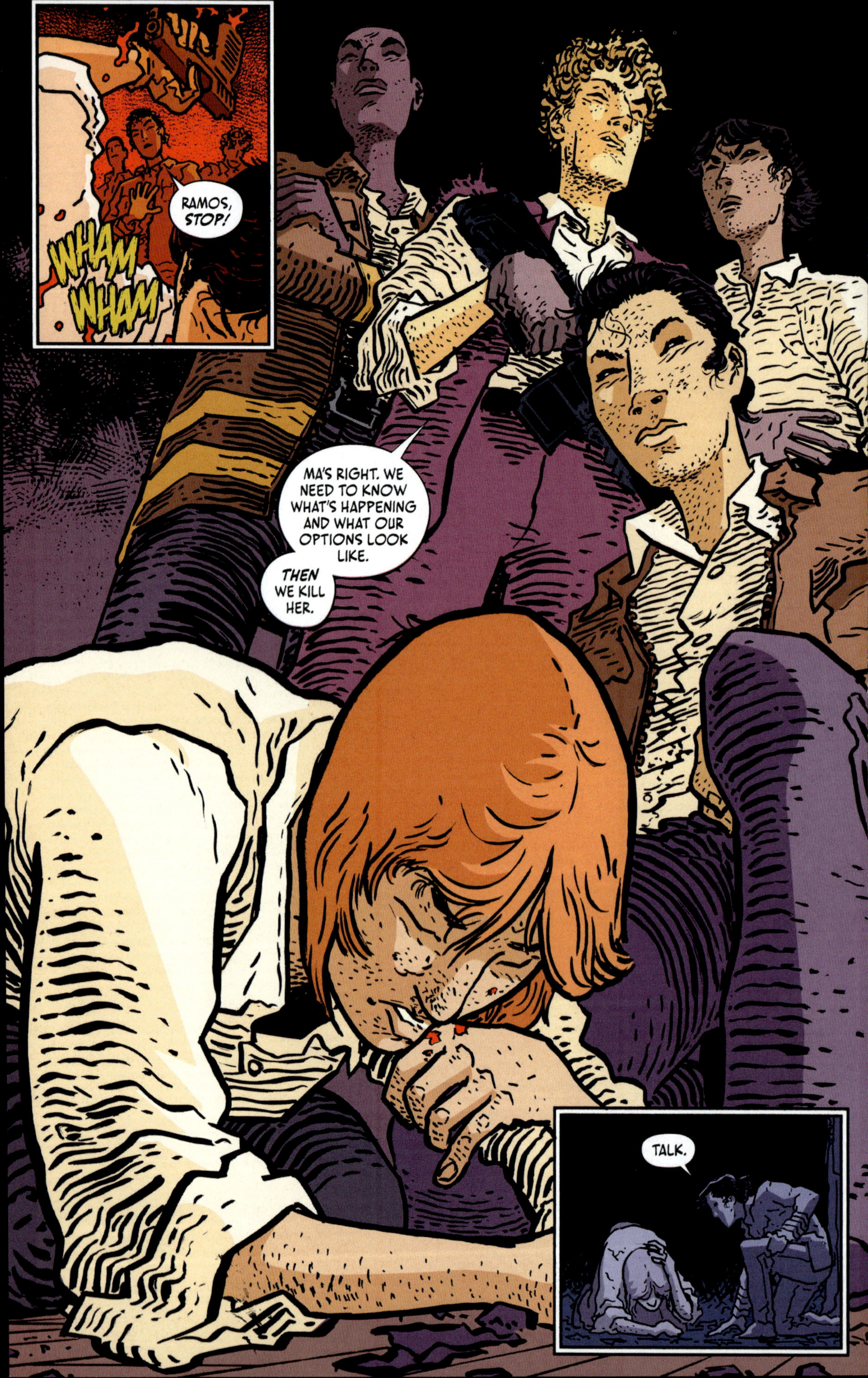
RAMOS, STOP!
WHAM WHAM
MA'S RIGHT. WE NEED TO KNOW WHAT'S HAPPENING AND WHAT OUR OPTIONS LOOK LIKE.
THEN WE KILL HER.
TALK.

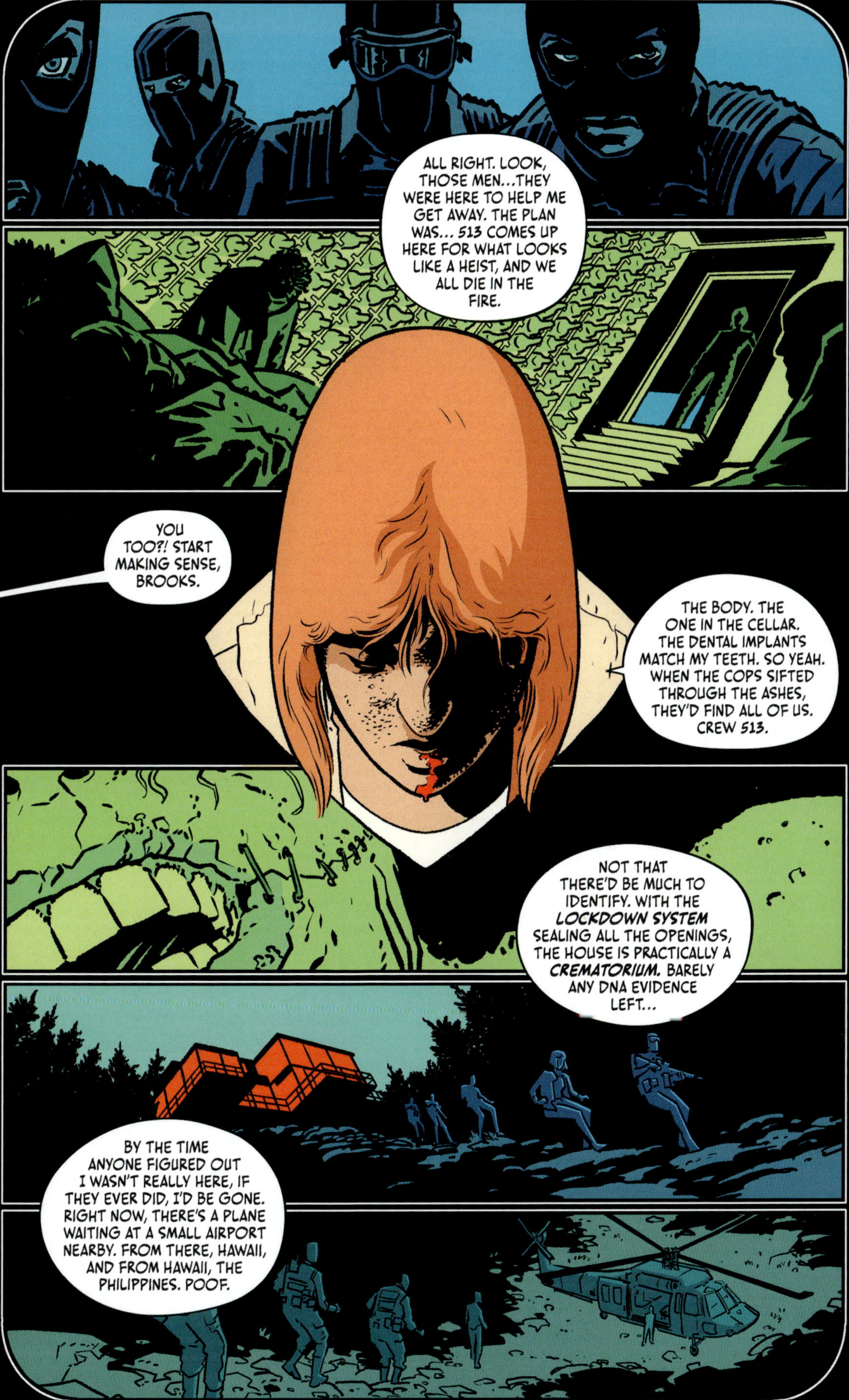
ALL RIGHT. LOOK, THOSE MEN...THEY WERE HERE TO HELP ME GET AWAY. THE PLAN WAS... 513 COMES UP HERE FOR WHAT LOOKS LIKE A HEIST, AND WE ALL DIE IN THE FIRE.
YOU TOO?! START MAKING SENSE, BROOKS.
THE BODY. THE ONE IN THE CELLAR. THE DENTAL IMPLANTS MATCH MY TEETH. SO YEAH. WHEN THE COPS SIFTED THROUGH THE ASHES, THEY'D FIND ALL OF US. CREW 513.
NOT THAT THERE'D BE MUCH TO IDENTIFY. WITH THE *LOCKDOWN SYSTEM* SEALING ALL THE OPENINGS, THE HOUSE IS PRACTICALLY A *CREMATORIUM.* BARELY ANY DNA EVIDENCE LEFT...
BY THE TIME ANYONE FIGURED OUT I WASN'T REALLY HERE, IF THEY EVER DID, I'D BE GONE. RIGHT NOW, THERE'S A PLANE WAITING AT A SMALL AIRPORT NEARBY. FROM THERE, HAWAII, AND FROM HAWAII, THE PHILIPPINES. POOF.

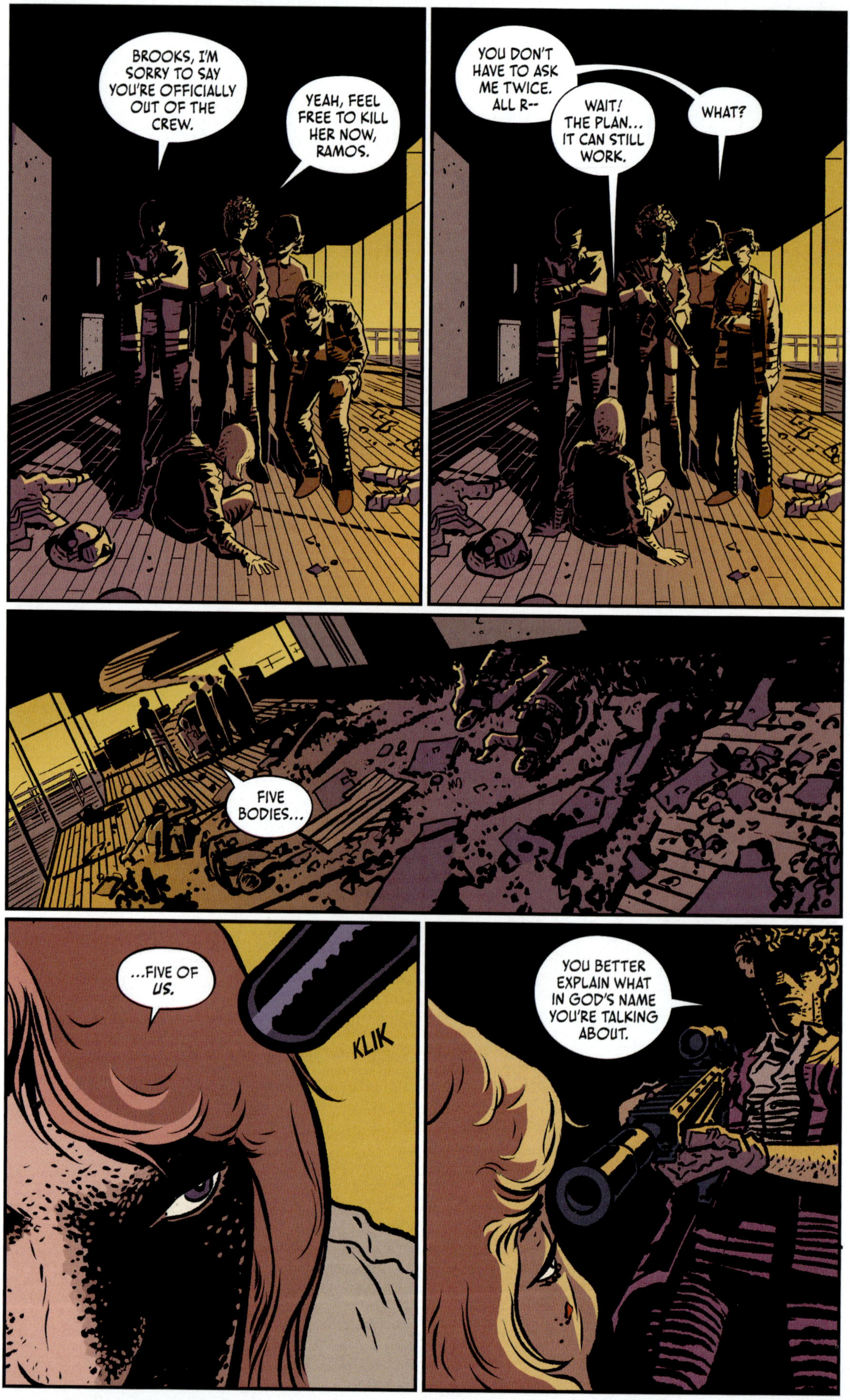
BROOKS, I'M SORRY TO SAY YOU'RE OFFICIALLY OUT OF THE CREW.
YEAH, FEEL FREE TO KILL HER NOW, RAMOS.
YOU DON'T HAVE TO ASK ME TWICE. ALL R--
WAIT! THE PLAN... IT CAN STILL WORK.
WHAT?
FIVE BODIES...
...FIVE OF *US.*
KLIK
YOU BETTER EXPLAIN WHAT IN GOD'S NAME YOU'RE TALKING ABOUT.

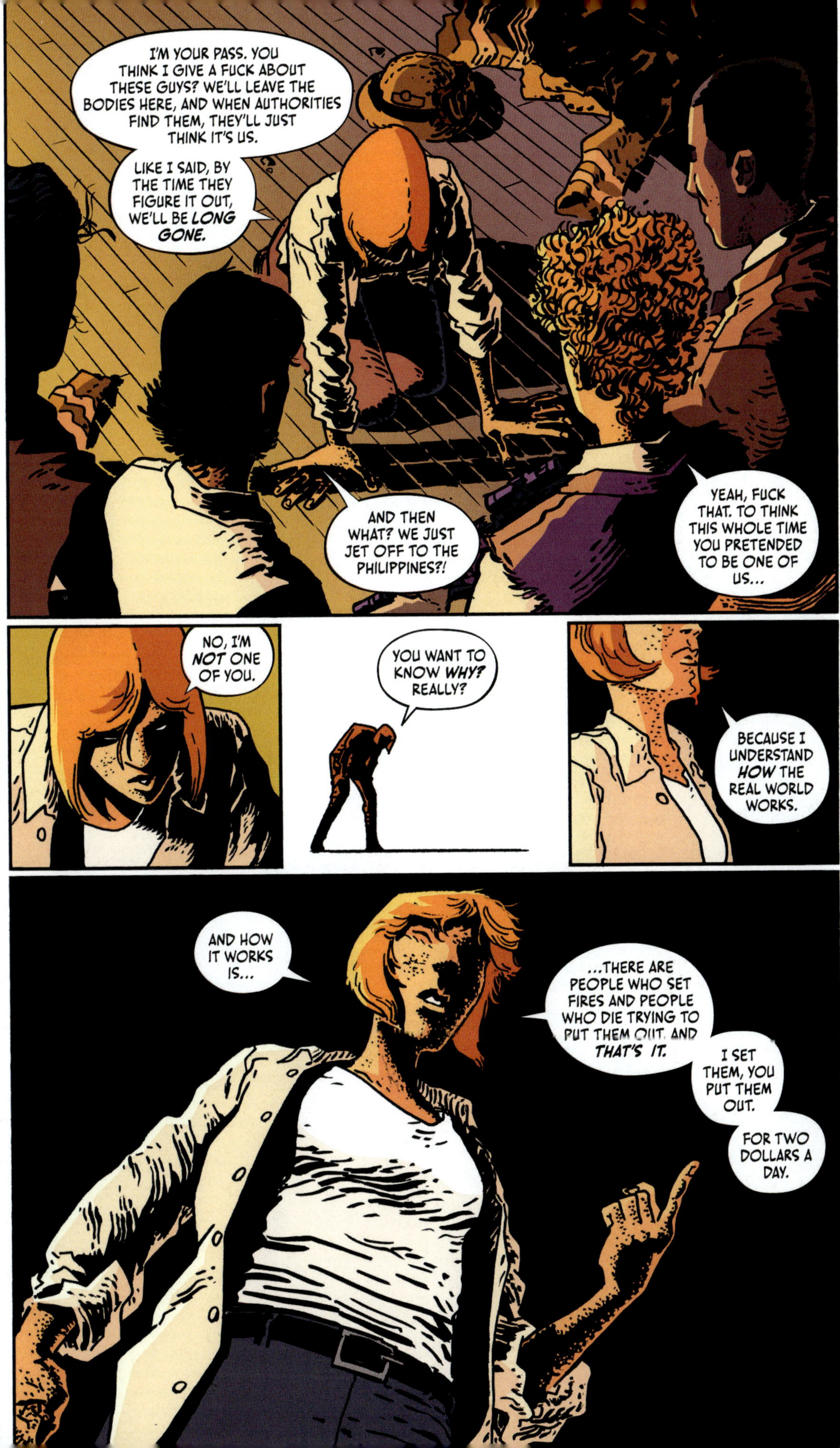

I'M YOUR PASS. YOU THINK I GIVE A FUCK ABOUT THESE GUYS? WE'LL LEAVE THE BODIES HERE, AND WHEN AUTHORITIES FIND THEM, THEY'LL JUST THINK IT'S US.
LIKE I SAID, BY THE TIME THEY FIGURE IT OUT, WE'LL BE *LONG GONE.*
AND THEN WHAT? WE JUST JET OFF TO THE PHILIPPINES?!
YEAH, FUCK THAT. TO THINK THIS WHOLE TIME YOU PRETENDED TO BE ONE OF US...
NO, I'M *NOT* ONE OF YOU.
YOU WANT TO KNOW *WHY?* REALLY?
BECAUSE I UNDERSTAND *HOW* THE REAL WORLD WORKS.
AND HOW IT WORKS IS...
...THERE ARE PEOPLE WHO SET FIRES AND PEOPLE WHO DIE TRYING TO PUT THEM OUT. AND *THAT'S IT.*
I SET THEM, YOU PUT THEM OUT.
FOR TWO DOLLARS A DAY.

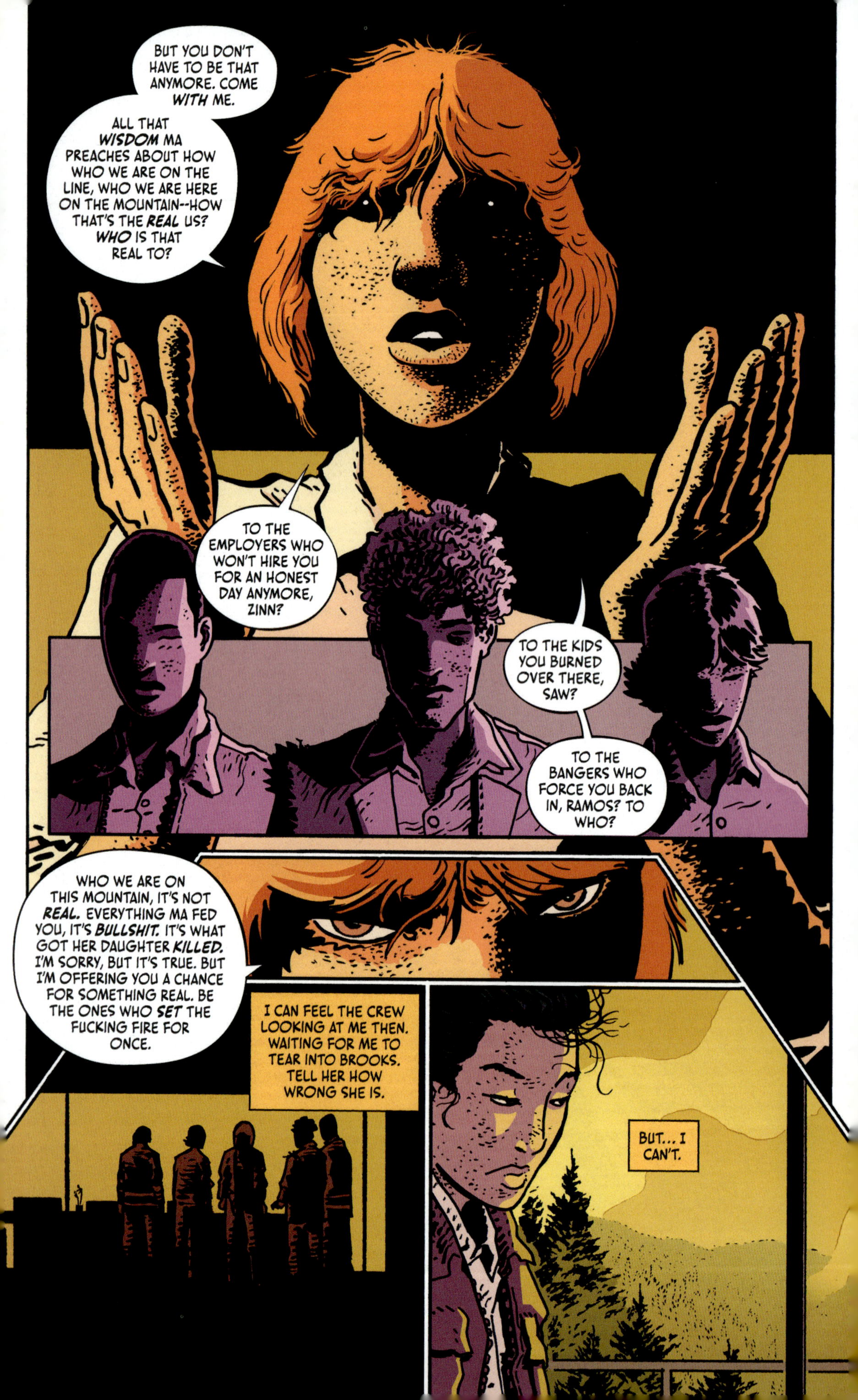
BUT YOU DON'T HAVE TO BE THAT ANYMORE. COME WITH ME.
ALL THAT WISDOM MA PREACHES ABOUT HOW WHO WE ARE ON THE LINE, WHO WE ARE HERE ON THE MOUNTAIN--HOW THAT'S THE REAL US? WHO IS THAT REAL TO?
TO THE EMPLOYERS WHO WON'T HIRE YOU FOR AN HONEST DAY ANYMORE, ZINN?
TO THE KIDS YOU BURNED OVER THERE, SAW?
TO THE BANGERS WHO FORCE YOU BACK IN, RAMOS? TO WHO?
WHO WE ARE ON THIS MOUNTAIN, IT'S NOT REAL. EVERYTHING MA FED YOU, IT'S BULLSHIT. IT'S WHAT GOT HER DAUGHTER KILLED. I'M SORRY, BUT IT'S TRUE. BUT I'M OFFERING YOU A CHANCE FOR SOMETHING REAL. BE THE ONES WHO SET THE FUCKING FIRE FOR ONCE.
I CAN FEEL THE CREW LOOKING AT ME THEN. WAITING FOR ME TO TEAR INTO BROOKS. TELL HER HOW WRONG SHE IS.
BUT... I CAN'T.

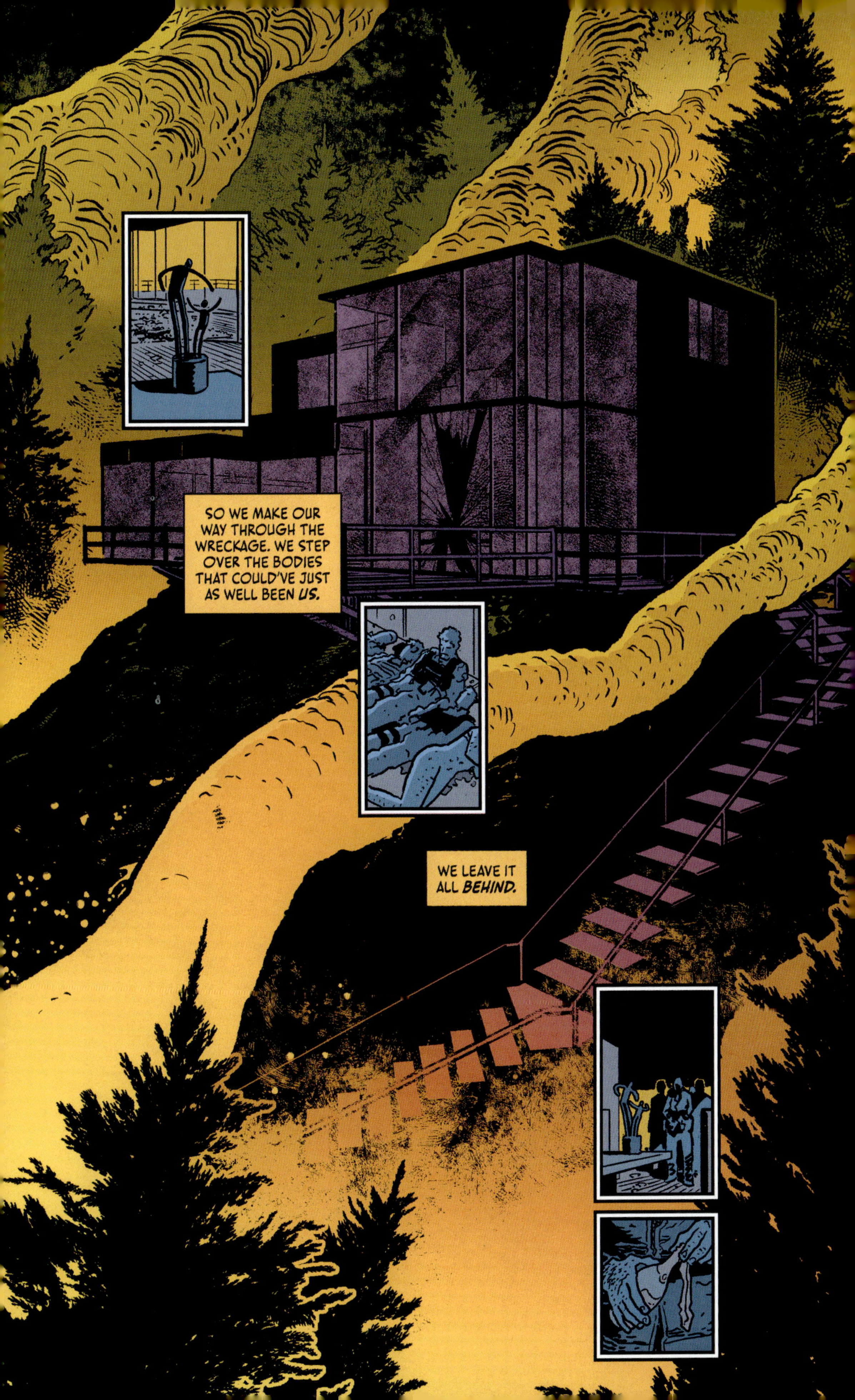
SO WE MAKE OUR WAY THROUGH THE WRECKAGE. WE STEP OVER THE BODIES THAT COULD'VE JUST AS WELL BEEN *US.*
WE LEAVE IT ALL *BEHIND.*

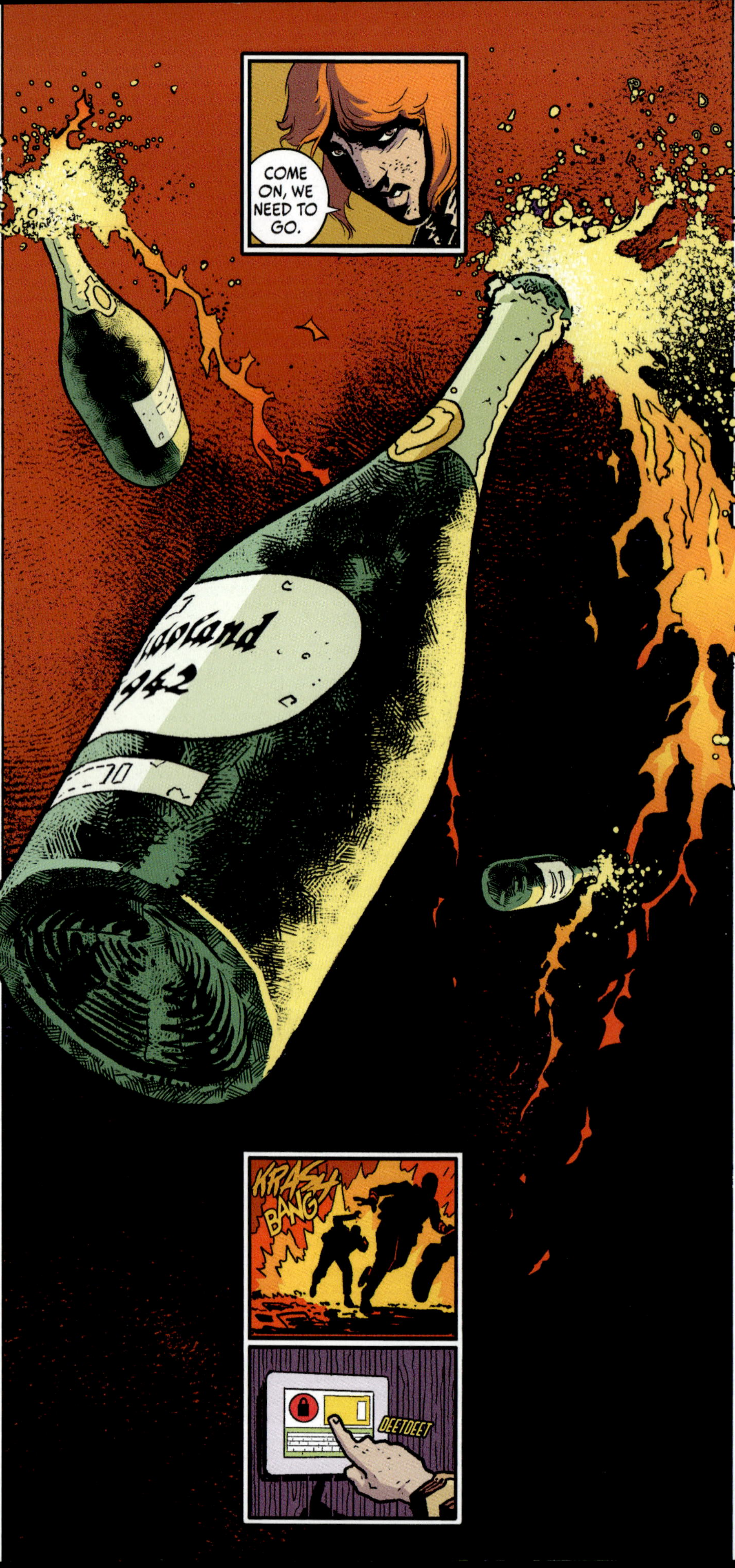

COME ON, WE NEED TO GO.
KRASH
BANG
DEETDEET

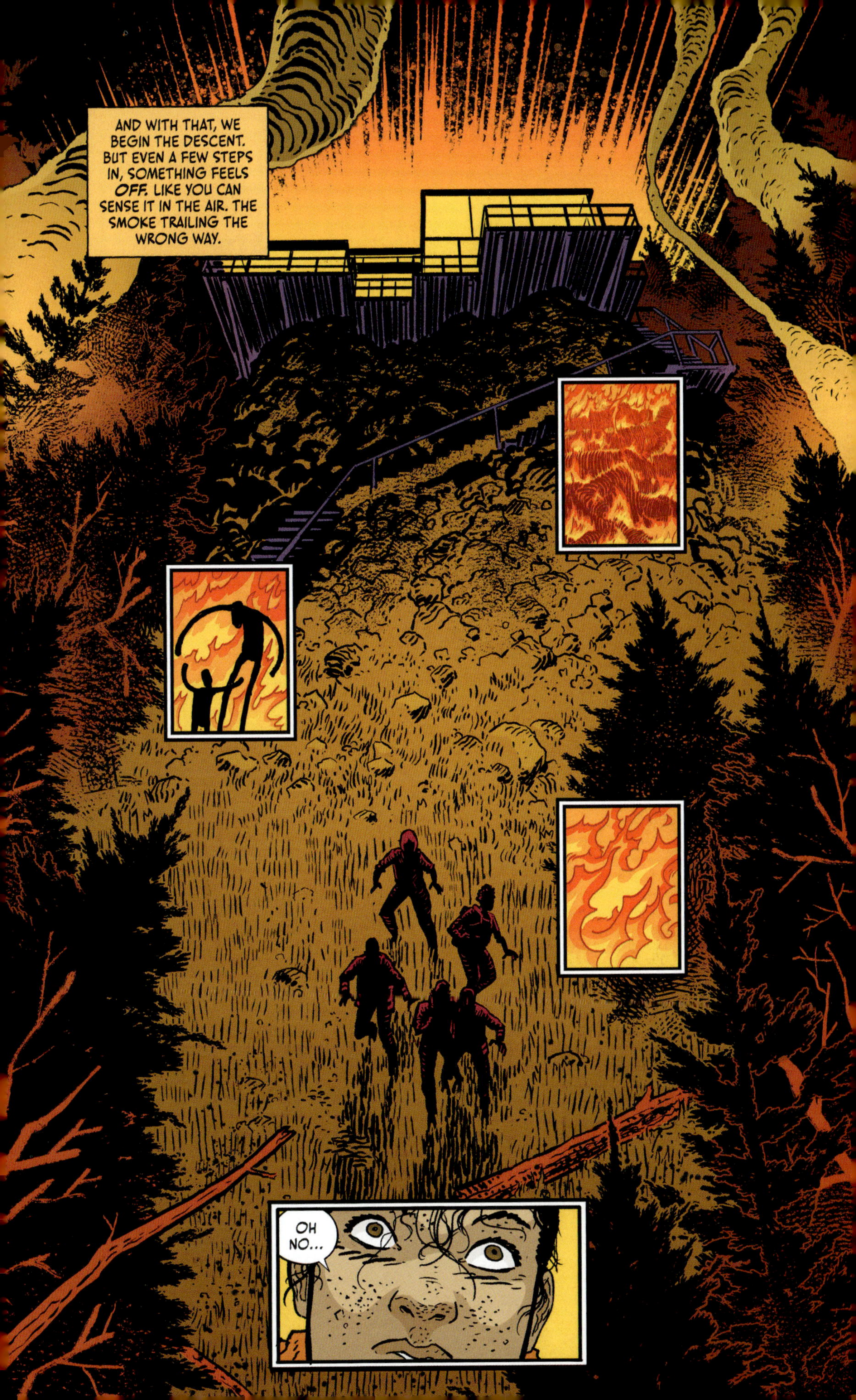
AND WITH THAT, WE BEGIN THE DESCENT. BUT EVEN A FEW STEPS IN, SOMETHING FEELS *OFF.* LIKE YOU CAN SENSE IT IN THE AIR. THE SMOKE TRAILING THE WRONG WAY.
OH NO...

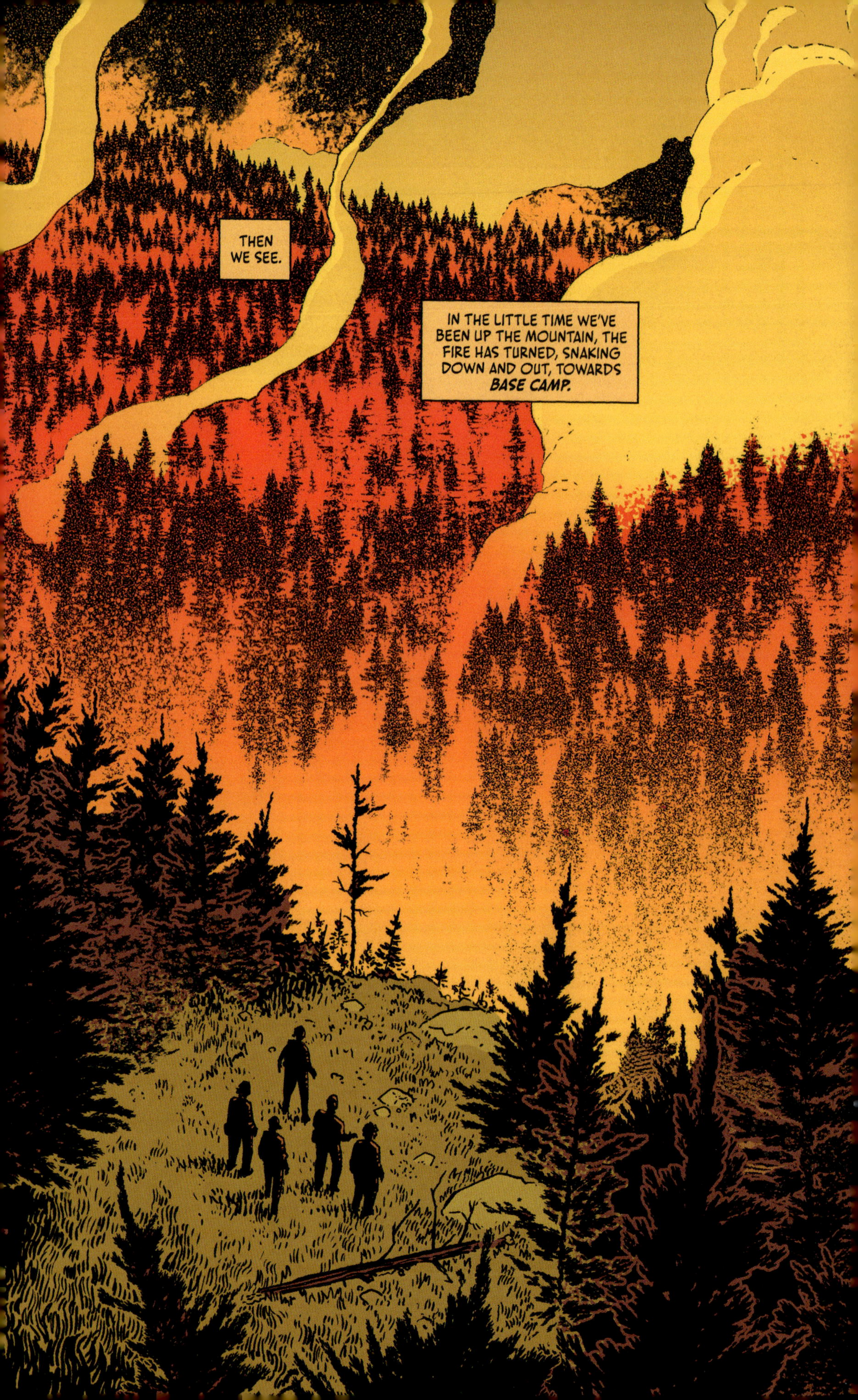
THEN WE SEE.
IN THE LITTLE TIME WE'VE BEEN UP THE MOUNTAIN, THE FIRE HAS TURNED, SNAKING DOWN AND OUT, TOWARDS *BASE CAMP.*

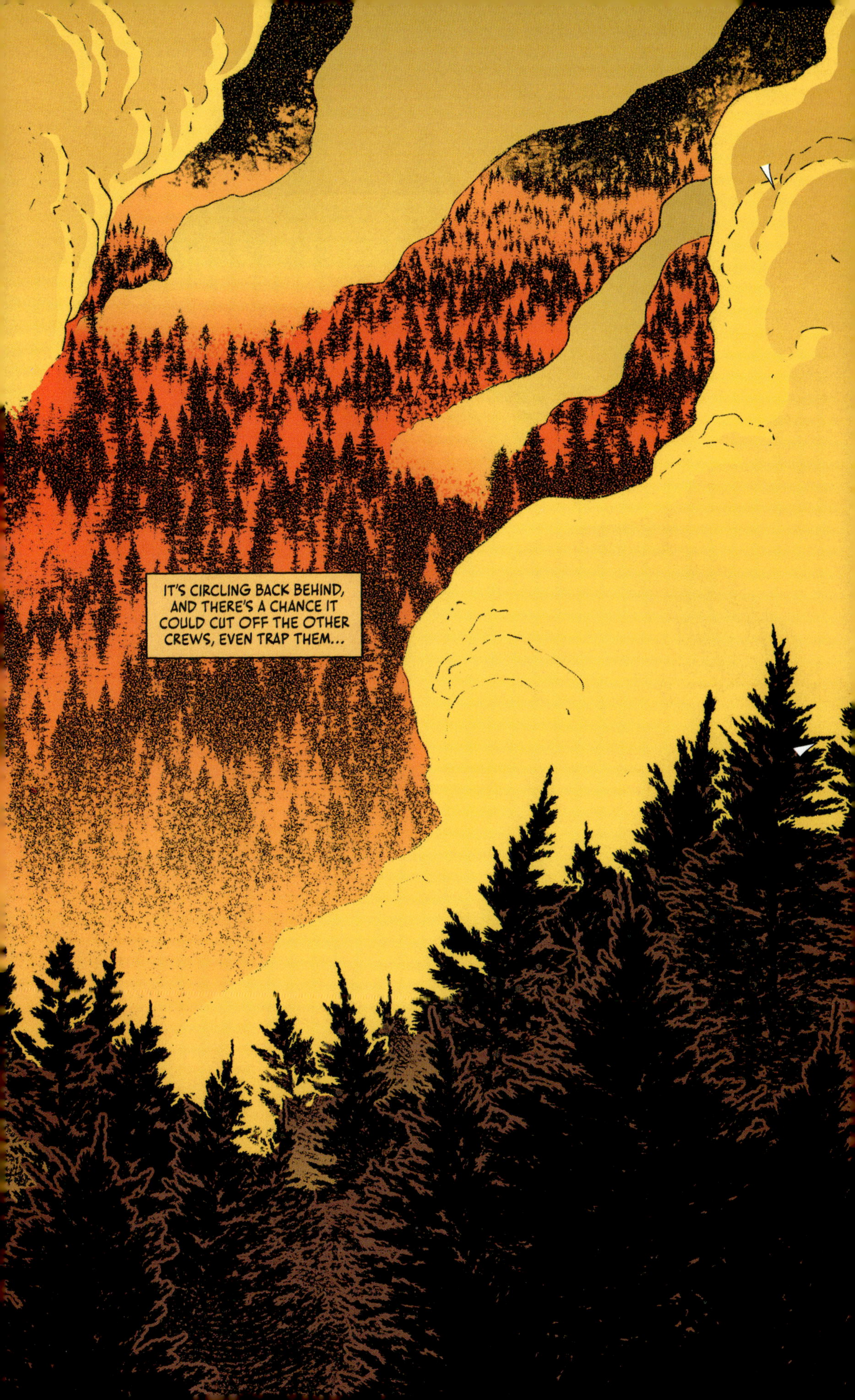
IT'S CIRCLING BACK BEHIND, AND THERE'S A CHANCE IT COULD CUT OFF THE OTHER CREWS, EVEN TRAP THEM...

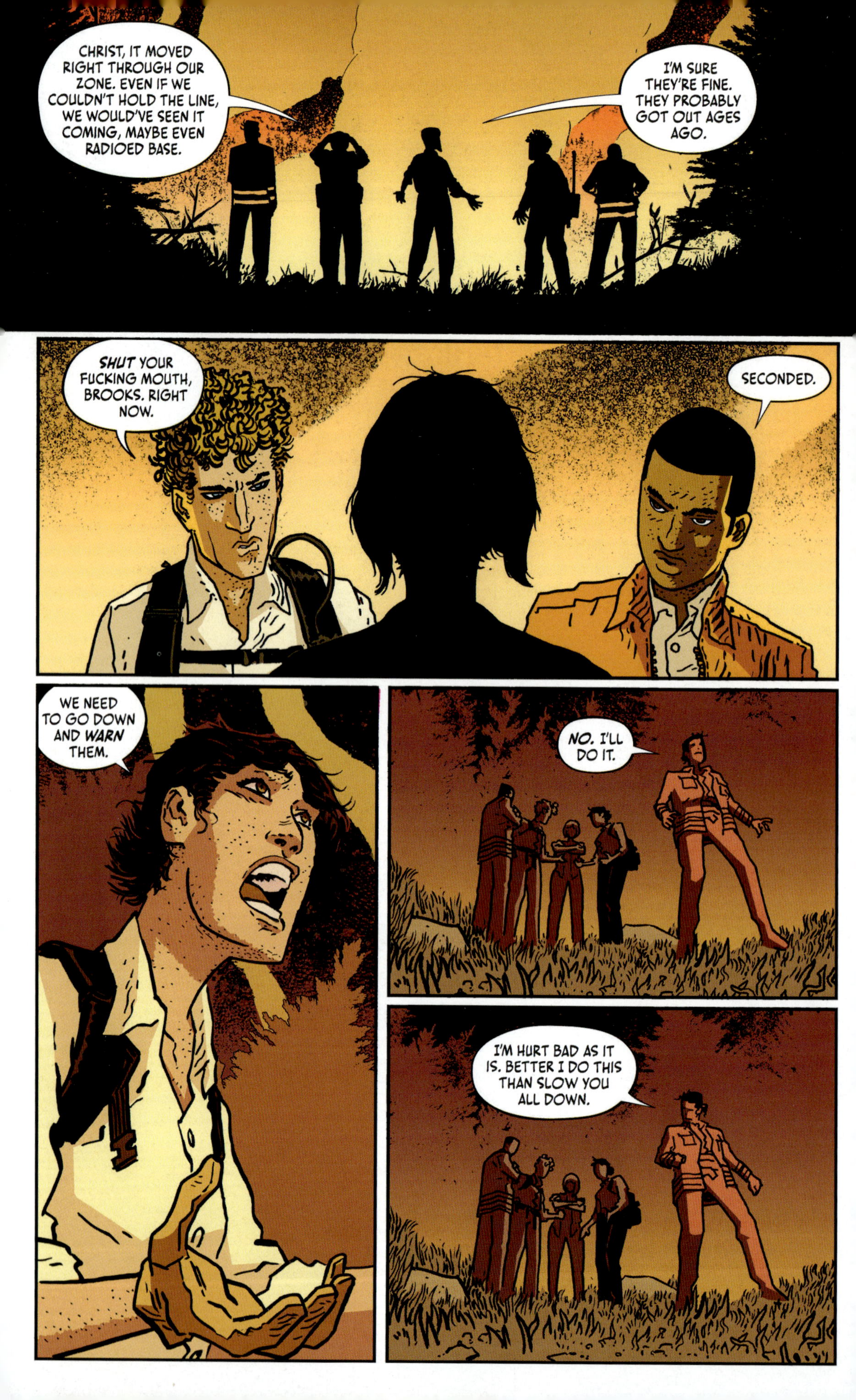
CHRIST, IT MOVED RIGHT THROUGH OUR ZONE. EVEN IF WE COULDN'T HOLD THE LINE, WE WOULD'VE SEEN IT COMING, MAYBE EVEN RADIOED BASE.
I'M SURE THEY'RE FINE. THEY PROBABLY GOT OUT AGES AGO.
SHUT YOUR FUCKING MOUTH, BROOKS. RIGHT NOW.
SECONDED.
WE NEED TO GO DOWN AND *WARN* THEM.
NO. I'LL DO IT.
I'M HURT BAD AS IT IS. BETTER I DO THIS THAN SLOW YOU ALL DOWN.

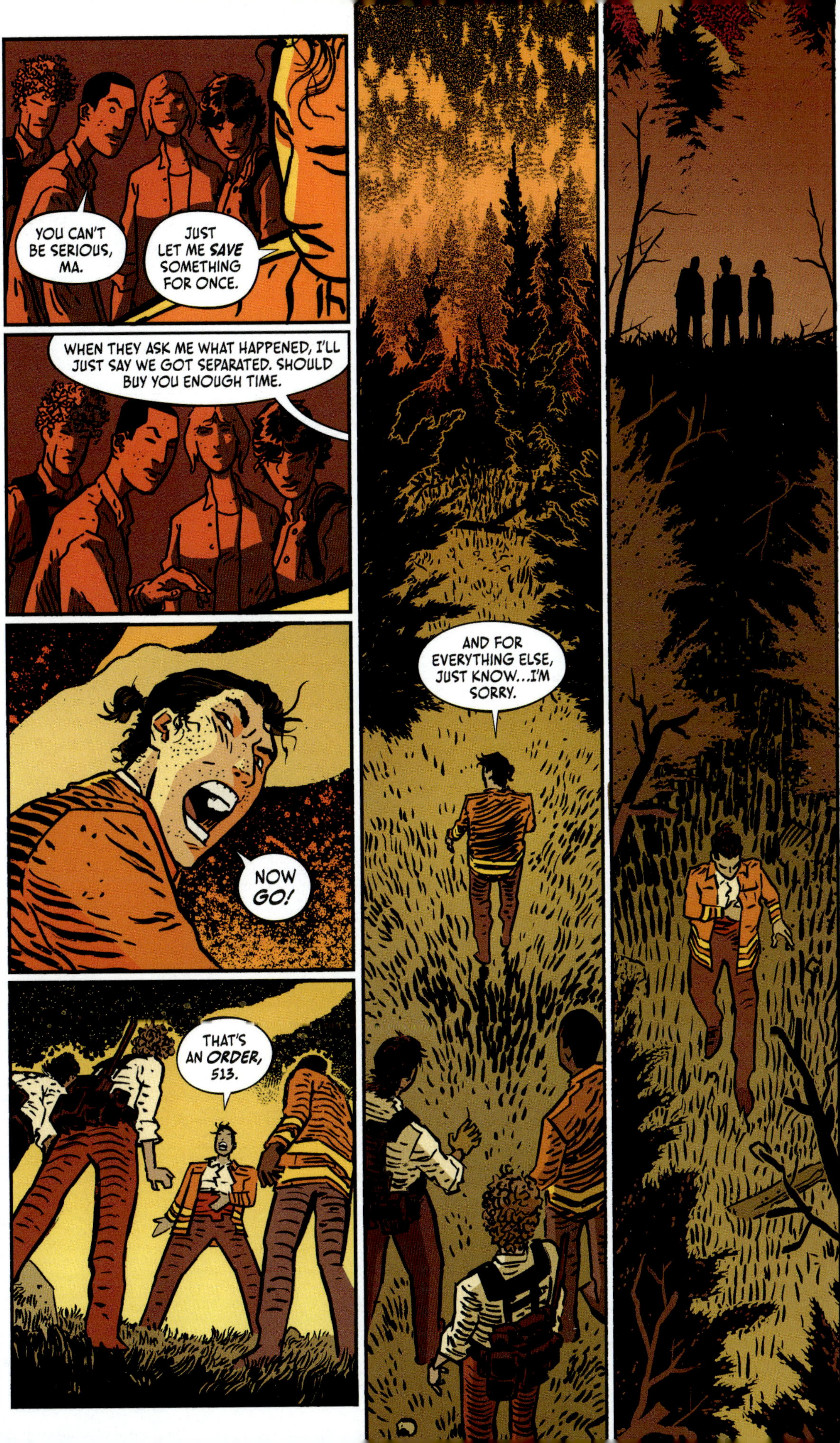
YOU CAN'T BE SERIOUS, MA.
JUST LET ME SAVE SOMETHING FOR ONCE.
WHEN THEY ASK ME WHAT HAPPENED, I'LL JUST SAY WE GOT SEPARATED. SHOULD BUY YOU ENOUGH TIME.
NOW GO!
THAT'S AN ORDER, 513.
AND FOR EVERYTHING ELSE, JUST KNOW...I'M SORRY.

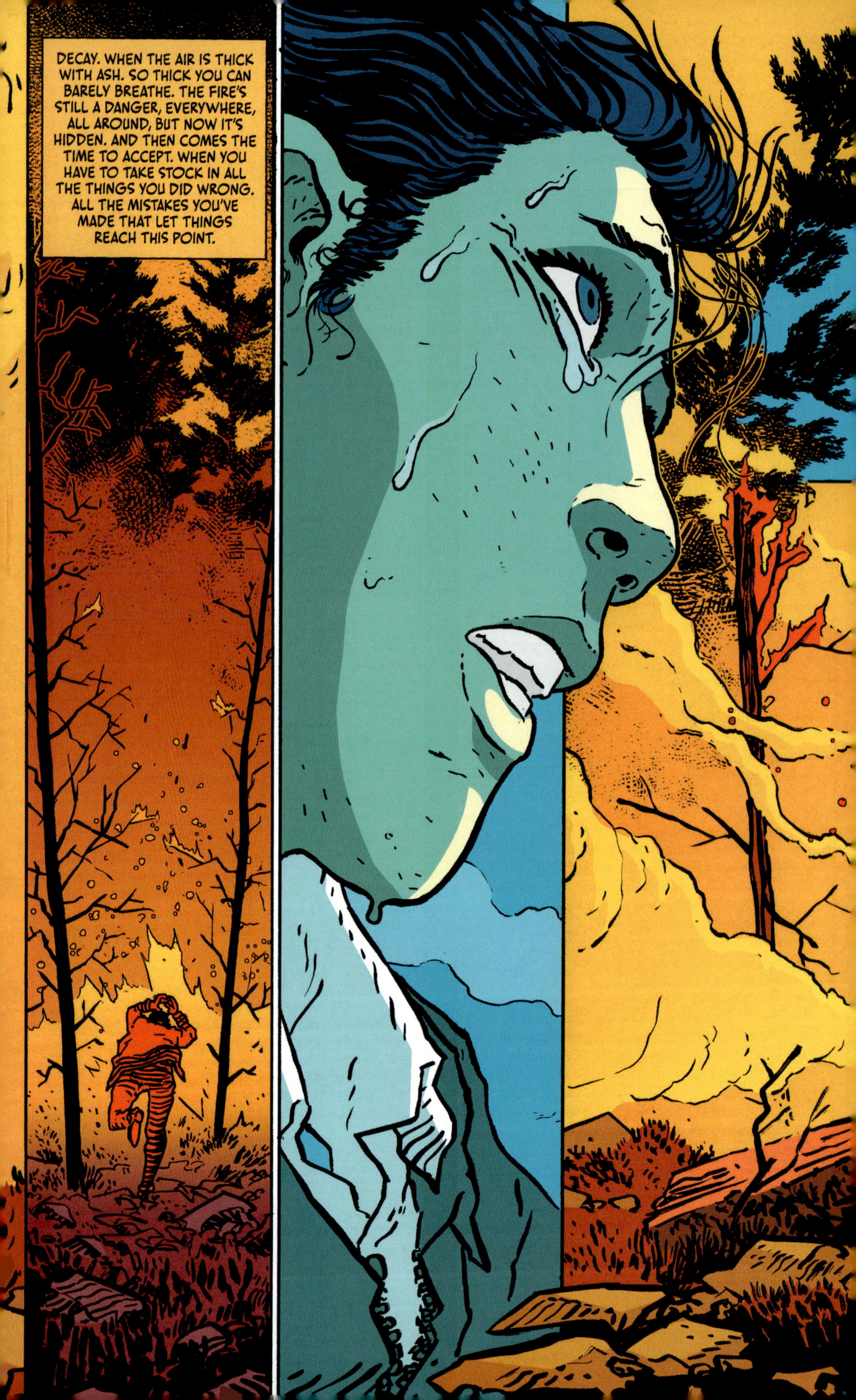
DECAY. WHEN THE AIR IS THICK WITH ASH. SO THICK YOU CAN BARELY BREATHE. THE FIRE'S STILL A DANGER, EVERYWHERE, ALL AROUND, BUT NOW IT'S HIDDEN. AND THEN COMES THE TIME TO ACCEPT. WHEN YOU HAVE TO TAKE STOCK IN ALL THE THINGS YOU DID WRONG. ALL THE MISTAKES YOU'VE MADE THAT LET THINGS REACH THIS POINT.

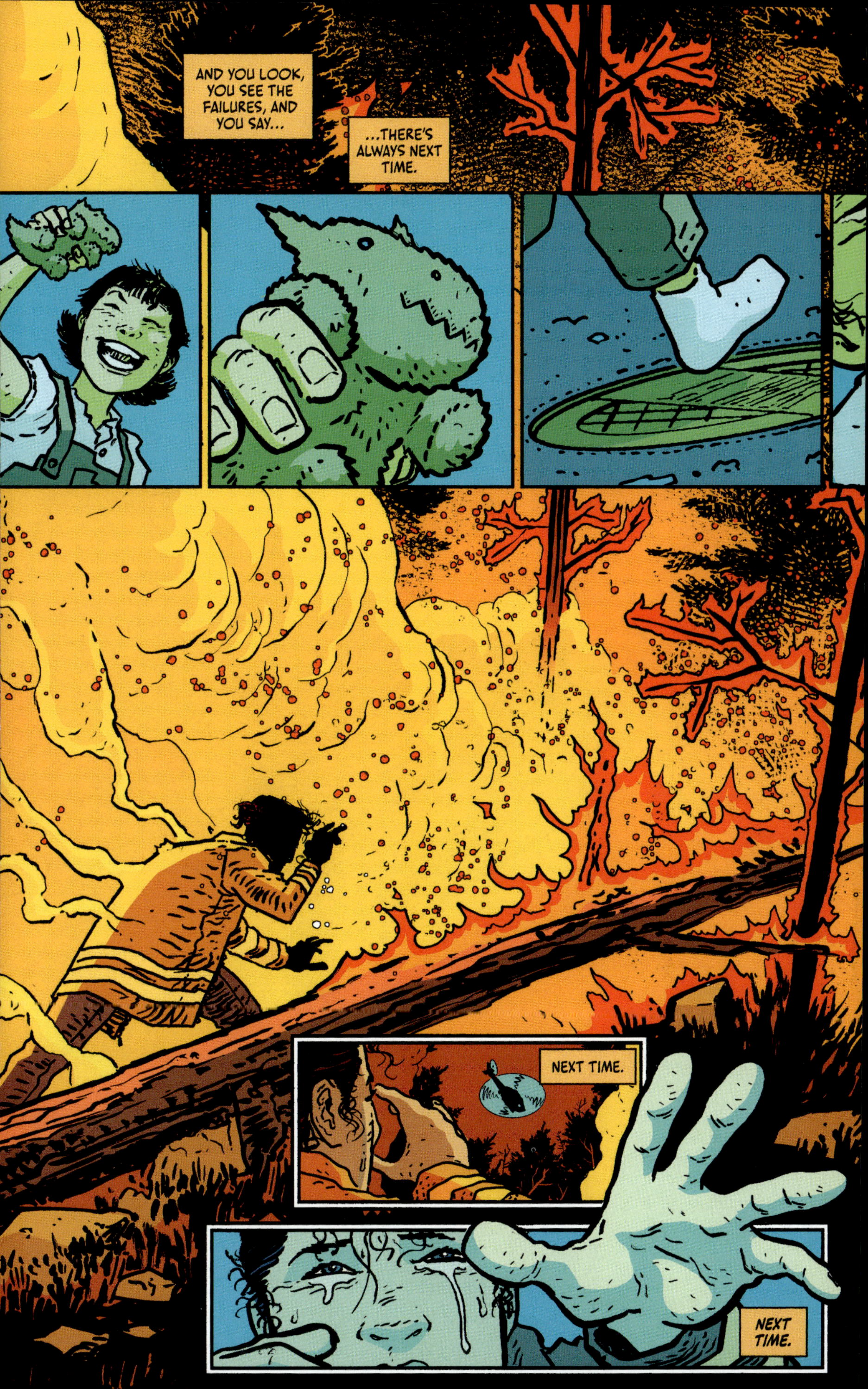
AND YOU LOOK, YOU SEE THE FAILURES, AND YOU SAY...
...THERE'S ALWAYS NEXT TIME.
NEXT TIME.
NEXT TIME.

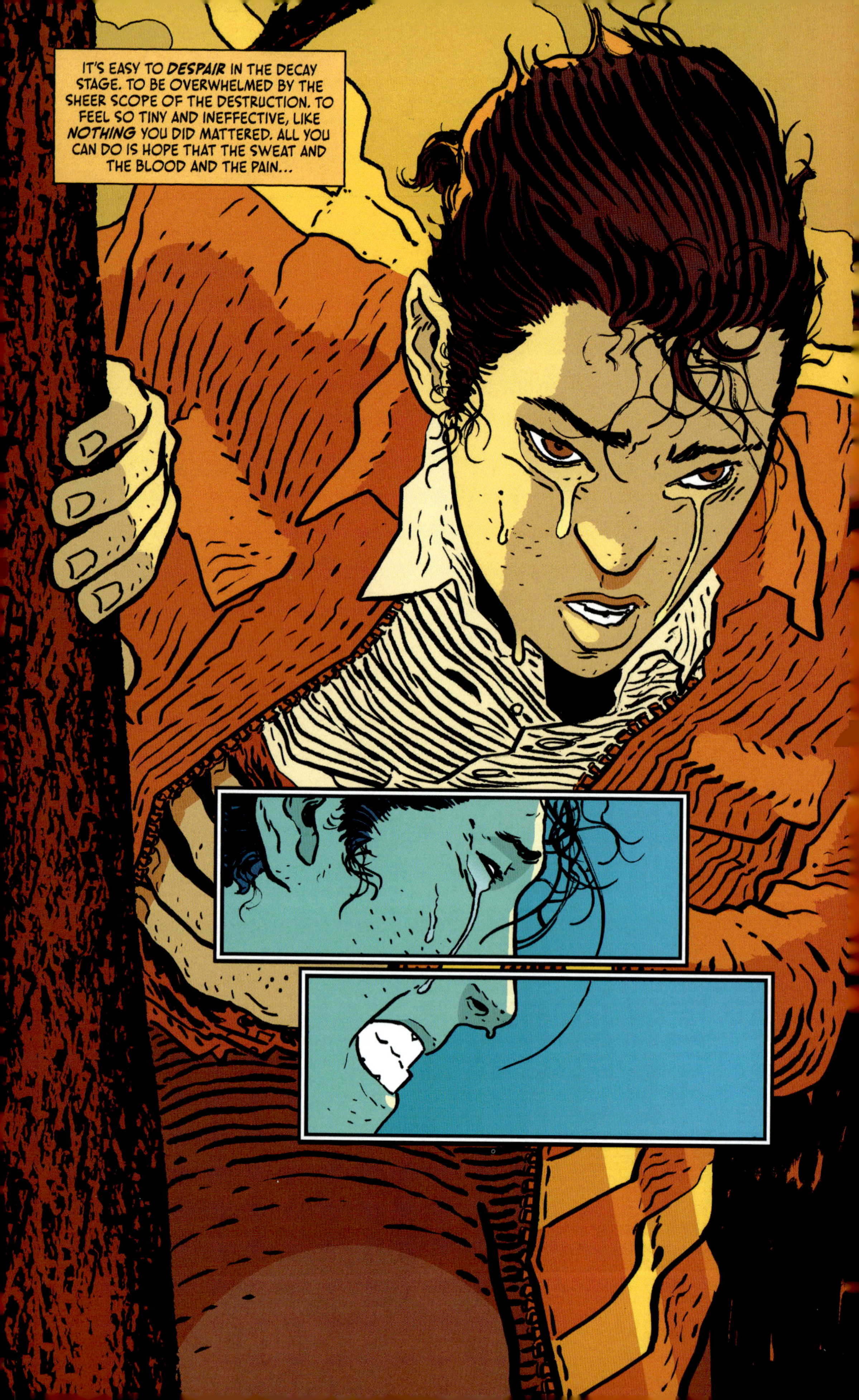
IT'S EASY TO DESPAIR IN THE DECAY STAGE. TO BE OVERWHELMED BY THE SHEER SCOPE OF THE DESTRUCTION. TO FEEL SO TINY AND INEFFECTIVE, LIKE NOTHING YOU DID MATTERED. ALL YOU CAN DO IS HOPE THAT THE SWEAT AND THE BLOOD AND THE PAIN...

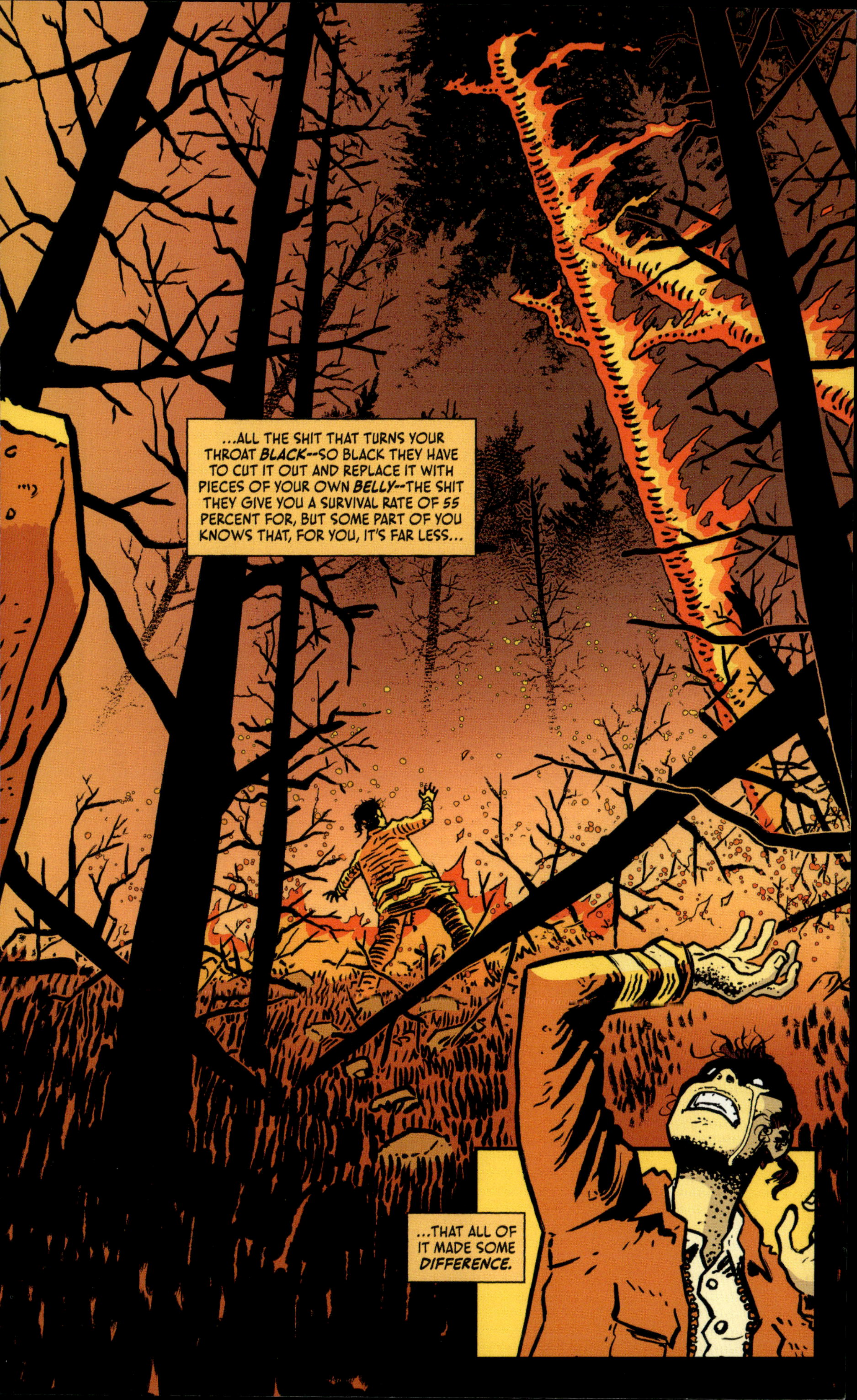
...ALL THE SHIT THAT TURNS YOUR THROAT *BLACK*--SO BLACK THEY HAVE TO CUT IT OUT AND REPLACE IT WITH PIECES OF YOUR OWN *BELLY*--THE SHIT THEY GIVE YOU A SURVIVAL RATE OF 55 PERCENT FOR, BUT SOME PART OF YOU KNOWS THAT, FOR YOU, IT'S FAR LESS...
...THAT ALL OF IT MADE SOME *DIFFERENCE.*

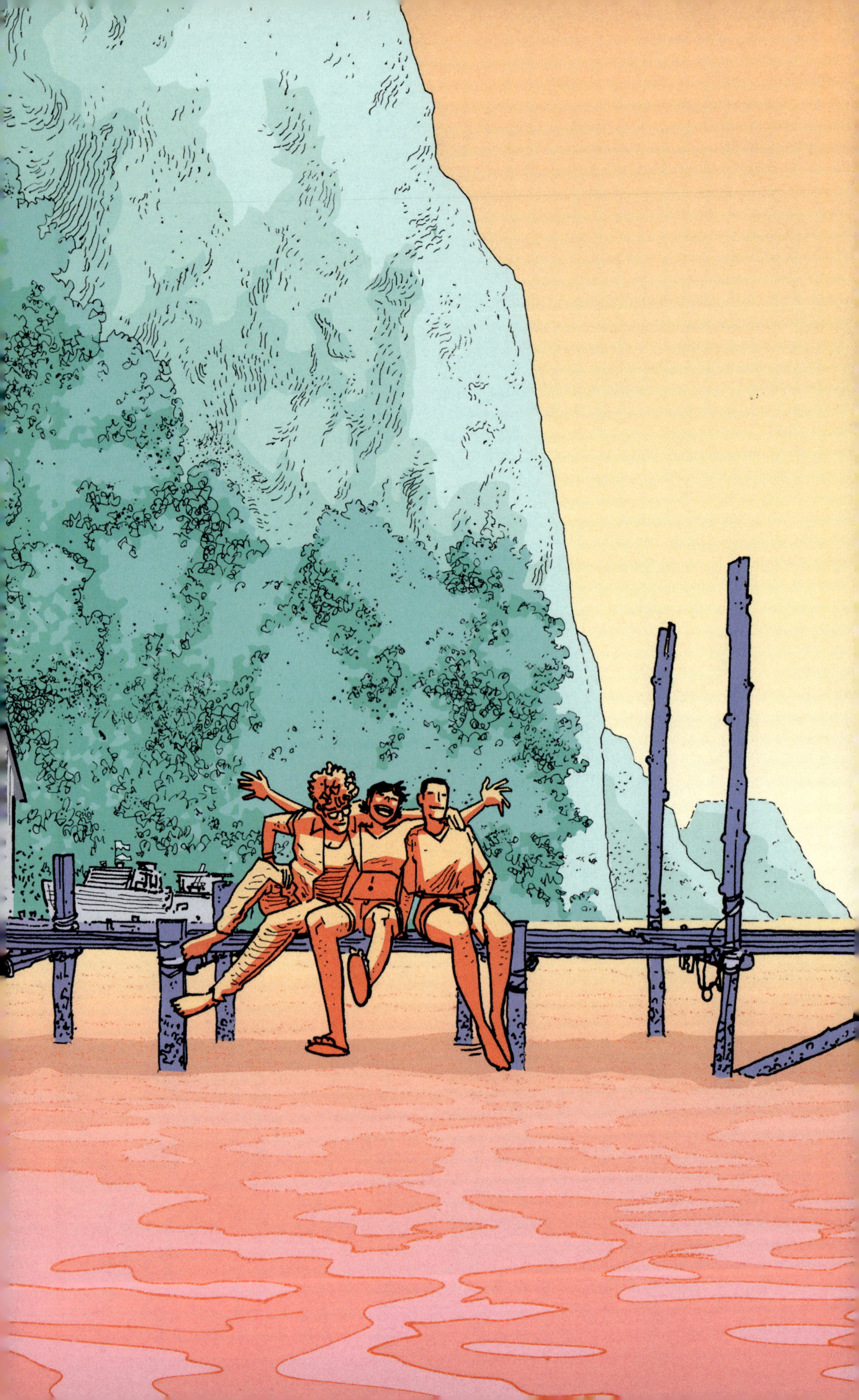

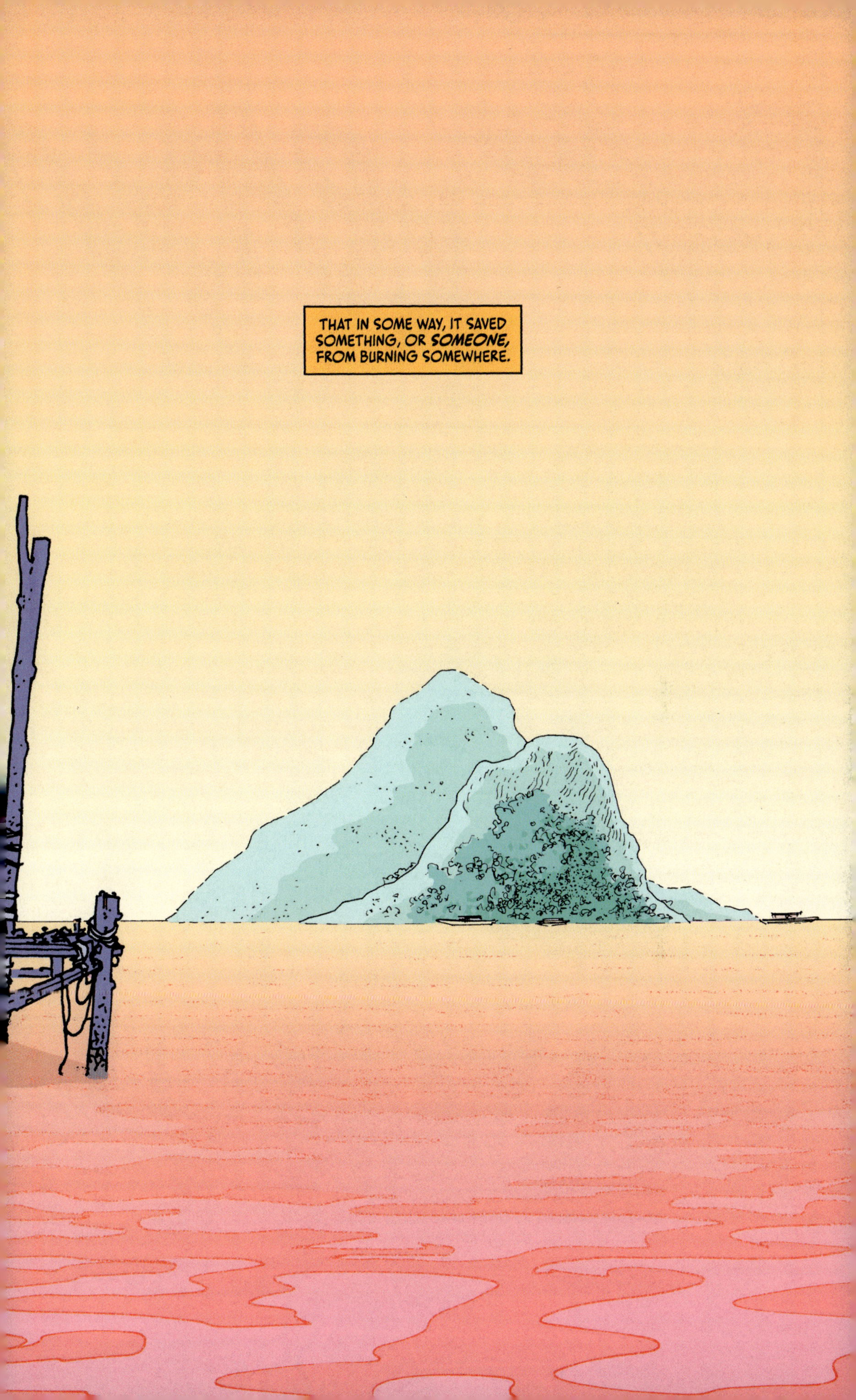
THAT IN SOME WAY, IT SAVED SOMETHING, OR ***SOMEONE,*** FROM BURNING SOMEWHERE.

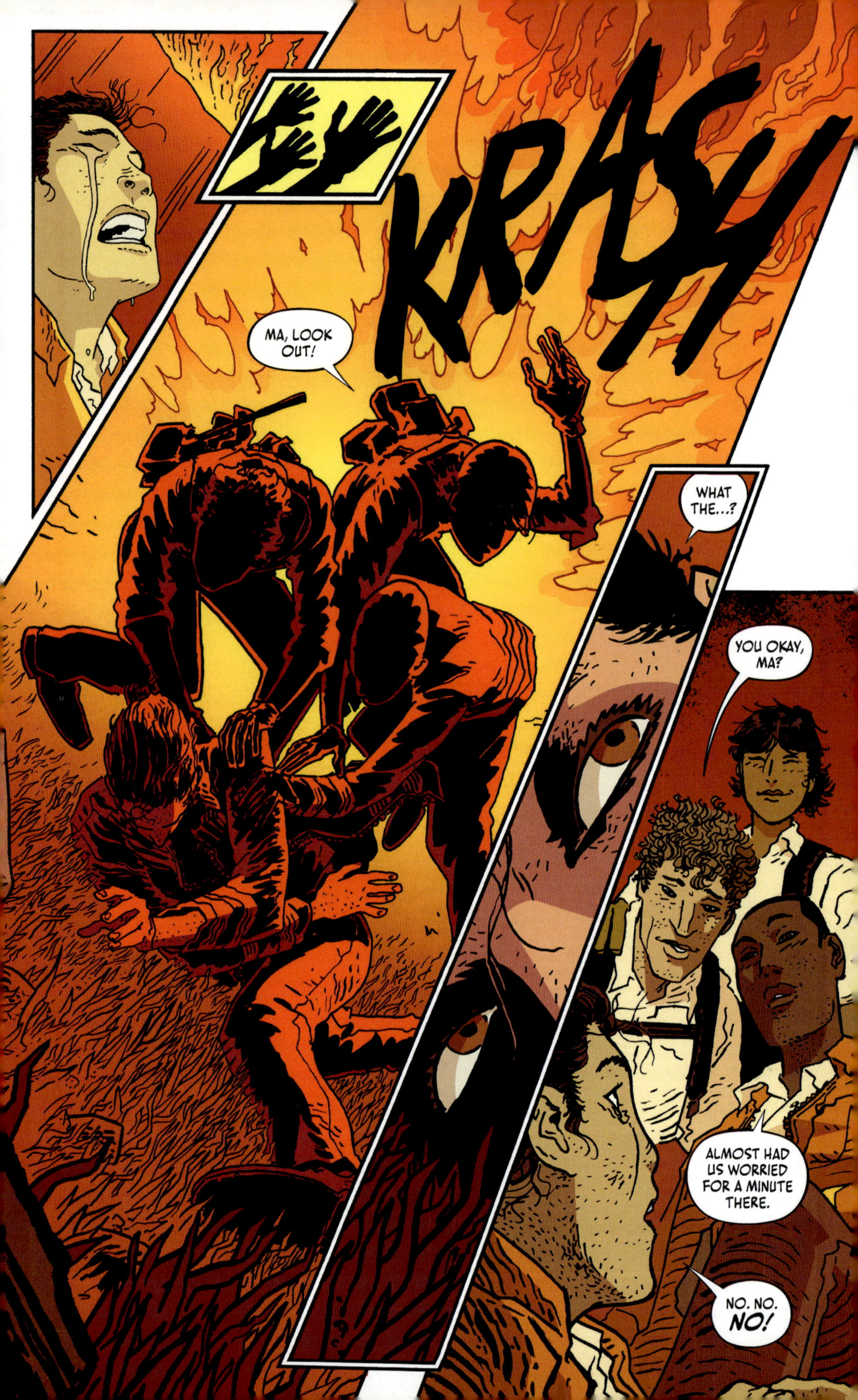
KRASH
MA, LOOK OUT!
WHAT THE...?
YOU OKAY, MA?
ALMOST HAD US WORRIED FOR A MINUTE THERE.
NO. NO. NO!

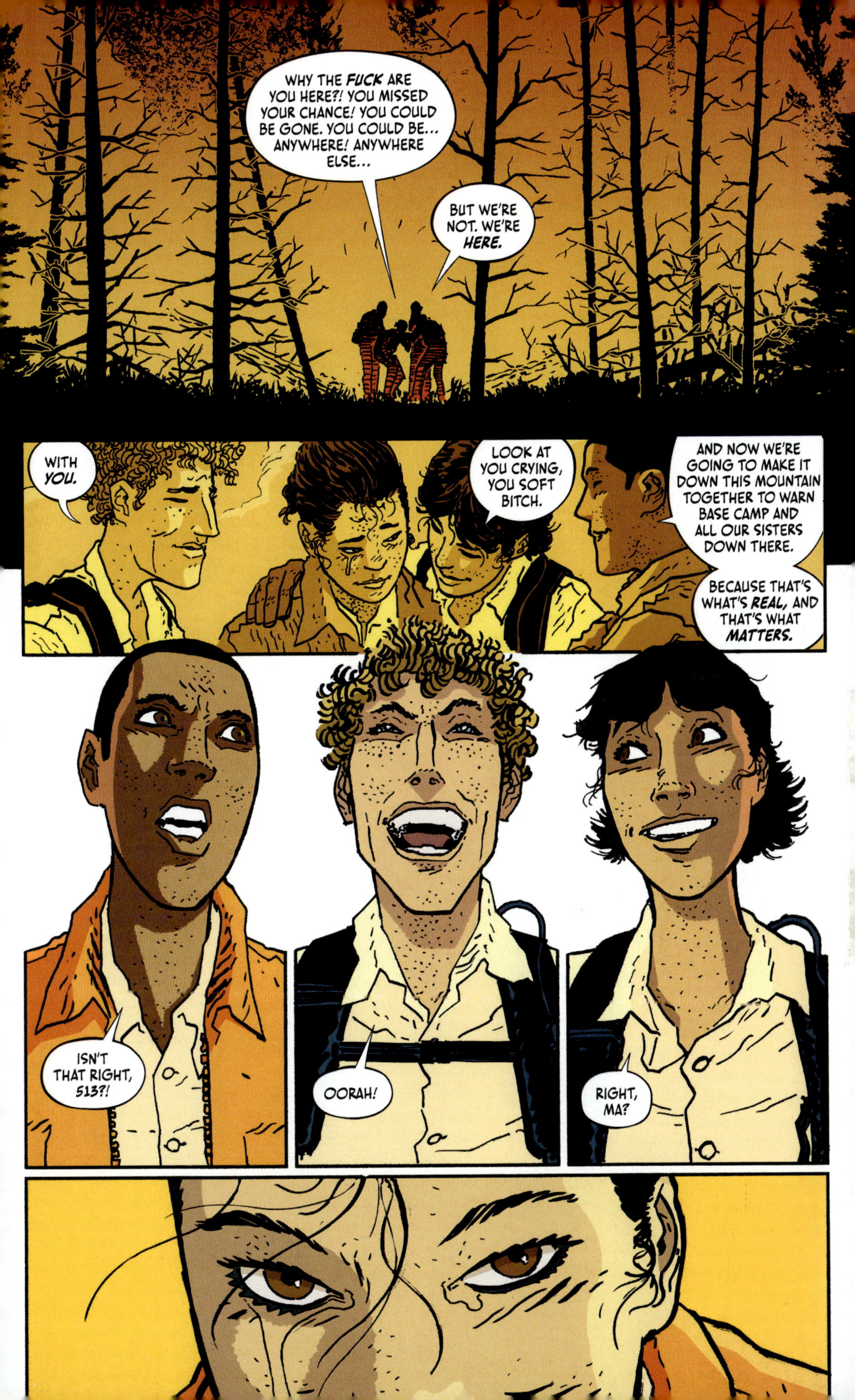
WHY THE FUCK ARE YOU HERE?! YOU MISSED YOUR CHANCE! YOU COULD BE GONE. YOU COULD BE... ANYWHERE! ANYWHERE ELSE...
BUT WE'RE NOT. WE'RE HERE.
WITH YOU.
LOOK AT YOU CRYING, YOU SOFT BITCH.
AND NOW WE'RE GOING TO MAKE IT DOWN THIS MOUNTAIN TOGETHER TO WARN BASE CAMP AND ALL OUR SISTERS DOWN THERE.
BECAUSE THAT'S WHAT'S REAL, AND THAT'S WHAT MATTERS.
ISN'T THAT RIGHT, 513?!
OORAH!
RIGHT, MA?

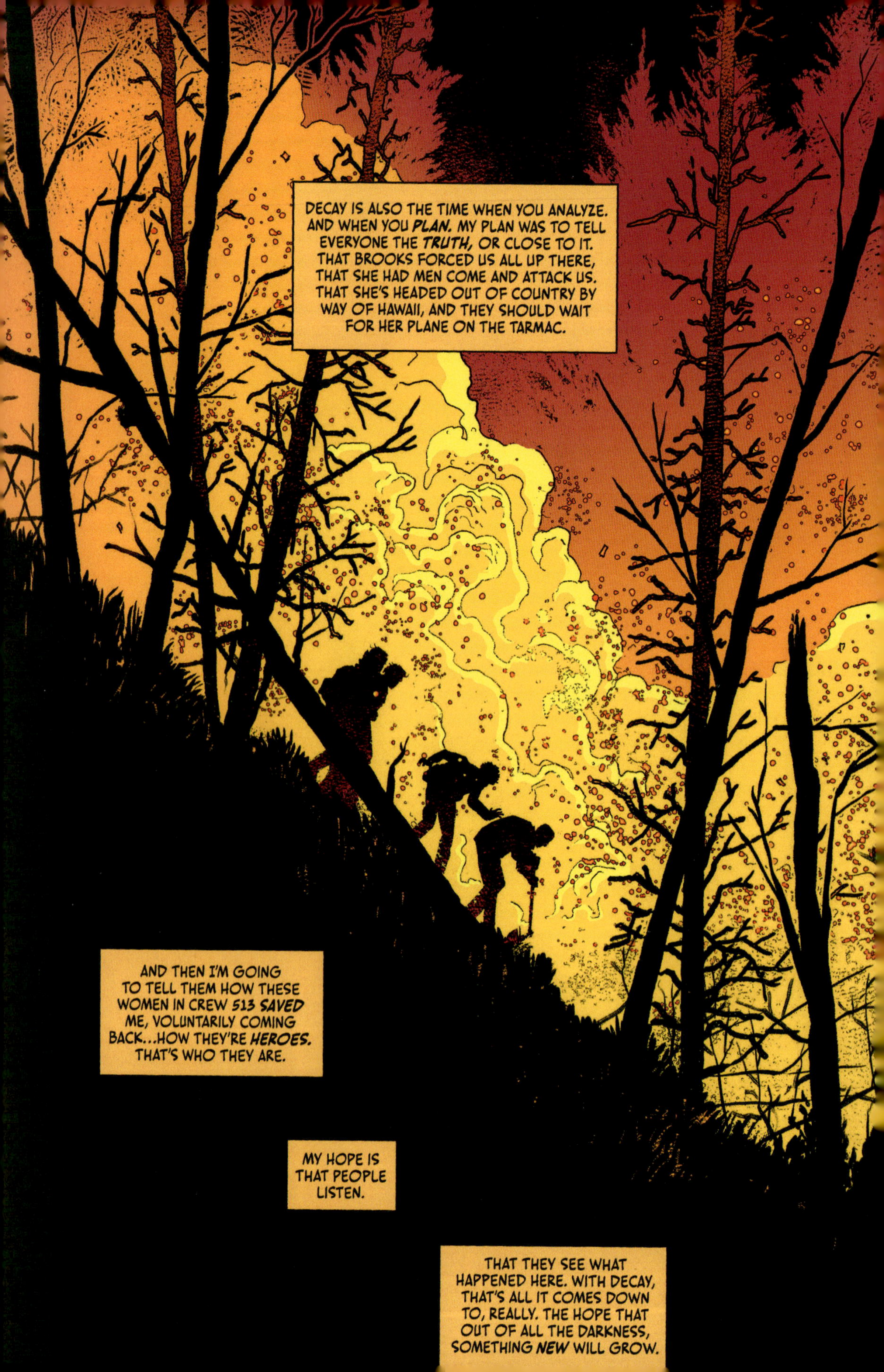
DECAY IS ALSO THE TIME WHEN YOU ANALYZE. AND WHEN YOU *PLAN.* MY PLAN WAS TO TELL EVERYONE THE *TRUTH,* OR CLOSE TO IT. THAT BROOKS FORCED US ALL UP THERE, THAT SHE HAD MEN COME AND ATTACK US. THAT SHE'S HEADED OUT OF COUNTRY BY WAY OF HAWAII, AND THEY SHOULD WAIT FOR HER PLANE ON THE TARMAC.
AND THEN I'M GOING TO TELL THEM HOW THESE WOMEN IN CREW 513 *SAVED* ME, VOLUNTARILY COMING BACK...HOW THEY'RE *HEROES.* THAT'S WHO THEY ARE.
MY HOPE IS THAT PEOPLE LISTEN.
THAT THEY SEE WHAT HAPPENED HERE. WITH DECAY, THAT'S ALL IT COMES DOWN TO, REALLY. THE HOPE THAT OUT OF ALL THE DARKNESS, SOMETHING *NEW* WILL GROW.

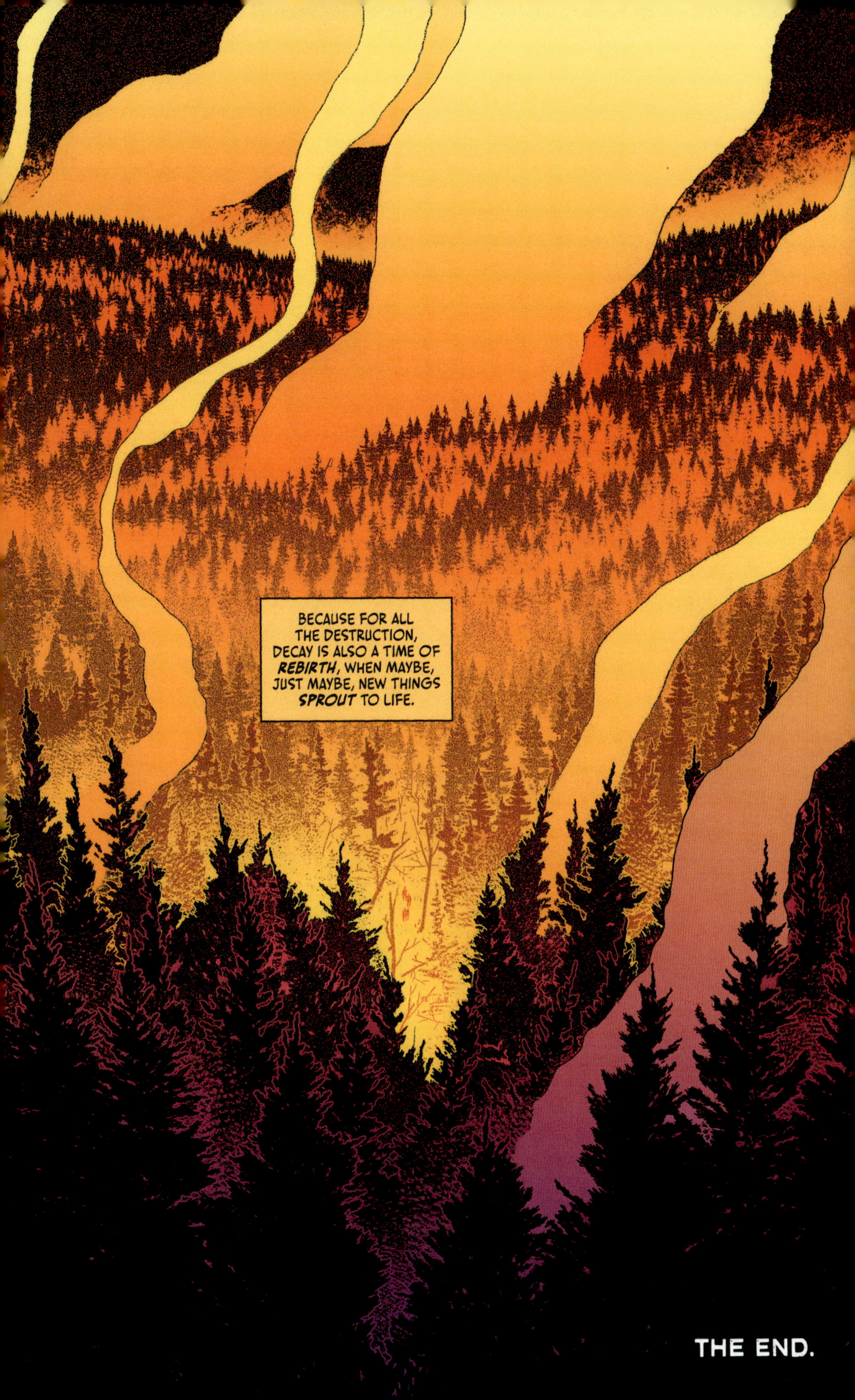
BECAUSE FOR ALL THE DESTRUCTION, DECAY IS ALSO A TIME OF *REBIRTH*, WHEN MAYBE, JUST MAYBE, NEW THINGS *SPROUT* TO LIFE.
THE END.

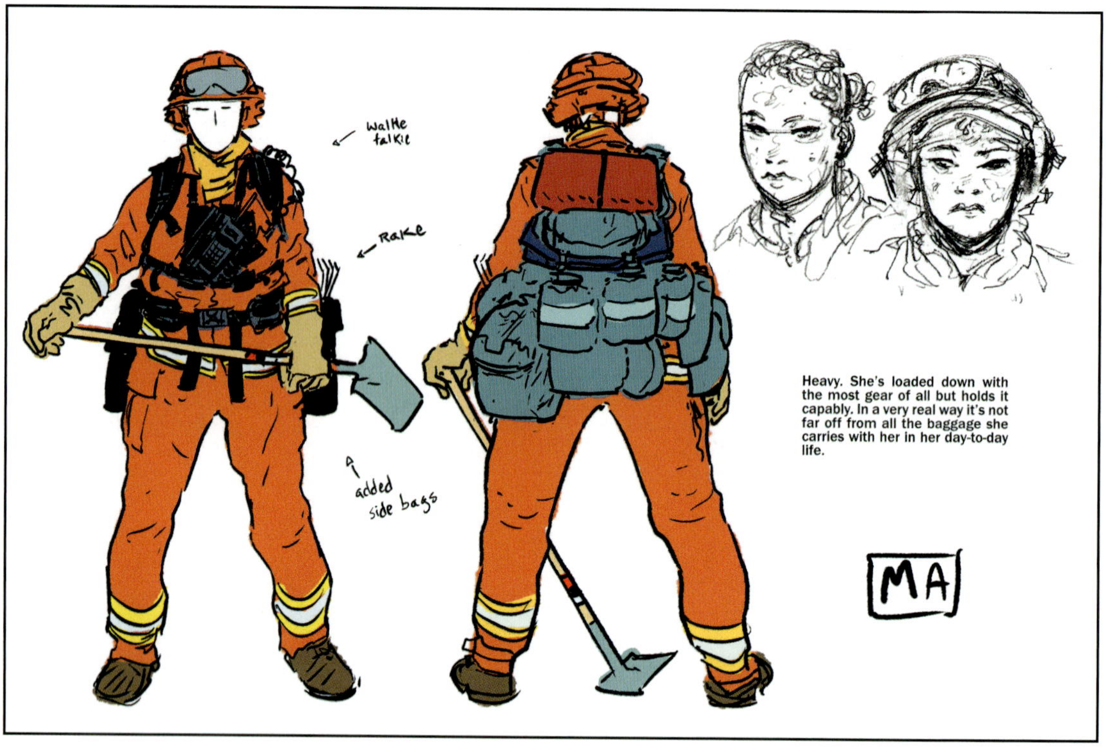
walkie talkie
Rake
added side bags
MA

Heavy. She's loaded down with the most gear of all but holds it capably. In a very real way it's not far off from all the baggage she carries with her in her day-to-day life.

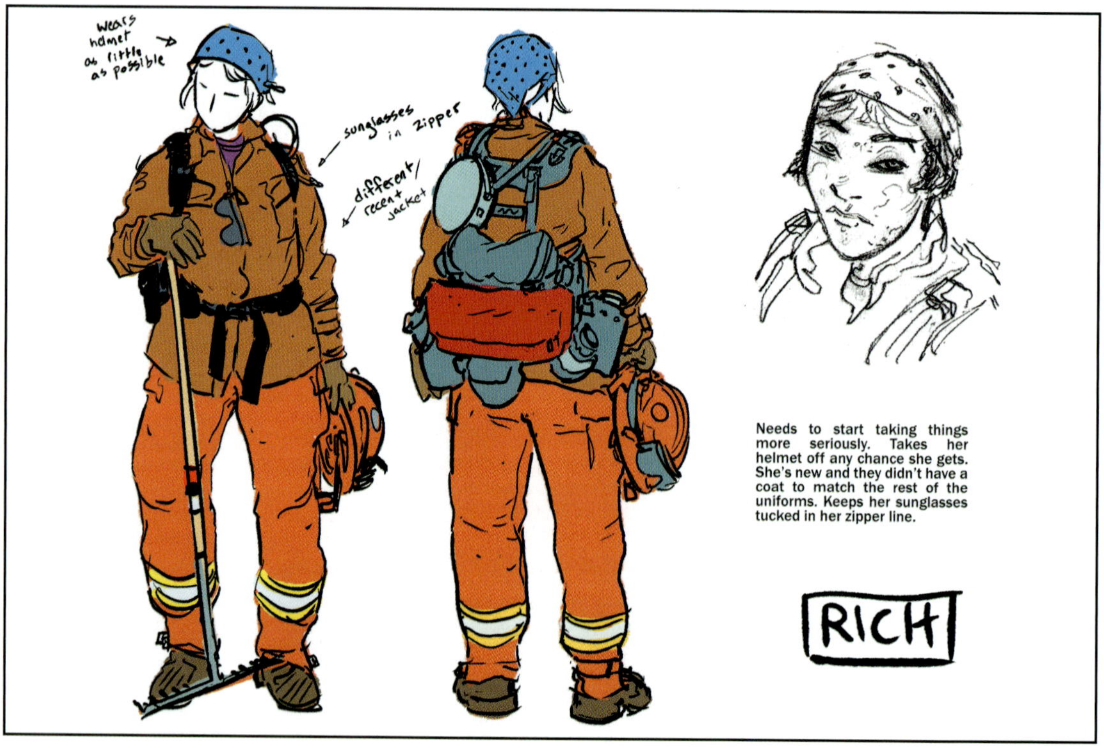
wears helmet as little as possible
sunglasses in zipper
different/recent jacket
RICH

Needs to start taking things more seriously. Takes her helmet off any chance she gets. She's new and they didn't have a coat to match the rest of the uniforms. Keeps her sunglasses tucked in her zipper line.

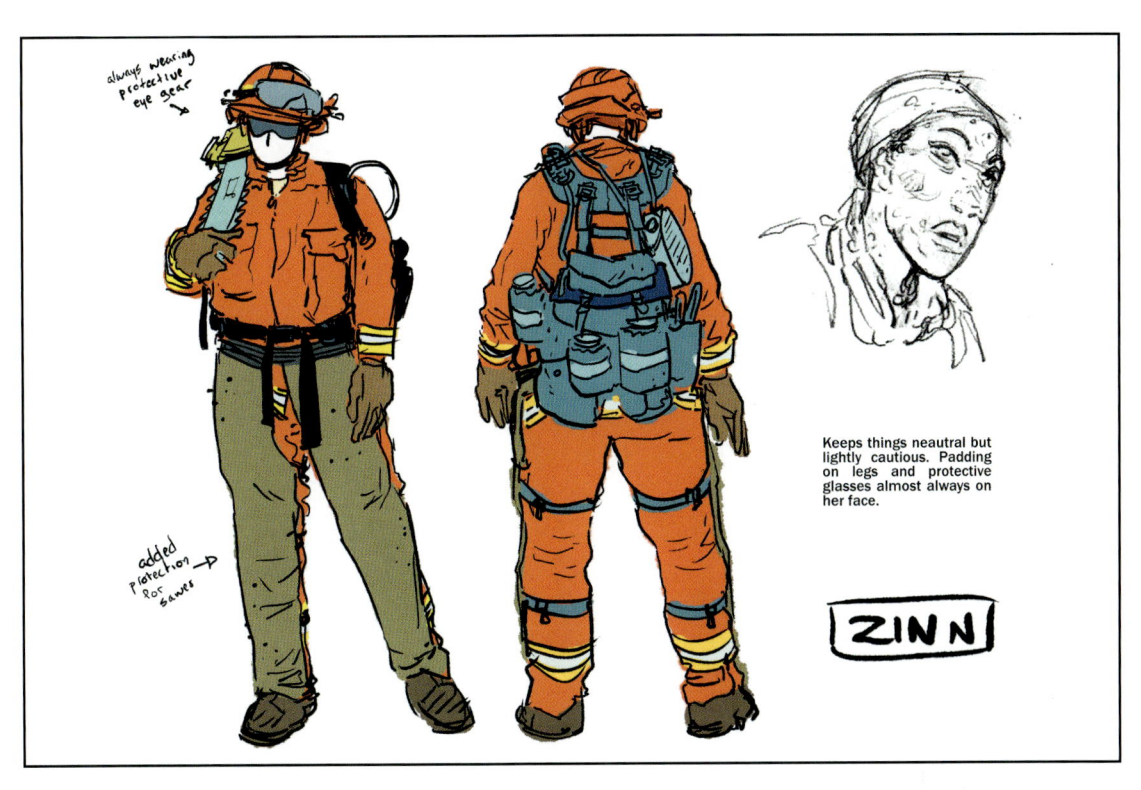

always wearing protective eye gear →

added protection for sawyer

Keeps things neautral but lightly cautious. Padding on legs and protective glasses almost always on her face.

ZINN

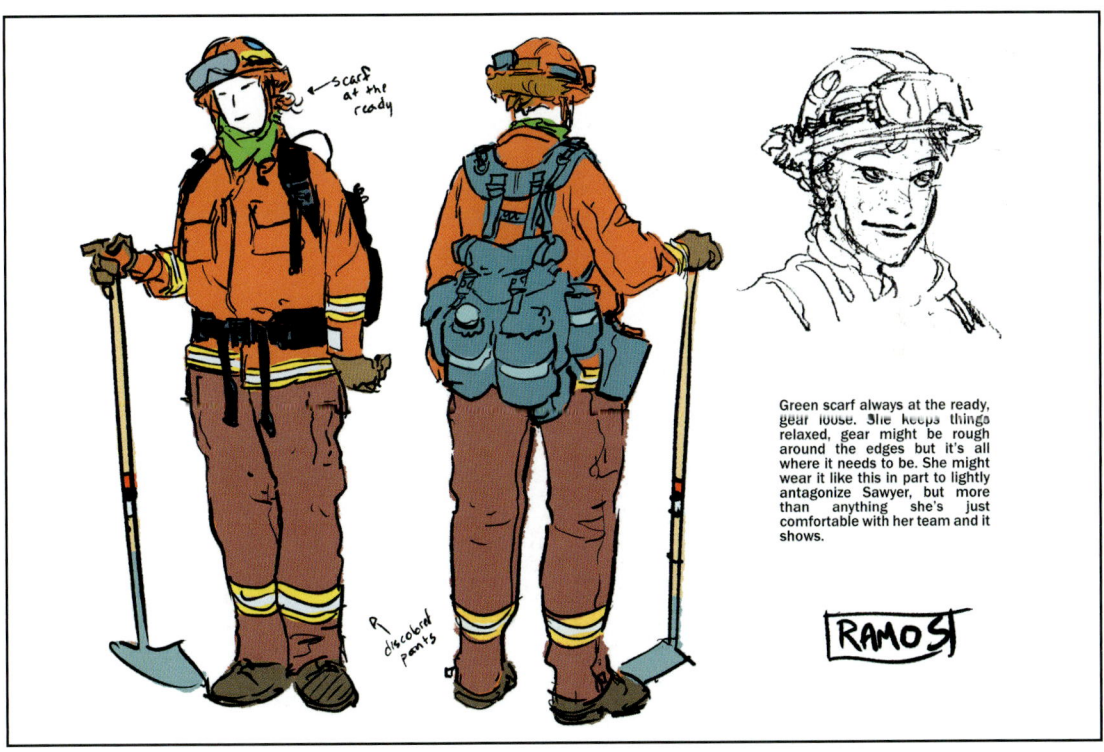

← scarf at the ready

discolored pants

Green scarf always at the ready, gear loose. She keeps things relaxed, gear might be rough around the edges but it's all where it needs to be. She might wear it like this in part to lightly antagonize Sawyer, but more than anything she's just comfortable with her team and it shows.

RAMOS

CHARACTER DESIGNS BY **HAYDEN SHERMAN**

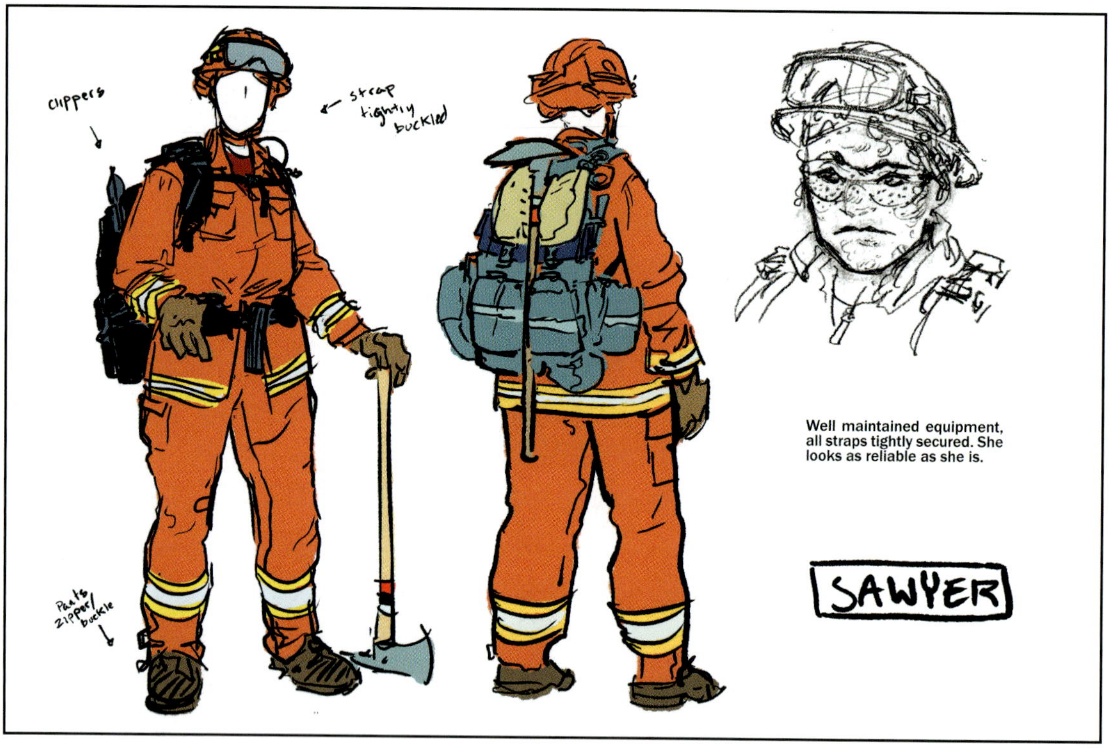
clippers
strap tightly buckled
Pants zipper/buckle
Well maintained equipment, all straps tightly secured. She looks as reliable as she is.
SAWYER

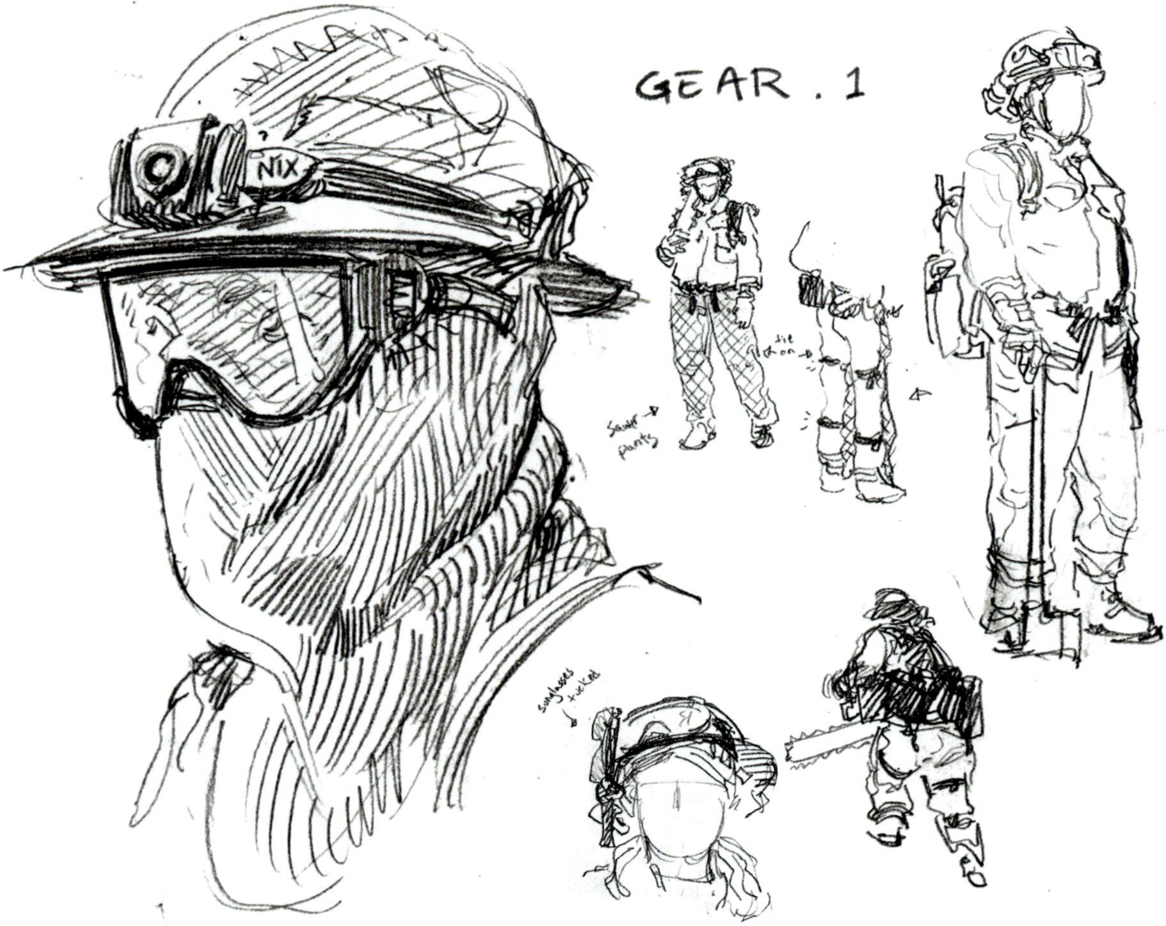
GEAR . 1
NIX
Sawyer pants
tie on
sunglasses tucked

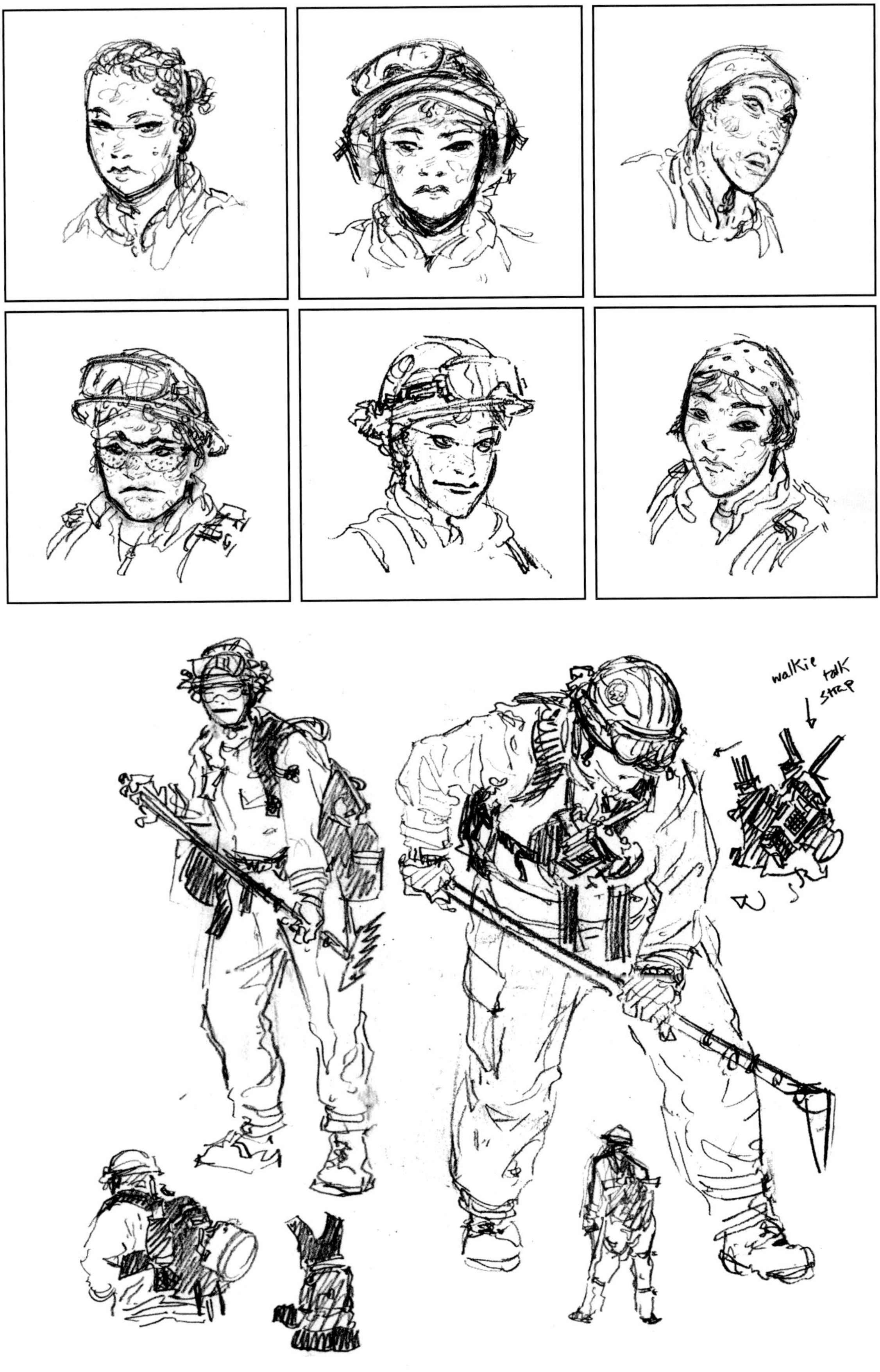
walkie talk STRP

DESIGNS BY HAYDEN SHERMAN

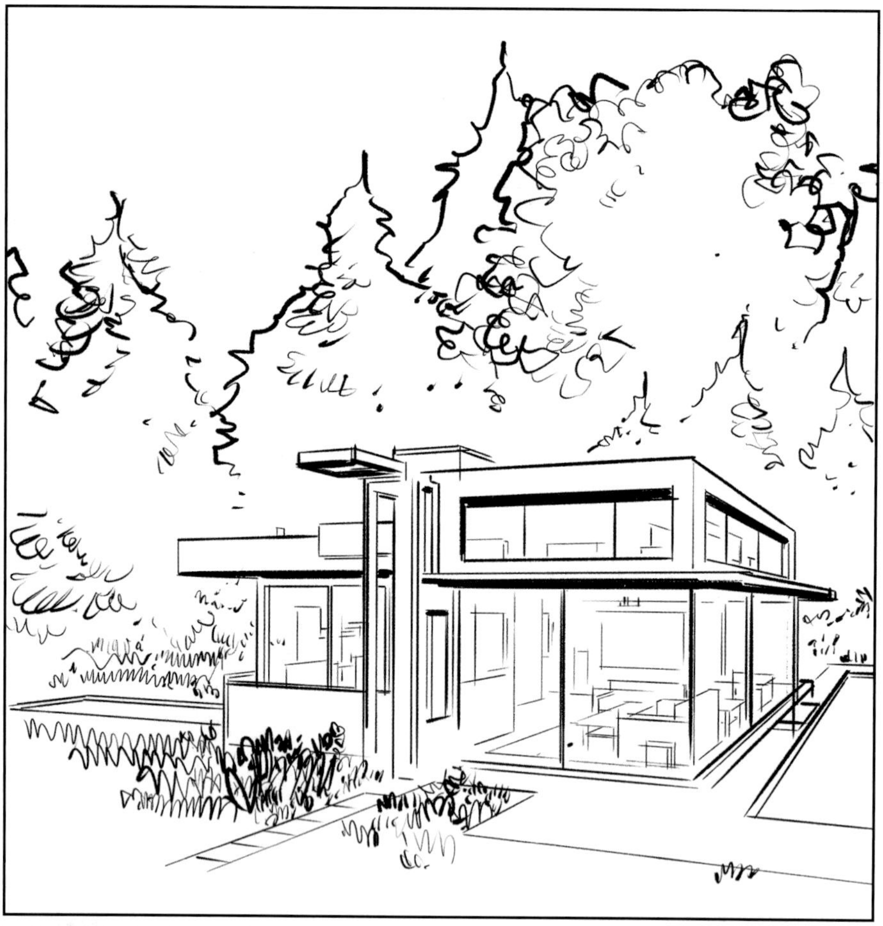

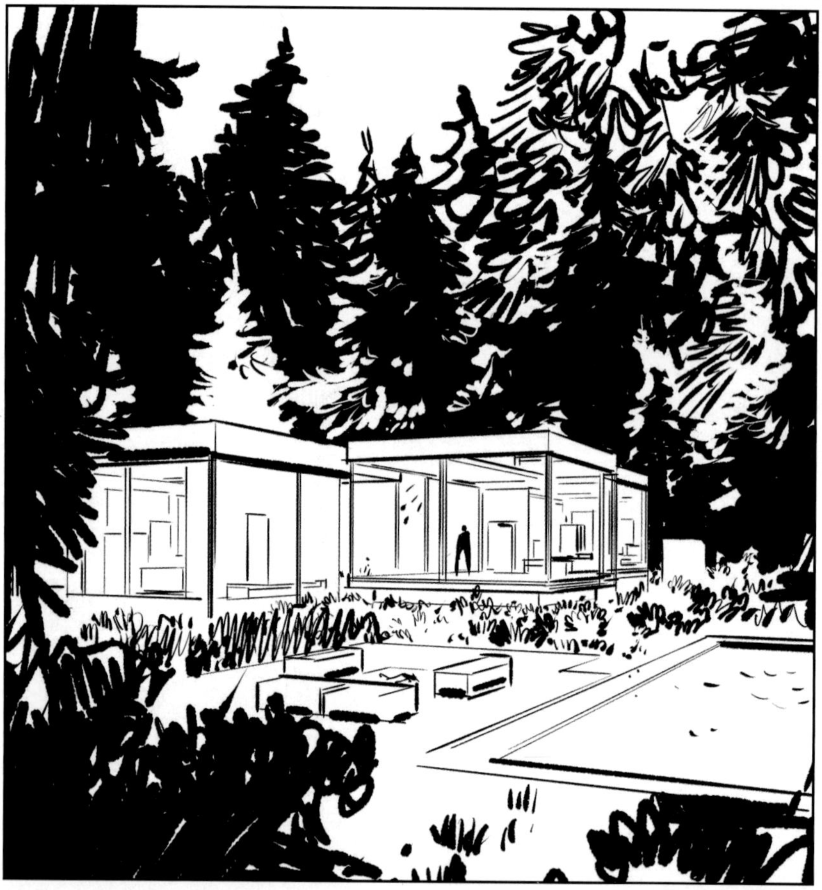

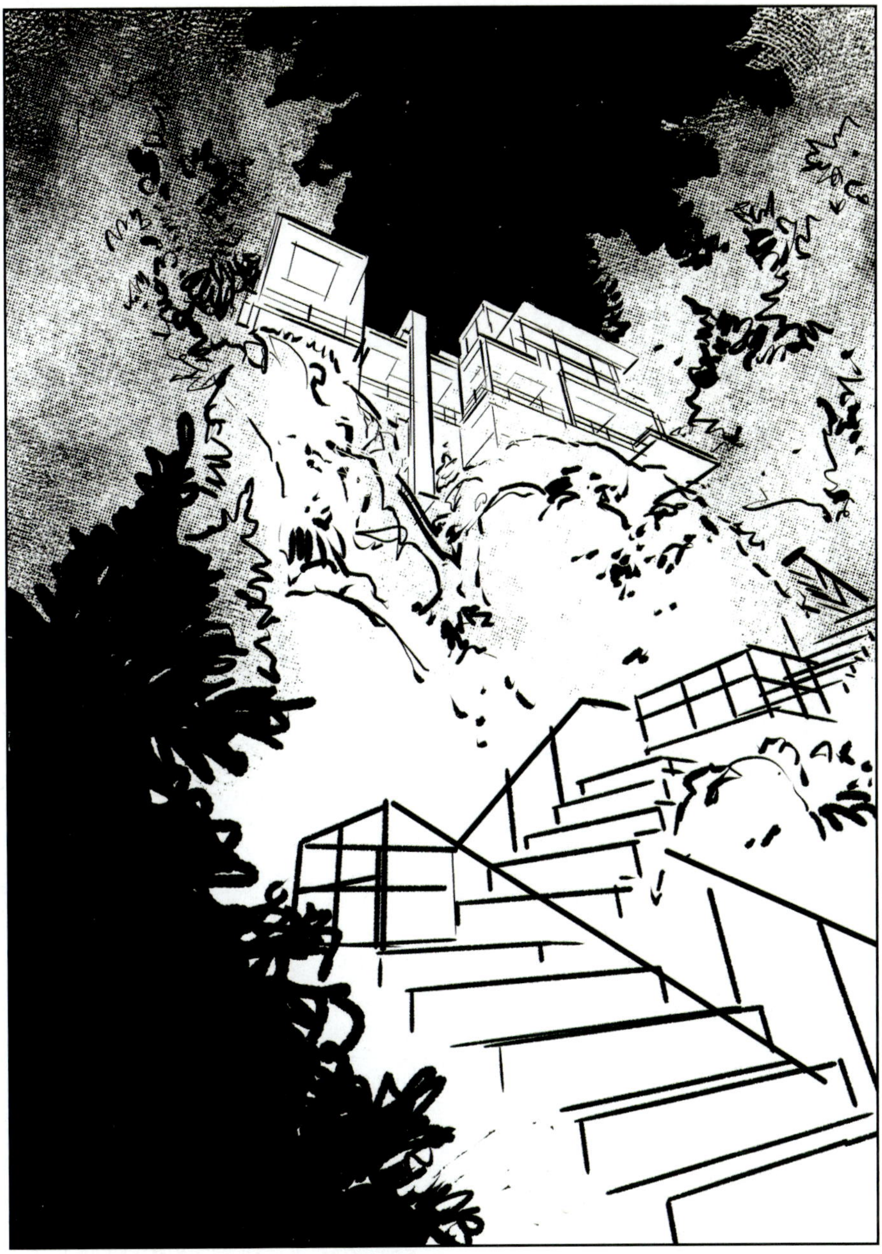

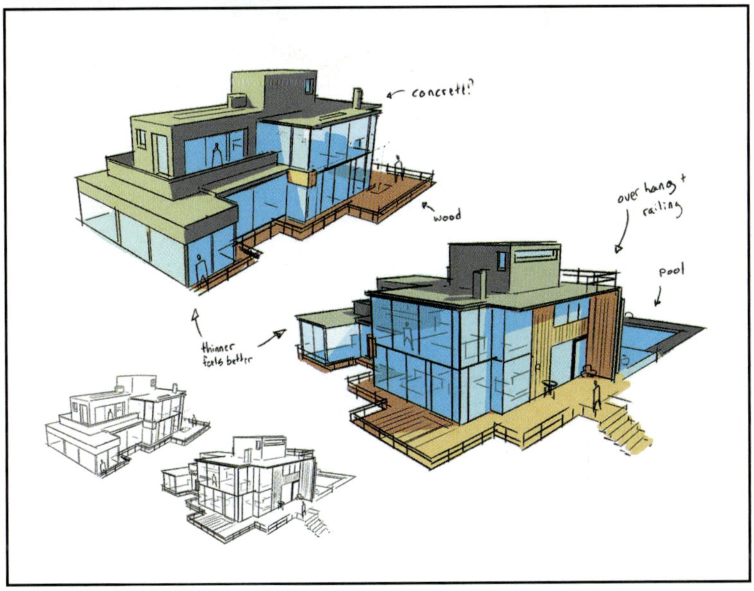
concrete?
wood
over hang +
railing
pool
thinner
feels better

UNUSED COVER CONCEPTS BY **HAYDEN SHERMAN**

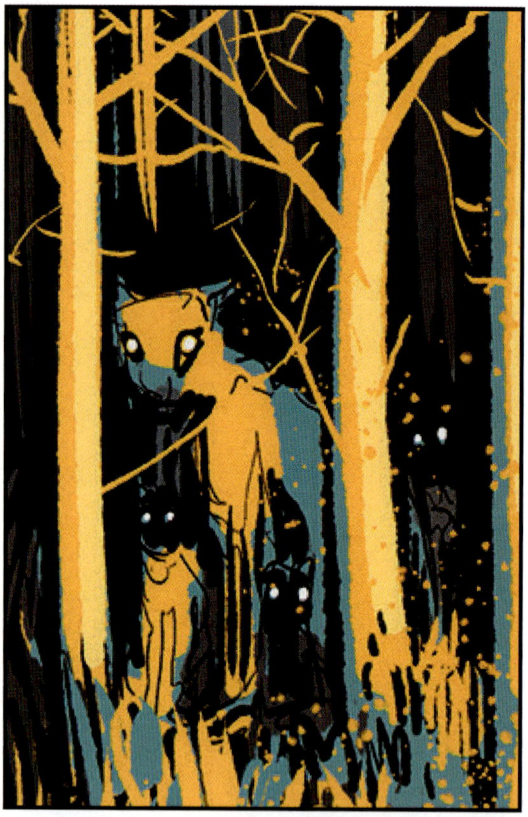

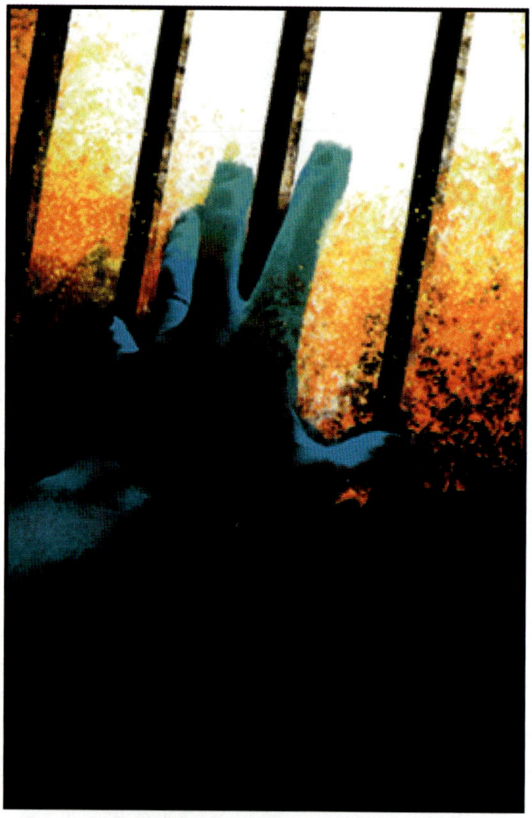

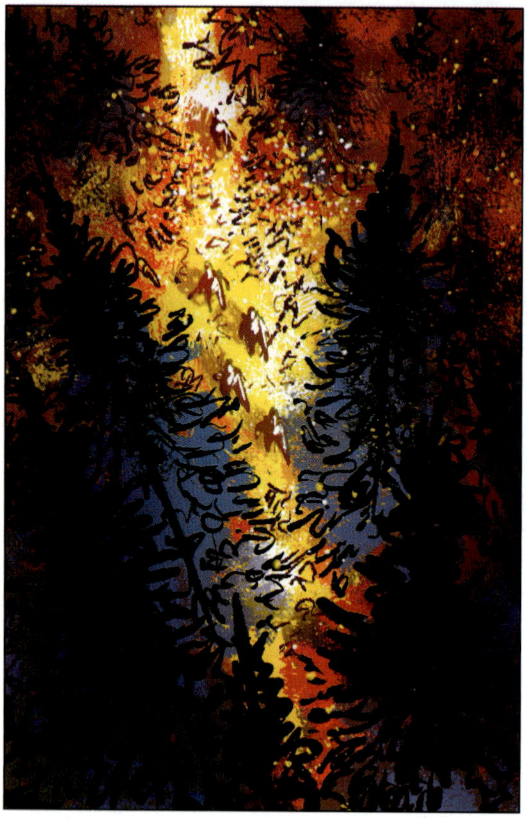

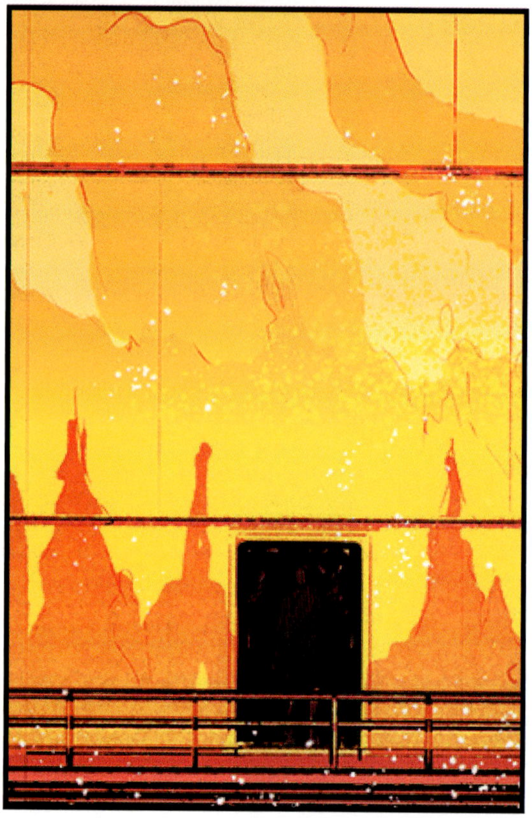

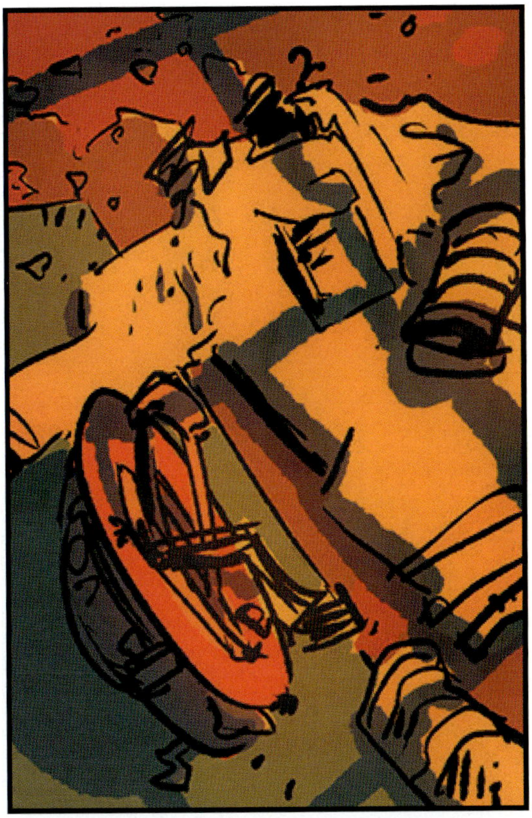
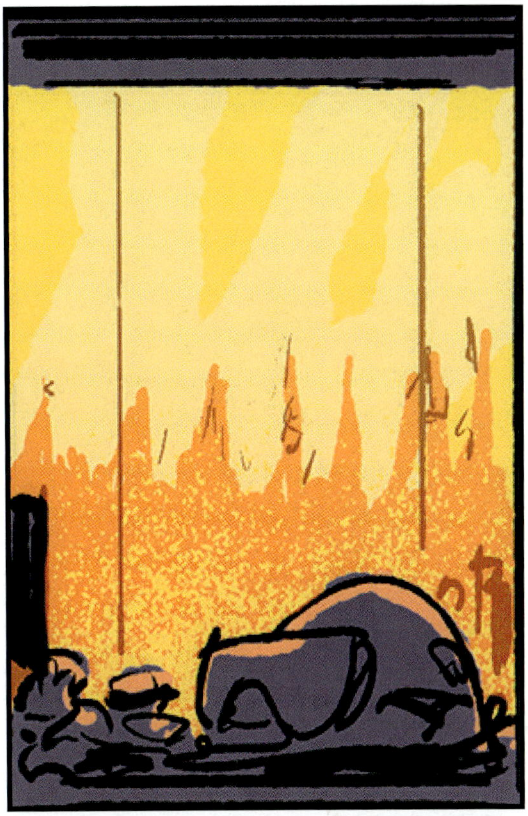
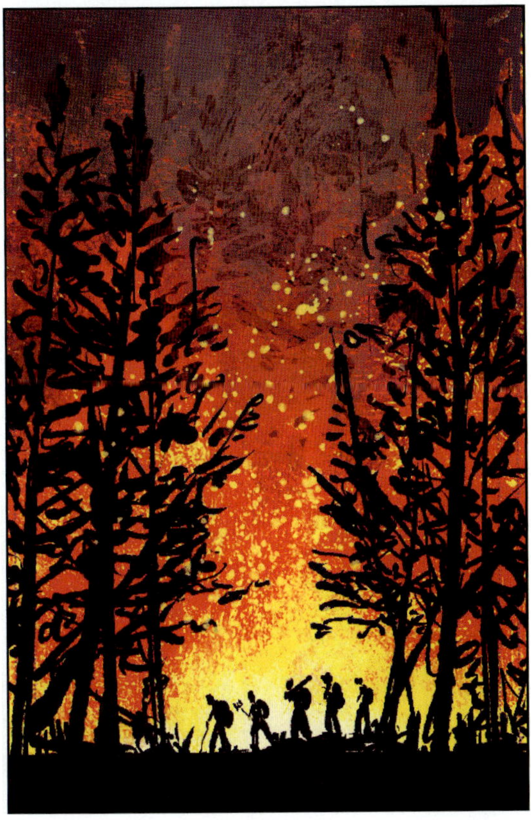
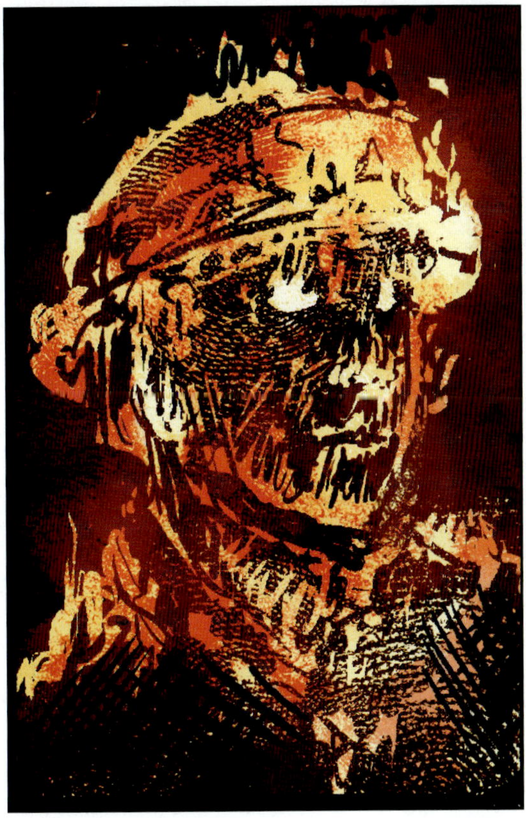

UNUSED COVER CONCEPT BY **HAYDEN SHERMAN**

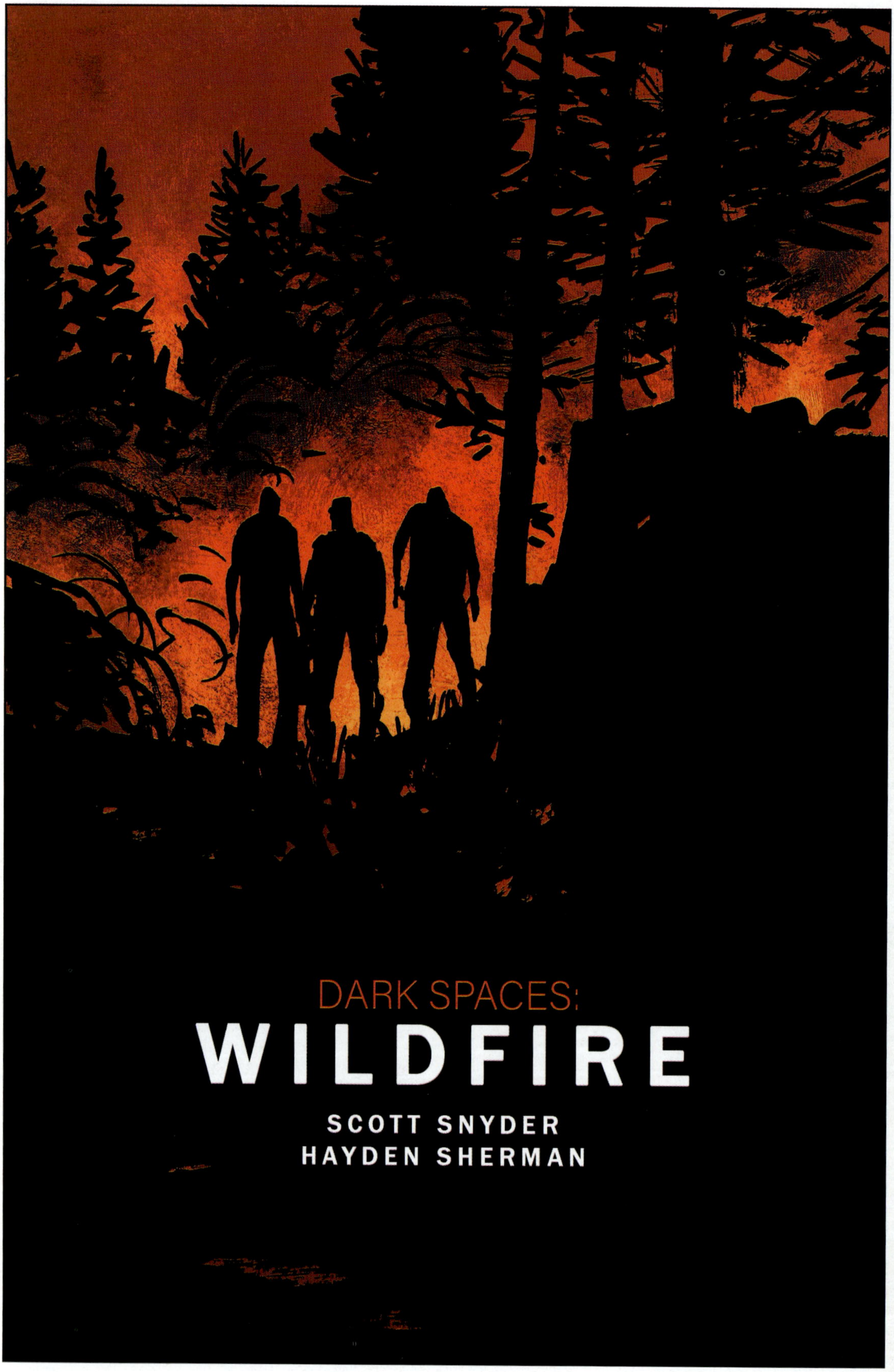

DARK SPACES:
WILDFIRE
SCOTT SNYDER
HAYDEN SHERMAN

DARK SPACES: WILDFIRE EXCLUSIVE COVER BY **HAYDEN SHERMAN**

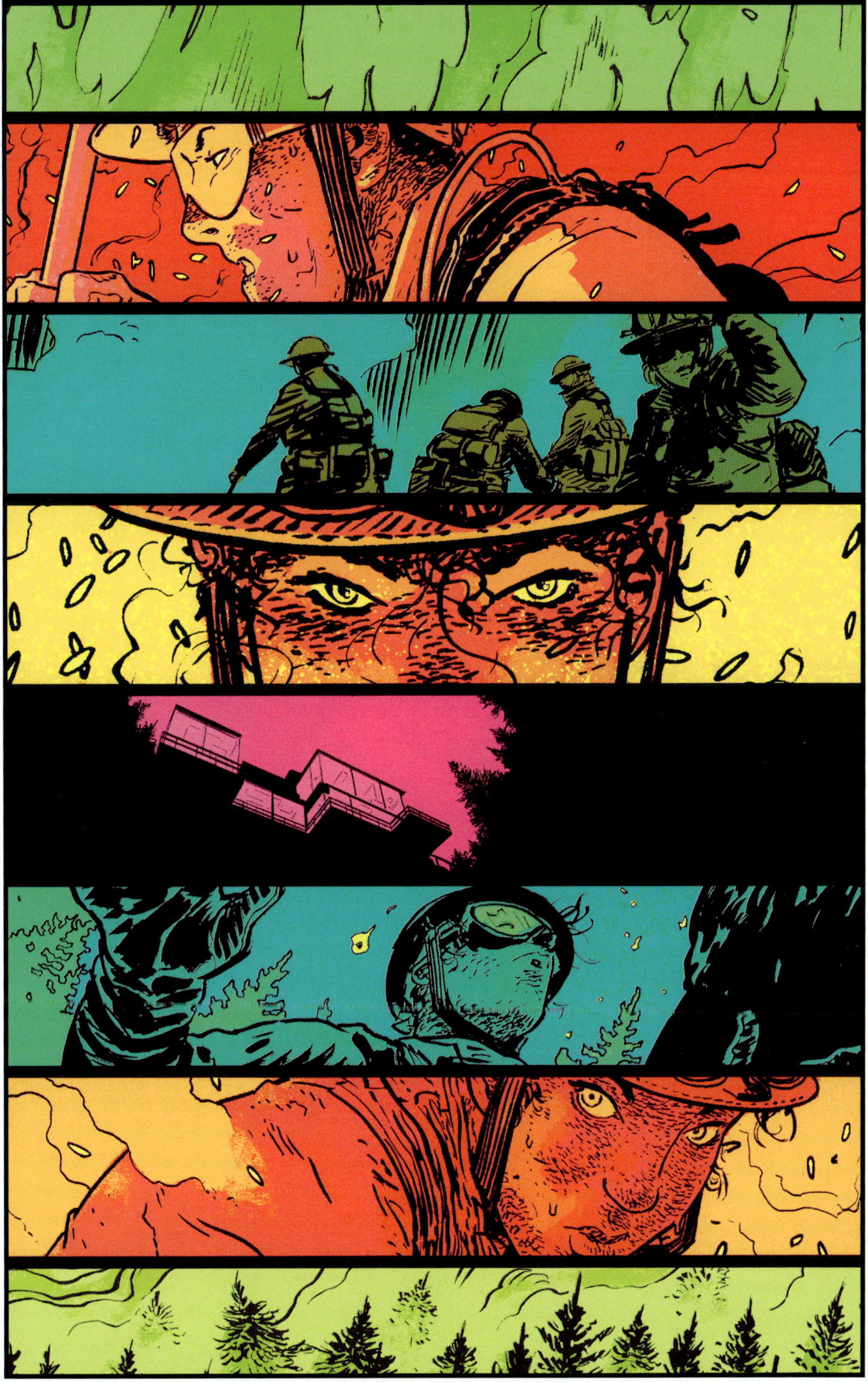

DARK SPACES: WILDFIRE #1 VARIANT COVER BY ANDREA SORRENTINO

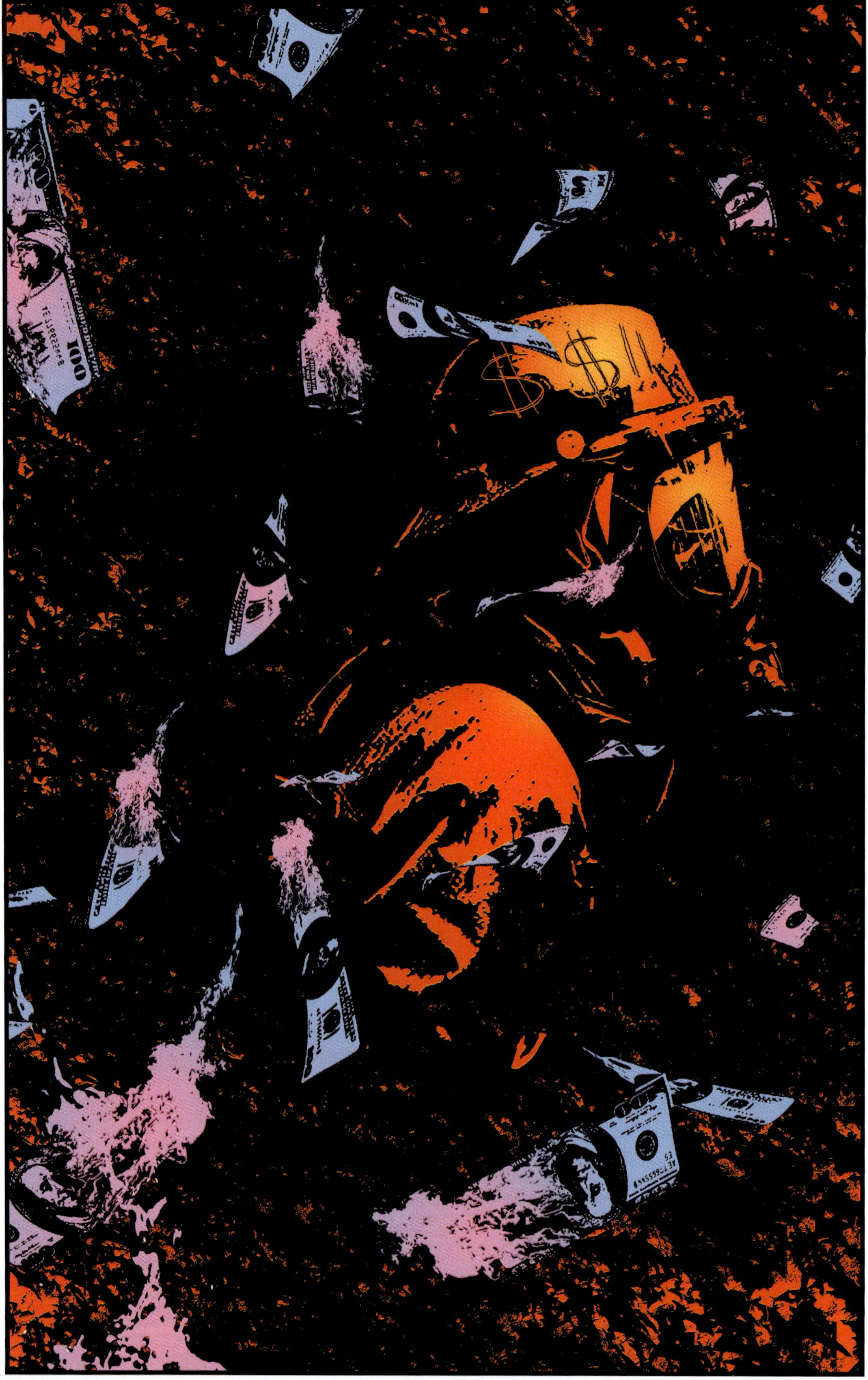

DARK SPACES: WILDFIRE #2 VARIANT COVER BY **ANDREA SORRENTINO** COLORS BY **JORDIE BELLAIRE**

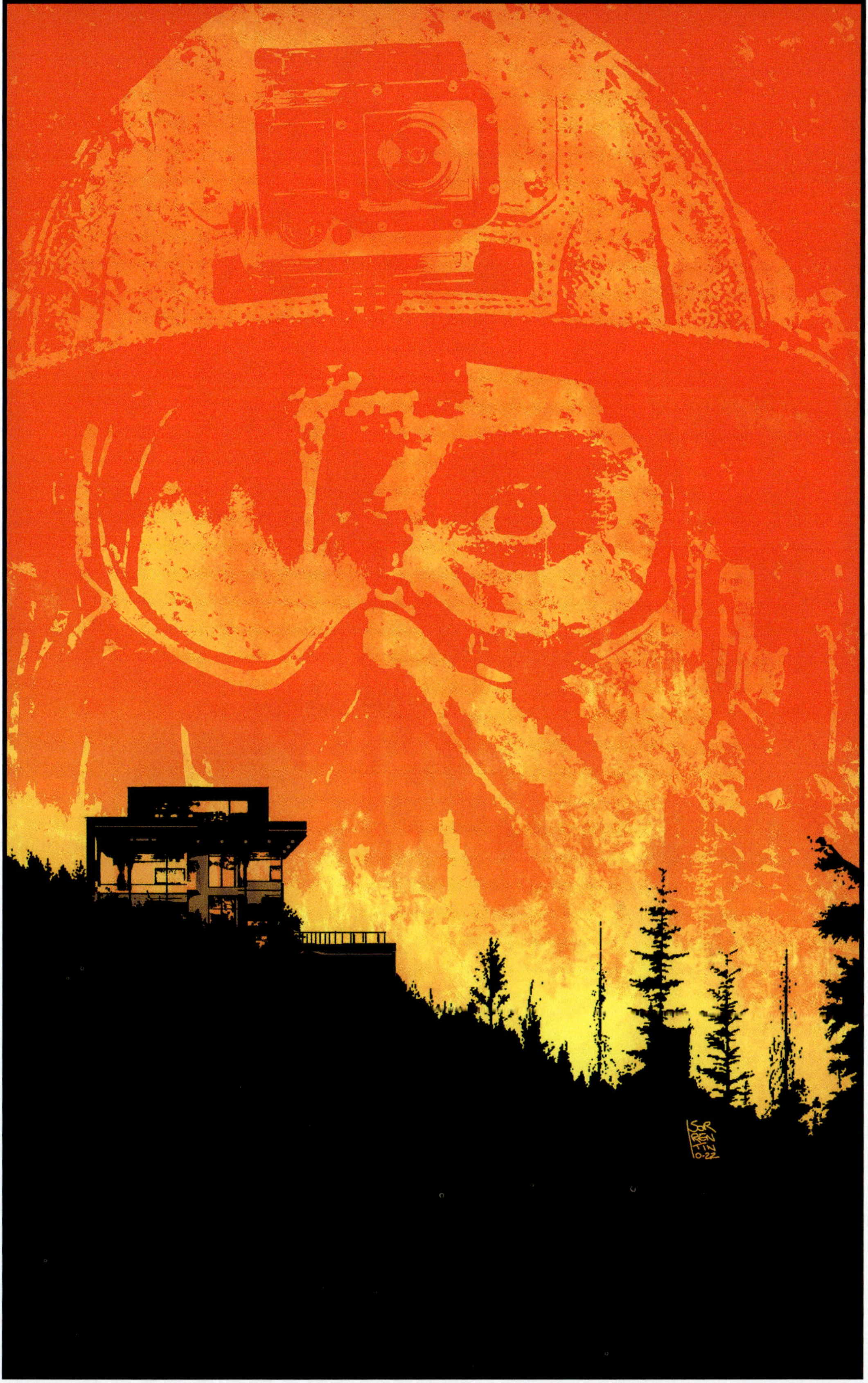
SORRENTINO 10-22

DARK SPACES: WILDFIRE #3 VARIANT COVER BY **ANDREA SORRENTINO** COLORS BY **JORDIE BELLAIRE**

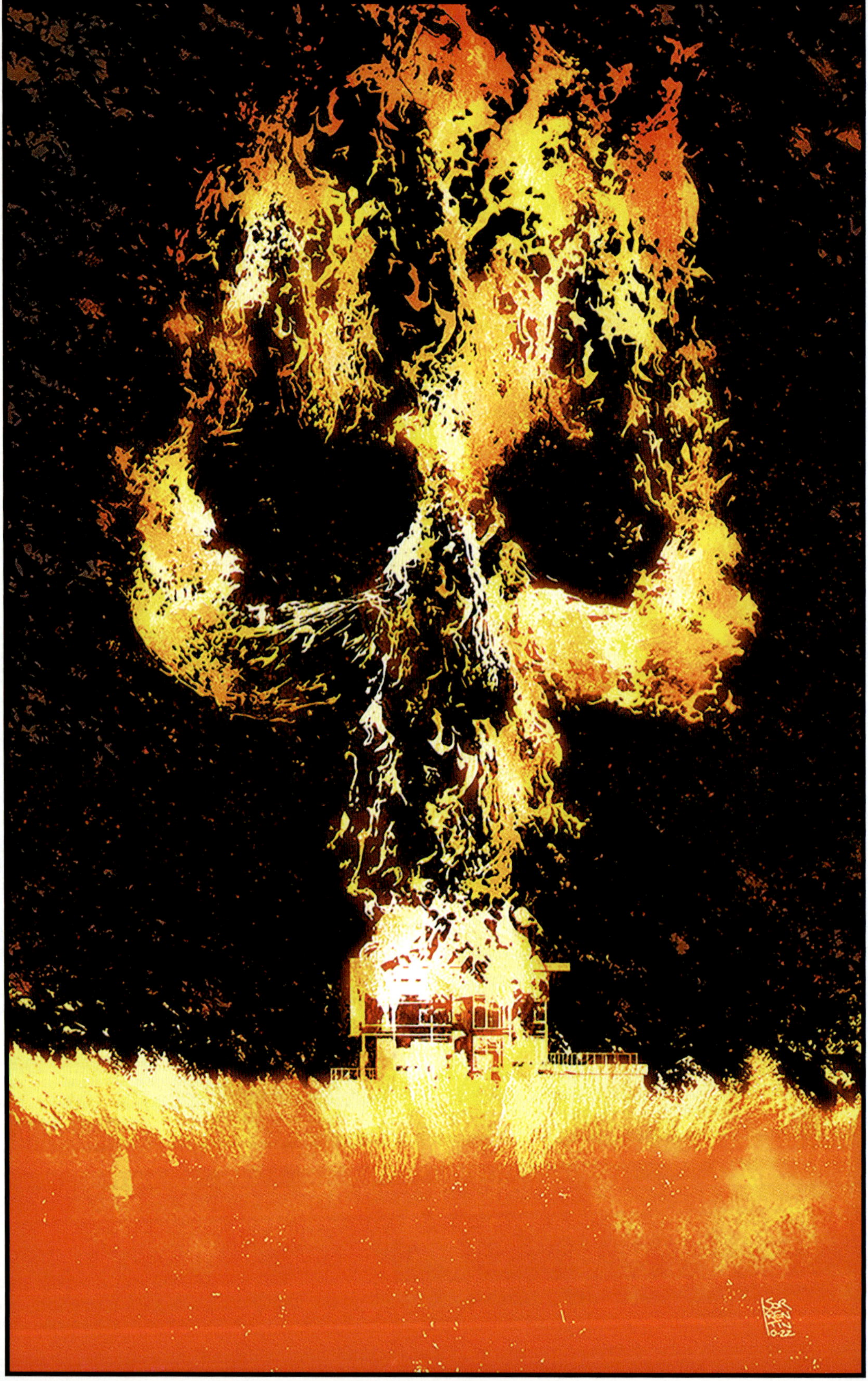

DARK SPACES: WILDFIRE #4 VARIANT COVER BY **ANDREA SORRENTINO** COLORS BY **JORDIE BELLAIRE**

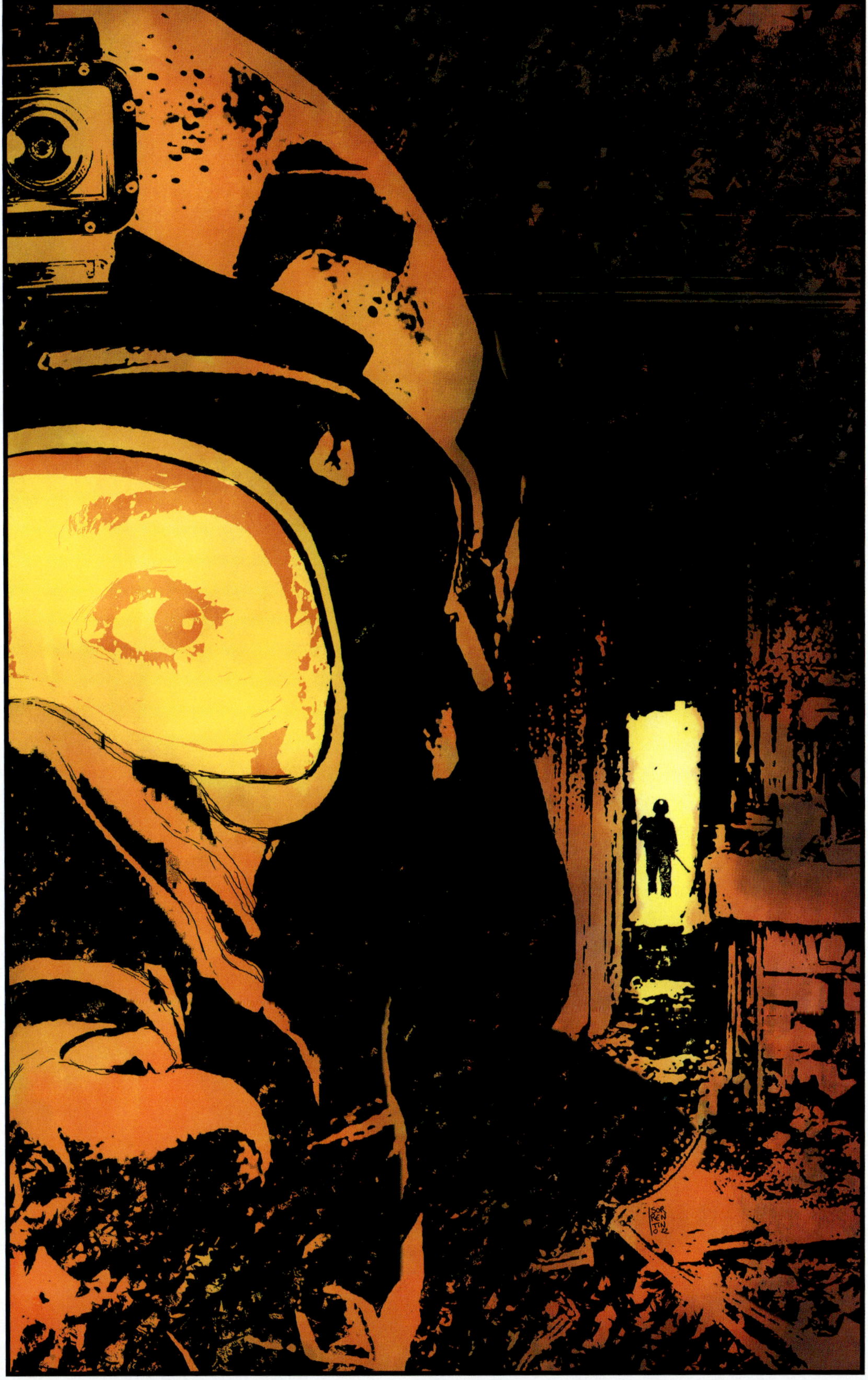

DARK SPACES: WILDFIRE #5 VARIANT COVER BY **ANDREA SORRENTINO** COLORS BY **JORDIE BELLAIRE**

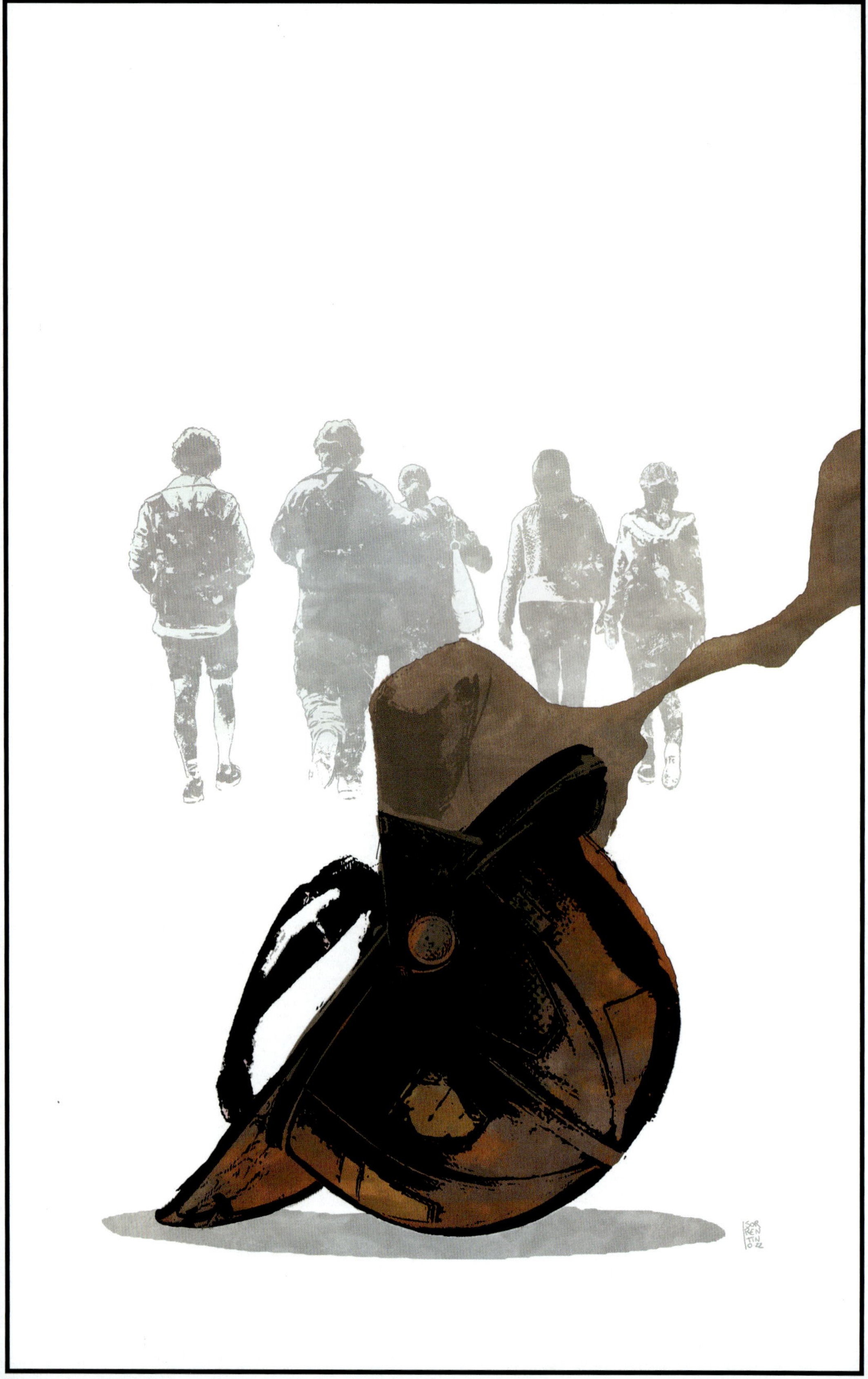

DARK SPACES: WILDFIRE #1 VARIANT COVER BY
LIANA KANGAS

DARK SPACES: WILDFIRE #1 VARIANT COVER BY
TULA LOTAY

DARK SPACES: WILDFIRE #2 VARIANT COVER BY
MORGAN BEEM

DARK SPACES: WILDFIRE #2 VARIANT COVER BY
MARIA LLOVET

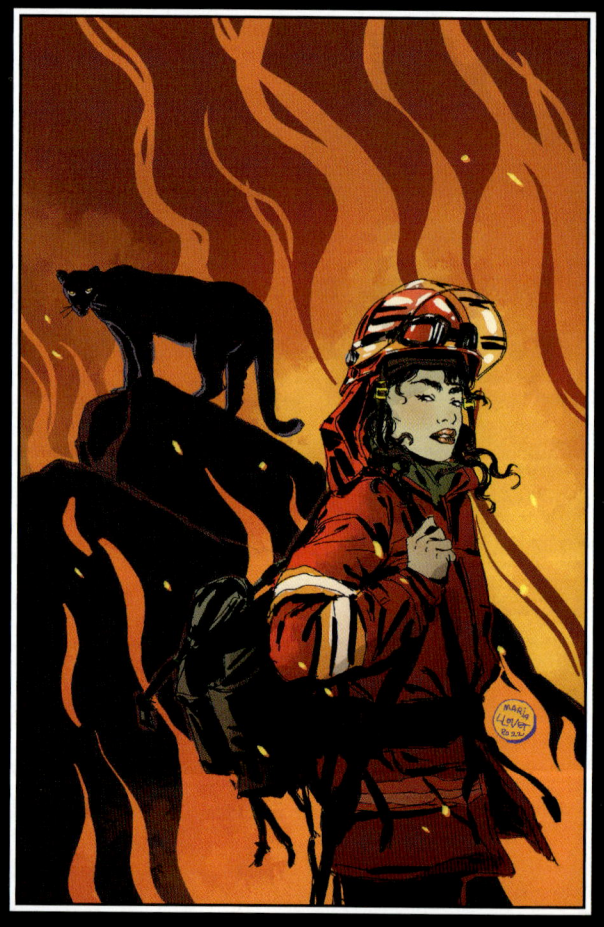

DARK SPACES: WILDFIRE #3 VARIANT COVER BY
GABRIEL RODRÍGUEZ
COLORS BY **JAY FOTOS**

DARK SPACES: WILDFIRE #3 VARIANT COVER BY
MOLLY MURAKAMI

DARK SPACES: WILDFIRE #4 VARIANT COVER BY
ANGEL HERNANDEZ
COLORS BY **RONDA PATTISON**

DARK SPACES: WILDFIRE #4 VARIANT COVER BY
LISA STERLE

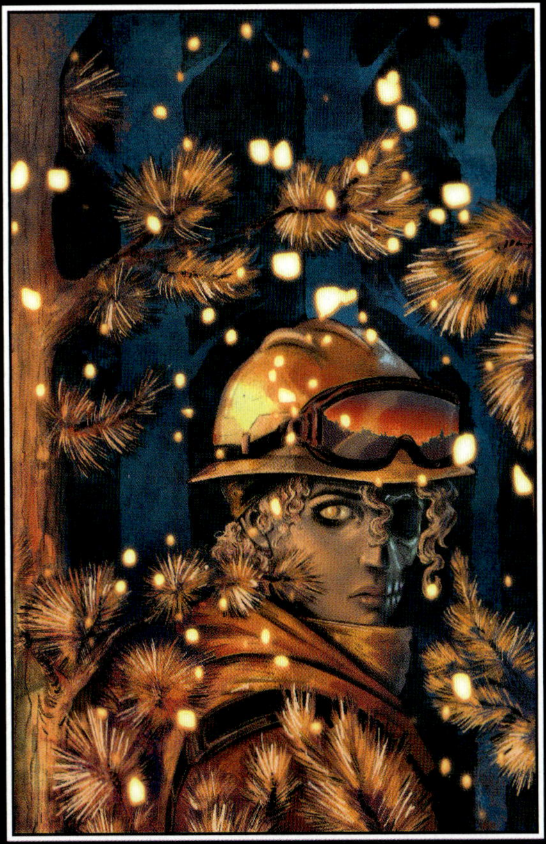

DARK SPACES: WILDFIRE #5 VARIANT COVER BY
SKYLAR PATRIDGE

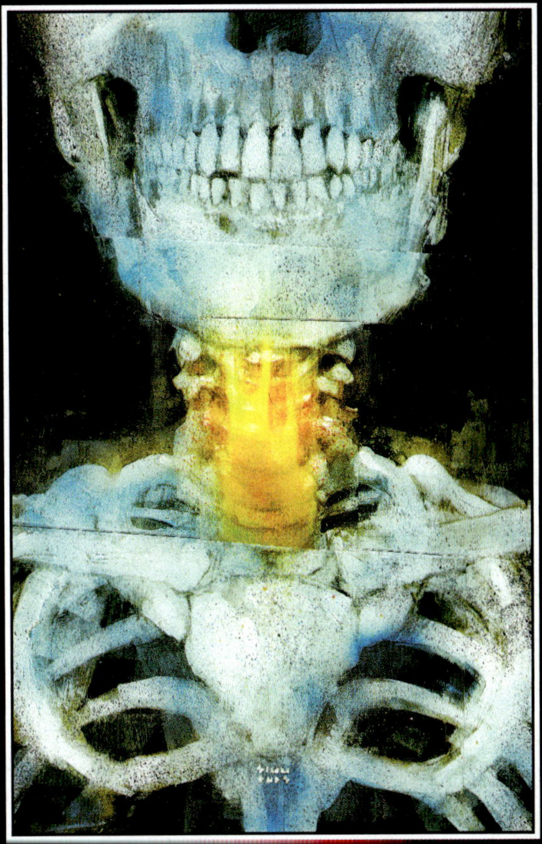

DARK SPACES: WILDFIRE #5 VARIANT COVER BY
MARTIN SIMMONDS

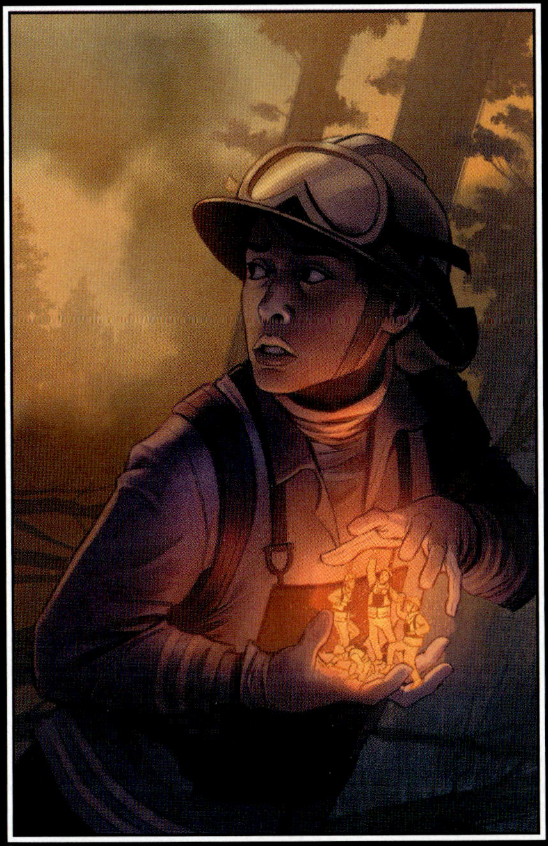

DARK SPACES: WILDFIRE #5 NYCC EXCLUSIVE VARIANT COVER BY
CAITLIN YARSKY

SCOTT SNYDER

Scott Snyder has been writing comics for over a decade. He is most known for various *Batman* titles, including the most recent *Dark Nights: Death Metal*, and creator-owned titles like *American Vampire*, *Wytches*, and *Nocterra*. His current focus is on his new creator-owned works like *Canary*, *Barnstormers*, *Dudley Datson*, and *Book of Evil*.

HAYDEN SHERMAN

Hayden is an award-winning comic artist whose work includes *Arkham Academy*, *Wasted Space*, and *Above Snakes*. They're a lover of sci-fi and fantasy who's very grateful to be drawing spaceships and cowboys for a living. Odd as it seems. They currently reside in Massachusetts, where they share an apartment with their significant other and an exceedingly dumb cat.